ESTOCADA

Graham Hurley is the author of the acclaimed Faraday and Winter crime novels and an award-winning TV documentary maker. Two of the critically lauded series have been shortlisted for the Theakston's Old Peculier Award for Best Crime Novel. His French TV series, based on the Faraday and Winter novels, has won huge audiences. The first *Wars Within* novel, *Finisterre*, was shortlisted for the Wilbur Smith Adventure Writing Prize. Graham now writes full-time and lives with his wife, Lin, in Exmouth.

www.grahamhurley.co.uk

By the same author

DI Joe Faraday Investigations

Turnstone
The Take
Angels Passing
Deadlight
Cut to Black
Blood and Honey
One Under
The Price of Darkness
No Lovelier Death
Beyond Reach
Borrowed Light
Happy Days

DS Jimmy Suttle Investigations

Western Approaches
Touching Distance
Sins of the Father
The Order of Things

Wars Within

Finisterre
Aurore
Estocada

FICTION

Rules of Engagement
Reaper
The Devil's Breath
Thunder in the Blood
Sabbathman
The Perfect Soldier
Heaven's Light
Nocturne
Permissible Limits
The Chop
The Ghosts of 2012
Strictly No Flowers

NON-FICTION

Lucky Break
Airshow
Estuary
Backstory

GRAHAM HURLEY

ESTOCADA

First published in the UK in 2018 by Head of Zeus Ltd

9 7 5 3 1 2 4 6 8

A catalogue record for this book is available from the British Library.

ISBN (HB) 9781784977894
ISBN (ANZTPB) 9781784977900
ISBN (E) 9781784977887

Printed and bound by CPI Group (UK) Ltd,
Croydon, CR0 4YY

Head of Zeus Ltd
First Floor East
5–8 Hardwick Street
London EC1R 4RG

WWW.HEADOFZEUS.COM

La Estocada (*Spanish*)

– stab, sword thrust, death blow

To
Richard Holmes
(1946–2011)

Part One

1

VITORIA-GASTEIZ, NORTHERN SPAIN, MARCH 1937

La estocada. The word fascinated him, taunted him, lurked playfully at the edges of every waking day, sometimes kept him awake at night. *La estocada.*

Georg's fault. He'd seen the posters that first month when they were flying out of rough airfields in the south. Within days Georg appeared beneath the cloth awning that served as a Mess. He had two tickets. Tonight, he'd said. I've talked to the *Oberleutnant*. We have permission. We'll take the motorbike. The one that works.

Seville in the hot darkness. The bullring full of nationalist soldiers off duty, sweating in the heat. The rich stink of horse dung and cheap tobacco. He watched the bull swaying left and right, pawing the ground, snorting, still tormented by the picadors. He couldn't remember the name of the matador – Rivera? Ordóñez? – but what mattered was the moment of the kill.

That first time it came more quickly than he'd expected. The matador seemed to barely move. Neither did the bull. It looked so easy, so artful, an arm's length between them, a moment of perfect grace as the long quick blade plunged downwards and the animal first shuddered, then buckled, his front legs giving way, blood frothing from the sudden slackness of his mouth.

He was still staring down at the bullring. *La estocada.* Get everything right, he thought, and the kill is yours.

*

Leutnant Dieter Merz jerked awake. It had been raining again during the night and his sleeping bag was wet through from holes in the canvas above his head. A shape crouched in the mouth of the tent. *Mein Katschmarek*, Dieter thought. My wingman.

'*Aufstehen.*' Georg Messner was wearing full flying kit and the summons to get up sounded urgent.

Dieter asked what time it was.

'Nearly seven. Our Spanish friends are planning an attack. You know that. They told us last night. The briefing starts in three minutes.' Georg tapped his head. 'Are you crazy or something?'

Crazy or something?

Georg had gone. Dieter struggled out of the bag. His flying suit – leather trousers, flannel shirt, leather jacket – was as wet as everything else. Outside, in the murk of yet another dawn on this godforsaken airfield, he heard the cough of an aero engine, then a clatter and a roar as a member of the ground crew opened the throttle. One of the new Bf-109s, Dieter thought. He was shivering now, his fingers barely able to manage the buttons on his shirt, his head still full of images from the bullring. A year ago, he'd believed the promises of eternal sunshine and a life so sweet you'd never want to leave. How wrong could you be?

He tugged on his boots and left the tent, stamping warmth back into his feet as he watched the 109 powering down. Dieter had been one of the first pilots on the squadron to fly the new fighter. He'd talked to one of the two engineers who'd shipped down from Stettin with the crated machines, a taciturn Berliner who'd cut his teeth with the Richthofen Circus in the war of the trenches. The engineer had squatted on the wing, talking Dieter through the controls. Be careful on take-off, he'd grunted. Plenty of throttle but full right rudder, otherwise this bastard will kill you. At the time, Dieter had assumed he was joking. Again, wrong.

A hut beyond the line of parked aircraft served as both a canteen and a briefing room. Dieter made his way through the scatter of empty tents and paused outside the door. A big iron stove had been installed in the first week of January, more than welcome as this coldest of winters at last came to an end. Smoke was curling from the stub of the stovepipe chimney and Dieter caught the sweetness of the burning wood in the swirling wind. Even now, in late March, the weather was unforgiving.

He paused, wiping the rain from his face. The door had never been hung properly and he could hear the *Oberleutnant* offering his assessment of yesterday's operational flying. He's started already, Dieter thought. *Scheisse.*

The big room was packed. Pilots occupied every available chair and others were sitting on the floor. Heads turned as Dieter pushed the door open. One of the younger flyers offered a nod of welcome, while Georg rolled his eyes. With his tangle of blond curls and his crooked smile, little Dieter Merz had become a talisman with this strange outfit, impish, popular with everyone, reliably different.

'You're late.' The *Oberleutnant*'s name was Gunther Lutzow. His inner circle called him 'Franzl'.

Dieter mumbled an excuse, found a perch on a nearby table. The *Oberleutnant* turned back to the map pinned to the blackboard. Dieter had lived with this swirl of contour lines for months now and was all too familiar with the scarlet crosses that tallied Republican positions in the mountains to the north. The towns of Elorrio and Durango, still held by Basque militiamen. Thin zigzag trenches in the harshness of the landscape, not easily bombed. Beyond the towering peaks lay a broadening estuary. Then came the sea.

The *Oberleutnant* was complaining again about the sloth of the Nationalist Army, the timidity of Franco's generals up here in the Basque Country, how nothing ever seemed to happen after the Condor Legion had done its work.

'Even our *Generalmajor* can't make a difference. He talks to Franco. Franco talks to his people up here. They promise an attack. Then another attack.' Lutzow made a gesture of contempt, half-turned towards the map. '*Nichts*.' Nothing.

There was a ripple of laughter. The *Generalmajor* was a tough, bear-like ex-fighter pilot who'd led the Condor Legion into Spain. As the face of the Third Reich amongst this bunch of Carlist fanatics, Hugo Sperlle was evidently running out of patience. Only now, it seemed, had his representations found a listening ear.

Lutzow permitted himself the ghost of a smile. He had news to impart.

'General Mola assures us that he'll be opening his offensive tomorrow morning,' he said. 'Our lads from Burgos will be bombing in relays. The objective is to fill the streets with rubble and bottle up the garrison troops before Mola's lot go in. Our job is to clean up afterwards. The problem with the 109 engines is unresolved. Therefore we'll stick to the Heinkels. Our allotted target? Durango.'

Heads nodded round the room. Most of these men had spent the last few months flying the Heinkel-51s, the latest of the *Luftwaffe*'s biplanes, robust enough in the air but a bitch to land. The two machine guns had to be loaded manually while still flying the plane, a chore that skinned the knuckles of even the best pilots. Worse still, the bomb load was pathetic: just six ten-kilo cylinders of high explosive, a mere calling card compared to the ordnance delivered by the big Ju-52s from Burgos.

Georg wanted to know what 'clean up' meant. He'd been a mathematician at university and his insistence on precision when it came to orders – as well as everything else in his life – was fast becoming a squadron joke.

Lutzow told him to hunt for targets of opportunity. Anyone in uniform with a white tunic on his back belonged to General Mola's army. Don't shoot him. Anyone else in uniform, go for the kill.

'And civilians?'

'We're there to make an impact.'

'With respect, sir, what does that mean?'

'It means that our job is to break these people's morale. First they get bombed. Then we strafe. Mola wants his men in Durango by dusk. If you're asking me whether that makes military sense, I have to say yes. Our job is to leave Mola with no excuses. He's relying on us and I have no intention of letting him down.'

Georg nodded and shot a look at Dieter. They usually flew as a pair on sorties in the old biplanes and Dieter had lost count of the times they'd pulled out of a bombing run because they couldn't be sure they were killing the right people. Everyone told each other that war was an imperfect art form, that mistakes were inevitable, but you could slow the biplanes to a near-stall in the interests of accuracy and at those kinds of speeds you were left with some very uncomfortable images if you got the targeting wrong.

Only last week, Dieter had machine-gunned a shepherd in imperfect visibility in the mistaken belief that his stick was a rifle and when he'd reported back, blaming the weather conditions, drifting mist on the mountainside had felt like the thinnest of alibis. Lutzow, to his surprise, had dismissed his qualms with a shrug. The fighting season may soon start in earnest, he'd said, and Franco wants to put the fear of God into these people. If his generals won't shift their arses, then I suspect the job falls to us.

Lutzow had returned to the map. The weather front responsible for the rain would have cleared to the east by mid-afternoon. Tomorrow morning, the Ju-52s from Burgos were scheduled to attack at 8 a.m., along with a squadron of Italian S-81s. The planes would be bombing in relays, offering no relief. The raid would open with sixty tons of high explosive dropped in just two minutes. Durango had no air defences but the Red infantry, tough Basque militiamen, would doubtless do their best to bring down the bulky biplanes with small arms fire. Lutzow didn't want that to happen.

'Get on top of these people.' His pointer found Durango on the map. 'Make them bleed.'

*

Breakfast that morning was a bowl of sweet coffee with thick slices of bread still warm from a bakery in the nearby town. Afterwards, Lutzow wanted them to take a look at Durango, high level, no hostile intent. He wanted them to plot attack lines, get a feeling for the topography of the place, imagine that they were garrison troops fleeing for the safety of the mountains. Where would these peasant militiamen hide? How best would Lutzow's flyers flush them out, line them up nicely, send them on their way?

La estocada, Dieter thought. The Legion wants us to toy with these people, bring them to their knees in an orgy of percussive violence, and then thrust the blade deep and put them out of their misery. He discussed the proposition with Georg and a couple of other pilots, sitting around the table closest to the stove. Georg, as literal as ever, viewed it as a matter of tactics. Tomorrow, by mid-morning, the last wave of bombers would have departed. Hopefully it would be a cloudless day. Attack, therefore, from just east of south, plane after plane, howling out of the brightness of the sun, invisible, terrifying.

One of the other pilots wondered how much of the town would be left by then. Dieter told him it wouldn't be a problem. He'd watched a lot of the bomber boys while flying escort duty on previous raids, and he'd got to know them even better when he'd taken a bullet in the radiator south of Burgos and made a dead-stick landing on their airfield when his engine had seized.

They were truck drivers in the air, he said. They were in the delivery business, flew in straight lines, held a steady altitude, but they were generous by nature and would do their best to leave a morsel or two for their fighter friends. That night in Burgos, once he was safely down, they'd broken open a case of Gewürztraminer the Mess Officer had been saving for Christmas, and all for the benefit of their newly arrived guest.

Georg, who'd heard all this before, told Dieter he was talking *Scheisse*. In Georg's belief, everyone had a reputation to make and everyone knew that the Junker pilots regarded themselves as the ultimate professionals. Late to the party, their own *Staffel* should concentrate on doing Lutzow's bidding, cleaning up after the main event. Did Dieter have a problem with that?

Coming from anyone else, this challenge would have triggered a serious head-to-head. Other conversations had come to a halt as pilots turned round to see what might happen next but the sight of Dieter Merz blowing his tall cadaverous wingman a kiss sparked a round of applause. Like Georg, these men called Merz *Der Kleine*, the Little One, and the nickname was salted with respect as well as affection, not simply because he was small and always held his corner, but because some of the stunts he pulled in the air defied imitation.

Berndt, a big-hearted Rhinelander of limited talents, had once tried a trick of Dieter's that involved a near-stall at a couple of hundred metres. Alas, he'd got it badly wrong. His Heinkel had burned on impact and they'd had to wait till nightfall to pull his charred body from the wreckage. After that, even Georg – who knew his friend Dieter better than anyone – had to agree that the little imp from Ulm properly belonged in a circus. *Der Kleine*. Seeing is believing.

*

The rain began to ease after lunch and by two o'clock the cloud base was beginning to lift until the frieze of mountains to the north was plainly visible. At Lutzow's insistence, the entire squadron – all eleven planes – were to fly in tight formation. He'd picked up a warning from *Jagdgruppe* headquarters that the Ivans were active in the sector immediately to the east and the last thing he wanted were needless casualties at the hands of the Russians ahead of tomorrow's operation.

Dieter, walking out to the waiting line of Heinkels, felt the first prickles of excitement. The Soviets were shipping their new monoplane, the Polikarpov I-16, into Spain. It was a stubby little aircraft, fast and agile, and Russian pilots flew in tight 4-ship formations, dancing through the screen of He-51s to get at the nest of German bombers inside. Dieter had flown against them on a number of occasions and knew the lumbering biplanes were no match for the I-16. The Republicans called them *moscas* or 'flies'. To the Nationalists they were *ratas. Rata* meant 'rat'.

Georg and Dieter shared the same ground crewman, a cheerful Bavarian called Hans who'd served his apprenticeship in the Bayerische Flugzeugwerke factory at Augsberg. Like everyone else on the squadron he knew that the only answer to the *ratas* was Willy Messerschmitt's new Bf-109, but just now there was still a serious problem with the engine.

Hans helped Dieter onto the lower wing of the He-51 and into the cockpit. Like Dieter, he was a big fan of American blues and they'd recently spent a wet evening together under canvas, listening to Dieter's collection of Mississippi Delta recordings. Back home, nigger music was banned. Out here, no one cared what you listened to.

'You hear about the Ivans?' Hans was storing boxes of ammunition for the two machine guns. 'Take care, eh?'

Dieter nodded, said nothing. Georg was already settled in the adjacent aircraft, engine running, ready to roll. Hans jumped down and stood back as Dieter went through his pre-start checks. The aircraft trembled as the engine fired, and moments later Hans offered a departing wave as Dieter joined the line of biplanes zigzagging across the still-wet grass towards the runway. The new airstrip at Vitoria was too narrow for formation take-offs and one by one the He-51s turned into the wind before final checks.

Dieter was number four in line with Georg behind him. He made a last adjustment to his goggles before his hand found the throttle. The He-51 was slow to accelerate, slow in the climb, slow in almost every other respect, but the big old biplane had taught Dieter everything he knew about surviving in the air and he'd come to love the feel of the machine beneath his fingertips. Halfway down the runway he eased the joystick forward, lowering the nose, bringing up the tail, and Dieter watched the onrushing line of trees beside the perimeter fence to judge the moment of take-off. One last bump and he was airborne, the biplane wallowing in the wake of the aircraft ahead. Dieter adjusted the trim and edged left for a smoother ride. A glance in the mirror confirmed that Georg was safely off.

The squadron tracked north, closing into a tight formation, fighting for altitude. The mountains lay ahead, a familiar line of granite-grey peaks, forbidding in the pale sunshine. There were valleys through these mountains and one of them led to Durango.

Dieter spotted the town a quarter of an hour later, a carpet of ochre roofs on the valley floor. The sunlight glinted on the broadness of the river and the big church at the city's heart threw a long shadow over the adjacent plaza. Up here at three thousand metres the blast of the air was icy but Dieter was still looking down as Lutzow led the squadron in a long shallow turn. Everything was toylike. The tiny trams on the broader avenues. The arches of the old stone bridge that spanned the river. And the black specks in the market square that had to be people. Were they aware of the distant clatter of aero engines? Were they looking up, their eyes shaded against the sun, wondering what to make of these silver fish swimming in the blueness of the sky? Had they any idea – any premonition – of what awaited them once Mola's offensive began to roll?

Not for the first time, gazing down, Dieter felt godlike, all-powerful. Flying had always set him free. He'd known that sense of liberation from the start, as a young cadet, barely seconds into his first two-minute flight in a training glider in the valley of the Upper Danube. It was a feeling he'd always struggled to put into words, all the more addictive because it grew and grew. To defy gravity, to have all three dimensions at your fingertips, to be free of any earthbound restraints, was an intoxication. It spoke of unlimited possibilities. There was nowhere he couldn't go, nothing he couldn't do. Flying offered a freedom so pure, so addictive, it had taken over his entire life.

Since that first moment of release in the tough little glider he must have spent thousands of hours in the air and every time he pulled back on the joystick and felt the aircraft come alive he'd known that nothing in the world could match this feeling. Except, perhaps, now: peering down at a town of ten thousand souls, the way a doctor might assess a patient before a major operation, armed with the power of life and death. Dieter half-closed his eyes, blurring the image below, wondering who might die, who might survive. War, as he was fast discovering, was a lottery. You could do your best to stack the odds in your favour but in the end there was no telling – no knowing – where and how you might die. Fighter pilots always dismissed this prickle of helplessness because they had to. Fighter pilots, after all, were immortal. There was nothing that could take you by surprise, no odds you couldn't overcome. That was the first law of aerial combat. Otherwise you were half-dead already.

Lutzow had begun to climb again, keen to examine the town from every angle. Dieter withdrew his head from the slipstream and pushed the throttle forward, easing the nose up. Then, from nowhere, came a blur of movement barely metres away, a momentary glimpse of a red star against a silver wing, and a lurch in the pit of Dieter's belly as the He-51 bucked in the slipstream of a Russian fighter. *Ratas* always hunted in packs. Where were the rest?

He couldn't see them. Time stopped. The biplanes around him were breaking away, minnows fleeing for the shelter of the reeds. Ahead, Georg had thrown his aircraft into a steep dive. Dieter followed, his body fighting the turn, his neck twisting left and right, his eyes everywhere, quartering the sky, desperate to anticipate the next attack. He found the *ratas* seconds later. There were three of them, line abreast, arrowing in for the kill. They were in good hands, and they had 100 kph on the He-51s. This was the Ivans' turn to play God.

Dieter tightened his harness. He lived for these moments, for the raw adrenaline rush, for the sweetness of teasing survival from the near-certain prospect of disaster. Three *ratas* was the minimum he could expect. There would doubtless be more.

Georg was pulling out of his dive, turning to meet the attack head-on. It was a brave move and the *ratas* split as they streaked past. Then came the chatter of machine-gun fire as they turned to close on another target. For a brief moment Dieter was alone in the sky, still plunging earthwards, the needle on the air-speed gauge pushing towards 470 kph. Any faster and the aircraft might break up. Any slower and he'd be easy meat for the marauding Ivans.

At two hundred metres, Durango had become all too real. Dieter hauled back on the joystick, levelling out. At this altitude he was nearly part of the traffic. A truck overladen with building materials, trailing smoke. A sea of white faces and pointing fingers in front of a roadside café. Two cars pulling in to the kerbside for a closer look. Then came the chatter of machine guns again, much closer. The aircraft shuddered under the impact but the engine churned on. Dieter killed the throttle and pulled back on the stick. Moments later, on the edge of a stall, he dropped the flaps. The *ratas* flashed past, pulling a tight turn for a second attack. Dieter kicked the full left rudder and pushed the throttle forward. By the time he emerged from the turn he was down to forty metres with nowhere left to go. Swooping even lower he sought the shelter of the river. Then came the machine guns again, the bullets pocking the water, before the stubby shadow of the Russian fighter swept over him, the pilot climbing away towards the mountains. Dieter eased up to clear the oncoming bridge, aware for the first time of the presence of another aircraft, barely feet from his starboard wing. He glanced sideways, blinked, then acknowledged the raised glove.

Georg.

*

On the *Staffel*'s return to Vitoria, it was *Oberleutnant* Lutzow's idea to settle 2.J/88's accounts with the Ivans. The squadron had lost two He-51s over Durango, and a third pilot was now in hospital with a bullet lodged in his thigh. He'd made it back to the airfield, but only just.

Dieter and Georg were sitting in the big tent that served as *Staffel* headquarters. Lutzow was bent over a map he'd spread on the table. The Russians flew from an airfield on the coast west of Bilbao. Lutzow estimated the flying time at fifteen minutes.

Dieter frowned. San Juan de Somorrostro was sixty kilometres away. It was well defended. At low level, the He-51s would be sitting ducks for ground fire.

'You'll be taking the 109s. Hans thinks he's found the answer to the engine problem.'

'Thinks?' This from Georg.

'He assures me it's solved.' Lutzow was still gazing at the map. 'You'll be taking off tomorrow morning at first light. The Ivans will all be in bed. Shoot their planes up and make sure they see you. We need to spread the word.'

'We've finished with the Heinkels?' Dieter this time.

'We'll see. Some kind of ground support role? Maybe. It depends.'

Georg wanted to know when more of the 109s would be arriving.

'Soon. A dozen of the "B" variant are shipping down. We fight fire with fire. No more easy pickings for the Ivans.' Lutzow at last glanced up. He was looking at Dieter. 'Someone told me Georg saved your life this afternoon. Is that true?'

Dieter didn't answer. Instead he wanted to know whether the new 109s would have radios. That way, next time, they might avoid getting bounced. Relying on hand signals from an open cockpit was no way to fight a war.

Lutzow held his gaze. He wasn't smiling. At last he folded up the map and nodded towards the open tent flap. He appeared to have no interest in radios.

'First light, gentlemen,' he said. 'This time we do the bouncing.'

*

Dieter and Georg played chess that night, three games straight, all victories for Georg. This had never happened before and it seemed to trouble Georg more than Dieter.

'Maybe you need a woman,' Georg said. 'Maybe that's it.'

'You think I could have done better over Durango?'

'I think you were crazy to dive like that. You were inviting him down. You were flying like a novice.'

'Maybe that's the way I wanted it to look. People make mistakes when they think it's easy.'

'Of course. But not that easy.'

'You're saying he shot me down? Something like that, I would have noticed.'

'I'm saying he got very, very close.'

'And then you saved my life?'

'The bastard broke off. It might be the same thing.'

Dieter was gazing at the chess board. Earlier, at dusk, he'd been for a run, two laps of the airfield in the gathering darkness. He did this every night, along with a set of exercises he'd gradually developed during his time in Spain. That way he slept better and gave himself a fighting chance with the Ivans.

Tonight, though, was different. There was a rumble of heavy artillery from the north where Mola's troops had opened their bombardment and from time to time he caught the scarlet shell bursts reflected on the belly of the clouds. In truth, Georg was right. He should never have found himself at twenty metres with nowhere to go.

'You think a woman might do it?' he asked.

'It's a possibility. Maybe your gypsy friend?'

Dieter shrugged. A couple of months back, he'd struck up a liaison with a local woman twice his age whom the squadron quartermaster employed to keep the mess quarters clean. She appeared in the evenings as well, and ghosted into Dieter's tent under cover of darkness. She had the chest of a diva and a fierce temper, and a pilot in a nearby tent, who knew a little Spanish, reported that after vigorous sex she'd scold *Der Kleine* over the state of his laundry.

Georg had always been amused by the story. Dieter's smile had melted a thousand hearts and even here, in the depths of the Basque Country, he could have any woman he wanted yet he'd clung to this strange relationship through the long winter nights, picking up enough Spanish to conduct a modest conversation.

One night, Georg had stooped into the tent to find Dieter cross-legged in front of this woman of his, replaying the day's flying for her benefit, knitting passes, and loops, and sudden reverses with his beautiful hands, laying his trophies at her feet. Was it praise he was after? Or reassurance? Or the kind of simple comfort he might have found from his mother?

Georg had no idea, but when the woman abruptly transferred her attentions to a good-looking braggart called Wolfgang, Dieter was broken-hearted. A week later she was barred from the airfield after rumours circulated that she was a Republican spy. This had all the makings of a scandal, with potential consequences for her two lovers, yet it was Dieter who ignored the advice of others and traced her to a dusty *barrio* on the edges of Vitoria, teeming with dogs and kids.

There, by his own account, he found the tumbledown but spotless shack she called home, knocked on the door and presented a bunch of wild roses. The man who accepted the flowers turned out to be her husband, a fact that didn't appear to trouble Dieter in the least. In this, as in many other areas of his life, *Der Kleine* remained an enigma.

'You want another game?' Georg nodded down at the board.

'No.'

'That woman still on your mind?'

'No.'

'Tomorrow, then? First light?'

Dieter held his gaze. Then reached out.

'Thanks.' He touched Georg lightly on the cheek. 'For this afternoon.'

*

Dieter was at the controls of the Bf-109 before dawn, listening to Hans's quiet explanation of what was going wrong with the engine. The radiator, it seemed, was malfunctioning towards the higher end of the rev counter. Hans had experimented with various replacement thermostats and finally settled on one that seemed to do the trick. Whatever else happened, Dieter was to keep monitoring the temperature gauge. Anything over the red line, abort the mission at once. Dieter nodded, guessing that dead-stick landings in an aircraft this powerful, and this heavy, would mean lashing himself to a brick.

'Any more good news for me, Hans?'

'*Ja*,' the engineer nodded at the firing button on the control column. 'At least you won't have to hand-load the bloody machine guns.'

Dieter and Georg took off at dawn, the first fingers of light creeping over the eastern horizon. The cockpit felt cramped, even to Dieter, and the rearward visibility was *Scheisse*, but it was an enormous relief to feel the surge of raw power as they climbed away on the compass direction that would take them to the airfield at San Juan.

In three short years, while the the rest of the world looked the other way, the engineers at the Bayerische Flugzeugwerke factory at Augsberg had conjured an aircraft that promised to match anything else in the sky. It wasn't perfect, far from it, but once you'd sorted out the prop torque and the narrowness of the undercarriage on take-off, it felt to Dieter like an eager yearling destined for glory. After the dowager embrace of the trusty He-51, this was an aircraft you'd be proud to showcase in any company. Better still, the needle on the temperature gauge was remaining comfortably below the red line.

Pre-take-off, Dieter had agreed to take the lead once the Ivans' airfield was in sight. Now, in the spill of yellow from the east, he dropped a wing as the airfield came into view.

From three hundred metres it looked as primitive as everything else in Spain. A village of brown tents had sprung up beside a long line of *ratas* parked in a shallow semi-circle. Even at low altitude, as he roared in over the dusty track that marked the airfield's perimeter, the snub-nosed aircraft looked too small to be real. To the north lay the coast and the broad inlet that led to Bilbao. Mercifully the gun pits that dotted the airfield were empty.

Dieter's thumb found the firing button. He slipped off the safety catch, dropped even lower and waited until the line of aircraft filled his gunsight before firing a long burst. A mechanic working an early shift on one of the planes ran for his life. Another, a little more brave, reached for what looked like a carbine. Before he could even raise the weapon, Dieter was gone, climbing into a steep turn before making another pass.

Dimly, amongst the long shadows, he recognised Georg stitching more bullets through the line of *ratas*, then it was his turn again. With one of the *ratas* in flames, he concentrated this time on the tented encampment. Men from the tents were running for cover. Some of them were naked. One of them stood and shook his fist. Dieter grinned. He could taste the sourness of cordite in the back of his throat. Another long burst from the machine guns. Tents collapsing. Bodies everywhere. One of these men nearly killed me, Dieter told himself. Thank God for Georg. Thank God for Willy Messerschmitt. Thank God for the chance to give these crazy Ivans a proper wake-up call.

After a third pass, back with the *ratas* this time, Dieter was out of ammunition. He climbed away from the airfield, watching another aircraft burn, and flew a long left-hand circuit until Georg climbed out of the drifting smoke below to join him. By the time they were back at Vitoria, there was real warmth in the sun.

Lutzow was waiting outside his tent for a full report. Georg, who liked to handle situations such as these, described rich pickings. Two aircraft certainly destroyed. Untold damage to many others. Dozens of men killed or badly wounded. Not a good day if you happened to be Russian.

'But they saw you? They saw what you could do?'

'They certainly did, sir. The ones who survived.'

'Excellent. The word will spread. That's all I ask.'

Dieter wanted to know what might happen next. It was nearly eight o'clock. The first wave of bombers would be minutes away from Durango. What now for the 109s?

'You've talked to Hans?'

'Yes.'

'And what does he say?'

'He says they're fine. He says the change of thermostat's done the trick. He's rearming and refuelling now. You want us to fly with the Heinkels?'

'Of course.' Lutzow offered a thin smile. 'Just in case the Ivans want some more.'

*

Flying with the Heinkels, Dieter and Georg agreed later, was no match for their expedition to San Juan. Throttling back, they weaved patterns in the sky overhead as the loose formation of biplanes droned north. Durango was visible forty kilometres away, a towering column of billowing smoke where the bombers had done their work. An *hors d'oeuvre* of high explosive, followed by a main course of thermite bombs to incinerate the wreckage. A tasty new offering for a totally new kind of war.

Closer, it seemed to Dieter that the church had been hit, and closer still – as the Heinkels prepared for their own attacks – he could make out streets full of rubble around the marketplace. Rescue parties were everywhere, running out hoses, fetching water in buckets from the riverbank, doing their best to control dozens of fires. None of them spared a cautionary glance at the skies above.

The lead Heinkels plunged towards the city centre, adding their own bombs to the chaos below, then breaking off at low level to machine-gun the rescuers as they ran for cover. Men and women fell. Kids, too. One man, a priest, had dropped to his knees in prayer. Dieter watched from a hundred and fifty metres as a line of bullets stitched towards him through the dust and then, as if by some miracle, stopped. Everywhere, farm animals from the market were running blindly in panic and as the smoke thinned beyond the outskirts of the city, Dieter spotted a lone cow, bellowing in the wilderness.

Then, quite suddenly, it was over. Half a dozen of the Heinkels had expended the last of their ammunition on refugees fleeing into the countryside. The rest of the aircraft were already heading south again, returning to Vitoria. Dieter and Georg caught them up. Of the Ivans, Dieter was glad to note, there had been no sign.

After landing, Dieter taxied back to the row of Bf-109s still awaiting modification. Hans helped him from the cockpit and then removed the engine casing to check on the ammunition bays. Puzzled, his eyes met Dieter's.

'Did you fire at all?'

'No.'

'May I ask why not? Lutzow's bound to check.'

'I was waiting for the Ivans,' Dieter said. 'But they never turned up.'

*

Four days later, Lutzow summoned the squadron to a meeting in the mess hut. The bombing of Durango had opened a new chapter in the war. The destruction of the church had killed fourteen nuns, the officiating priest and most of the congregation. Hundreds of other civilians had fallen to the Ju-52s and the strafing Heinkels. With the Führer's birthday only weeks away, the success of the Legion had sparked celebrations in certain quarters in Berlin yet the Nationalist generals, once again, had called a sudden halt to the offensive. The resilience of the Basque forces in the mountains, it was said, had surprised them. The Reds were bleeding heavily but refused to give in.

Lutzow's map was back on the blackboard. He used the pointer to jab at the Nationalist positions around Durango. To his disgust, the Condor Legion were dropping bombs for no reason at all. Kill hundreds of civilians, and still Franco's generals refused to drive their men forward. Hopeless.

A pilot at the back of the room raised a hand. He wanted to know where the war might go next.

'Good question.' Lutzow returned to the map. 'In time even General Mola will move. The axis of advance is this way, along the river.' The pointer tracked north, then paused eleven kilometres from the coast. 'My guess is that we bomb again, perhaps here, to bottle up the Reds as they retreat.'

Dieter had a poor view of the map. He asked for the name of the town. Lutzow obliged with a weary sigh.

'Guernica,' he said.

2

DROCHAID, 12 NOVEMBER 1937

Tam Moncrieff lay in the dampness of the heather, his binoculars trained on a herd of deer grazing in the valley below. He'd been stalking them since sunrise, following their slow passage along the further bank of the river, making notes on the behaviour of the younger animals, on who bossed whom, on which of the young does was first to the best pasture, on which one took fright at the slightest hint of danger.

In all there were nine beasts, including three females and a magnificent stag the estate's ghillie had christened Hermann. The nickname, far from subtle, was intended to raise a smile amongst a party of German industrialists booked in to enjoy a week's recreational slaughter on the modest Moncrieff estate. They were due to fly into the windswept airfield at Aberdeen at the weekend. Tam's notes, together with the ghillie's inexhaustible fund of stories, would serve as an appetiser when they settled around the dining room table for supper ahead of their first day in the field.

Moncrieff's shotgun lay beside him. He killed for the pot, mainly pigeons and woodcock and the odd hare. All that would come later in the day when his interest in the deer was exhausted, but the knowledge that he had a weapon at hand was oddly comforting.

He'd learned to shoot properly in the Royal Marines, a decade and a half of ceaseless challenge that had brought him to the edge of middle age. At thirty-three, with the rank of Major, he'd been assured of further promotion if he'd been prepared to sit behind a desk, grow slowly fatter and joust for territorial advantage with the other high-flyers in the endless corridors of the War Ministry. None of these prospects held the slightest attraction for Tam Moncrieff and so here he was, back in the Cairngorms, cooking for his mad father, chopping logs for the fire, scaling a ladder to replace yet another length of guttering, while at the same time trying to tease the beginnings of a business from the glorious creatures below.

Week-long shoots with full board had been his mother's idea. Bedridden with cancer of the liver, one of her last conversations with Tam had been sparked by a visit from a longstanding friend with a much larger estate in the Borders. The McClennans, she whispered, were making a great deal of money out of business people from down south eager for a taste of life in the wild. They charged their clients ridiculous fees, even when they returned from the shoot empty-handed, and it seemed they were only too happy to pay.

Tam, at first, had dismissed the idea. He knew his mother was frantic to find ways to fill the gap in her husband's life once she'd gone, as well as giving him an income to live on, but the fact remained that both the house and the grounds were in the saddest of states. Who on earth would be prepared to part with even a modest sum for a week of draughty bedrooms, leaking roofs, uncertain plumbing and unceasing rain?

His mother, who was only spared the grave by her sheer strength of will, had brooked no argument. If you love me, she'd said, you'll at least give it a try. And so Tam had put his reservations to one side and set to.

To his astonishment, the gamble had paid off. Sadly his mother was dead before the first party of guests was due but Tam had rallied support from women in the village to take a paintbrush to room after room. In the meantime, working every hour afforded by the thin winter daylight, he'd spent a sizeable portion of the money left to him by his mother on a programme of badly needed repairs that restored the roof, the windows and an abandoned stable to some kind of order.

To his slight surprise, he'd enjoyed the work. Making do with his own company had never been a problem. Indeed, he relished the busy silence of The Glebe House. Perched on the roof with a mouthful of nails in the freezing wind he could take his hammer to yet another slate and then lift his head to savour the view down the valley towards the looming frieze of mountains dusted with snow. As a child growing up in the draughty chill of The Glebe House, these mountains had always fascinated him. Smooth, bare and humpy, they looked like the work of a giant on a beach, and as winter gave way to spring and the melt came, he'd taken advantage of the extra daylight to tidy up the pointing on the chimney stacks.

The first paying guests had arrived in a charabanc from the station on a glorious afternoon in early April. The stalking party, jowly men with ready laughs, came from an aluminium-rolling mill in the West Midlands. Their first breakfast featured bowls of steaming porridge, a platter of Arbroath kippers, and what Tam's newly acquired cook termed 'an Ulster fry'.

Despite the efforts of the past few months, there was still no disguising the fact that The Glebe House had seen better days, but the men from the Black Country appeared to love it. It was, they said, just the thing. They felt both replete and very much at home.

Tam remembered the arrival of the morning papers. A lengthy article in *The Times* had sparked a passionate debate about the awful reports emerging from Northern Spain. A town called Guernica had been more or less destroyed by German bombers from the Condor Legion. One or two of the men around the table considered the incident to be regrettable, wondering aloud what other atrocities Mr Hitler might have up his sleeve, but the overwhelming consensus was that this – from the business point of view – was very good news. The destruction of an unknown town in the Basque Country was proof that a new kind of war was on the way. A war of fighters and bombers. Hundreds of them. Thousands of them. All made of aluminium.

That first morning around the breakfast table had stayed fresh in Tam's memory. He could still hear the laughter and feel the warmth that bonded these blunt businessmen so eager to stretch their legs and bag a beast or two. It meant that his mother had been right. It meant that the house and the estate, a lifeline for Tam's bereft father, would remain in the family. And when, at the week's end, one of the happy guests slipped Tam a handsome tip for the cook and the housekeeper, he'd taken careful note of the muttered advice that came with it. You know where the real money is these days? Get some of those rich Germans across for a spot of shooting. They'll pay through the nose. You'll make a fortune.

As it happened, Tam spoke half-decent German, thanks to his father's insistence that his son should learn the language. This was back in his schooldays. The Huns might be on their knees after the war, his father had warned, but you'll never keep these people down. Tam hadn't enjoyed university at all, but the two years he'd spent studying German before he bailed out and joined the Marines had given him a real taste for the language. He liked the challenge of the grammar. He enjoyed taking a great bite out of a sentence laden with impossibly long words and then giving them a thorough chew. And most of all, on his visits to Berlin and Munich, he enjoyed being able to eavesdrop on conversation after conversation.

On the whole he'd found the Germans a strange people, a breed apart, and the more he had to do with them the less sure he became that he'd ever properly get their measure. There was much to admire about German *Kultur*, not least their beer and their music, but it was rare to leave a conversation without a gruff lecture about the iniquities of recent history. How they'd been cheated of victory in the last war. How they'd been bullied into humiliation and poverty by the peace treaty that followed. How they'd very nearly been delivered into the hands of the Communists. Only now, thanks to the Nazis, was the rest of the world to discover that Germans were capable of anything. He'd first heard the boast in a Munich *Bierhalle* and for whatever reason it had refused to go away. A people besotted by their own destiny, he'd concluded, and largely deaf to the opinion of others.

Tam was back at The Glebe House by late afternoon. He'd bagged a rabbit and a couple of pigeons in the walk down through the woods and he left them in the stable out of reach of the dogs. A car he'd never seen before was parked on the patch of gravel in front of the house and when he went inside he found a stranger sitting at the table in the dining room. He was tall, well-built. He had heavily lidded eyes deep-set in a sallow complexion. A mane of greying hair swept back over the collar of his shirt. The house was full of the sweetness of fresh baking and the stranger was picking up crumbs from his plate with a moistened finger as Tam shut the door.

'Mr Moncrieff?' He got to his feet and extended a hand. 'My name's Sanderson. You'll forgive me for intruding.'

'You've come for the scones?' Tam was looking at the empty plate.

'A windfall, Mr Moncrieff. One would have been sufficient. Three was your housekeeper's idea. In my defence, she insisted.' He smiled for the first time, and then patted the flatness of his belly. 'Gluttony, I'm afraid. Rude to say no.'

Moncrieff held his gaze. The newcomer was wearing a well-cut tweed suit that accentuated his powerful frame and there was a hint of a Scots accent in his voice. Edinburgh, Tam thought. Either a lawyer or a businessman.

'So why are you here?' Tam nodded towards the gathering dusk outside the window. 'We normally take bookings by post. Or sometimes on the phone. You could have spared yourself the journey.'

'That's kind of you. But I'm afraid we need to talk.'

'About what?'

'About you, Mr Moncrieff.'

*

Sanderson was gone within the hour, declining an invitation to stay for supper. He'd been less than precise about the details but he assured Tam that he'd come with the authority of his masters down in London. His line of business, a phrase he chose with some care, enjoyed a loose connection to the War Office. He was part of an outfit that belonged to none of the mainstream armed services but had won itself a degree of independence. The work was complex and demanding and much of it took place abroad, and even when they took a scalp or two their efforts went largely unsung. They lived in a world of constantly moving targets, and untold frustrations, and all too often your only guarantee of survival was to be even more devious than the enemy. Yet to sup at this table, he hinted, could be a pleasure as well as a privilege.

Enemy? Tam had said nothing. He knew enough about the upper reaches of the military to recognise the markings of the priesthood to which Sanderson, if that was his real name, belonged. He clearly worked for one of the intelligence organisations and he was here on a fishing expedition. He'd been sent to take the measure of the ex-Marine, sample his language skills and judge his fitness to serve in a higher cause. This wasn't a job interview. Sanderson was far too subtle for that. Instead, he'd made Moncrieff aware that he might be able to offer King and country much needed assistance in ways that had nothing to do with conventional warfare. In short, he was being assessed as a potential spy.

The conversation at an end, Tam had walked him out to the car. A driver materialised from nowhere, emerging from the car to open the rear door. Tam paused in the darkness and then shook Sanderson's outstretched hand.

'Who gave you my name?' he asked.

'Gunther Nagel.'

'Gunther's due here at the weekend. He's been before. He runs one of the Krupp factories in Essen.'

'That's right. He said it was a pleasure to meet you. And for the record, he was very impressed.' He paused. 'He believes I'm with the Foreign Office, by the way. I wouldn't want him to think anything else.'

Without a word of farewell Sanderson ducked into the car. Seconds later it was disappearing down the drive that led back to the village and the main road out towards Aberdeen. Tam watched until he could hear nothing but the wind in the trees. Then – from the house – came the first chords of the evening, the violin still wildly out of tune, and a soft chuckle from the cook as she poured his father's second whisky.

Tam listened for a long moment, then stepped back inside the house and put his head round the door of the big kitchen to say hello. The old man glanced across, unshaven, painfully thin. He was wearing a threadbare dressing gown over his pyjamas and he badly needed a haircut. He broke off playing and let the bow dangle from one bony hand.

'Your name, sir?' He was frowning, annoyed by the interruption.

Tam stared at him. For a second or two, he assumed that this was some kind of joke, but then he realised that his father meant it.

'My apologies.' Tam forced a smile, already backing into the passage. 'I didn't mean to intrude.'

*

Gunther Nagel's second visit to The Glebe House was an enormous success. He arrived with a small party of favoured executives and news from the Reich, which he shared with a degree of incaution that took Tam by surprise. At the supper table that first night he boasted that factories the length of the Ruhr were producing everything from tanks and heavy artillery to armour plate for the new *Kriegsmarine*. Capital funding was suddenly no problem and higher wages on the assembly lines had filtered down to the working man. The shops were well-stocked, the kids couldn't wait to get into uniform, and the Rhineland, peaceably German once again, was thriving. In short, National Socialism had restored German fortunes and German pride, just the way the little corporal had always promised. So much for Versailles. So much for the Bolsheviks. Here's to the one alliance that will really matter. *Das Dritte Reich mit Grossbritannien.*

At the time, reaching for his glass, Tam had said very little but three days later in failing light Nagel managed a fine shot that brought down the biggest of the estate's stags. Tam and his German guest strode together through the soaking heather to inspect the steaming corpse. The ghillie had got there first but took a respectful step back when the two men approached. Nagel squatted briefly beside the dead beast, his rifle cradled in his arms, insisting on a photo. Afterwards, shaking the rain from his cape, he fell into step alongside Tam for the long walk back to The Glebe House.

By now it was nearly dark. Nagel, still beaming from the kill, began to enthuse about the challenges awaiting him in Essen. A new steel alloy on which Krupp had just secured a world patent. Calls from the generals in Berlin for yet more battle tanks for the new Panzer divisions. When Tam enquired lightly where all this frenzied rearmament might lead, Nagel paused in the gloom, beckoning Tam closer with a sudden grin. The gesture was conspiratorial, the offer of news you'd only share with a trusted friend.

'Those bloody Czechs,' he said, 'will be the first to find out.'

*

A week and a half later, nearly December, Tam was summoned to London. The telephone call came from Sanderson. Tam left The Glebe House in darkness the following morning and drove himself to the station in Laurencekirk. A watery sun rose as the train clattered over the Tay Bridge but it was raining long before they crossed the border. The ten-hour journey was interminable, the fug in the compartment laden with pipe tobacco, an overweight Labrador sprawled beside the door.

Tam resisted the occasional conversational advance from his fellow passengers, staring out through the smeary window at the deadness of winter. The smoky heart of Newcastle and the flat, wet fields further south were an invitation to think in earnest about the decisions that might face him over the coming couple of days. Did he really want to step back into the world of the military? A world where he'd no longer be his own boss? A world where he'd have to do someone else's bidding?

In truth, he'd loved much of his time as a bootneck, especially the early days when the Royal Marine instructors – with a mystifying belief in this towering ex-university student – had set him challenge after challenge. He'd risen to all of them, surprised and gladdened that his body had proved so infinitely capable, but there'd come moments when his growing self-belief hadn't been quite enough to overcome the inner conviction that what he was doing was crazy.

One night in the Western Highlands he and his troop had scrambled for six hours in full combat order up and down a particularly unforgiving three thousand foot peak. The tussock at the bottom of the mountain was sodden, a trap for the unwary, and by midnight half a dozen young marines were hobbling along with ankle injuries. Then, in the windy darkness, lashed by sudden squalls of rain, came the sudden relief of a metalled road.

Seconds later the CSM had barked at the men to take the next couple of miles at the double, a heavy jog. Backpacks swaying, rifles clutched to chests, the untidy column began to lengthen out. Thinking back, Tam could still feel the rasp of breath in his lungs and warning stabs of pain from his right knee. The moorland road went on for ever until, quite suddenly, the CSM brought them to a halt. The clouds had parted. The rain had stopped. In the light of the full moon a bend in the road had revealed the long white curl of a dam still in the process of construction.

The CSM told them to take a good look. This, it turned out, was the final test. Another minute's rest and they'd be doubling down the road to the dam. Happily, he said, retaining walls at the top of the dam had yet to be built. Two hundred paces, same speed, would take them over the roughly poured concrete to the other side. The allotted path, a couple of feet wide, hung over a three hundred foot drop. One mistake, one moment's lack of concentration, and the consequences wouldn't bear thinking about. Keep it steady. Keep it simple. One step at a time. Good luck, eh?

The moment they started moving again, Tam had recognised the logic of this grim coda to a truly miserable night. This was the way it would happen for real. In battle there'd be precious little time to think and absolutely no room for debate. You were exhausted, you hurt all over, but unless you made one final effort, you were dead. And so he got to his feet, stirred his aching limbs into a poor imitation of a jog and headed down towards the dam.

Years later, he could still feel the ridges of the concrete through the leather soles of his boots, still tell himself not to look down at the fathomless drop, still remember the jolt of purest fear when his foot slipped on a slick of mud and his whole body lurched sideways towards the beckoning darkness, still hear the muted cheer from twenty-six exhausted recruits the moment everyone was safe on the other side.

The CSM had doubled across with them, bringing up the rear. The young marines were still huddled together, their white faces daubed with camouflage grease. The CSM went from man to man, a hand on a shoulder, just a hint of a smile. Even now Tam could feel his presence and the inner glow that came from knowing they'd somehow passed into another place.

Another place.

The train had come to a stop. Grantham. The passengers on the seats opposite Tam shuffled together to make room for a clergyman who took the seat beside the window. He sat down, his suitcase stowed on the netted rack above his head, his raincoat carefully folded on his lap. A whistle blew and the train began to move. Tam stared out at the emptying platform, aware of his vision beginning to blur. It was late afternoon. The station was wreathed in smoke from the engine. Then he became aware that the clergyman was studying him with some care. He was Tam's age, maybe slightly older.

'Do you mind me asking you a question?'

'Not at all.'

'Has something upset you?'

'No.' Tam shook his head. 'What gives you that idea?'

'Your eyes are a little moist.' He smiled. 'Windows to the soul.'

*

As requested, Tam made contact with Sanderson from a telephone box on King's Cross station. The train had been delayed north of Watford. It was already ten past nine.

Sanderson supplied the name of a restaurant. Told him to take a taxi.

'This late?'

'This late.'

The phone went dead. On the station forecourt Tam joined the queue for taxis. The rain had stopped now and a bitter wind was rippling the puddles at the kerbside.

The restaurant was in Bloomsbury, barely a mile south. The menu beside the front door promised a rich assortment of offal. Tam stepped inside, glad of the warmth, aware already of Sanderson's presence at a table towards the back of the room. With him was an older man, pale face, dark suit, waistcoat, signet ring. The two of them appeared to be sharing a joke. Sanderson looked up and gestured Tam over. A waiter took his coat and overnight case.

'Name's Ballentyne.' The stranger was on his feet. 'Call me Andrew.'

He was slighter than Sanderson and a good deal older. His face was gaunt with exhaustion but there were laugh lines around his eyes and his handshake was warm. Tam wondered where he belonged in this strange new world. A colleague of Sanderson's, perhaps? His boss? Someone from yet another corner of the intelligence world?

Sanderson offered no clues. Tam found himself looking at a menu. The kitchen closed at ten and time was moving on.

He settled for devilled kidneys and a medley of vegetables. It seemed Sanderson and Ballentyne had eaten earlier. Sanderson was already addressing the evening's business exactly the way he'd done it at The Glebe House. No small talk. No polite exchange of life's smaller courtesies. No time, as a good friend of Tam liked to say, for enjoying the view. Instead, with a sudden lift of an eyebrow, the curtest of questions.

'Are we au fait with the political situation?'

'Where?'

'Here might be a good place to start.'

Tam wondered whether to lie. A busy life in the depths of the Cairngorms left precious little time for keeping abreast of events in London. Should now be the moment when he made his excuses and left?

'I rely on the wireless,' he said carefully, 'and the newspapers. Just like everyone else.'

'Which newspapers?'

'*The Times*, mainly. But to be honest, we have it delivered for the benefit of our guests.'

'Shame on you.' Ballentyne was gazing at his empty glass. 'I use mine to light the fire.'

'Me, too. Next day.'

Ballentyne's laughter broke the ice. He called the waiter for a couple more brandies and watching him, Tam realised that – wherever Ballentyne belonged – he probably outranked Sanderson.

'Is this about politicians?' Tam was looking at Ballentyne. 'Only I'd hate to waste your time.'

'Not at all, my friend. Our only interest in politicians is when things go wrong. Happily, left to their own devices, we can largely ignore them. They come with democracy. It's a cross we have to bear.'

'So what's gone wrong?'

'Excellent question. Very astute. Oliver?'

Tam made a mental note of the Christian name. Sanderson was studying his hands.

'You'll understand this is strictly confidential.' His head came up. The coldest eyes, more grey than blue. 'Halifax was in Germany a couple of weeks ago. You may have read about it.'

Tam shook his head. Lord Halifax was a senior member of the Cabinet, thin, horse-faced, nearly as tall as Tam. In photographs he always towered over everyone else. Even Neville Chamberlain, the Prime Minister, was dwarfed by his presence.

'My father regards him with awe,' Tam said.

'For his conduct of affairs?'

'For his shooting. I understand he has a withered arm.'

'True.' Ballentyne this time. 'But that doesn't excuse what happened in Germany.' Halifax, he said, shared his passion for field sports with Hermann Goering. Goering, as well as raising a decent air force from the ashes of Versailles, was the *Reichs-Jägermeister.*

'Master of the hunt?' The translation came easily to Tam.

'Exactly. This is a man who can't resist a title, or a uniform. He's also getting very fat, which isn't at all the Halifax style. But our German friends think our esteemed Foreign Secretary might enjoy a couple of days in the field and they're right. We understand he did well. In fact, better than well. What's more alarming is what happened afterwards. Some of us have been privy to the intercepts. Oliver?'

'Halifax went down to Bavaria. They made a great fuss of him, as well they might. Hitler has a place in the mountains, the Berghof. When the weather's kind, we understand the views can be sensational.'

'Halifax told you this?'

'No. More to the point is what happened inside. Hitler leads a different Germany, a Germany Redux. I'm sure that won't have escaped your attention. He's got the place working. He's also casting eyes at some of his neighbours. We naturally have an interest in maintaining the peace. The last war cost us all a great deal of blood and a great deal of treasure. Marching into the Rhineland we can live with. It was his in the first place and since then things have been quiet for a while. The last thing we need now is Hitler and his pals knocking the furniture around. That, in essence, is the message Halifax was supposed to deliver.'

'And?'

The two men exchanged glances, then Sanderson made room on the table as the waiter arrived with the brandies. Of Tam's meal, there was still no sign.

'When it comes to diplomacy,' Ballentyne said carefully, 'Hitler has his own style. To be blunt, we tend to play the gentleman. We're used to dealing in nuance. We expect everyone else to be as understated as we are. With Herr Hitler, that may turn out to be a major mistake.'

'So what happened?'

'The pair of them talked about Central Europe. We have interests there and so do the Germans. Hitler believes that language is the key to everything. If you happen to speak German, then wherever you live should belong to Berlin.'

'Like Austria?'

'Of course. And the Sudetenland. And parts of Poland. Versailles put bandages over bits of Europe. Hitler wants to rip them off.'

'By force?'

'I'm afraid so. And the sooner the better.' Ballentyne smiled. 'Didn't your mother tell you that? The quicker you rip the thing off, the less it hurts?'

Tam nodded, thinking suddenly of Gunther Nagel. Those bloody Czechs, he'd said.

'Europe's coming undone.' Tam reached for a bread roll. 'Is that what you're saying?'

'Indeed. Which is why our Foreign Secretary found himself up in the mountains at the Berghof.'

The conversation, Ballentyne said, had lasted a couple of hours. Halifax, in his courtly way, had stressed the importance of leaving the post-war settlement alone. Hitler, never one to mask his ambitions, had pressed Germany's interest in her neighbours.

'Not quite our style, of course. But at least the man was honest.'

'And Halifax?'

'Halifax. . .?' Ballentyne offered a despairing shrug. 'Halifax was loath to upset him. Told Hitler not to ignore the possibility of treaty changes. Said that anything was possible. . . but not quite yet.' He shot a look at Sanderson. 'Am I right, Oliver?'

'More or less. The phrases that matter are *peaceful evolution* and *the passage of time*. They're both in the confidential minutes.'

'So why are we so surprised?' Tam looked from one face to the other. 'And why does any of this matter?'

'Because it's sending the Germans exactly the wrong message. There's a pattern here. Hitler's a gambler. He's always raising the stakes. He did it in the Rhineland. It turns out that a single French division could have sent him scuttling back to Berlin with his tail between his legs but that never happened. The man's clever. He's shrewd. He looks at us across the table and he sees what's in our eyes and he acts accordingly. They invited Halifax over to test the water. They want Austria. They want the Sudetenland. God knows, they're probably after the rest of Czechoslovakia as well. So who's going to stop them? The French? They're a basket case. A new prime minister every month and no one with any appetite for war. The British? Who knows. So Hitler decides to get Halifax across. And ask him a question or two. Put him under a little pressure. See how he reacts.'

'He plays the gentleman.'

'Exactly. Which is less than useful when you're dealing with gangsters.'

Tam's meal had at last arrived. Ballentyne insisted he tuck in. While Tam forked the kidneys on to the bed of mashed potato he wondered how much of this conversation he could trust. The word *gangster* was perhaps a little excessive. It was hard to associate the likes of Gunther Nagel with Al Capone but there were moments during the industrialist's recent stay when Tam had overheard brief exchanges between Nagel and his colleagues, companiable in-jokes that suggested they had the measure of Germany's new masters. If that was the case, and if Hitler was as aggressive and ruthless as Sanderson and Ballentyne were suggesting, then complacency was the last thing that anyone, German or otherwise, could afford.

'You think Hitler is a real threat?' Tam was looking at Ballentyne.

'I'm afraid we do, Tam. Diplomacy was invented to put people like Hitler in a box but regrettably that doesn't appear to be working. It took him half a morning to see through Halifax, and to be frank he'll do the same with Chamberlain. We believe Mr Hitler is a man who will stop at nothing until someone he respects, someone he believes, someone he's afraid of, tells him no. At the moment, we're playing by nursery rules. We believe in Nanny. We believe in the voice of reason. Hitler doesn't. Some people, some of his own countrymen, think he's mad. Some of these folk are kind enough to share their thoughts with us. To be blunt, they have serious concerns about their leader.'

'What do they say?'

'They want our help. They choose to believe that we and the French are there to keep the peace in Europe. Alas, our lordly envoy has just handed Mr Hitler the keys to the castle. Even the Germans, even Hitler, can't believe it. So unless we table the military option, and unless we mean it, the wretched man will barge in and help himself. Sadly, it's as simple as that.'

'We go to war? For Czechoslovakia?'

'We draw a line in the sand. We say so far and no further.'

'You mean with regard to Austria?'

'Perhaps.'

'And Czechoslovakia?'

'Definitely.'

'And we'll really do that? Put forces in the field? Stop him?'

Ballentyne didn't answer. Instead, it was Sanderson who pointed out how Britain had lowered its guard since the war, how pitifully thin our defences had become, how it might take years of heavy investment – millions and millions of pounds – to stay in step with Hitler's Reich. The *Wehrmacht* and the *Luftwaffe*, he said, were in the rudest of health. These people couldn't wait to test all those shiny new toys, all those impatient stormtroopers, on their immediate neighbours. While the best we could do was to despatch the likes of Halifax and cross our fingers and pray for the best.

'So it's hopeless? Is that what you're saying?'

'Not exactly. . .' Sanderson glanced across the table at Ballentyne. '. . . Andrew?'

Ballentyne, signalling again for a second brandy, took his time.

'We understand you speak fluent German,' he said at last.

'That's true.'

'You have a military background. That's important, too.'

'May I ask why?'

'Because we've taken a look at your service record. It appears you have a gift for making a wide range of friendships. In our view, that's a talent beyond price.'

Tam was lost. While it was true that he'd emerged from the Marines with a select circle of friends, people he'd trust with his life, he'd never regarded himself as in any way unusual. Hard physical challenges bred loyalty of a special kind. That, in Tam's view, had nothing to do with the word *talent*.

Ballentyne read the confusion on his face.

'Bear with us. . .' he said. 'You relate to people easily, especially the kind of folk we might have in mind. You share with them a certain background. They'll know that at once. They'll sense it. On the other hand you appear to be equally at home with the other kind of people who pay you a fortune to kill things, people like Gunther Nagel. That's unusual, believe it or not. And it's something we'd be foolish to ignore.'

'So what are you asking me to do?'

'In the first place? Very little. You have a business to run. We understand your father isn't the man he once was. We need you to go back to Scotland, to have a think about this conversation, and to be ready – we hope – to run an errand on our behalf.'

'Errand?'

'Let's call it an operation.'

'Alone?'

'Maybe. We haven't decided.'

'When would this happen?'

'Probably in the New Year.'

'Where?'

'Czechoslovakia.' Ballentyne leaned forward over the table. 'Oliver's right, Tam. Sadly we're under-prepared for Mr Hitler. . . and more to the point we know very little about the

Sudetenland. We need someone with your kind of background to take a proper look. Most of the Sudetens speak German. That's where the trouble begins. And that's where you might lend a listening ear. We have an excellent military attaché in Prague but we need a second opinion. Does that sound something that might attract you?'

3

NAGASAKI, JAPAN, 22 MARCH 1938

Oberleutnant Dieter Merz had been waiting in the garden for nearly an hour. A light snack had just arrived, presented with a smile and a delicate bow from the prettiest of the household's three maids, but the two-day journey from Tokyo over atrocious roads had robbed Dieter of his appetite.

Now he put the bowl of *miso* carefully to one side. After nearly three months in Japan, he still found it near-impossible to fathom the tangle of tiny courtesies that governed this strange society: how to indicate respect, how to salt gratitude with something more than obsequiousness, how to avoid the million ways of giving offence. One of the older hands in newly appointed *Reichsminister* Von Ribbentrop's Foreign Office in Berlin, himself blessed with perfect pre-Nazi manners, had warned of the many traps that lay in wait for the unwary Westerner. Never forget that these are an island people, he'd said. They keep foreigners at arm's length, even when you happen to be their guest.

And so it had proved. After an elaborate round of largely pointless meetings in Tokyo with middling figures in the Japanese military, Dieter had been despatched down here, to the city of Nagasaki on Kyushu Island, to spend a little time with a fighter pilot his own age. Seiji Ayama had just returned from an attachment to a squadron tasked with escorting Mitsubishi bombers attacking targets on the Chinese mainland after the Japanese invasion. Details had been hard to come by but intelligence contacts in the *Abwehr* had briefed Dieter that the Japanese were having a hard time against the Chinese air force. The Chinese flew the Russian I-16, the deadly little *rata*, and after his year in Spain, battling against exactly the same fighter, Dieter was keen to compare notes.

'You don't like the soup?' A woman's voice. In heavily accented but grammatically perfect German.

Dieter half-turned on the bench, shading his eyes against the brightness of the spring sunshine. She was tall for a Japanese, and slim. Every woman he'd met in Japan had bowed as a gesture of introduction. No bow.

Dieter struggled to his feet. Offered a name. Apologised for not finishing the soup. The woman was watching him with interest.

'You have a problem? Here?' She touched her own back below the waist.

'I have.' Dieter nodded, surprised by the directness of the question.

'So what happened?'

'I had to bale out of an aircraft. I made a bad landing.' He shrugged. 'They mended most of me. Not all.'

'You can still fly?'

'Of course. Why do you ask?'

'Because my brother wants to fly with you. My name is Keiko.' She gestured at the bench. 'Please sit down. My brother apologises. He's been delayed. He'll be here soon. You like what we have here?'

Dieter gazed out at the view while Keiko settled beside him. The Ayama family owned steel mills across the country but had made their home in Nagasaki, on the steep hillside overlooking the broad estuary of the river. The house was big, exquisitely furnished, and the garden had been designed in the Japanese style, every view framed by delicate explosions of pink blossom from carefully placed stands of cherry trees. From across the water, where giant shipyards lined the further bank, came the muted roar of heavy engineering. A wartime economy, Dieter thought. Not just here but in city after city along the coast.

'Did your parents build the house?'

'My grandparents. In summer it can get hot. Too hot. Up here you can breathe.'

'So you grew up here? As a child?'

'Yes.'

'And you still live here?'

'No.'

Dieter wanted to find out more. Unusually, this woman seemed at ease with the give and take of Western conversation.

'You've spent time abroad?' he asked.

'No.'

'So how do you speak German so well?'

'Because I listen hard, study hard. Speak other languages and people take you seriously.' She was very close. Sea-green eyes in the paleness of her face. 'You speak Japanese?'

'I'm afraid not.'

'No matter. Here—'

From a bag she produced a newspaper and handed it to Dieter. On the front page, lapped by a sea of inky Japanese text, was a photo of Adolf Hitler on a huge dais, taking the salute. Columns of troops receded into the far distance. The pavement beyond the marching soldiers was black with onlookers. Most of them were women and most of them had their arms extended in an answering salute, their faces contorted in the kind of wild ecstasy that increasingly badged the regime.

'Vienna,' Dieter said. '*Anschluss*.'

Anschluss meant annexation. Ten days ago, *Wehrmacht* troops had crossed the border and occupied Vienna. Austria was now part of the Greater Reich.

'You know what we say about Germans?' Keiko tapped the paper.

'Tell me.'

'We say that they always help themselves. And you know what else we say? We wonder what the rest of the world should make of it.'

'They stand aside. . .' Dieter said carefully, '. . . and watch.'

'For now.'

'Of course.'

'But this?' She nodded down at the paper. 'You think the British and the French will accept such a thing?'

Dieter didn't know but after his weeks of stiff diplomatic exchanges the opportunity for a real conversation was too good to miss. Keiko was bent towards him. She wanted an answer. He half-turned and looked her full in the face. He owed his presence here in Japan to the recent treaty between the two countries, a gesture calculated – in a phrase from Dieter's letter of appointment – to cement the union at an operational level.

'You invaded China last year,' he pointed out. 'You helped yourself.'

'Our generals invaded China. Not me.'

'You disapprove?'

'Of the consequences? Of course. What happened in Nanking was shameful. Some of the military people should be locked up.'

'You'd put them in a prison?' Dieter blinked.

'I'd put them in a zoo. They belong with the animals. They *are* the animals.'

Dieter nodded. Nanking was on the Chinese mainland. He'd heard rumours about atrocities but nothing more.

'And your brother? What does he think?'

'My brother is a rich man's son. With wealth comes blindness. He lives for flying. He sees what he wants to see. Nothing else.'

'And you?'

'I see everything.' For the first time, she smiled. 'You know about reiki?'

'No.'

'It's a therapy, a treatment, a way of making people better.'

'You do it?'

'Yes.'

'And it works?'

'Yes. Tell me more about your back.'

Keiko was listening carefully to Dieter's account of the moment his aircraft had taken a direct hit over the mountains in Northern Spain and the dizzying blur of events that had followed. With the aircraft's engine on fire and the fuel tank still half-full he'd rolled the aircraft on its back, wrestled the canopy open and released his harness. Briefly in freefall, with less than five hundred metres in hand, he'd managed to open the parachute but had landed badly amongst rocks on the mountainside.

Mercifully, it was a couple of Nationalist troops that had got to him first. The force of the landing had knocked him unconscious and his next real impression was a pain beyond description in his ribs and lower back as they carried him down the mountain. Two weeks immobilised in a hospital in Burgos had done very little to ease the pain but the Spanish doctors had certified him fit to travel, with no damage to the spinal cord, and an eight-hour flight had taken him to a hospital in Stuttgart where surgeons had operated on his lower spine. After that, thank God, he'd begun to recover.

'You were flying the 109?' The question came in Japanese. A male voice. Keiko supplied the translation.

Dieter looked round. A stocky young man in a blue Western suit was standing behind the bench. He had a shock of black hair and wide grin.

Dieter confirmed he'd been flying Willy Messerschmitt's new fighter.

'The canopy is shit, yes?'

'Yes.'

'It opens sideways. But only sometimes. Yes?'

'Yes.'

'So maybe that makes you lucky. My name's Seiji.' He patted Dieter on the shoulder. He appeared to have heard the whole conversation and made sense of most of it. 'You know what they say about pain in this country? That it's just an opinion. I like that. But then I've never fallen out of an aircraft.'

He roared with laughter at his own joke, ignoring his sister's wince of disapproval. It was nearly lunchtime. There was a favourite restaurant in the city that always looked after him very well. They'd take one of his father's cars. The three of them would feast like kings and afterwards there'd be time for some flying.

'You're OK with that?'

'Of course. Dual controls?'

'It's a trainer. A Yokosuka. Nothing special but no one shoots at us either.' Another bark of laughter. 'You like beef steak? Come. . . '

The restaurant was fifteen minutes away in the heart of the city. To Dieter's slight surprise, Keiko took the wheel of the big Packard. Seiji sat beside her, his body half-turned in the passenger seat. He wanted to know everything about the flying in Spain, about the Condor Legion, and about what Dieter had made of the little Russian fighter that had so tormented the Japanese bombers. The questions bubbled out of him, a torrent of Japanese accompanied by brisk, savage chopping movements with his right hand, while Keiko did her best to keep up. After a while, Dieter caught her eyes in the rear-view mirror and he knew at once that the tiny shake of her head was an apology. Outside the restaurant, she helped Dieter from the car and gave his arm a squeeze as they headed across the pavement.

'My brother is a child,' she whispered. 'Tomorrow we'll take him to the zoo.'

*

The restaurant was busy, diners sitting cross-legged on *tatami* mats while women in exquisite kimonos emerged from a screen at the back with trays of steaming food. By now Dieter was used to the sense of theatre that attended so much of Japanese life but this felt like something special. Eyeing a pile of clams at a nearby table, he felt the first stirrings of an appetite.

Seiji had reserved a table. When a waitress appeared with a menu, he waved it away. He wanted to know whether Dieter liked fish.

'Very much.'

Seiji said something to Keiko, who nodded and then turned back to the waitress. Seconds later, she was gone.

'My brother always knows what he wants,' Keiko murmured. 'My father says it's part of his charm.'

'Is he right?'

'That's for you to judge. I just hope you like oysters. And crab. And tuna with wasabi mash. Seiji loves giving presents. This is one of them.'

Seiji had called another waitress over. She fetched two beers and poured them with a delicacy that brought a smile to Dieter's face. This was a long way from the beerhalls of Hamburg or the dark *Gallego* bars he and Georg had patronised in Vitoria.

Seiji had settled behind the table. He wanted to propose a toast.

'We're still flying this afternoon?' Dieter nodded at his glass.

'Of course. Happy landings.'

Seiji swallowed most of the beer in a couple of gulps and wiped his mouth on the back of his hand. He wanted to know more about the *ratas* in Spain. How good were the Russians? And what did they make of the new Bf-109?

Dieter took the question at face value, addressing himself to Keiko, pausing to let her translate. The Russians, he said, flew like Cossacks. Their discipline in the air could be poor. They were easily distracted. But they were brave to the point of madness and pushed their little fighters to the limit.

Seiji followed the translation with a series of nods, his big-boy grin ever wider. Madness was a good word, the right word, the perfect description. These people were crazy. The last fight he'd had, a huge battle just north of Peking, he'd watched a single *rata* make attack after attack on the Japanese bombers. He'd been close to this lunatic, close enough to glimpse the big square goggles, the tan helmet, the light blue flying suit, close enough to snatch a deflection shot as the Russian banked and sped away. Seiji's hands weaved above the table, reliving the encounter, and then his fist smacked into his open palm as he got to the point of the story.

'Bam!' he yelled, followed by a volley of Japanese.

Diners stirred at nearby tables. Most of them looked like businessmen. Dieter glanced at Keiko.

'What did he say?'

'He said the Russian flew into the bomber. On purpose. He said he probably ran out of ammunition.'

Dieter returned to Seiji. He'd heard similar stories in Spain and had always wondered whether they were true.

'Did this happen often?'

'All the time. The Russians hate us. Life is cheap in a war like this, even your own.'

'You'd do the same thing? If you ran out of ammunition?'

'Never. Where's the satisfaction? Who would you tell afterwards?'

He roared with laughter, rocking back and forth on the *tatami* mat. He wanted to know about the 109.

'The Russians avoid us. Most days I never fired a shot.'

'Not so crazy, then, the Russians.'

'Not at all. All we had to do was take off, make an appearance, simply be there. Our bomber boys love the 109. The moment they saw us, they knew what it meant. No Ivans. Just a nice sunny day and the eggs on the target and an easy cruise back.'

'Eggs?' Keiko was frowning.

'Bombs. One night we drove over to their airfield. . .' Dieter was still looking at Seiji. 'They bought us beer all night because they thought we were magicians, casting spells on the Ivans, and they never wanted the magic to stop.'

'And what did you say? About the magic?'

'We told them our glasses were empty. Then we told them our secret. That everything depended on beer. Life is simple, we said. No beer. No magic. No magic and the Ivans will be all over you. It was a game, of course. The bomber boys are lions in the air. You need to be brave to have their kind of patience. But they bought us beers all night. And so the magic worked.'

Seiji waited for the translation and then slapped the table, rocking back and forth again.

'Beer,' he said. 'We need more beer.'

*

It was mid-afternoon before they left the restaurant. Keiko took a rickshaw back to the house while her brother retrieved the Packard. Dieter had counted the beers during lunch and wondered whether they were still going to fly.

The traffic was light. The wind had strengthened and a roadside park was carpeted with cherry blossom. Dieter sat back, watching a child as she splashed through the fallen leaves.

Without Keiko, conversation was limited but nothing stopped Seiji giving it a try.

'My sister? You like?'

'Very much.'

'Beautiful?'

'Very.'

'Bad girl. . .' he looked sideways and grinned. '. . . Tokyo. . . very bad girl.'

Dieter held his glance. More in hope than expectation he realised he urgently needed to know more.

'Bad girl?'

'Sure.' The word carried an American inflection.

'How?'

Seiji struggled to find an answer. 'Bad,' he repeated. 'Plenty bad girl.'

'So why Tokyo? She lives there?'

'Sure.'

'Is she married?' Dieter tapped the third finger of his right hand.

'Husband?' Seiji barked with laughter, swerving to avoid an old man on a bicycle. 'One time, yes.'

'No more?'

'No. My father. . .' He shook his head in mock despair.

'Your father what?'

Seiji didn't answer. At a crossroads beside a line of kerbside stalls he turned left, down towards the river. Then he reached across and put his hand on Dieter's arm.

'You like her?' he asked again.

'Yes.'

'Good.' He nodded. 'Very good.'

'Why?'

'Because she. . .' he frowned, hunting for the right tense, '. . . is liking you.'

'How do you know?'

Seiji shook his head. Then came the grin again and the big white teeth, and Dieter caught a gust of stale beer as he failed to stifle a yawn.

'*Very* bad girl.' Seiji pulled the car to a halt and gave Dieter's arm a reassuring squeeze. 'Very, *very* bad.'

Dieter was looking at a wooden pontoon that stretched out into the river. At the end of the pontoon, bobbing in the choppy green water, was a seaplane. It looked tiny in the brightness of the afternoon light. The fuselage aft of the big radial engine was streaked with oil and the unsecured rear cockpit cover, flapping in the wind, gave the machine an air of faint neglect. For Seiji, thought Dieter, this was a toy he'd once played with in his bath. He hoped to God his new friend would lose interest in showing it off.

Far from it. Seiji led the way down the pontoon. Dieter could feel the heave and suck of water beneath his feet. At the end of the pontoon, Seiji stepped uncertainly on to the lower wing and removed both cockpit covers before folding them flat and tossing them down to Dieter.

'Car.' He pointed towards the Packard.

Dieter carried the covers back along the pontoon. The Japanese were a race who set great store on the smaller courtesies. Even with a drunken pilot at the controls, refusing this invitation to fly was unthinkable.

The car was unlocked. Dieter left the covers on the front passenger seat and searched for something to keep him warm.

On the rear parcel shelf he found a long scarf. It was red, the softest wool, and the moment he wound it around his neck he knew it belonged to Keiko. It was a strange smell, a bitter sweetness he couldn't quite place, and under the circumstances – given what might happen next – he couldn't think of anything more appropriate to wear. Already, he'd sensed she was the beginning of something exotic, something utterly unexpected. If Seiji got it wrong on take-off, at least he'd carry this scent to the afterlife.

Back at the seaplane, Seiji had clambered into the rear cockpit. He had his head down and he appeared to be wrestling with something at his feet. Dieter was still freezing in the wind, trying to calculate what might happen next. The wind was blowing square across the river. Here in the heart of the city the river was barely a kilometre wide and the land on the other side shelved steeply upwards. In an ageing biplane, from a grass airstrip, Dieter wouldn't have hesitated to give it a try. He'd never flown in a seaplane in his life but one glance at the bulky floats told him that the machine would be infinitely less nimble. How brave – or how immortal – would you feel after five bottles of Asahi?

Still staring across the water, Dieter heard a snatch of Japanese and then a cackle of laughter from the rear cockpit. Seiji, just for a second or two, seemed to have mistaken the slight figure in the crimson scarf for his sister. Not a good sign.

Seiji was signalling for Dieter to swing the prop. Even on dry land, this called for a degree of caution. Dieter sat on the end of the pontoon until his feet found the float. The moment he transferred his weight, he felt the little plane nose down.

He reached back for support from the bottom wing, steadied himself, then inched forward again. Swinging the prop under these conditions called for perfect balance. At best, he'd probably fall in. At worst, once the engine caught, the wooden propeller would chop him to pieces.

Mercifully, Seiji just wanted to purge the cylinders of oil. Dieter did his bidding each time the Japanese circled his finger in the air, hauling on the prop until the last of the cylinders was empty. Ignoring the stabs of pain from his lower back, Dieter returned to the pontoon, stepped on to the lower wing, and then lowered himself into the front cockpit. A single glance took in the controls and gauges. Joystick, airspeed indicator, throttle, rudder pedals, rudimentary compass, the bare minimum you'd need to get yourself airborne and return in one piece. This, he told himself, was flying in the raw.

Dieter strapped himself in. Whoever normally flew in the front was a great deal fatter. He heard the engine cough once, then again, and suddenly – after the long months of convalescence – he was back in a world he understood, his face buffeted by the blast of air from the prop, his nerves tingling at the scent of aviation spirit and hot oil.

He felt a tap on his shoulder. Seiji. Dieter strained against the straps, trying to look backwards, caught the gloved hand, the raised thumb. He answered the only way he could, his own thumb vertical, a gesture – he later realised – of resignation. Bad things happened all the time. He just hoped this wouldn't be one of them.

Seiji had slipped the ropes securing the seaplane to the pontoon. A surge of throttle inched them forward until he had the searoom to pull the little plane into the wind. Dieter settled lower in the seat, Keiko's scarf heaped around his neck. As far as he could see, there was no conflicting traffic on the river. Hunched even lower, he tried to pick an impact point on the far side of the river between the scratches on the tiny disc of windscreen. Given a choice, he'd have settled for one of the sturdier pine trees. The impact alone would spare him burning to death.

Seiji opened the throttle. The engine, to Dieter's surprise, responded at once. The plane already felt light as a feather, bouncing along, picking up speed, pushing the water aside. Fat drops on the windscreen blurred his view. Then came the moment of release, a tiny lurch upwards, and the river had suddenly let them go. Briefly ashamed by his lack of faith, Dieter raised his hand again, thumb and forefinger ringed, a private gesture of approval or perhaps deliverance.

Seiji steadied the seaplane, gaining height before he dipped a wing and began to track south down the river towards the open sea. Perfectly trimmed, this was a plane that would have looked after itself but Seiji flew like a fighter pilot, his fingertips alive on the joystick, a fidget at the controls, constantly adjusting in search of exactly the right balance between the tug of the engine, the suck of gravity and the buffet of the wind.

From a thousand metres, gazing down, Dieter could make out the scatter of houses on the terraced hillsides that fell away towards the river, the landscape pinked by cherry blossom. They looked like shell bursts against the darker greens and browns and Dieter was suddenly back in the mountains of Galicia, a year earlier, prosecuting a foreign war that had nearly killed him, when he felt another tap on his shoulder. Seiji again. Wanting him to take over.

Dieter stared down at the joystick. This was the first time he'd been at the controls of an aircraft since his accident. Even flying to Japan as a passenger, a six-day journey hopscotching across the globe towards the wide sweep of Tokyo Bay, he'd felt an anxiety that had never troubled him before. Falling out of an aircraft, he told himself, was an abrupt reminder that in any serious argument the forces of gravity always won.

His right hand settled around the joystick, thumb on top, wrist loose, the lightest touch, trying to feel his way back into what he'd always done best. The rev counter showed 2,150 rpm. Airspeed was 138 kph. They were heading seven degrees west of south. Dieter smiled, touching all these familiar bases, making himself at home, building a kinship with this ugly little duckling that had so far proved so responsive. He inched the joystick forward and fed in a little left rudder to keep the slip ball in the middle of its small glass tube. The nose dipped and he held the turn until he felt the buffet of his own slipstream, a perfect 360 degree turn with no loss of height. The compass needle settled once again on the original heading. Easy, he thought, his whole body flooded with something he recognised as relief. His touch was still there. He hadn't lied to Keiko. He could still fly.

Minutes later, hugging the coast as it curled away towards the east, he thought about Georg. The last time they'd been together was in the hospital in Stuttgart. Georg had arrived with a supply of Dieter's favourite chocolates, as well as a bottle of schnapps, and it turned out that he'd been posted to an airfield in the north of Germany where the *Luftwaffe* trained their pilots for the bomber fleet, and at first Dieter had difficulty understanding why on earth Georg would abandon a fighter

Jagdstaffel for the tedium of the delivery business. Wasn't he bored to death? Wouldn't he miss the excitements of the hunt?

Not at all. Far from it. The official letter of appointment to the Führer's elite *Reichsregierung* had found Georg in Spain where he was still flying against the Reds. His masters in Berlin had selected him for the tiny corps of pilots qualified to ferry Hitler and other luminaries around the country. Membership of this airborne elite came with a huge increase in pay and a series of other perks but in the opinion of his squadron commander, Gunther Lutzow, this was irrelevant. What mattered was that Georg was exactly the man for the job. Hitler was lucky to have him.

At the time, still trying to come to terms with his injuries, Dieter had mustered a smile and limp applause, but the more he thought about it, the more he recognised the logic of the promotion. Georg had the lowest blood pressure of anyone he'd ever met. He flew like an angel. He was utterly dependable. And he showed every sign of being able to ignore all the nonsense that went with the upper reaches of the regime. Good luck, he'd said, giving Georg's hand a squeeze. Let me know what those bastards are really like.

Dieter felt a tap on his shoulder. It was Seiji again, directing his attention to the fuel gauge. The tank was three quarters empty. Dieter loosened his straps and half-turned in the seat, gesturing down at the joystick. You take control. Seiji shook his head and then pillowed it against his gloved hands. Too much Asahi. Time for a nap. You fly us back.

Dieter stared down at the control stick. He was freezing cold. There were bits of him that would never be right. He'd never landed a float plane in his life. Yet here was someone with trust enough in him to get them both back to the comforts of the pontoon. Had word of his adventures in Spain got as far as Nagasaki? Was this rich kid, with his four months combat record, a little in awe of *Der Kleine*'s twenty-seven kills? Dieter shrugged. He didn't care. Get them both down in one piece and he might be through the door that would take him back to proper flying.

Out here, above the ocean, he could see the whitecaps driven by the strengthening wind. Now and again, the little plane bucked and dropped a wing in yet another gust. The wind direction, as far as he could gauge, hadn't changed. His only landing option was the same kilometre of semi-sheltered water that lay off the pontoon. That meant a steep approach across the city itself, shedding height towards the river, flying as low as he dared until the final moment when he pulled back on the stick and returned the little plane to the water.

And so it went. Visibility on the approach to the city was perfect: scudding white clouds against the blueness of the sky. He flew into the estuary, comforted by the steady cackle of the engine, slowly losing height over the big estates that overlooked the river. Somewhere down there, he told himself, is Seiji's property. Might Keiko be there? Might she be out in the garden, peering upwards? Might she recognise the little silver fish with its big bootees? Dieter dropped another hundred metres and waggled the wings just in case, a manoeuvre which brought a bark of laughter from the rear cockpit. Then, quicker than he'd expected, Dieter found himself over the city centre.

A more cautious soul would have made a turn to the east, maintaining height, giving himself more room for the final approach, but Dieter was starting to panic. This had never happened before, not once, and it took him a second or two to make sense of the symptoms. His mouth was suddenly dry. His heart was racing. His hand was gripping the control stick the way a novice might, white knuckles that spoke of nothing except the imminence of disaster. All he could think of was the moment when he rolled the 109 on its back, thumped the canopy release, and fell into a wilderness of pain and blackness.

He'd spotted the pontoon and the Packard parked beside it. For some reason the car's door was open. He didn't know this plane at all, didn't know its limits, hadn't a clue about the control inputs it simply couldn't cope with, and that ignorance, that recklessness, simply confirmed the inevitable. Aloft, you got no second chance. This time, he thought, it was truly over.

Easing back on the throttle, he side-slipped, letting the aircraft drop. The prop began to windmill, the rush of air falling off. Below, Dieter was dimly aware of traffic coming to a halt, of a rickshaw driver pointing skywards, of a woman gathering her little girl in her arms. Too low? Dieter prayed not. He could practically touch the red tiled roofs, spot the birds' nests in the gutters, taste the woodsmoke curling from an on-rushing chimney. He fed in a little throttle and kicked the float plane straight before an instinctive tweak on the joystick spared him a collision with the tallest of the electricity poles. Seconds later the pontoon was a blur of faded planking beneath them and there was nothing but water ahead. Dieter closed his eyes, easing back on the control stick, letting the aircraft look after itself, knowing that somehow he'd survived.

The landing itself felt brutal, a sudden lurch as the floats bit into the curling wavelets, but the aircraft quickly settled down and when it felt right Dieter used the rudder to circle back.

Finally secured against the pontoon, Dieter cut the engine and let Seiji help him out of the cockpit. His lower back was on fire. His legs were trembling. He felt physically sick. He clambered awkwardly down on to the pontoon, sucking in the cold air. Seiji took a tiny step backwards and offered a deep bow. Dieter didn't know whether it signalled admiration or relief but either way it didn't matter. At all costs, despite the churning in his belly, he had to save face.

'Thank you for that.' He nodded towards the little plane.

'You like?'

'Very much.'

He extended a hand. Seiji didn't move.

'Tomorrow.' Seiji nodded towards the tall figure standing beside the Packard. 'She takes you to the zoo.'

4

LONDON, 7 APRIL 1938

Tam Moncrieff's sister Vanessa lived in a three-storey Regency mansion in the heart of Belgravia. The house had served for generations as the London home of the Nairn dynasty, a Scottish family with extensive estates in the rolling Border hills south of Edinburgh. As a young graduate, fresh out of St Andrew's University, Vanessa had been hired to tutor the two Nairn children in Spanish and Italian. Six years later, after the sudden death of Alec Nairn's wife, she became Lady Nairn.

Tam and Vanessa had never been close. Tam had met Lord Nairn only once, on the day of their wedding. He was nearly twenty years older than his new bride, tall and conversationally distant, and Tam had always struggled to understand why Vanessa had taken him for a husband. Watching them together at the lavish reception after the service, it was difficult to detect any real warmth between the newlyweds and when they'd appeared later in the evening to lead off in the first reel, the mismatch was painfully obvious. Faced with his wife's vivacity, Alec Nairn was shy as well as physically awkward. He plainly loathed highland dancing and quickly excused himself to spend the rest of the evening with a table of old friends, all male.

At the time, to Tam, this had felt like the grimmest of omens but nearly a decade and a half later the marriage appeared to be in rude health. Mutual friends praised Vanessa for bringing Alec out of himself. The Nairns had even become something of a fixture on London's social circuit. Only last week, waiting for a dental appointment, Tam had leafed through an ancient copy of the *Tatler* and found himself looking at a photograph of the happy couple in the steward's enclosure at Henley. The news that Alec Nairn had once won a rowing blue at Oxford was another surprise.

The house was in Upper Belgrave Street. Tam had never been here before. Three steps took him up from the pavement to the front door. He rang the bell and then stepped back. Ionic columns supported the handsome portico. A fresh coat of paint gleamed on the tall Georgian windows. This was a world away from the make-and-mend of The Glebe House.

The door opened. It was Vanessa. She was wearing a pair of ancient corduroy trousers and a bulky old pullover darned at the elbows. The last time they'd met was a couple of years ago in Edinburgh. Tam had just left the Royal Marines and was visiting a stockbroker in a bid to tease some order into his father's financial affairs. Emerging from the office with nothing of any value accomplished, he'd found his sister sipping a glass of sherry in the waiting room. Vanessa had looked up at him, making no attempt to get to her feet.

'What on earth are you doing here?' she'd said.

Seconds later, summoned to the inner sanctum, she'd left Tam with an image of a stylish woman in her early forties with a blaze of red curls and a face that needed no make-up. Since he could remember, his sister had always had the physical presence to make any man take a second look, a fact that made the choice of Alec Nairn even stranger. Was it his money? His title? The thousands of acres of prime Berwickshire? Or what?

These were questions that Tam had never been able to answer. Now, on the doorstep, she offered him a brief frown.

'You're late,' she said. 'We agreed eleven.'

Tam didn't answer. The occasion demanded a handshake, at the very least, maybe even the briefest peck on the cheek, but his sister had already turned on her heel and was leading the way into the depths of the house.

'Alec's out,' she said over her shoulder. 'He's not very keen on family occasions.'

'Is that what this is?'

'Of course. You want to talk about dad. That's what you said on the phone.'

Tam found himself in a sunny drawing room at the back of the house. The windows offered a view of a generous garden, trees already in full leaf, and a pair of spaniels lounged in front of a spitting wood fire.

'Alec gets chilly, even in this weather.' Vanessa was looking for another log. 'I think it must be his age. One day I might open a convalescent home. Tea?'

Without waiting for an answer, she left the room. Tam heard the low mumble of conversation from across the corridor and the fall of water into a kettle. Then Vanessa was back. She peeled off the pullover. Underneath was a plaid shirt several sizes too big for her. The sleeves were rolled up, revealing a man's watch on one wrist and a collection of silver bangles on the other. Tam's gaze seemed to amuse her.

'I've been out in the garden.' She nodded towards the window. 'Paid help costs the earth and it's getting worse and worse.'

'You're running out of money?'

'I'm running out of patience. You pay these bloody people a fortune and end up doing the job yourself. People expect everything these days. Not just money but conversation. The last man we had used to spend his summers down in Kent. If you want to know about hop-picking, just ask.'

She shook her head, uninterested in a reply, and made space for a tray of tea in the hands of a youngish woman with a sallow complexion and huge brown eyes. She offered Tam a nod and a smile and left.

'That was Maria. She's Italian, comes from a little village down in the south. A woman of low expectations and immense wisdom. We talk and talk and talk. She's a treasure, that woman. If you want the truth, she's the only person who keeps me sane.'

'And Alec?'

'Alec is Alec. One acquires good habits and bad habits. In Alec's case, mercifully, it's the former. Fondness is all. He's back for lunch so we don't have much time. Sugar?'

Tam nodded, wondering what had happened to her accent. Only a trace of her native Scots seemed to remain. Was this what happened if you lived in Belgravia? Acquired a title? Consorted with the rich?

She wanted to know about their father. On the phone, Tam had used the word 'deranged'. What, exactly, did that mean?

'He's crazy. He's been losing touch for a while but recently it's got worse. Most mornings I suspect he doesn't have a clue who he is. He's as thin as a rake, won't eat proper food, won't look after himself. When I try and have a conversation, he just talks about Mum. He thinks she's living in the attic. He's certain she's refusing to come down and talk to him. And that makes him cry.'

'How horrible. What does the doctor say?'

'The doctor says he's got dementia.'

'Then I suspect the doctor's right. Dementia's everywhere. Alec's got chums who think Belgravia's something you pour on roast beef. Well done to you for looking after him.'

Chums was new, a word he'd never heard her use before. Along with the accent, she seemed to have become someone else. The next few minutes, Tam knew, were going to be far from easy. Way back, when they were kids in Scotland, she'd had a family nickname.

'He needs proper care, Nessie.'

'Then put him in a home.'

'I can't. He'd hate it. It would kill him.'

'Then get someone in to help.'

'I can't do that, either.'

'Why on earth not?'

'Times are challenging. We're trying to run a business.'

'You've come to ask for money?'

'I've come to tell you that our father's very ill. The least we owe him is company.'

'But you're there. You're on the spot.'

'Not for much longer.'

She frowned. She had a thorn in one of her fingertips. Sucking it, she suddenly looked like the child he remembered from his nursery days, for ever looking for ways to hurt him.

'You're suggesting he comes down here? You think we can look after him?'

'Yes.'

'Impossible. Alec wouldn't have it. And neither would I.' She was staring at him. 'Are you serious? About Dad?'

'I'm afraid I am.'

'Then where are you going? What's so special it can't wait until. . .' she shrugged, '. . . he doesn't need you any more?'

'I'm afraid I can't tell you.'

'Really? It's some kind of secret?'

'In a way, yes it is.'

She nodded and then reached for the teacup, balancing it carefully on her knee. She didn't bother to hide her irritation.

'You're really going away?'

'Yes.'

'Abroad?'

'Yes.'

'For long?'

'I don't know.'

She took a sip of tea, and then another, studying him over the rim of the cup.

'It's Germany, isn't it? It has to be. You speak the language. Don't deny it. Just nod.'

'Speaking the language?'

'Going off to Germany.'

Tam held her gaze, giving nothing away. Within minutes they were back in the chokehold of the long-ago relationship they'd never properly resolved. Older, stronger and always more devious, she'd made bits of his childhood a nightmare he never wanted to revisit.

'We had the ill-fortune to meet the German ambassador last year,' she said. 'You've heard of Brickendrop?'

'Brickendrop?'

'Von Ribbentrop. He lived round the corner here while they were messing about with the embassy. Alec thinks it must have been that wife of his behind it all. They took three of those gorgeous old Nash houses in Carlton House Terrace and knocked them into one. They tore the places apart, absolutely ruined them. It must have cost millions, literally millions. They threw a huge party the day after the Coronation. Fourteen hundred of us. It was mediaeval. It was like one of those French levees. We were there to pay homage. What a truly ghastly night.'

'But why Brickendrop?'

'Because the man has no tact, no judgement and certainly no taste. He was here for less than a year. He speaks decent English but that only made things worse because he could never hide behind an interpreter. Count the number of people he offended and there'd be no one worth knowing *left* in London. Why on earth did they send him in the first place? What does a man like that tell you about his masters?'

Tam said he'd no idea. He badly wanted to bring the conversation back to his poor, mad father but Vanessa hadn't finished. Alec, she said, was close to certain individuals in the Foreign Office. People in the know had concluded that Ambassador Brickendrop had the ear of Hitler, who regarded him as a wondrous discovery, a kind of secret weapon to inflict on the English.

'First Brickendrop,' she said. 'Then the *Luftwaffe*. Gloomy, I know, but everyone's saying it.'

Tam sensed she was softening. Her conviction that her brother might be up to no good in Germany seemed to have put him in a new light.

'Are you some kind of spy?' she said. 'Only we'd rather like that.'

'We?'

'Alec and I. Alec thinks we're all heading for the clifftop, especially now that fool Halifax is at the FO. God knows, Alec is probably right. Anything you might do in that regard, we'd be very grateful.'

'You could look after Dad for a bit,' Tam said. 'That would help.'

She nodded, took another sip of tea, stirred one of the spaniels with her foot, said nothing. Then her head came up.

'How long do you think he's got?'

'Dad?'

'Yes.'

'Couple of months? Maybe less?' Tam had no idea.

'Does he speak Italian at all? Might Maria look after him?'

'He barely speaks English.'

'Do you think he'd recognise me?'

'He might. He might not. Would it be easier if he didn't?'

For the first time, Tam had sparked a smile. He leaned forward, returning his cup to the tray.

'You're happy for this conversation to remain confidential?' he asked.

'Of course.'

'You mean that?'

'Absolutely.'

He studied her for a moment. Her eyes were gleaming. He put his hand on hers. She didn't flinch.

'As it happens, it's not Germany,' he said. 'But unless Dad comes to you and I know he's safe, it won't happen. Your decision, Nessie. Yours and Alec's.'

She nodded. She looked transformed.

'The answer's yes,' she said. 'Give me a couple of days to sort things out.'

'And Alec?'

'He'll agree.'

5

TOKYO, 13 APRIL 1938

Dieter and Keiko never made it to the zoo in Nagasaki. The morning after the flight in the seaplane, Dieter lurked in the house overlooking the river, expecting Keiko or her brother to appear with the news that the car was once again awaiting them for the trip into the city. Neither showed up, not that day or the next. Instead, a senior manager from the steel mill took Dieter on an extended trip around the biggest of the shipyards across the river, eager to show off the industrial lead that Japan had established amongst her neighbours in the Eastern Pacific. The biggest oil tankers. The fastest construction times. The most ambitious five-year plan.

Coshed by superlatives, Dieter dined alone that night, raising his head at the long empty table to contemplate the view. By now he knew enough about this strange country never to trust the surface of things. What you saw, what you heard, was seldom the whole truth. The programme for his three-month assignment was littered with invitations – a *Sakura* ceremony up in the hills around Naga, an oyster festival on the island of Miyajima, an incomprehensible Noh play he'd sat through in a freezing venue in Kyoto. He'd emerged from each of these events impressed by the costumes and the ritual and the rapt attention of the audience but convinced more than ever that the Japanese had wilfully put themselves beyond reach. Maybe it was centuries of physical isolation from the rest of the world. Maybe they were just more comfortable keeping the rest of the planet at arm's length. But either way, as the family maid appeared with yet more *miso,* it was hard not to feel a sense of being somehow short-changed. Maybe the invitation to the zoo had been a joke. Maybe the zoo didn't even exist. And maybe, more to the point, he might never lay eyes on Keiko again. A pity, he thought, pushing aside his empty plate.

Within days he was back in Tokyo. He attended a courtesy briefing at the War Ministry that paid a great deal of attention to Japan's growing fleet of aircraft carriers. Through a translator who looked not a day older than her charges, he did his best to address a huge class of schoolchildren in a Tokyo suburb about everyday life in Germany. On successive evenings, he gave his escorts the slip and did a modest tour of the bars in the Ginza area of the city. With the weather still cold, Lohmeyer's restaurant offered a reliable goulash but Dieter preferred a seedy little bar called Fledermaus, favoured by drinkers from the more louche corners of the German business and diplomatic community. Then came the summons to his own embassy. With the end of his assignment in sight, there was to be an evening reception for some of the Japanese military who had looked after the young German flier.

The German Embassy lay in Tokyo's diplomatic quarter, a handsome colonnaded building set in lavish gardens. That evening, the military attaché was in charge. To Dieter, Eugen Ott had always been a grim-faced presence amongst the rest of the staff but his career prospects had recently brightened with the departure of the Ambassador, Herbert von Dirksen, for a new position in London. Eugen Ott had been in post for four years in Tokyo and his fluent Japanese made him the favourite to replace the outgoing chief. Ott had never succumbed to Dieter Merz's charm and relations between the two men remained icy.

Dieter's appointment appeared to have the backing of Joachim von Ribbentrop, now *Reichsminister* for Foreign Affairs back home, and Ott knew better than to incur the wrath of so powerful a champion, yet in his view Merz had never cut the kind of figure the new regime deserved. Ott's reservations had nothing to do with Merz's combat record – the boy was obviously an accomplished killer – but in conversation he seemed to lack the assertiveness and the sense of innate entitlement required to impress the Japanese. The boy needs to grow up, he'd confided to his secretary. No wonder fellow pilots in the Condor Legion had called him *Der Kleine*.

Tonight's embassy function took a while to catch fire but Ott himself was circulating with bottles of champagne specially imported from von Ribbentrop's family business and by mid-evening the big first floor reception room was alive with conversation. To Ott's visible surprise, Merz was popular with the Japanese. They seemed to regard him as a favourite son, someone they could share a joke with, throw an arm around, recount moments during some embassy-planned tour or other when they'd both strayed from the official briefing and surrendered to the craziness of events. This degree of informality, from Ott's point of view, was slightly unsettling and he was tight-lipped when he ordered Merz to stay behind after the departure of the last guest.

Ott worked from an office on the ground floor. The shelf behind his desk featured photographs of his wife and his dog, an enormous Alsatian called Werner who prowled the corridors of the embassy at weekends, terrorising the duty typists.

Dieter was eyeing a humidor that lay beside the telephone. He'd enjoyed the evening immensely. All he needed now was one of Ott's big fat Cuban cigars.

Ott wanted Dieter's thoughts on the success or otherwise of his assignment. Within a week, the young fighter pilot was due to ship back to Europe. What did he make of what he'd seen?

Dieter saw no point in disguising the truth. He'd seen what his hosts had wanted him to see. The air force were good in certain areas, less so in others. They were finding it heavy going against the Chinese but they were quick to learn and much of their equipment was first class. If they had a real problem, said Dieter, then it surely lay further down the supply chain. Warfare these days was a glutton for raw material – especially oil and rubber – and the Japanese were lacking in both.

'So how do you think they'll manage?' enquired Ott.

'Either they'll keep buying overseas or they'll go to war.'

'You mean a wider war? Not just the Chinese?'

'Of course.'

'So what choice will they make? In your opinion?'

'They'll go to war,' Dieter said. 'They'll ask nicely for whatever it is they want and when the answer is no they'll help themselves. It's cheaper that way and a lot more tidy. The

Dutch have the oil and the British have the rubber. If I were living in Singapore or Jakarta just now I'd probably be booking a passage home.'

'How can you be so certain?'

'Because I'm German.'

'What does that mean?'

'It means I understand their problem. It's means and ends. These people draw the straightest lines. You can see it in their architecture. They think the way they build.'

'And we do the same?'

'Yes. Except our buildings are uglier.'

'I see...' Ott was toying with a paperknife. There was a tiny swastika on the handle. At length, he looked up. 'And have you shared these thoughts with your new friends?'

'On the contrary. They told me.'

'About Singapore? Jakarta?'

'About the oil and the rubber. It's a shopping list. The rest you can work out. All you need is a map.'

Dieter let the exchange hang in the air. He'd had a great deal of time to think about these issues over the past three months. His conclusions had done nothing for his relationship with this man but he didn't care. The worst that could happen was a scathing report to the Foreign Ministry in Berlin but if his days as a would-be diplomat were numbered then nothing could be sweeter. Representing the Reich in Japan had been a struggle from first to last and once his body and his nerves were truly healed he'd be glad to get back to a trade he understood.

Ott mentioned a senior Japanese commander, Vice Admiral Kiyoshi. He'd been on this evening's invitation list but had sent his apologies at the last minute. Dieter shrugged. He'd never even met Vice Admiral Kiyoshi.

'I'm afraid that's not the point,' Ott grunted.

'It isn't?'

'No.'

There was a smile on Ott's face. Dieter didn't know why. At length Ott asked whether he'd heard of a ship called the *Soryu*.

'Of course. It's an aircraft carrier.'

'Exactly. Kiyoshi wants to show it off.'

'Who to?'

'You. The ship's on manoeuvres off Tokyo Bay. I'm afraid the weather isn't all it might be but Kiyoshi wants to put you in one of their torpedo bombers tomorrow morning and pay a visit.'

'You mean land on?'

'Of course.'

'Fine.' A second shrug. 'I've never been on a carrier. I'll enjoy the trip.'

'I'm afraid it's not quite that simple. They want you to pilot the aircraft.'

'You mean fly it?' Dieter was staring at him.

'Yes.'

'Why?'

'Because they're impressed by what you've been up to in Spain. Because they heard about your little escapade in the seaplane in Nagasaki. Five beers? And a near-perfect landing? They think you're pretty special in the air. And I'm sure they're right.'

It took a second or two for Dieter to marshal his thoughts. The best part of a bottle of champagne didn't help.

'Impossible.' Dieter shook his head. 'You need to be trained for that kind of flying. Give me a month with the right people. Then I might say yes.'

'I'm afraid that's not an option. Not in this country. Think of it as an honour. Believe me, this is an invitation we cannot afford to turn down.'

'I'm alone in this aircraft?'

'To the best of my knowledge there are three of you.'

'Dual controls?'

'I'm afraid I have no idea.'

Dieter looked away. He could visualise the approach, a strange aircraft at his fingertips, the carrier rolling and heaving, a single chance to get down in one piece.

'What if I get it wrong?'

'You won't. One of the other two is your friend from Nagasaki.'

'Seiji Ayama?'

'Indeed. I gather it might have been his idea in the first place. I'd take it as a compliment if I were you. What kind of pilot volunteers for a suicide mission?'

Ott pushed his chair back and stood up, sparing Dieter the Hitler salute. There was no warmth in his smile.

'There's a car outside.' He nodded at the door. 'Good luck for tomorrow.'

*

The car was waiting at the kerbside beyond the guard at the embassy gates. The Japanese driver watched Dieter making his way carefully down the steps to the street and then emerged to open the rear door. Dieter recognised the scent before he caught sight of the face.

'Keiko,' he said.

She was in the back of the car. She nodded down at the empty seat beside her. Her brother, she murmured, sent his apologies for not being able to make it to the embassy function. She was wearing the red scarf he'd borrowed the afternoon he went flying with Seiji in Nagasaki. She was smiling.

'Where are we going?'

Keiko didn't answer. The car began to move without a word to the driver. Dieter's modest hotel was a five-minute walk from the embassy but the driver turned right instead of left, joining a major road still thick with traffic. Dieter sat back, gazing out at the swirl of pedestrians, too numbed to bother asking again where they were headed or what Keiko was doing in the car.

All he could think about was the torpedo bomber and that inexplicable tangle of circumstances that would – come tomorrow – put him in the pilot's seat. He knew a great deal about surviving in the air, often against near-impossible odds, but that very same knowledge told him that tomorrow's challenge was close to impossible. Landing Seiji's seaplane, after months out of the cockpit, had shaken him badly. He'd misjudged the approach. Worse still, within touching distance of disaster he'd come close to folding his hand, pushing back his chair and leaving the game. He could still taste that feeling of helplessness, of resignation, and it terrified him. Putting down on a carrier, especially in bad weather, would be suicidal.

The car had left the main road and plunged into a maze of side streets. Dieter found himself looking at a narrow, single-storey house wedged between a garage and what looked like a furniture store. Keiko was already on the pavement, holding the door open.

'Come,' she said.

Dieter did her bidding. She closed the rear door behind him and murmured something to the driver. Dieter heard a clink of coins before the car drove away. A thin-looking cat had appeared from nowhere, winding itself around his ankles. Gusts of wind lifted a sheet of abandoned newsprint from the throat of a nearby alley, ghostly in the hot darkness. The air smelled of gasoline.

Keiko had opened the front door to the house. She gestured him in. Dieter found himself in a room bigger than he'd expected: *tatami* mats on the floor, a bamboo screen towards the back, the tang of citrus from a lemon tree beneath the window, shadows dancing in the candlelight. A low shelf ran along one wall, home to a line of tiny sculptures flanked by the candles, and a long tapestry hung on another wall. The room had a grace and simplicity Dieter had come to expect from the countless family visits he'd paid but it had something else as well, something that went hand in hand with this woman who seemed to have nested deep inside him. *Mystery* was too small a word but just now he was struggling to find another.

Beyond the screen was an open door. Keiko disappeared for a moment and then returned. She was holding a pair of pyjama trousers and a loose, sleeveless jacket.

'Please. . . '

She gave him the garments and nodded at the mattress on the floor. Then she was gone again.

Dieter was looking at the cat. It sat on a low table beside the biggest of the candles and seemed to be watching him. Was it the same cat he'd seen in the street? Or was it as spectral, as unreal, as everything else had suddenly become? Dieter lived on his instincts. But his instincts, those nerve ends he'd never had cause to mistrust, had abruptly let him down. In ways he found impossible to understand, he was totally lost. *Reiki*, he thought, studying the mattress on the floor. This must be where she works.

Keiko again. She was offering him a glass. He took it. Sipped it. Hoping for *sake*, he was disappointed. Water.

'What do you want me to do with these?' Dieter still had the pyjama trousers and the jacket.

Keiko didn't answer. She began to undress him. He was wearing *Luftwaffe* dress uniform, the material stiff under her busy fingertips. Finally he stood naked before her. She turned him round in the candlelight, the way she might have inspected an object that had attracted her at an auction, something she might end up putting a bid on. Her touch was light, her eyes mapping the surgical scars on his lower back.

'This hurts? Here?'

'A little.'

'And here?'

'Yes.'

'Bend for me, please.' Dieter did his best. 'That's difficult?'

'Yes.'

'Reach for the left. Now the right. Spread your legs. Bend down.'

Her voice was soft. She appeared to know exactly what she was after. What little Dieter knew about *reiki* suggested it was a spiritual thing, a laying-on of hands, some mysterious transfer of energy, but this procedure belonged in a clinic. Except for the cat, Dieter might have been back with the army of surgeons and nurses in Stuttgart who had restored him to some kind of working order.

Finally, she was finished. She asked him if he was cold and whether he wanted to put the garments on. He shook his head.

'You want more?' She nodded at his empty glass. 'Water is important.'

'Why?'

'It purifies you.'

'Then the answer's no.'

She held his gaze for a moment. Not a flicker of amusement.

'Lie down, please.' She nodded towards the floor. 'On your back.'

Every mattress Dieter had tried in Japan was hard. This was no exception. He did his best to make himself comfortable. Being naked had never embarrassed him, but he was aware of Keiko's eyes on his body.

'You're beautiful,' she said. 'You look like a child.'

Dieter smiled. Other women in his life had said something similar. *Der Kleine.*

Keiko sat cross-legged at his head, her upper body bent over him, the paleness of her face ghostlike in the darkness. Dieter felt her hands cupped on his temples, the softest touch, the tips of her fingers lingering for a moment then moving on, very slowly, pausing for minutes at a time, looking – it seemed to Dieter – for some purchase on what she might find inside his head.

'Who matters to you?' she asked at last.

Dieter blinked. He liked the silence. He liked the way his body was surrendering to the candlelight, and the unexpected warmth of her touch. The question broke the spell.

'My father.' Dieter closed his eyes.

'Why?'

'Because he was a like a god in my life. Because I worshipped him.'

'He's gone?'

'Yes.'

'How?'

'He died after an accident. It wasn't his fault.'

'He was a flier? Like you?'

'Yes. He flew in the war. Afterwards he taught others.'

'Including you?'

'Yes. He was a fine teacher. The best. He taught me that anything is possible as long as you want it badly enough.'

'So what did you want?'

'I wanted to fly. I wanted to be free.'

He was staring up at her. Her very presence beside him had triggered memories buried deep in his brain. He began to tell her about his home town. Ulm, he said, lay beside the upper Danube. The river was still an infant here, a mere trickle compared to what it would become further downstream, but the city boasted the tallest Minster in Europe. As a child, his father had taken him up to the very top of the tower. He still remembered counting the steps. There were seven hundred and sixty-eight. At the time, the ascent had felt like a game, no stopping allowed, a long, long climb, ever higher, the roughness of the bare walls cold under his touch, his legs on fire, his young lungs bursting while his father quietly urged him ever upwards in the gloom.

Then, quite suddenly, they were out in the open. It was early spring, the air crystal-clear after a series of showers, and in the far distance, away to the south, his father's pointing finger had found the Swiss Alps. The blur of snow-capped peaks on the far horizon meant nothing to Dieter. What was far more interesting was the sight of a huge bird, ungainly, cartoon-like, slowly circling the cathedral spire. From this height, nearly a hundred and fifty metres, he was looking *down* at the bird and he raced round the viewing gallery on his tired little legs, keeping the creature in sight.

'It was a stork,' he said. 'You know about storks?'

Keiko smiled, said nothing. Her hands were mapping the flatness of Dieter's belly. When he began to stir, she leaned back.

'Tell me about storks,' she said.

'They were huge. Enormous. You saw them all the time in the marshes by the river. They built nests the size of bicycle wheels, maybe bigger, often on church towers, anywhere safe, anywhere they could bring up their young. My father had a pair of binoculars. We'd ride into the country, along by the river, along by the places where they hunted for food, and then we'd find a nest and the young waiting, and we'd watch the storks flying back, the way they circled the nest, the way they lost speed, their legs out, their wings spread, a perfect landing every time. At school I'd draw pictures of storks. At night I'd dream about them.'

Dieter was smiling at the memory. Keiko wanted to know more about his father.

'He taught me to fly,' he said again. 'He taught me how to *become* the stork. That's all you need to know.'

'You miss him?'

'Of course.'

'And your mother?'

'She left us.'

The questions stopped. In the silence, Dieter could hear the cat washing itself. He opened his eyes. Keiko's face was very close. His father had survived for three days after the crash. At the hospital in Ulm, Dieter hadn't left his bedside. At fifteen it was still OK to know nothing. Except that death had no place for a man like this.

'I told him,' he whispered.

'Told him what?'

'I told him he was a god. It made him laugh. I was holding him when he died. I think he was happy.' He paused, swallowed hard. 'He had a spare flying suit which came to me. I tried it on but it was much too big. I loved that suit. I gave it to a friend of mine in the end. Georg. He still wears it.'

'It was just you, then? You and your father? After your mother left?'

'Yes. Just him and me. When he was dying he told me he'd flown with the Richthofen Circus during the war. He'd kept it a secret all that time. Richthofen. Another god.' Keiko was back beside his head. Dieter stared up at her. 'And you know another thing he told me? When he was dying? He told me never to believe in fear. Only consequences.'

'But you have fear now. I can feel it.'

'Really?'

'Yes.'

Dieter thought about the proposition, then shook his head. 'It's not fear,' he said. 'It's something else.'

'Like what?'

'Resignation. Which is probably worse.'

'Why?'

Dieter didn't answer, turning his head away. In Spain, he'd flown reconnaissance missions against foreign warships trying to keep the Republican port of Bilbao open. One of them was a huge British battleship. He could see it now, dwarfing the screen of smaller destroyers fussing around it. He'd never seen anything bigger in his life yet this grey giant was still troubled by the long Atlantic swells, wallowing beneath Dieter's starboard wing.

Tomorrow, he knew those same implacable weather gods would kill him. The barometer dropping. The ocean beginning to stir. The aircraft carrier heaving and pitching as the weather took a turn for the worse. Low cloud base. Maybe rain. The wind tossing him around like a leaf in the storm. One chance. Just one. One chance to drop the aircraft on the deck and come to a halt. But that would never happen because the odds were impossible. At best, he'd hit the throttle and stagger into the air like some wounded bird and stay aloft for long enough to fail all over again. At worst, they'd topple off the flight deck that first time and die in the roaring darkness beneath the oncoming carrier. Consequences, he thought. And maybe a surprise reunion with his father. Would he still be bandaged up? Or might the angels have made him whole again?

He told Keiko about the carrier. He wanted to reach up to her. He wanted to hold her. Not because he was frightened but because life had suddenly locked a door behind him and thrown away the key. Did this strange sorceress with the magic in her fingertips believe in immortality? Was she aware that a corner of paradise was reserved for fighter pilots? Did it even matter that three young men would end their lives in a brief spasm of terror, their lungs filling with water, the pressure bursting their ear drums as the aircraft sank into the depths?

Keiko seemed to recognise the darkness in his eyes, the bewilderment behind the gathering frown. She asked him to turn over. Some time later, he didn't know when, he felt one of her hands on the base of his spine, while the other found the nape of his neck. After a long pause she drew her hands together, a combing motion, up and down the length of his torso three times. Then she got to her feet and stepped away a moment before the rough knap of a blanket settled around him. Finally darkness came as she extinguished the candles one by one, the soft pad of her footsteps receding into the depths of the house. Dieter closed his eyes, surrendering to a deep and dreamless sleep that seemed to last forever.

*

Morning was a thin stripe of sunlight on the *tatami* mat.

'Here. . .' It was Keiko again. Green tea in a delicate porcelain bowl.

Dieter struggled to sit up. For the first time since he'd bailed out in Spain the stiffness in his lower back had gone. Already, he was looking for his uniform. Keiko nodded towards the window.

'Seiji is waiting outside. He has a car. And he wants me to give you this.'

The bundle under her arm was a flying suit. Dieter was to put it on. The briefing for the morning's flight would take place at an airfield down by the water.

'When?'

'As soon as you get there.'

'And the weather?'

'*Scheisse.*'

Dieter winced. Then he heard footsteps crossing the road and moments later the door burst open. A torrent of Japanese accompanied by some forceful sign language announced the arrival of Seiji. Keiko was right. The weather was shit and they were already late for the briefing. Time to go.

*

They drove to the airfield on the edge of Tokyo Bay. The road led through an industrial estate, a wilderness of black puddles between factory after factory. Tangles of telephone wire hung from roadside poles, swaying and dipping in the gusty wind.

Seiji was having trouble with the single windscreen wiper. Bent over the steering wheel, his face inches from the glass, he wanted to know about his sister.

'Good?'

'*Wunderbar.*'

The news seemed to please him. He wound down the window and cursed an old man doing his best to balance a clutch of bamboo canes on an ancient bike. The weather, if anything, was getting worse.

Dieter wanted to know whether they'd still be flying. The question drew an emphatic nod.

'No problem,' Seiji said, flashing a grin.

*

The briefing, conducted in a leaky wooden hut, was in Japanese. Dieter did his best to make sense of the chalked lines on the big blackboard but failed completely. A small yellow oblong appeared to represent the aircraft carrier. A nest of Japanese ideograms seemed to contain comms information laced with approach vectors and wind speeds. Outside on the hardstanding, their bulk blurred by the rain streaming down the windows, were five torpedo attack bombers.

The briefing over, the crews gathered briefly in the lee of the hut before making a dash for their aircraft. Aside from the pilot, each bomber had a commander and a rear-gunner who doubled as the wireless operator. Dieter was staring at the nearest of the five aircraft and for the first time he realised that it was carrying a torpedo.

Seiji was taking a furtive last drag on a cigarette cupped in his hand. Dieter pointed out the torpedo. Why turn an already risky landing into a suicide bid?

Seiji was frowning. Landing? Using both hands, Dieter mimed the approach to the carrier until Seiji finally understood.

'You think we *land*?' He gestured at the weather and then barked with laughter.

'So what happens?'

'We *hit* the carrier.' He nodded towards the closest aircraft and smacked a fist into the softness of his palm. '*Bam*.'

Within minutes, they were airborne. To Dieter's enormous relief, it was Seiji at the controls; Seiji leading the loose little formation out over the heaving greyness of Tokyo Bay; Seiji taking the aircraft down to twenty metres as the looming bulk of the *Soryu* emerged from the murk.

By now, Dieter had recognised his real role in this little exercise. Not for a moment had there been the slightest chance of Vice Admiral Kiyoshi risking a precious aircraft and a precious crew under conditions like these. On the contrary, *Oberleutnant* Merz was here strictly as a spectator, as a respected fighter pilot who was about to witness the sheer reach of the airborne arm of the Imperial Navy and report back to anyone in the West who might care to listen.

So how come the nightmare images that had haunted him the last twelve hours? The inner conviction that his time was finally up? Eugen Ott, Dieter thought. The bastard was trying to intimidate me, trying to scare me, trying to extract an ounce or two of sweet revenge for the times when I might have been more polite, more deferential, less sure of myself.

That in itself was bad enough. But what was infinitely worse was the fact that Dieter Merz, one of the Condor Legion's genuine stars, had allowed himself to fall for the ruse. Combat pilots owed their very survival to lightning reflexes and an absolute faith in their own immortality. Yet *Der Kleine* had been cowed by a man who flew nothing more intimidating than a desk.

The torpedo bomber was closing fast on the aircraft carrier. Seiji's bulk filled the windscreen and from the seat behind him Dieter's field of vision was less than perfect but through the side windows he could see the other aircraft in the group, a loose 'V' formation just metres from the boiling sea, and already he had an instinctive feel for the engine's potential to get him out of trouble.

He reached forward, tapping Seiji on the shoulder. They were flying the training version of the torpedo bomber with dual controls.

'Me!' Dieter shouted.

'You?' Seiji half-turned, straining against his harness. Then he nodded at the fast-approaching carrier. 'You want?'

'*Ja*.'

Dieter's hand had already closed around the joystick. For a split-second, he felt the competing pressure of Seiji's input, then control was suddenly his. By now, Dieter estimated the carrier at less than a kilometre. The other aircraft would be taking their lead from Seiji. Only when Dieter hit the torpedo release and pulled the bomber into a steep climb would the rest of the attack group follow.

Five aircraft, Dieter thought. Fifteen lives. Countless relatives. Not to mention a serious international embarrassment if he got it wrong.

Dieter held his nerve. Seiji appeared to be singing to himself. The air speed indicator was reading 371 kpm. At speeds like this, any room for error had ceased to exist.

Dieter's left hand closed on the throttle, keeping it hard against the gate. He took the aircraft even lower and then came the moment when his whole world darkened, an unforgettable shade of aircraft-carrier grey, and his left hand found the release lever alongside the throttle.

He pulled hard, feeling the aircraft lurch upwards after shedding the weight of the torpedo, and he hauled back on the stick and braced himself for the gut-wrenching suck of the sudden climb. The engine howled as the aircraft fought for altitude and for a split-second Dieter thought he might have left it too late but then came a blur of gleaming wet flight deck and the briefest glimpse of a figure in blue overalls gazing skywards before the *Soryu* was behind them.

Dieter was grinning. He could have been doing this forever. He could have been a fully trained torpedo pilot. He was back in control. Eugen Ott was part of a world that would never be his. *Wunderbar.*

They were at seven hundred metres before Seiji took control again. The torpedoes were armed with smoke warheads and already the rear-gunner had reported four hits.

'*Banzai*!' Seiji was roaring with laughter. 'We sank her good.'

6

CLACTON-ON-SEA, 28 APRIL 1938

Tam Moncrieff took the train to the coast, a two-and-a half hour journey that clattered through wind-rippled fields of early wheat to a handsome new station on the coast. He'd never been to Essex before and he was struck by the bigness of the sky and glimpses of white clapboard cottages as the train sped through village after village. Towards the end of the trip the railway line briefly followed a river. The tide was low and there were flocks of wading birds feeding on the gleaming mud banks. Beyond the reed beds on the far side of the river the broad blades of a windmill were slowly turning and that same sea breeze, still hinting at winter, greeted him as he emerged from the station at the end of the line.

A ten-minute walk took Tam to the seafront. From the carefully tended gardens on the clifftop he gazed down at the pier. It was still too early for the holidaymakers but there were knots of fishermen at the seaward end, while a workman on a ladder beside the entrance was giving the fascia a coat of paint.

Tam had seen Sanderson again last night. Turn right on the seafront, he'd said, and follow the promenade as far as you can. You're looking for a place called Jaywick. They've got a little miniature railway there for when it gets busy in the summer. Ask for Karyl.

Tam found the railway without difficulty. There was no sign of a train but an attempt had been made to mock-up a crude station guarded by a hut that appeared to serve as a booking office. Beside the hut, sitting in a deckchair, was a slim woman in her twenties. Blonde curls were escaping from a knotted scarf and her bare legs were tanned beneath a loose cotton skirt. A roll of tickets lay on her lap but the cashbox between her feet was empty.

Tam asked where he might find Karyl. The woman peered up at him, shading her eyes, asking him to repeat the question. Her English, she said, was no good. She was trying her best but she found the language hard.

'Your native language?'

'Czech.'

'You speak anything else?'

'German.'

'Then German it is.' Tam smiled. 'I'm looking for Karyl.'

'He's in hospital.' Her German was perfect, barely a trace of an accent.

'Sick?'

'He fell off a ladder.' She tapped her knee. 'And broke his leg.'

Tam gazed round. Jaywick was a work in progress. A network of concrete slab roads stretched in every direction. According to a battered hoarding, this was an investment opportunity for buyers looking for a home by the sea. Builders were busy weatherproofing the wooden shells of half-built chalets, and one backyard boasted a line of washing, but there was an emptiness about the place suggesting that business was slow.

Tam squatted beside the woman. For the first time, he noticed the towel and what appeared to be a costume drying in the sun.

'You've been swimming?'

'Of course.'

'What's it like?'

'Cold.' She pulled a face. 'And muddy.'

'So where's the train?'

'That's broken, too. Everything's broken. Karyl. The train. Everything.'

'So why are you selling tickets?'

'Because it's my job. You want one?' She nodded down at the roll of tickets. 'One penny. Two rides. Maybe three if Karyl stays in hospital too long. He's the only one who knows about the engine.' She paused, fingering the tickets, then forced a smile. 'Four rides? Five? Your choice.'

Tam hesitated a moment. According to Sanderson, Karyl Novakov was a refugee from Czechoslovakia. He'd arrived via the British embassy in Prague, securing his entry to Britain with the aid of certain information. He'd spent more than a decade as a driver on Czech Railways, mainly freight trains, and had an encyclopaedic knowledge of the state of the Czech economy. He also had a brother who was serving in the Army, manning the fortifications along the nation's western border. Which was why Tam had come to find him.

'Is the hospital here? In Clacton?'

'No. It's in another place. Many miles away.'

'You go to see him? Pay visits?'

'Never.'

'Why not?'

'We have no money. Without money, you sit here in the sunshine and sell tickets for the train that doesn't work.' She extended a hand and allowed Tam to pull her to her feet. 'My name is Renata. You have money?'

'I do.'

'Then maybe we go and see Karyl. Come – '

She stooped for the cashbox, collected the towel and her bathing costume, and set off across a patch of wasteland. Tam followed her, trying to avoid drifts of rubble amongst the ankle-high weeds. Away from the protection of the sea wall the wind was cold again. They crossed the road, stepping around a manhole without a cover. A coil of thick electric cable lay at the foot of a wooden pole.

'Here – '

The first chalet was already showing its age. The door frame was sagging and one of the window sills had begun to rot. Renata produced a key. Watching her, Tam detected a sense of resentment or maybe impatience.

'I'm hungry,' she said. 'I need to eat. Come.'

She opened the door and stepped inside. Tam followed. The chalet smelled of damp and blocked drains. The exterior walls were crude, timber shingles nailed on to a wooden frame, and Tam could see daylight through the cracks. The wind keened between the ill-fitting shingles and not a stitch of carpet or matting softened the bare wooden floors. He shivered. It was colder inside than out.

Renata had paused in the tiny hall. There were three doors, none of them properly shut. She nodded at the one on the left.

'In there,' she said.

'In there what?'

'Karyl.' She threw him a look. 'He told me someone was coming. That must be you.'

For a moment, Tam was wrong-footed. He'd bought the hospital story. He'd believed her. Now this.

He pushed the door open and stood back for a moment, uncertain what to expect. The room, tiny, was dominated by a double bed. Beneath the blankets someone was beginning to stir. First a head of hair, greying, unkempt. Then a face darkened by a week or so of stubble, and a single hand crabbing across the edge of the blanket. For the first time, Tam noticed the line of empty bottles neatly stacked against the wall.

'You're Karyl?' he enquired in German.

The name drew a grunt of assent. Karyl rubbed his eyes and then farted before rolling over. There was another bottle on the other side of the bed, a quarter full this time. Karyl retrieved it, examined it carefully, and then drained it in a single gulp before wiping his mouth with the back of his hand.

'You come from London?'

'Yes.'

'Your country is shit.' Karyl waved the empty bottle at nothing in particular. 'This. Outside. The weather. The people. The food. Everything is shit.'

Tam held his gaze. There was a poster taped to the wall over the bed, the only splash of colour in a moonscape of grey. No wonder the man drank.

'Jáchymov?' Tam was looking at the poster. Green hills rolled away into the blue distance. Closer, in a deep valley, red-tiled houses caught the sun.

'You know this place?' Karyl hadn't moved.

'Never had the pleasure.'

'Good food. Good people. Good everything.' He began to cough, his skinny frame bent double, then spat into a corner of the room.

Renata appeared in the open door and took Tam by the arm. The strength of her grip surprised him.

'Please. Enough.'

She led him into another room that evidently served as a kitchen. A wooden table with one leg chocked with books. A stool. A single chair. Something was bubbling on the two-ring electric stove and it took a moment for Tam to realise it was water.

'I make you tea. Please – ' She nodded at the chair.

Tam settled on the stool. He wanted to know how Karyl had known about this visit of his.

'We have a radio.' She nodded at the cupboard over the sink. 'You want to see it?'

She fetched it out. It looked military. Tam dimly remembered something similar from his earliest days in uniform.

'What else did they give you?'

'Money. They give us a little money every week.'

'And Karyl drinks it?'

'Yes. Most of it.'

'He's your husband?'

'That was another Karyl. Before the drinking.'

'So why does he get so bad? With the drink?'

'He's sick for home.'

'Jáchymov?'

'Yes. That's where we lived.'

'So why leave? Why come here?'

She studied him a moment, then turned away.

'Karyl was a good man,' she said at last. 'He worked hard. He loved the railways. He went everywhere, all over the country. Some weeks he never came home but we were happy.'

'You have children?'

'One. She died. . .' She gestured at her throat.

'Diptheria?'

'Yes.'

'Recently?'

'Two years ago. Horrible. After that there was nothing for us.'

'So you came here.'

'Yes.'

'When?'

'In the winter.'

'To sell tickets for a train that doesn't work?'

'Yes.'

'To people who aren't here?'

'Yes.'

Tam nodded, said he understood, offered his sympathies. Renata shrugged. Then she returned the radio to the cupboard and found a curl of sausage and the remains of a loaf of bread. From the bedroom came another bout of coughing.

Tam said no to the sausage. Then he asked whether Karyl would like to go home.

'He can't.'

'Why not?'

She wouldn't say. She washed a second cup and dried it carefully before shaking tea leaves into a strainer. The tea was the colour of teak and tasted of smoke. Tam rather liked it.

'I've come to talk about Karyl going back,' he said.

'I know.'

'With me.'

'Yes.'

'And now you're telling me that can't happen.'

'Yes.'

'So what do we do?'

The question drew another shrug. She used the tea leaves for a cup of her own. Two brimming spoons of sugar. Then she looked up. She wanted to know exactly what Tam wanted.

'I need to get to know your country. I need to look at the fortifications on the border. I speak no Czech. That's where Karyl can help.'

'You want company? Someone to make it easier?'

'Yes. And somebody,' he frowned, 'who knows the people I should talk to.'

'What kind of people?'

'People who know what's really going on.'

'You mean in the Sudetenland?'

'Yes.'

She nodded, taking it all in. She was staring at the cup.

'You really have money?' she asked at last.

'Yes.'

'How much money?'

'That doesn't matter. Not at the moment.'

'You think? You really think that doesn't matter?' She was staring at him now, her face suddenly flushed with colour. 'You know how we come here? You know the promises they make? How we shall live like kings? How Karyl will love the little train? The beach? The sea? The sunshine? How many friends we shall make? What a time of it we shall have?' She gestured around. 'We live in a prison. We have nothing. People check on us all the time. Run away and they'll put us in prison for real. Maybe that's what you should have done from the start. But you know what they say about the English? In my country?'

'Tell me.'

'They tell us never to trust the English, especially the English smile. They tell us that English is the language God created for liars and thieves. They say the English never tell you the truth.'

Tam let the sudden gust of anger subside. Sanderson had been sparing with the details but to the best of Tam's knowledge the offer of work on this godforsaken building site had come from a syndicate in the City, brokers who were bankrolling the wilderness of chalets outside. Somewhere this handsome young couple could settle down. Somewhere safe they could call their own. Plus a job which Karyl would adore. In Sanderson's view, a near-perfect solution.

'I'm sorry,' Tam said again. 'Maybe it's best I go.'

'No.' She shook her head. 'I don't want that.'

'What do you want?'

'We came here to help. That's what we said in Prague, when we went to your Embassy. And it's true.'

'Help how?'

'Help you. And help us back home. Austria will never be enough for the Germans. It's us next.'

'But Karyl can't help. Just look at him.'

'I do. Every day. Every night. But there are two of us. And one isn't sick.'

Tam studied her carefully. She held his gaze.

'You and me?' he asked at last. 'Is that what you're saying?'

'Yes.'

'You know the Sudetenland well?'

'We lived there. We got married there. In Jáchymov.'

'You still know people?'

'Of course.'

Tam nodded. Then came another thought.

'What about Karyl? Who looks after him?'

'Karyl won't know I've gone. He lives in a world of his own. There's a woman he likes, too.' She threw a glance at the window. 'She's English. She drinks nearly as much as he does.'

Tam nodded. They might be gone a while. Did that matter?

She stared at him for a long moment and then began to laugh.

'After this? Are you serious?' She gestured around again and then reached for the roll of tickets. She tore one off and slipped it across the table. 'We have a deal?'

'We do.'

'And I can trust an Englishman?'

'You don't have to.' It was Tam's turn to laugh. 'I'm a Scot.'

*

Tam was back in London by mid-evening. It was by no means clear whether or not he had the authority to hire a companion for the days to come but he was prepared to fight for the offer he'd made. Speaking German with Renata had clarified the territory they shared. He admired the way she'd handled herself. She was an outsider in a society she had every reason to mistrust, and he suspected he could put her determination and her anger to good use.

It was Sanderson who'd given him directions to a Mayfair pub. The Punch Bowl was a picturesque Georgian relic wedged between two towering apartment blocks. At half-past eight drinkers had spilled out on to the pavement, briskly corralled by three uniformed policemen. Tam shouldered his way through the crowd. Access to the pub was barred by yet another policeman.

'I'm afraid not, sir. Bit of an incident.'

Beyond the policeman, Tam caught a glimpse of upturned tables and what looked like a body on the wooden floor. A doctor was returning instruments to a leather bag. Of Sanderson there was no sign.

'Tam?' The lightest touch on his shoulder.

Tam spun round. Instead of Sanderson, he found himself looking at Ballentyne.

'Oliver has been called away. Pressing business in the Far East. He sends his apologies. I'm afraid you'll have to put up with me.'

Ballentyne led the way across the road and headed north through the maze of streets towards Grosvenor Square. It appeared that an argument at the bar had got out of hand and from his perch at the back of the pub Ballentyne had enjoyed a ringside seat for what followed. One of the two men was an American. The incident had lasted no more than thirty seconds. In Ballentyne's view, the man on the floor was probably dead.

'Beware who you pick a fight with,' he murmured as they paused on the kerbside for a passing taxi. 'These days that's something worth keeping in mind.'

Tam smiled but said nothing. He liked Ballentyne. He had a lightness of touch that was lost on Sanderson. This was only their second meeting but he was more certain than ever that Ballentyne, so ordinary in his appearance, so easy to overlook, was running the show.

'Over there, my friend. Top floor, I'm afraid.'

Tam was looking at a newish block of flats, brick built. Ballentyne had the key to the front door. A lift was waiting behind an iron grille but Ballentyne took the stairs. Floor after floor smelled of serious money: carefully chosen art on the walls, stands of late daffodils on occasional tables, everything spotlessly clean. On the sixth floor Ballentyne produced another key.

'I don't live here, in case you're wondering. We like to think of this as part of the estate.'

The phrase meant nothing to Tam. So far, neither Ballentyne nor Sanderson had told him to which part of the intelligence world they belonged, and neither had he been minded to ask. His years in the military had taught him a number of lessons and one of them, just now, was all too apposite. If there was good reason to know, they'd tell him. Otherwise, he'd remain in the dark. The one surprise was the news that Sanderson was some kind of businessman. Where, exactly, did he fit in Ballentyne's world?

The flat was furnished like a good quality Edinburgh hotel suite: polished wooden floor, thick-piled, patterned rugs in rich reds and blues, and a low occasional table in what looked like mahogany. Ballentyne took Tam's coat and then inspected the contents of a drinks cabinet.

'I'm assuming Scotch,' he said. 'Last time I was here they had a couple of decent malts. This one?' He was peering at the label on the bottle. 'Ardbeg?'

'Perfect.'

Ballentyne found two glasses and poured. So far, Tam had yet to describe his expedition to the seaside. Ballentyne pulled the curtains and settled himself in one of the two leather armchairs before offering a toast.

'To Renata,' he said. 'I'm glad you've had the pleasure.'

Tam gazed at him. For the second time that day, he'd lost his place in the plot.

'You've met her?'

'Not face to face, alas. They had a couple of interviews on arrival, both down in Kent. I monitored the second one. Karyl, to be frank, is a disappointment. Renata is anything but. Quite why she married him remains a mystery. In my judgement she was put on earth for the benefit of an organisation like ours. Good fortune is something we should never take for granted. I'm pleased you two got along.'

'How do you know that?'

'She made contact after you left. She seems to trust you. God knows, she might even like you. More to the point, she's well connected. Did you discuss any of that?'

'Not really.'

'Then allow me to explain.'

Renata, he said, had spent her formative years in Prague, daughter of a Czech physicist who taught at the university. Naturally, given his background, he was keen for Renata to take a degree but after a term and a half in the Faculty of Law, she'd dropped out.

'She wanted to be a journalist,' Ballentyne was smiling. 'Made a real nuisance of herself. That's how she came to our attention.'

Renata, he said, had done her best to find a post with the established newspapers in Prague but had finally made a reputation of sorts by supplying stories for the underground press. In the early thirties, he said, Czechoslovakia was quite the place to be, a boisterous little democracy, the love child of the Versailles Treaty.

Tam smiled. It was an arresting phrase and it reminded him of a conversation he'd had only recently with Gunther Nagel and his German hunting party. These men were no strangers to Prague. Wonderful architecture, they'd said, with women and beer to match.

'So how old is she? Now?'

'Twenty-nine, according to her passport. Looks younger, I know.'

'And she stuck with the journalism?'

'Yes. Until Karyl came along.'

Ballentyne appeared to know her story by heart. He confirmed that they'd met in the Sudetenland, a little place called Jáchymov. Karyl, who worked on the railways, loved American jazz. A long evening in a pub near the station and they began an affair. Renata had a soft spot for communism, as well as Charlie Parker, and Karyl – with his good looks and his proletarian passion for the footplate – had the perfect credentials.

'How do you know all this?'

'She wrote a book about it. Little novella. *Roman-à-clef.* All the clues are there, very lightly disguised.'

'It was published?'

'Yes. Small circulation but a modest success. By the time she wrote it I'm guessing the marriage was in trouble. She called it *Changing Trains*. This is a woman with a sense of humour.'

Tam was thinking about their first conversation, her luckless husband in a faraway hospital, nursing a broken leg. More fiction.

'So why has she stayed with him? Does the book explain any of that?'

'In a way, yes. She loved him once and she meant it. Nowadays she seems to regard the drinking as an illness, which I imagine makes her a nurse as well as a wife. During the second interview she was alone and she made it quite plain that we'd only get the benefit of her services if we looked after Karyl.'

'And you'll do that?'

'Of course. There's an institution not far from Colchester. They have a bed waiting for poor Karyl once you're both operational.' He paused, fingering the rim of his glass. 'I understand your father has moved in with your sister. Might that be correct?'

'It is. I brought him down a couple of days ago. My sister said you'd paid a visit, just to vouch for me. Am I right?'

'Indeed. A bit of an intrusion, I'm afraid, but we thought it might help.'

'It did. She was most impressed.'

'A pleasure, Tam. We like to keep things tidy.'

Tidy. Tam reached for his glass. Very slowly, the way these people liked it, the pieces of the jigsaw were slipping into place. First write yourself a script. Then turn your mind to the casting.

'So why Renata?' He was looking Ballentyne in the eye. 'And why me?'

Ballentyne had evidently been expecting the question. He got to his feet and fetched a thin manila folder from his briefcase. Then he returned to the armchair. To date, Tam had been spared any kind of detail about what lay in wait for him. All he'd been asked to guarantee was three weeks of his time and a modicum of discretion. In return he'd be well paid with an unspecified bonus on his safe return. The phrase *safe return* had given Tam pause for thought but the unknown had always attracted him and he knew he could look after himself in most circumstances.

Ballentyne opened the file and extracted two photographs, laying them carefully on the low table between the two chairs. Then he directed Tam's attention to the smaller of the two shots. Tam picked it up. It had been scissored from a newspaper. A tall figure in Army uniform was pictured amongst a group of other men, two of them in evening dress. Tam recognised Goebbels, dwarfed by the bulk of the officer beside him. Imposing face, strong jaw, eyes locked on some distant object.

'This is Werner von Blomberg.' Ballentyne tapped the photograph. 'Good war. Did well after Versailles. Threw his hand in with the Nazis. Until very recently, Army Commander-in-Chief.'

Tam took a longer look at the figure in the photograph. A line of medals hung from the chest of his tunic. He held himself erect, unsmiling, aware of the presence of the camera.

'So what happened?'

'He upset his lord and master. Life in the Reich must be hell. Hitler holds himself aloof and the rest of them – Himmler, Goering, Goebbels – fight like mediaeval barons. Some of the conversations we've had recently are difficult to credit. One moment of weakness, one indiscretion, one misjudgement and the game's over.'

'Conversations with whom?'

'Germans. Mainly diplomats. Sometimes the odd businessman. The people we talk to are old school. They never really wanted Hitler in the first place but they assumed that power would clip his wings. As it happens, they were wrong. The man is a lunatic. That's their word, not ours.'

'And Blomberg?'

'Blomberg's a Prussian. He knows where the real power lies but he's never stopped being a soldier. Hitler held a conference in Berlin back in November. Blomberg was there. Hitler shared his plans for the next couple of years. He wanted space in the east for the Germans to breathe and he wanted the Army ready to march. There was no timetable, no deadline, but the implications were obvious. Blomberg was appalled. So were a number of others.'

'Why?'

'Because the implications were obvious. Czechoslovakia had to be the target but any war with the Czechs would bring in the French and the Russians and quite possibly us. Blomberg's a professional soldier. He counted up the number of divisions on either side and he didn't like what he saw. His big mistake was telling Hitler. Blomberg had no objection to grabbing someone else's country. He just needed time to get the Army in shape, to bed in the new equipment, to do the thing properly. This distinction was lost on Hitler. Orders are orders. If the Führer says march, you march. The Himmlers and the Goerings spotted their opportunity. Blomberg did his best. The man was brave but badly wounded. They picked him off.'

'He's gone?'

'Yes. The poor soul had the misfortune to fall in love. His wife had died recently and Hitler consented to be a witness when he married for the second time. Alas, the bride turned out to have once worked as a prostitute. That, at least, was Goering's story. We think the evidence was cooked up but that's commonplace now. Hitler, of course, was outraged and when he wanted the marriage annulled, Blomberg resigned.'

Tam's eyes drifted to the other photograph, a studio portrait this time, a different face – thinner, more vulnerable – but the same buttoned tunic, the same high collar, the same stiff pose.

'Werner von Fritsch,' Ballentyne murmured. 'Blomberg's Number Two. His enemies dredged up some tramp or other who insisted Fritsch had paid him for sex. Fritsch denied everything and was halfway to proving it when Hitler staged a little diversion. This was last month. You might remember.'

'Austria? *Anschluss*?'

'Exactly. Germany loses its head, goes mad with joy, all those swooning *Mädchen*, and nobody cares a fig for either Blomberg or Fritsch. Hitler can do no wrong and no one seems to mind when he assumes leadership of the Army for himself.' He offered Tam a thin smile. 'Dictator might be too small a word when it comes to Mr Hitler. The man now controls everything. That meeting in November troubled the generals. They despatched an envoy, a businessman we happen to know well. He brought a number of facts to our attention. One of them was a remarkable degree of unanimity about Germany's current direction of travel.'

'Meaning?'

'There's a degree of alarm amongst the top military.' Ballentyne's eyes drifted back to the photos. 'Blomberg and Fritsch have been thrown to the wolves. Other generals are still in post. Loyal to Germany? Yes. Loyal to Hitler?' He shrugged. 'Who knows. . .?'

'This is some kind of plot?'

'Not so far. Not to our knowledge.'

'But it might be?'

'Indeed. They could try and talk Hitler round but I doubt that's an option. He only listens to people who agree with him. Just now all the signs are that he's determined to march into Czechoslovakia. The generals think that's madness, far too premature, but to make the man see sense you need to shout at him. That's not the generals' style. Neither, alas, is it ours.'

Tam nodded. When Ballentyne reached for the bottle of malt, he declined a refill.

'So what exactly do you want me to do?'

'We want you in the Sudetenland. There are people you'll need to meet, people who have no truck with the Germans, and Renata knows most of them. We have a good man at the embassy in Prague, Harold Stronge, the military attaché. He'll open more doors. The word from Prague is most comforting. The Czechs have a decent army and their equipment is first class. This is kit they produce themselves, which is one of the reasons Mr Hitler wants to lay hands on all those factories. They've also had the foresight to build defence works in the west. We want you to take a look at all that, have a conversation or two, confer with Stronge, and then make a judgement for yourself.'

'To what purpose?' This, to Tam, was the crux of the matter. There was nothing in the assignment that he couldn't handle, especially with someone like Renata alongside him, but what was the point of it all?

'We live in difficult times, Tam. Politicians only see what they want to see. In the opinion of some of us, the country is flying blind. You, believe it or not, can add something new to the mix. You have the right credentials, the appropriate skills. People will trust you. Exactly the way we trust you.'

'People here?'

'Of course.'

'People you want me to talk to afterwards?'

'Indeed.'

'What kind of people?'

'People with influence. People who can make a difference. Democracy is a deeply beguiling proposition, but I'm afraid we're babes in the wood when it comes to dealing with the likes of Mr Hitler.'

'You want to turn me into some kind of messenger? You want me to bring back glad tidings?'

'We want you to help build a case for standing by the Czechs.'

'As simple as that?'

'As difficult, and as complex, and as important as that. We have the connections. We can open doors in appropriate places. But we need to have someone independent, someone plausible, someone who's been there, someone who *knows* at the table. Intelligence, I'm afraid, has lately become somewhat debauched. The professionals have a tendency to serve up their masters' favourite dishes. That's the last thing we want.'

'We?'

Tam's question hung in the air. Not for the first time, he was beginning to wonder exactly which part of the intelligence empire was so keen to acquire his services. Ballentyne made no effort to supply an answer. He was running his fingertips lightly round the rim of his glass. He appeared to be waiting for a decision on Tam's part. Was this the moment when he could make his excuses and leave? Collect his mad father, take the midday train, and get back to a business that still needed a great deal of attention? Or was the prospect of the coming weeks already too tempting to turn down?

'Well?' Ballentyne had emptied the glass.

Tam was smiling. The most important decisions in life were always the simplest. Just one detail still bothered him.

'So why did you send me to meet Karyl and not Renata today? Do you mind me asking?'

'Not at all. We wanted you to make your own sense of the situation, of their wretched little ménage down there.' Ballentyne uncapped the bottle again. 'And you did it rather well.'

7

BERLIN, 6 MAY 1938

Dieter Merz had been waiting nearly an hour before Georg turned up at the wheel of one of the new rear-engined Volkswagens. It was black. Two parps on the horn brought Dieter onto the street. Georg reached over and opened the passenger door. He wanted to know what Dieter was doing in a luxury apartment off Friedrichstrasse.

'It belongs to the Foreign Ministry. I'm keeping it warm until they decide what to do with me.'

'Their decision or yours?'

'Theirs. I've told them I'll never make a diplomat but no one at their level ever seems to listen.'

'But you're supposed to be a fighter pilot.'

'Am I?'

Georg didn't answer. Instead, he shot Dieter a look and then gunned the engine and pulled into the traffic. It was a beautiful Berlin day, cloudless, just a hint of breeze, and Dieter sat back, enjoying the ride.

'Where are we going?'

Georg named a restaurant beyond the Tiergarten. He promised Dieter they pickled Baltic herrings like no one else in the city.

'I can't stand herrings. You know that.'

'Sure. But Beata adores them. You two need to meet.'

'Her name again?'

'Beata.'

'Is that why you're wearing a ring?'

'Yes. The wedding's in a couple of weeks' time. If you're doing anything else, cancel it.'

Dieter stared at him. Georg was as brusque and matter-of-fact as ever. Not a flicker of excitement.

'You're *marrying* her?'

'That's the plan. She's a Catholic. Very staunch, unlike me. She wants to do it properly.'

Dieter was still trying to absorb the news.

'You've known her long?'

'Eight weeks.' A ghost of a smile. 'Maybe nine. This way no other bastard will ever get a sniff. Not even you.'

The restaurant was packed, a tribute – Dieter assumed – to the herrings. There was a waterfront terrace at the back and Georg had booked the table in the corner. Dieter settled into his chair, enjoying the view of the Spree, while Georg went inside to make a telephone call. A young couple on the far bank were deep in conversation while an old man on a bench beside the water appeared to be asleep. Beata, he thought, savouring the word. Beata and Georg.

Georg was back within minutes. From his wallet he produced a slightly creased black and white photo and laid it carefully in front of Dieter.

'She can't come,' he announced. 'She sends her apologies, says she was looking forward to meeting you. You'll have to make do with this for now.'

Dieter studied the photo. Severe features, sensible glasses, carefully tended hair, just the hint of a smile. If Georg had been born a girl, he thought, he'd end up looking exactly like this.

'Beautiful.' He punched Georg lightly on the arm. 'You're a lucky man. Does she have a job?'

'She's a physicist. She works at the KWI.'

Dieter took another look at the photo. The Kaiser Wilhelm Institute was only interested in the cream of the Reich's scientific talent. The KWI was where the nation's best brains tore up the old theories, licked their pencils and started all over again.

'She must be a genius.' Dieter was smiling. 'You'll never keep up.'

Georg ignored the jest. He called a waiter and ordered beers. Enough of Beata.

'I flew Ribbentrop back from Munich a couple of days ago,' he said. 'Your name came up. The man's a fool, of course. God knows how he made it to Foreign Minister but he seems to hold you in some regard.'

'I'm flattered. What do you make of him?'

'He's a true believer. When he was Ambassador in London he was to and fro all the time, couldn't bear to be away from his lord and master. That man can't get further up the Führer's arse. He's like a woman with him. He's besotted.'

'So what did he say? About me?'

'He seems to think you did well in Japan. Very well. Or maybe it was the little souvenir you brought back. He couldn't remember her name. I said I'd ask you personally.'

Dieter had turned away. He was watching two newcomers to the bench across the river. They were in SS uniform. One of them wore the insignia of a *Hauptsturmführer.* He bent to the old man and gave him a shake. Then he hauled him to his feet and pushed him on his way before sitting down.

'Her name's Keiko,' Dieter said softly.

'What kind of name is that?'

'It's Japanese. It means a child full of sunlight.'

'And is she?'

'Yes. And I'll tell you something else. She does a healing thing with her hands.'

'Should I be surprised?'

'I mean it. Not just the injury but here, too.' Dieter tapped his head. 'Some of the games the embassy people play, you need a friend to keep you sane.'

'*A friend to keep you sane?* Christ, what's this woman done to you?'

'Good question.'

'You have an answer?'

'No.'

Dieter explained about the trick that Eugen Ott had pulled, pretending to volunteer him for a carrier landing in the knowledge that his rogue fighter pilot would have twelve hours to imagine the consequences.

'Ott didn't like you?'

'He hated me. I wasn't seven feet tall. I didn't dress properly. I didn't say the right things. It didn't help that he can't stand Ribbentrop.'

'Neither can anyone else. Doing what I do, you get to hear what the people at the top really think of each other. This town is like a battlefield and the war hasn't even started yet.'

'You're serious? About a war?'

'Of course. It's bound to happen. It's inevitable. You just have to listen to the radio. Hitler can't help himself. Once you get the taste for conquest it never goes away. After Austria, he was walking on water.'

'And you think people want a war? A proper war?'

'That's a different question.' Georg produced a cigarette case Dieter hadn't seen before. 'Tell me about the Japanese.'

'They were fine. Crazy people, especially in the air, but OK. I had some good times.'

'And the carrier? What made you think you couldn't do it?'

Dieter was still watching the SS men on the bench. The old man had disappeared, limping away without a backward glance. In another life Dieter would have stripped to his underwear, swum the river and given them both a good kicking.

'I lost my nerve a couple of weeks earlier,' he murmured at last. 'If that sounds like a confession, I'm afraid it is.'

He described taking the controls in Seiji's seaplane at Nagasaki, his first time since the accident, and the moment on the final approach when he saw the rooftops swimming up towards him and felt the cold sweat on his face.

'I got it wrong, Georg. I was flying like a novice. Hopeless. And I was frightened, too.'

'*Frightened?*' Georg offered a cigarette. Dieter shook his head. 'What did the guy in the back think?'

'He was drunk. I don't think he was even watching. Like I said, these people are crazy. Some days you'd think that dying doesn't matter. Not to them, anyway. As it happened, he's Keiko's kid brother. That's how we met.'

'And you have,' Georg was frowning, 'a thing going?'

'We have nothing going. Except I've agreed to look after her.'

'Where?'

'Here. The Japanese fixed for her to come back with me. They found her a job in their embassy.'

'That's where Ribbentrop laid eyes on her. Even her German impressed him.'

The waiter arrived with the beers. Dieter watched him, saying nothing. The last couple of days Keiko had stayed the night in the apartment, occupying the spare bedroom. At dawn, both mornings, Dieter had blinked awake to find her bent over him, her fingers exploring the hollows on his face. On the bad days in Japan, and there were many, he'd begun to accept acute pain as a permanent part of his life but Keiko, in ways he failed to understand, first softened the pain, then made it go away.

Dieter reached for his beer. The SS men were on the move.

'Do you believe in magic, Georg?'

'No.'

'Then maybe you should.'

*

After the meal, Georg drove Dieter out to the airport where Hitler's personal transport was based. The *Regierungsstaffel* occupied a discreet corner of the hardstanding, hidden from the sweep of the terminal. Major construction was under way to make Tempelhof the biggest airport in Europe and cranes towered over the building site. The road from the Reich Chancellery and the major ministries had also been improved over the last year to make life easier for the VIPs shuttling back and forth. The two sentries at the gate gave Georg the Hitler salute as he slowed to show his ID. Dieter had only his *Luftwaffe* pay book. The older of the two sentries made a careful note of his name and service number. Then a brief word from Georg was enough to get him nodded through.

Georg was living in a sunny first floor room in the accommodation block behind the biggest of the maintenance hangars. Dieter eyed the aircraft parked out front as they walked across the hardstanding. Three of them were Ju-52 tri-motors, adapted as VIP transport. The fourth, bigger, was new to Dieter.

'Focke-Wulf *Condor*,' Georg said. 'This is a prototype. They've fitted it out to cross the Atlantic. Lufthansa want to run a service to New York. Extra fuel tanks and a lot of patience for the crossing if you happen to be a passenger. It's a prestige project and some of my customers have got their eye on it.'

'Like?'

'Who do you think?'

'Ribbentrop?'

'Of course. Carrying the flag in his new job, he thinks he's pretty special. He wants armour plating and some newfangled automatic parachute. As long as he's still in favour, he'll probably get it.'

Dieter nodded. The more he was learning about the upper reaches of the Reich, the more he understood the need for armour-plating. Georg was right. These people were permanently at war.

Upstairs in his room, Georg brewed coffee while Dieter inspected more photos of his friend's bride-to-be. Georg had never had any time for sharing inner secrets, something he regarded as a mark of personal weakness, and Dieter was surprised by the warmth in his voice. At the very least, this was an indication that Beata had somehow penetrated the seeming indifference that served as Georg's personal armour plating.

'Sometimes you get lucky,' he said. 'I couldn't believe her when we first met and that feeling's never gone away. It's fine for you. You always fall on your feet. Me? I'm choosy.'

'Meaning I don't care?'

'Meaning it matters less. Women? Aircraft? Bits of Spain you wouldn't inflict on your dog? You cope. You always cope. You make the best of it. Often more than the best of it. I'm different that way. Things have to be right. Especially when it comes to women. Take Beata. You know the moment she had to become my wife? It was the second time out together. We were in a little place in the country. I'd been there before. It was quiet and it was nice. Excellent food. Wonderful *Schnitzel*. The kind of welcome you can depend on. Except they'd just built some barracks in the woods nearby, some training facility or other, really young kids, first-timers, out on their own, rough, ignorant, foolish. It was evening. Three of them came in for a drink. One of them was drunk already. A local said something he didn't like and suddenly we're looking at a fight. I got up, of course. The local man was at the next table. Then Beata told me to sit down. I couldn't believe it. Sit down, Georg. Leave this to me. And you know what? She talked to the oaf, calmed him down, made him ashamed of himself, insisted he bought the poor man a drink. We got drinks, too. He had to stand us a bottle of *Sekt*. Beata again. She wouldn't take no for an answer.' He shook his head. 'What a woman.'

Dieter smiled. This, from Georg, was a major speech but he could visualise the scene, Georg watching the incident unfold with something close to disbelief, reluctant as ever to trust anyone else. He'd always been a stranger to both risk and the workings of fate, insisting that a wise man learned to depend only on logic and good sense. But now there was this Beata in his life, opening doors he never knew existed.

'How old is she?'

'Twenty-five.'

'Older than you.'

'Yes.'

'Has she had boyfriends before?'

'I've no idea.'

'You haven't asked her?'

'No. What would be the point?'

The question, so unforced, was deeply revealing but Dieter knew he meant it. Beata's previous life would probably remain a secret. All that mattered was the fact that she'd slotted so neatly into Georg's plans. They would doubtless be perfectly matched, have three brilliant children, and would cherish each other for ever. Dieter could think of worse outcomes but not many.

Georg wanted to talk about the wedding. Dieter's stories about the aircraft carrier and the seaplane had disturbed him.

'Why?'

'Because I have something in mind. A present, if you like.'

'For Beata?'

'Of course.' He poured the coffees and brought them over to a small table beneath the window. 'She knows what I do. She knows I fly all these big names around. But what she doesn't know is what I was up to before. She knows about Spain and the Legion and some of the times we had but I don't think she's ever really grasped what it means to be a fighter pilot.'

'Then take her up. Borrow a trainer. Put her in the back. Show her what you can do, what it feels like.'

'I'm not sure that would be wise. She had a trip in a glider once. She said it made her ill.' Georg glanced up. He was toying with his coffee cup, a moment of indecision, trying to frame a question or perhaps a favour. Not at all the Georg Dieter remembered.

'You told me you were frightened,' Georg said at last.

'Of what?'

'Flying. You told me at the restaurant. You told me you'd lost your nerve.'

'That's true. I did.'

'So why did that ever happen? Haven't you asked yourself?'

'Of course I did.'

'And?'

'I don't know the answer. Falling out of the 109 didn't help. And nor did what happened afterwards. You end up being someone a bit different. It takes getting used to. Keiko says I'm living with a stranger. All I have to do is ask him to leave.'

The thought put a frown on Georg's face. This kind of talk, to him, was plain crazy.

'So who is this stranger?'

'Me, Georg. It's me. I'm the stranger.'

'So how do you get the stranger to leave?'

'I've no idea. But she's definitely working on it.'

'You feel better?'

'Much better. There are kinds of pain you never want to live with. Just now they're heading for the door.'

'And this is Keiko's doing?'

'Yes. Entirely. It's a skill she has. A technique. In a moment you're going to ask me whether I'm grateful. The answer is yes but if you want the truth it's much worse than that. I think I'm in love with the woman.'

'Because she's making you better?'

'Because she's a mystery. Because I don't understand her. And because I could probably spend the rest of my life trying.'

'*The rest of your life?*'

'Make that a couple of months. Maybe longer. Whatever. I don't know. All that matters is she cares enough to try and get me back in the air.'

'That's what you want?'

'Of course. Diplomacy, all that Reich shit, must have its rewards. But they're lost on me.'

'Have you talked to anyone about what happens next?'

'Not really. Not formally. So far I've been on leave. Next week I have to report to the Air Ministry. You know the way it works. The decision will be theirs.'

'They'll check you out. Make sure you're safe.'

'Of course.'

'That might take a while. Maybe there's another way. Maybe I can talk to one or two people. Just a private word. Someone like Goering.'

'Goering?' Dieter blinked. 'Why would you want to do that?'

Georg reached for his beer. Then came the look again, weighing up the wisdom of some inner decision.

'The wedding is the weekend after next,' he said. 'That gives you ten days to get back in a serious aircraft. It has to be a 109. The new "E" series is a beauty. Power you wouldn't believe and lots more range. The boys in Spain can't believe it. There are a couple of Emils over at Johannistahl. They're still using them for tests. The right word in the right ear and I could get you in the cockpit by Thursday.'

'But why the hurry?'

'I just told you. The wedding. I want Beata to see what flying really looks like. I want it to be a present, a surprise.'

'You mean a display?'

'Exactly. Her parents have a summer home on the lake at Gatow. We're having a celebration in the garden after the ceremony. You could display for twenty minutes and be back with us within the hour. As I said, it would be a present. You wouldn't even have to wrap it up.' Georg extended a hand. 'Deal?'

8

KARLOVY VARY, SUDETENLAND, 6 MAY 1938

Tam Moncrieff took a train to Folkestone late that same afternoon. The ferry cast off as dusk began to gather and it was dark by the time he landed in Boulogne. Ballentyne had provided him with a railway ticket through to Karlovy Vary in Czechoslovakia. The ticket, to his mild surprise, entitled him to a private sleeping berth and he awoke as the train shuddered to a halt in Frankfurt the next day. By mid-afternoon he was queuing for passport checks on a windswept platform on the Czech border, listening to fellow passengers from Nuremberg discussing how much quicker the crossing might be once the Führer sorted the situation out.

The situation. Renata, according to Ballentyne, had gone ahead. Tam hadn't seen her since their encounter on the Essex coast but he was assured that she'd be on the platform at Karlovy Vary to meet the train. Over a breakfast of boiled eggs and slightly burned toast in the Mayfair safe house, Ballentyne had wished him luck with the programme of discreet meetings that Renata had already arranged. These were Czechs with their fingers on the fitful pulse of the infant democracy and would doubtless tell him a great deal about morale, as well as prospects for the near future.

Now, as the train clattered into the Sudetenland, Tam sat by the window trying to avoid the attentions of a small but persistent dachshund belonging to an overdressed woman who must have been in her late fifties. Impressed by his German, she seemed to believe he came from the Rhineland and because she'd never laid eyes on his passport he was content to leave it that way. Deception, he told himself, had to become a way of life. Why not start now?

The Sudetenland lay in the rolling green hills south of Dresden. This part of Czechoslovakia, the ancient lands of Bohemia and Moravia, was full of German-speaking Sudetens who looked to Berlin rather than Prague. There were more than three and a half million of them and lately, under the leadership of a vocal Sudeten politician called Konrad Henlein, they'd made it plain that they wanted to rid themselves of the heavy hand of the Czech government. In the eyes of most observers in Paris and London, this was the perfect overture to Hitler's next move into Central Europe, and only days ago, in front of an enormous crowd in Karlovy Vary, Henlein had tabled a set of unnegotiable demands to set the Sudetens free.

Tam had managed to absorb this much in a briefing from Ballentyne but what remained unclear was the attitude of the Western democracies in the face of such pressure. Would the French honour their treaty obligations to the Czechs in the event of a German invasion? And if so, would the British support the French? Ballentyne, as imperturbable as ever, had smiled at the questions. In his view, the future, like the past, was a river. Where it flowed next depended on circumstances, some foreseen, others not. Tam, in a phrase he wouldn't forget in a hurry, might become one small but important particle of those circumstances. Good hunting. And God bless.

Renata was waiting beyond the ticket barrier. Tam scarcely recognised her. The tan she'd acquired had deepened and something had happened besides that. Back on the Essex coast in Jaywick, she'd been on the shortest of fuses, an angry woman short-changed by false promises and beached by a situation beyond her control. Now, she looked transformed.

'This is Edvard,' she said simply.

A tall, bony figure stepped out of the shadows beside the left-luggage office. His work trousers were giving out at the knees and a button was missing from his once-white shirt but his smile warmed the space between them. He might have been a day labourer with a pound or two in his pocket and the prospect of an interesting evening to come. He radiated a sense of anticipation that Renata appeared to share.

Edvard seized Tam's bag and led the way out of the station. The plaza outside was already full. Making his way through the waiting crowd, Edvard plunged into a maze of narrow streets on the far side of the square. One alley led to another. The press of people began to thin. At length, alone in a cul-de-sac lit by a single street lamp, Edvard rapped at a door. At length it opened. Tam glimpsed a scrawny arm and a woman's face before his bag disappeared inside and the door slammed shut.

'This is where you live, my friend. The lady of the house is very accommodating. Anything you need,' Edvard grinned, 'within reason.'

Edvard's German, heavily accented, was otherwise perfect. He checked his watch and conferred briefly with Renata before giving her a hug and disappearing back towards the mouth of the alley. She watched him go, a smile on her face, and then turned back to Tam.

'Tonight the Nazis are holding a rally. We need to be there. Afterwards Edvard has someone you must meet. Come.'

It took nearly half an hour to get back to the centre of town. The streets were choked and once they got to the square itself there was barely room to stand. A band were playing on a hotel balcony and the women in the crowd had linked arms, swaying with the music. Renata slipped her arm through Tam's, joining in, swapping some joke or other with the women behind while Tam's gaze sought out the faces upturned to catch the spotlights roaming across the vast gathering. Most of the men looked a little like Edvard: lean, fit, scruffy, poorly shaved. Many of them wore swastika armbands and the moment a figure appeared on the planked scaffold that served as a stage, a deep roar gathered in the belly of the crowd.

'*Hen-lein!*' they shouted. '*Hen-lein!*'

Some of the men were punching the air, a gesture that seemed to link the Communist salute to something darker from the other side of the frontier. Tam had last witnessed scenes like this in Germany, a decade and a half ago, when he'd sampled a rally or two during his stay in Berlin. This was in the early years of the Nazi movement. The capital had been full of working men, by no means convinced about the NSDAP brawlers in their fancy uniforms, and night after night political rhetoric had given way to violence as the Brownshirts and the Reds squared off.

Then, Tam had marvelled at how volatile and how easily manipulated a crowd could be. Given a decent orator, a man of passion, a man who knew how to use language and gesture, ten thousand people became putty in his hands. Much later, back from Germany, Tam had watched the same dark magic at work at the Nazi rallies so meticulously staged in the cradle of the regime at Nuremberg. Even on newsreel films, even in the smoky darkness of an Edinburgh cinema, you were a fingertip away from abandoning every shred of rationality. The pillars of light, he thought. The forest of raised arms. The sheer theatricality of the moment, scored for abandon and the most terrifying ecstasy. The Nazis knew how to make love to crowds, how to toy with them, how to raise them to a howling climax, orchestrated by the demonic tub-thumping figure on the spotlit rostrum.

Was Henlein this good? Could he mould the crowd the way his master in Germany did? By now he'd started speaking and Tam knew at once that the answer was no. Effective? Yes. Well-informed? Undoubtedly. But there was something missing, perhaps a sense of ruthlessness or maybe ownership. At Nuremberg, the crowd belonged to Hitler. It was his business to cast a spell on them, something he perfected in speech after speech. The soaring rhetoric, the wild theatrics, the moments of bathos when he risked seconds of total silence, carried not a scintilla of self-doubt. He was the man in charge. He was the leader. He was there to point the way to a glorious future, purged of countless enemies. Henlein, on the other hand, was a bureaucrat, a man of facts and figures, far more cautious, infinitely more reasonable, and probably hamstrung by the smallness of his part in the enfolding European drama. Ballentyne had hinted that this grey-suited man on the stage up front was in the pocket of Berlin. And watching him, Tam sensed that Henlein knew it.

The speech, compared to Hitler's diatribes at Nuremberg, was mercifully brief. Henlein took the crowd through the Eight-Point Declaration he'd drawn up just a week and a half earlier. This was the gun they were holding to the heads of the Czechs in Prague, a ruthless bunch of Slav patriots with their collective foot on the neck of the Sudetenland. These people, Henlein said, had badly misjudged the Sudetens. They'd underestimated their loyalty to the mother tongue and the mother country. In the name of the hated Versailles Treaty, they'd tried to fob them off with vassal status. But the Sudetens, millions of them, knew better than that. Because Prague was on the wrong side of history and unless they conceded on every point then history, in ways that Henlein declined to describe, would exact a savage price.

This was code for a brutal intervention, Panzer tanks on the border, violence in the streets, and afterwards a taste of the surprises Hitler had already unleashed on the ridiculous Schuschnigg in Vienna. At the mention of the Austrian Chancellor, parts of the crowd erupted and for the first time, watching other faces around him, Tam sensed that what probably lay in store for Karlovy Vary and the surrounding towns and villages wasn't entirely welcome. These people still belonged to the last surviving democracy in Central Europe and no matter what the Sudeten National Socialist Party might think, ownership of a vote that truly meant something, that might decide the way you wanted to live, was still precious.

Tam felt a tug on his arm. It was Renata. Time to go. Tam carved a path through the crowd as Henlein was reaching the end of his speech. A gaggle of toughs guarded the street that

Renata wanted to take. These men, all armed with cudgels, weren't young. One of them looked Tam in the eye. He tried Czech first, then German.

'Where are you going, comrade?'

The word 'comrade' was the clue. The man spat it out. Only Reds left an occasion like this early.

'Die Glienicker.' It was Renata. 'There's a meeting we have to attend.'

'Where's Die Glienicker. . .?' The man was still looking at Tam.

'I'm afraid I've no idea.'

'Where are you from?'

'England.'

'So why are you here?'

'I'm not sure that's any business of yours.'

'Wrong, my friend. You have a passport?'

'Not on me.'

'Every visitor has a passport.'

His eyes flicked left. Two of his colleagues stepped forward, grabbing Tam by each arm, and forcing him against a shop front. Tam resisted the urge to fight back. Given the odds, this was neither the time nor the place to bring his visit to an early end, and so he allowed himself to go limp. The glass on the shop front was cold against his face. There were summer flowers inside, bright explosions of yellows and reds. Unseen hands were all over his body, patting him down, searching through his pockets, and he was thankful that he'd stowed his passport in the bag he'd left at the house. He could hear Renata behind him, arguing with the men in Czech. He didn't understand a word. Then, abruptly, he was free again.

The man who'd done all the talking was very close. Tam could smell alcohol on his breath.

'Be careful, comrade. And say thank you to the lady.'

*

They finally made it into the street, heads down, hurrying away from the roar of the crowd as Henlein reached the end of his speech. There was comfort in the cobblestones underfoot and the knowledge that they seemed to have escaped intact.

'Not quite.' Renata pulled him into the shelter of a bar on the corner of a side street. 'I had to show them my ID. They took the details.'

'That's all they wanted?'

'Of course not. They wanted to know about you. I told them you were English. When they asked what you were doing in Karlovy Vary I said you were gathering material.'

'For what?'

'A book.'

'And they believed you?'

'Of course they didn't. It was the best I could do.' There was a hint of reproach in the wanness of her smile. 'You might want to think of a book you'd like to write. Because they'll probably be back.'

Tam shrugged and ordered two brandies. Just now he could conjure nothing from his imagination except the certainty that the next few days and maybe weeks were going to be tougher than he'd anticipated. *Enemy territory* was a dramatic phrase but he could think of nothing more apt.

'Does any of this nonsense surprise you?' Tam nodded towards the open door. The street outside was beginning to fill with people, mainly men, a blur of swastika armbands in the gathering darkness.

'I grew up in Prague,' Renata said. 'Prague is different. These are country people. They happen to speak German, but don't be fooled. They'd like a nice little corner of Czechoslovakia for their own, but that doesn't open their doors for the likes of Hitler. If we stick together, if we keep the Germans out, there might be a future for us all. Otherwise,' she shrugged, reaching for her glass, 'the whole country will be speaking German. *Prosit.*'

Tam returned the toast. He knew it was the least he owed this woman. He'd listened to her voice when she was talking to the bully boys back at the rally. Not a single tremor. Not the least sign of nervousness. Deeply impressive.

'Tell me about Edvard. You've known him long?'

'Yes. He was a friend of Karyl's. He came from a village on the other side of the mountain from Jáchymov. His dad was a farmer. Two bad harvests in a row and he had to look for a job. In the end he found work on the railway. That's how he met Karyl.'

'And now?'

'Now he does something else.'

'Like what?'

Renata shook her head. 'Some other time.' She nodded at Tam's glass. 'Drink up.'

They made their way back to the house they'd visited earlier. This time it was Edvard himself who opened the door. Tam could smell onion soup and glimpsed a kitchen beyond the curtain at the end of the tiny tiled hall. A woman stood at the stove, stirring a huge saucepan of soup with a wooden spoon. Her name was Haninka and when she turned round, wiping her hands on her apron, she had a face that belonged to a different century, roughened by a life of hard physical work. When Edvard said something in Czech, nodding at Tam, she threw her head back and cackled with laughter. Three surviving teeth and eyes a milky blue.

'She's Edvard's mother,' Renata murmured. 'His father's dead.'

'And Edvard lives here?'

'Sometimes, yes.'

Haninka spooned the soup into the waiting bowls. The taste of the soup and the warmth of the bread that came with it took Tam back to The Glebe House: the same shadowed spaces, the same burble of conversation. Renata and Edvard were talking in Czech, with occasional glances in Tam's direction. There was a complicity between them that went further than mere friendship. No wonder Renata had been so eager to come home.

'So you met our Nazi brothers.' Edvard's smile had settled on Tam.

'I did.'

'Then you have my sympathies. Henlein leads these people by the nose. He's selling them goods unseen. Who in their right mind agrees a bargain like that?'

It was a country phrase and it brought another cackle of laughter from his mother. She forced more soup on Tam and scolded Renata for not feeding him up. Her thickly accented German, to Tam, was close to incomprehensible but every time she looked at Renata the seamed old face lit up.

Edvard had produced a bottle of wine. Three glasses and a teacup appeared on the rough wooden table. This time there was no toast, just an exchange of nods. Tam's glass was the biggest. He took a sip, then another. It was undrinkable.

Haninka was bent over the stove. From the oven came a dish of potatoes crusted with cheese. She put it in front of Tam. Renata told him to eat.

Tam did her bidding, helping himself. Suddenly there was a bowl at his elbow and he watched the old woman's rough fingers dust the steaming cheese with paprika. After the wine, the fiery potatoes came as a relief. He was thinking about a second helping when Edvard stiffened at the table. Moments later he was at the front door. Tam heard a low mumble of conversation, then Edvard was back in the room with a guest.

The newcomer was small, robustly built, with a shock of curly black hair and a sallow, indoor face. His black suit was giving out at the elbows and the heel of one of his boots flap-flapped on the flagstones as he approached the table. His eyes were huge, moving slowly from face to face. He was carrying a stained hessian bag which he gave to Edvard. Tam judged his age at thirty, maybe a year or two older.

'My name is Spielmann,' he announced. 'We will speak in German.'

Without waiting for an invitation, he made himself comfortable at the table and seized the bottle of wine. Fat, stubby fingers. Bitten nails. In the absence of an extra glass, Tam pushed his own across. Already, he sensed that this man's sudden arrival was far from unexpected. His gaze settled on Tam.

'Your name, sir?' His fleshy lips were moist from the wine.

'Tam.'

'Mr Tam. . .' He nodded, enjoying the feel of the word in his mouth. 'I come from Dresden. You know Dresden? Perhaps not. A beautiful city.'

As it happened, Tam had been there twice, once for more than a week. He began to enthuse about the city – the walks beside the Elbe and the view of the Frauenkirche from the Neumarkt – but Spielmann wasn't interested. A second bottle of wine was making the rounds. He intercepted it before it got to Renata. Already he'd dismissed the offer of food and Tam began to wonder how much else he'd had to drink.

'You know what I like to do in Dresden? More than anything? I like to fish. And you know why I like to fish? Because of this book.' He muttered something to Edvard, who fetched the hessian bag. From the bag he produced a book which he pushed across the table. The book, in English, must have been fifty years old. The spine was broken and many of the pages were loose. Leafing carefully through, Tam found himself looking at sepia photos of fishing ports on the east coast, mainly Grimsby and Hull. The harbours were thick with drifters, tiny workboats relying on sail, and at the back of the book he found a section devoted to Fraserburgh, a harbour he knew well, up on the coast beyond Aberdeen. Spielmann's eyes never left his face.

'The women,' he said. 'Look at the women.'

Tam turned a page. The photographer had abandoned the busy clutter of the granite quay for the nearby sheds where dozens of women filleted the catch. To the rear of the benches where the women worked was a big area where the fish were auctioned every morning. The sheds had been enlarged after the Great War and Tam had been here himself on countless occasions, buying cod and herring for The Glebe House.

'You speak English?' Tam looked up.

'*Nein*. No English. But I have this.' His hand plunged back into the bag. This time Tam was looking at a flensing knife, the wooden handle worn with use. Spielmann began to slash at the space between them, filleting some imaginary fish, telling Tam how he'd spent long days on the Elbe above Dresden, catching shad and carp and even once a salmon and how he'd taught himself to use the knife the way the ladies in Britain did, so much flesh, so few bones, and so *quick*.

'So, Mr Tam, you find me a job, *ja*?' He nodded at the book. 'With the ladies, *ja*?'

'You mean in England?'

'*Ja*. You know what I am? Apart from a fishing person? I'm a Jew, Mr Tam. Here, take a look – '

The bag again, and a yellow star, hand-sewn, tossed down on the table like the Joker in some imaginary card game.

'You know who makes the star for me? My mother. She hates the ones they give you. Factory stars. Stars probably made by Jews. That's the kind of game they play. The Jews make the stars, thousands of them, millions of them, one star for every Jew. But me? I have a special star. From my mother.'

Spielmann was beginning to lose control. He was sweating heavily and his hands were shaking and Tam wondered how many times he'd been through this routine. There was a madness about the man, barely disguised, and when at last he fell silent it was only to wipe the spittle from his lips.

'Life was tough in Dresden? For Jews?'

'Impossible. Life is impossible. Where you can go. Where you can shop. Which part of the tram is yours. Who you can talk to. And what happens when they find you without your precious badge.' One pudgy hand closed over the star. 'There's nothing left for Jews, Mr Tam. Where I come from it's standing room only. And you know the worst of it? People don't care. Everyone else, they look the other way. Why? Because they're frightened. Frightened and maybe ashamed.' There was an edge of accusation in his voice. 'So what do you do, Mr Tam? If you're Jewish and you catch fish and find a book like this, and a knife like this, and you think that maybe one day you can find yourself in a place like that?' He nodded at the open book. 'My mother tries, Mr Tam. She tries very hard. She knows an old man in Dresden who speaks English. I ask him to write me a letter. I send the letter to the person who wrote that book. I tell him about my knife and my fish and about everything I've learned. And you know what happens? Nothing. No reply. No job. Nothing.'

'The book is very old,' Tam said gently. 'The author will be dead.'

Spielmann swept the fact aside. He didn't want any kind of debate. What he wanted was a new life where strangers wouldn't spit at him on the street and where his mother wouldn't live in fear of an early morning knock on the door.

'You know where I went after Dresden? When it got so bad? I went to Vienna. Imagine. Vienna. It was Christmas. There were funfairs. I make some friends. No one likes the Jews but there are Austrians who keep their feelings to themselves and so I start to think that things aren't so bad after all. I take my knife to a shop in the market that sells fish. I even find myself a job in the back of the market where no one can see how Jewish I am. That was good. That was better than good. Just me and the knife and the fish, and the fish don't care about Jews and neither does the knife. But then last month the Germans come again, and there are old women, Jewish women, Jewish professors even, on their knees on the pavement scrubbing and scrubbing, and I look at what's happening and I realise it's even worse than Dresden. You happen to be Austrian, you get a rifle and a uniform. Me? I get a yellow star and a brush for the pavement. And so one night I start walking again, walking and walking, always at night, always east, the wandering Jew, and one of those nights I cross the border high in the mountains and I find somewhere to live and even a little work again but everyone says the Germans are coming, the Germans are following me, and so here I am, meeting the Englishman, meeting Mr Tam, telling him my story, knowing that everything's going to be fine.'

He reached for his glass, visibly exhausted. Then his eyes settled on Edvard and he forced a crooked smile before nodding towards the door.

'You want me to go now? Have you heard enough?'

9

DAHLEM, BERLIN, 12 MAY 1938

Joachim von Ribbentrop lived in an impressive three-storey villa, lapped by an enormous lawn, in the wealthy Berlin suburb of Dahlem. It was a house that spoke of power as well as money, with room for tennis courts and a swimming pool, but what struck Dieter most of all was a collection of kids' bicycles propped beneath a huge willow tree. This was a family property, proof that even at the very top of the Reich there still existed an appetite for the messiness of real life.

The invitation to Dahlem had come from Ribbentrop's wife, Annelies. On the prompting of her husband, she'd evidently phoned the Japanese Embassy and spoken briefly to the ambassador. Adolf, their fourth child, was having a party. Still very young, he was already fascinated by the faraway countries his papa described on his return from yet another diplomatic mission. The presence of Keiko would be the perfect surprise and if her consort, the young flier who'd done so well in Japan, cared to attend as well then so much the better. Dress would be casual. Presents should be modest. Guests would be away by late afternoon.

The question of dress had preoccupied Keiko for several days. Dieter knew by now that she'd turned her back on the formalities of Japanese public life but, given the spirit of the invitation, she'd decided to wear a full-length kimono in smoky vermilion that she'd borrowed from the young cultural attaché at the embassy. The kimono was complemented by a delicate *kanzash*, black and gold, pinned to fall free from the hair she'd so carefully piled around her head, and she also carried a fan in bright spring colours with a shadowy bird motif that only appeared once the fan was fully spread. She wanted this hint of magic to work with children, especially the younger ones. At four years old, Adolf might be the perfect audience.

A car from the Foreign Ministry had called at the apartment off Friedrichstrasse to pick them up. Now, Dieter stood aside as the driver helped Keiko from the big Mercedes. For the third day running Berlin was enjoying cloudless skies and Dieter could hear children's laughter drifting from the open windows on the ground floor. A woman rounded the corner of the house. She was middle-aged, thin-lipped, watchful, with a face untroubled by the sun. The sight of the kimono, to Dieter's amusement, sparked a smile.

'Perfect,' she said. 'Joachim promised me something special. Young Adolf will be so excited. I'm Annalies, Joachim's wife.'

She extended a hand in greeting and then led them into the house. To Dieter's surprise, Keiko seemed born to this new role. She took tiny steps, a fixed smile on her face, her long body perfectly erect. Moments before they mounted the steps, Dieter softly called her name and when she glanced back he mimed applause.

'*Wunderbar*,' he murmured.

She acknowledged the compliment with the faintest nod of her head and then opened the fan to hide her blushes. Another geisha trick, Dieter thought. Perfectly executed.

Once through the ornate front door, the big hall smelled of furniture polish and fresh flowers. Art hung on the walls, the pictures slightly too big, the frames slightly too heavy. There was a clutter of antique furniture and a huge bust of Hitler in polished black granite. This was a house, Dieter thought, designed to make a statement about its owners. According to Georg, the regime had been kind to the Ribbentrops and here was the proof.

The birthday boy appeared, open-mouthed at the sight of Keiko. He was small for his age, blond and a little shy. He tried to stifle a fit of the giggles and at first he hid his face as Keiko bent to shake his hand.

'This is Herr Merz,' she said. 'Herr Merz flies aeroplanes.'

The mention of aeroplanes widened his eyes. A little girl had appeared, evidently Adolf's sister. She had none of her brother's shyness and she seized Keiko's hand and pulled her towards an open door beyond the stairs.

'*Komm*,' she squealed. '*Komm mit mir*.'

Taken hostage, Keiko disappeared. Adolf was still gazing up at Dieter.

'Can you come upstairs?' he asked. 'To my bedroom?'

His mother had been called to the phone. Dieter waited for her to finish. He needed to consult about this pressing invitation. Annalies enquired how much patience Dieter had. Reassured that patience and Dieter were best friends, she wished him luck. Adolf, she said, was obsessed by aeroplanes. Be firm if he gets too excited.

The child's bedroom was on the first floor, an L-shaped space with a view over the swimming pool at the rear of the property. Wooden models of planes, exquisitely painted, hung on threads of cotton from the ceiling and there were more aircraft, metal this time, carefully arranged on a sheet of brown paper on the floor. The paper had been crayoned with runways and space for a control tower, part of this child's fantasy world, but pride of place belonged to a Ju-52 parked on the low table beside the bed. Adolf was already sprawled beside his model aerodrome, tenderly fingering one of the new Stukas.

Dieter squatted beside the Ju-52. The ribbed metal fuselage carried a name. *Wilhelm Siegert*. Dieter recognised the name. Siegert had been an ace during the Great War.

'That's my daddy's aeroplane.' The child was gazing at it.

'You've been inside?'

'Yes.'

'Flying?'

'No.'

'Have you ever been flying?'

'No. What's it like?'

Dieter smiled at the question. If he got the answer right it would explain a very great deal.

'What does your daddy say?'

'He says it's noisy.'

'He's right. It is. What else does he say?'

'Papa says it's very quick. He says you can get to England in less than three hours.' He frowned. 'What's England?'

Another good question. Dieter's gaze drifted to a framed photograph on the chest of drawers showing Ribbentrop in full dress diplomatic uniform in a gathering of notables, similarly attired. One of them, he suspected, was the English king who'd fallen in love with an American and lost his throne.

'That's England.' He nodded at the photo.

'No,' the boy shook his head. 'That's my daddy.'

Dieter tried to explain but Adolf had lost interest. He wanted to know what kind of aeroplane his new friend flew. Dieter glanced at the metal models on the makeshift airfield.

'This one.' He picked up a Bf-109. 'It's called a fighter.' He performed a loop or two, the fuselage lightly grasped between his finger and thumb. The boy watched him, entranced.

'Again,' he said. 'Do it again.'

Dieter stood up this time, starting by the door. Thanks to Georg, he'd taken up one of the new 'Emils' only yesterday, flying from the research field out at Johannisthal. One of the test pilots had briefed him on the differences he should expect from the uprated engine and had asked him about Spain. Dieter had been happy to talk about the tactics they'd learned to expect from the Russian pilots, and how more speed and more agility could only make life even tougher for the Ivans. The 109 he was flying had a full tank of fuel and he'd been able to spend more than an hour in the air, pushing the machine – and himself – to the limits. To his intense relief, the confidence he'd once taken for granted – that feeling of total command – hadn't deserted him, and the neatness of his landing on the shorter of the two runways had won a pumping handshake from the watching test pilot when he climbed down from the cockpit. Even his lower back, he realised later, had been free of pain.

Now, easing the toy fighter up from the carpet, he tried to share some of that same flight with young Adolf. The battle to keep the 109 straight on take-off. The feeling of raw power when he climbed away from the airfield. And the moment when he half-rolled off the top of a loop and came screaming down towards the big hangar where he knew the test pilot and a small gaggle of others were watching. He'd made a low pass at no more than twenty metres, half an eye on the speed indicator, judging the moment when he'd have to pull up to clear the swelling bulk of the biggest hangar. In the dive he'd reached 710 kph which was faster than he'd ever managed before and even 600 kph straight and level would have been inconceivable in Spain.

Adolf wanted to know whether Dieter had killed people.

'Fighting, you mean? In the air? In combat?'

'Yes.' He tried to mime the chatter of a machine gun but the rat-tat-tat got stuck in his throat. 'Other planes. Baddie planes. Not our planes.'

Dieter nodded. He'd shot down lots of those baddie planes.

'How many?'

'Lots.'

'How many?'

'Twenty-seven.'

'*Twenty-seven?*' The boy clapped his tiny hands, and then seized another of the little models. It happened to be an He-51, the sturdy biplane that had been a mainstay of the Condor Legion. 'I'm a baddie. Shoot me down.'

Dieter studied him a moment, wondering quite how far he should allow this game to go, and then he began to explain the moves young Adolf should make as Dieter's 109 crept ever closer. Drop a wing. Look for cover down there, towards the nest of shoes. Push the plane harder. Climb. Roll. Pretend you're a fish. Wriggle free. The boy loved the charade, breathless with excitement, trying to kick Dieter with his bare feet when he got too close, but then the end came, all too sudden, when Dieter out-turned him by the wardrobe and shot him down.

'It's over?' The boy was staring at Dieter. He was close to tears. 'I'm dead?'

'I'm afraid so.'

'But how did you do that? What's it called?'

Dieter smiled at him, extended a hand, promised a rematch any time he wanted, but the boy wasn't listening. He still demanded an explanation. How come it was over so suddenly? What was the trick Dieter had pulled?

Dieter couldn't come up with an answer. Then he remembered the word he'd learned with Georg in Spain: the matador in the bullring, the glint of light on the plunging blade, and then the wounded animal on its knees, the sand pink with blood.

'*Estocada*,' he said. 'It's called *estocada*.'

The boy was staring at him. He liked the word.

'*Es-to-ca-da*,' he repeated carefully.

They had another dogfight and this time Dieter was careful to let the child win, but Adolf knew he wasn't really trying. He landed his own plane back on the pretend airfield and headed for the door. His big brother was downstairs. His big brother knew everything. He'd even flown in Papa's plane. Let's see what Dieter could do against Rudolf.

Dieter listened to the footsteps running along the landing and back towards the head of the stairs. From the window, he gazed down at the swimming pool, wondering whether the water was heated or not. Then two figures came into view, walking slowly side by side. One of them was Keiko. She was laughing. The other was Ribbentrop, young Adolf's papa. He was wearing a grey business suit with a party badge in the lapel but it was recognisably the same figure who featured in the framed photo on the child's chest of drawers: the trademark stiffness, the same slight bend of the upper body, the same stern frown, his hands clasped behind his back.

Beside the pool, the two figures stopped. Ribbentrop seemed to be explaining something about the way it worked, pointing at a grille at the further end. Then he turned back to Keiko and reached for the *kanzash* she'd pinned to her head. It was a delicate gesture for a big man, full of wonderment, and in that brief moment Dieter realised that Ribbentrop, too, was helpless in the presence of this woman. She'd taken a tiny step backwards. She'd splayed the fan. She'd turned her face away. But then came the sound of laughter again from the side of the pool, the pair of them sharing a joke, two voices, impossibly in tune.

Young Adolf had returned. His elder brother, it seemed, had no time for kids' games. The child picked up the 109 and began to fly it round the room. Still beside the window, Dieter was aware of his presence but couldn't take his eyes off the couple by the pool. They were on the move again, Ribbentrop pointing to a summer house at the far end of the garden. Keiko, hanging on his every word, fell into step beside him.

They crossed the lawn, more laughter, and then Ribbentrop paused to stoop to the flower bed that edged the summer house. The roses were in their prime, the deepest shade of red, and the big man's fingers brushed bloom after bloom before making his selection. He presented it to Keiko with a smile and a courtly bow. She studied it a moment, holding it delicately between her long fingers, and then lifted it to her nose. Whatever she murmured appeared to delight her companion. Ribbentrop whispered something in her ear and then produced a key to the summer house. Moments later, they were gone.

Adolf had joined Dieter at the window. He, too, was staring at the summer house.

'That's Papa's special place,' he said in wonderment. 'No one goes in but him.'

10

PRAGUE, 16 MAY 1938

The British military attaché in Prague occupied a cubbyhole of an office on the second floor of the embassy in the area of the Old Town that dropped down towards the river and the Charles Bridge. Harold Stronge was a soldier's soldier, terse, businesslike, a man for whom real life held few surprises. When he closed the door and wedged himself back behind the tiny desk, Tam caught a hint of weariness in his voice.

'On the small side, I know. It doesn't impress our Czech friends either.'

Ballentyne had set up the meeting and Tam knew at once that the presence of someone from the shadowy world of Intelligence in this city was far from welcome. On the other hand, Stronge appeared to have been briefed about Tam's pedigree.

'How well do you know these people? Sanderson? Ballentyne? All those chums of theirs?'

'Scarcely at all.'

'They tell you much? About their little set-up?'

'Barely anything.'

'I'm not surprised. These people operate in the dark, write their own rules, help themselves to whatever they choose. When it suits them, they keep their heads down, claim all kinds of immunity. God knows, medals are in short supply just now but if things ever brighten up I'm sure they'll be first in the queue at the bloody Palace.'

He enquired, by name, about a couple of officers in the Royal Marines. Tam, who knew both men well, realised he was being put to the test. After several minutes of conversation, with Tam doing most of the talking, Stronge seemed to relax. His attitude to Tam had visibly softened. If anything he seemed saddened that a man with a decent military background should have fallen into such poor company.

'Did your keepers tell you about Maček?' Maček was the Czech Colonel assigned to liaise with the Western Armies. He spoke both English and French and could, according to Stronge, expect to be seriously disappointed in either language.

'Nice chap, though. Seriously good egg. Something of a realist, too, and in these parts that can be rare. I'm afraid the best we can do for him just now is play the gentleman by not promising too much. Are you getting my drift?'

'I've got nothing to promise,' Tam said. 'I'm here to take a look, see what these good folk are up to, then report back. Anything else is beyond my pay grade.' It was a small lie, and Stronge knew it.

'Anyone tell you about their kit? Our Czech friends?'

'A little.'

'It's first class. Better, to be frank, than most of ours. Tanks, artillery, aircraft. . . they make this stuff themselves and they do it well. They're also bloody motivated, which is another advantage. This is a rough neighbourhood. It pays to look after yourself.'

Tomorrow, he said, he and Tam were due to join Maček for a tour of the western fortifications. Stronge had yet to visit the sensitive areas up on the border but he knew that the Czechs were putting a lot of effort into keeping the Germans at arm's length.

'My spies tell me you've been in the Sudetenland.'

Tam detected just the hint of a smile.

'That's right.'

'Karlovy Vary. Henlein. All that lunatic company he keeps.'

'Correct.'

'So what did you make of them?'

Tam took his time in answering. Already, after barely a week, that first evening in Karlovy Vary seemed to belong to another life. Since then, thanks to Renata and Edvard, he'd met countless men and women, most of them appalled by where the Sudeten push for independence might leave the rest of Czechoslovakia.

'These are people who want to fight,' he said carefully.

'Happy to fight?'

'Not at all. Far from it. Need to fight would be closest. They understand the Germans and they're not fooled.'

'Meaning?'

'Meaning they take Hitler at his word. He wants their country. He's said so. He thinks it's his due. Which leaves them no choice but to say no.'

'By resisting.'

'Of course.'

'With whose help?'

'Ours. And the French.'

'And you really think that will happen?'

'I've no idea. But I somehow doubt it.'

'And they share that feeling?'

'Yes. That's what disturbs me most. They're aware of the treaties, the pledges, the words on paper. If it comes to a fight, a real fight, they know they'll need us. I just hope we turn up.'

Stronge nodded, saying nothing. There might have been that same faint smile back on his face but Tam couldn't be certain.

'Interesting,' Stronge said at length.

'Interesting how, Colonel?'

'Interesting how quickly we exceed our briefs. By your own account you came here to compile a report. Yet already you're offering an opinion. Do I blame you? Not in the least. Do I think you're right? As it happens, I do. These are decent people, most of them. They deserve our support. But do you think either you or I will make a ha'pence of difference?' He shook his head. 'Sadly not.'

*

Tam spent the evening with Renata in a bar across the river. By now he knew he'd been right about what had really brought her back to Central Europe. She and Edvard had been close for years and now that closeness had matured into something deeper. This was a man, she said, who enabled her to live with her conscience. Edvard had known her husband longer than she. He knew Karyl like a brother. And that was important because, like Renata herself, he'd suspected for years that his drinking was turning him into someone else, and that there was no way back.

'You have a conscience about Karyl?'

'Of course. I keep it in here.' She tapped her head. 'Maybe I'm fooling myself. Maybe it's just an excuse. But it's easier to betray a stranger than a friend.'

'A stranger? Karyl? Is it that bad?'

'Worse. One day I realised I didn't even like him any more. He never beat me. He never even threatened me. He just became a sad old man. He smells, too.'

'And Edvard?'

'Edvard never gives in. And Edvard is an optimist. Two reasons why Karyl always told me he was crazy. So maybe Edvard's not so crazy. Not once you get to know him. Rare? Yes. But not crazy.'

She seemed happy with the thought, ducking her head to mask a grin. Then her head came up again. She wanted to know about Tam. Did he have a wife? Children? This was the first indication that she had any interest in his private life and Tam didn't know whether to be flattered.

'Neither,' he said. 'I have a father who's lost his mind and a business that's doing its best to make me as crazy as he is.'

He told her a little about The Glebe House, and his mother's dying wish that he should try and make the place pay. To date, bookings had exceeded his expectations but he'd never underestimate the challenge of turning a profit. To his surprise, she seemed genuinely interested.

'So tell me about Scotland. What's it like?'

'Empty.'

'And you like that?'

'Very much. That's where I grew up. You learn to fend for yourself. Maybe that's why I never settled down. I like my own company too much. Or maybe I'm just scared of taking the risk.'

'The risk is everything. Get it wrong and it can be horrible. Get it right and you're the happiest person in the world.'

'And you and Edvard?'

'We've got it right.'

Tam nodded, said nothing. Edvard had been due to meet them at the bar around eight. It was already close to ten.

'So where is he?' Tam asked at last.

'I don't know. He was in Jáchymov this afternoon. It's only a couple of hours away. He should be here by now.'

Jáchymov was in the Sudetenland, Karyl's home town. Tam remembered the poster over the bed in the Jaywick chalet. Edvard, according to Renata, also came from the area, back in the days when his father was still farming.

'So what's so important that takes him back to Jáchymov?'

'You want the truth? It's difficult. It's complicated. Maybe it's best we,' she shrugged, 'talk about something else.'

Tam held her gaze. She wanted to tell him more, he knew she did. Already he felt a duty of care towards her. If he ever got married and had a daughter, he hoped she'd turn out to be someone like this.

'You know what Edvard's doing in Jáchymov?'

'Of course. He tells me everything.' She stole a look around the bar. At this time of night, it was beginning to empty.

'You want another drink?' Tam nodded at her glass.

'No.' She beckoned him closer. 'You know about Jáchymov? About the quarries?'

'No.'

His reply appeared to confuse her. She checked again. When he shook his head for a second time she seemed to believe him.

'The rocks there are radioactive,' she said. 'Many of the men get sick. Some of them die. One time they tried to make a business out of it, radioactive soaps, wristwatches that glow in the dark, but that's all stopped. Edvard worked there for a couple of weeks but some of the older men frightened him with their stories. Breathe the dust and you'll never make fifty. That's what they told him. And that's why he went to the railway.'

'The mines are still open?'

'Yes.'

'And they crush the rocks? Sell the ore?'

'Yes.'

'So who buys it?'

She hesitated, looking round again. 'The Germans,' she said. 'They came with a big order last year. They want to ship the stuff back home. No one knows why.'

Tam nodded. This had to be uranium. One of Gunther Nagel's shooting party had mentioned it at The Glebe House. He and Tam had shared a malt or two after dinner. The German had a brother who was a chemist, working on some project or other, and uranium had featured in the conversation. Apparently it had special properties, lending itself to all kinds of possibilities, but it was hard to lay hands on.

'There are other quarries like this in Czechoslovakia?'

'No. Only Jáchymov.'

'Elsewhere, maybe? Austria? Germany itself?'

'I asked the same questions. Edvard says not.'

'So that must make Jáchymov pretty special. If you know what to do with this stuff.'

'Of course. That's what I told your Mr Ballentyne. When he came out to Prague to meet me.'

'When was this?'

'Last year. That's how we got the permits to come to England. I thought you knew about all this.'

'About the permits? The mine?'

'Yes. And about Karyl.'

'Karyl?'

'He's Jewish. That's why we had to leave.'

Tam absorbed the news. The gaunt face on the pillow. The line of empty bottles. All the clues to a life cast adrift. He checked his watch. Nearly half-past ten.

'So tell me what Edvard was doing in Jáchymov this afternoon,' he said.

'I can't.' She shook her head.

'Was it to do with the mine?'

'Please. . .'

'Was he meeting someone?'

'Yes.'

'Do you know where?'

'Yes.'

'Where?'

'Why do you ask me?'

'Because I want to help.'

'You think something's happened? To Edvard?' She was looking alarmed.

'I don't know.'

The answer didn't please her. Finally she bit her lip. None of this was easy.

'A hotel,' she said with some reluctance. 'The Hotel Kavalerie.'

'And do you know this person he was planning to meet?'

'No.'

'Do you know anything about them?'

She was staring at him now. The drumbeat of his questions had put something new in her eyes, something Tam hadn't seen before. Fear.

At length, she ducked her head.

'He was an American,' she muttered. 'That's all I know.'

*

Next day Tam was due to visit the fortifications on the western frontier and he was on the road with the military attaché by first light. Stronge's assistant had phoned Tam's hotel and left a message. The Colonel had to be back in Prague for a function in the evening and thus he had no alternative but to insist on an early start. As a small consolation he'd bring a bite to eat for breakfast.

An hour and a half from Prague, the road west plunged into an area of dense woodland. Stronge spotted a forester's track and pulled over. Even this early, the sun was warm through the dapple of leaves overhead, and the glade was alive with the busy hum of insects.

'Bully beef, I'm afraid. One day our commissary might start buying local produce.'

Stronge extracted two thick sandwiches from a wrap of greaseproof paper and passed one over. Tam took a bite. He was sitting on his folded greatcoat, his back against a tree. The bread was as indigestible as the bully beef.

'Tell me about Jáchymov,' he said.

'You mean the bloody mine?' Stronge needed no prompting. 'I thought your people were the experts?'

'They probably are. But you need to be in the priesthood to share all this stuff. I do what I'm told. Everything else goes over my head.'

Priesthood raised a smile. Tam was beginning to suspect that he and Stronge might end up allies in this strange war, poking about for scraps of other people's intelligence and then comparing notes to tease out some kind of truth.

'The locals have been mining in the mountains for centuries,' Stronge said. 'They were after silver to begin with. Then came the uranium. Marie Curie ring any bells? Turn of the century? Radium?'

Tam nodded. He'd gleaned this much from Renata. The pre-war health spas in the foothills around the town centre. The belief that the mysteries of radioactivity might work some therapeutic miracle or other.

'Are we talking uranium?' Tam needed to be sure.

'We are.'

'So who owns this stuff?'

Stronge said he didn't know. He'd produced a silver toothpick, wincing as he probed a tender spot between his back molars. If, by chance, Tam ever needed the services of a decent dentist in Prague, he knew just the man.

'You're changing the subject.'

'I am.'

'Why?'

'Because you're here to look at the bloody defence works not quiz me about subjects I frankly don't understand. Has it come to my notice that our friends across the border have an interest in uranium? Yes, it has. How? Because your lords and masters have been moving heaven and earth to find out why.

Forgive me, but it's those same people who appear to be paying your wages, which makes this seeming ignorance of yours all the more puzzling.'

'I'm a new boy. I just told you. I get to see the stuff on the lower shelves. Eyes only. No touching. Whatever else they've got is locked away. And I'm guessing that includes uranium.' Tam tossed the remains of his sandwich towards a pair of watching squirrels. 'Might the Americans be involved here?'

'In Jáchymov, you mean? God forbid. The Yanks want nothing to do with Czechoslovakia these days which is a bit rich in my book because Woodrow Wilson bloody invented it. Why do you ask?'

Tam didn't answer. Instead he stretched himself full length on the warm moss and shut his eyes. Renata had left him at the bar last night and departed to make a phone call. She was currently staying with a friend in Prague but she'd promised to get in touch again after his return. By then, she assured him, she'd have laid hands on Edvard.

Tam felt a shadow looming over him. Stronge stooped to retrieve the greaseproof paper. Then he paused, looking down at Tam.

'Why would the Americans have any interest in Jáchymov?' he asked. 'What on earth gave you that idea?'

*

The Czech fortifications on the western frontier had been the work of several years, a succession of strong points offering mutual support and interlocking fields of fire. Each of these strong points, reinforced in metres-thick concrete, formed a link in a chain that stretched for countless kilometres. Turn the lie of the land to your advantage, deny the enemy the high ground, funnel his approach by tank obstacles, thickets of barbed wire and artfully sited minefields, and you ended up with a series of killing zones the Czechs could pound into oblivion.

The theory, elaborated with some passion by Colonel Maček, sounded invader-proof but Tam knew enough about the untidy realities of combat to recognise that no plan, no matter how well conceived and engineered, survived contact with the enemy. All morning they drove from strong point to strong point in convoy with their Czech host. They explored underground galleries, peered through range-finding periscopes, watched young trainees serving the new Skoda artillery, and finally emerged into the brightness of the late spring sunshine to gaze across the wooded Bohemian hills towards Germany. Somewhere beyond the haze, thought Tam, were tens of thousands of men in *Wehrmacht* grey. Their appetites whetted by the easy stroll into Austria, they couldn't wait for the next country to serve itself up. Vienna. Prague. Maybe even Budapest. Where would it end?

Colonel Maček, for one, had no doubts. He was a small, neat little man with a crooked smile and a black leather wallet bulging with photos. Over canteens of mushroom soup and thick slices of wild boar sausage, he shared these photos with Tam and Stronge. He had three daughters. Two of them were in their late teens and, in Stronge's happy phrase, they both looked 'real poppets'. No way was their proud father going to let them anywhere near a German, uniformed or otherwise, and the battle for their virtue would begin and end here, where Czech cunning and Czech resolve would stop any invader in his tracks.

'We may be the youngest country in Europe,' he kept reminding Stronge, 'but our days in the nursery are over. All we ask from our allies is a little understanding and a little support. When it comes to fighting, if it comes to fighting, we can take care of ourselves.'

The soup and the sausage had been accompanied by two bottles of a local wine, red, rough, but more than welcome. Walking back to the car, having bade farewell to Colonel Maček, Stronge's mood had mellowed. Like Tam, he understood only too well that battle had a brutal logic all of its own. Morale mattered. Command mattered. And so did countless other factors that lay beyond the careful calculations of the military draughtsmen responsible for designing the Czech defences. If only victory went to the most deserving, Tam thought.

Back at the car, Stronge paused to raise his binoculars and take a final peek at the last of the forts they'd visited.

'So what will you tell your people back home?' he asked.

'Officially?' Tam shrugged. 'It's impressive. You can't deny it. Lots of the kit is brand new. They seem to have the training taped. Their command set-up looks pretty effective. And you'd never argue with the siting and the design. I can think of any number of reasons why the Germans might have a real fight on their hands.' He shot Stronge a look. 'If only we were in the same position.'

'But?'

'But nothing. You asked me a question. That's my answer.'

'And you think it's the answer your masters are after?'

Tam ducked his head a moment, said nothing.

'Well?' Stronge was still waiting for an answer.

'I'm sure it'll be music to their ears.' Tam reached for the car door. 'Any chance of dropping me off en route?'

*

It was late afternoon by the time they got to Jáchymov. The spa town lay in a narrow valley shadowed by the mountains on every side. The sunshine had brought out the locals and the cafés in the middle of the town were as busy as in Prague. Directions from a passer-by led them to a narrow cul-de-sac, nearly a mile out of town. The silence was unbroken the moment Stronge killed the engine, except for the burble of water from a nearby spring. If you were looking for somewhere for a discreet conversation, thought Tam, you could do worse than the Hotel Kavalerie.

Stronge made a telephone call from the tiny desk that served as the hotel's reception area, warning his secretary he might be a little late for his evening engagement. Then he turned back to Tam, one bony hand outstretched.

'It's been a pleasure,' he said. 'And I mean that. You'll keep in touch? I'd appreciate it.'

He pumped Tam's hand and then he was gone. Moments later, Tam heard the engine cough and there was a rumble from the exhaust as Stronge headed back towards the town.

'You're staying here?' The woman who had given Stronge the telephone had re-emerged from her office. 'You need a room?'

Tam shook his head. The fact that the woman was speaking German probably meant she took him for a tourist, maybe some Sudeten from one of the bigger cities looking for a bit of peace and quiet, or a wallow in one of the town's thermal baths.

'You get many foreigners here? Do you mind me asking?'

'Sometimes.' The woman shrugged. 'What sort of foreigners do you mean?'

'Germans?'

'Of course. They love it here. Their money goes a long way.'

'Business people? Holidaymakers?'

'Both.' She was frowning now. 'Are you police?'

'No.'

'So why so many questions?'

'I'm trying to find a friend of mine. I was supposed to meet him here last night but I got the date wrong. My mistake.'

'You have a name?'

'Edvard.'

'I meant a surname.'

'No.'

'You're telling me he hasn't got a surname? This friend of yours?'

Tam was cursing himself. He should have thought this thing through. He spread his hands wide, apologised for wasting the woman's time. Maybe he'd got the wrong hotel.

The woman was studying him carefully. For some reason she was still prepared to help.

'Describe him. This friend of yours.'

Tam did his best. Tall. Thin. Black hair. Not so well dressed.

'He smiles a lot? Your friend?'

'All the time.'

'You're right. He was here last night. Room 17.' She reached for the hotel register. 'His name's Kovač. Would you like me to write it down?'

Tam nodded. She wrote in capital letters, the way you might for a child. Tam waited for her to finish.

'Was he alone? Mr Kovač?'

The woman wouldn't answer. Not at first. Then she returned the pen to the inkwell and looked up again.

'Is that important? Does it matter to you?'

'Yes, I'm afraid it does.'

'Then the answer is no. He met someone else.'

'You saw this other person?'

'No. The two of them had a meal here. On the terrace. I have a copy of the bill.'

'Somebody served them? A waiter, perhaps?'

'Of course.'

'And the waiter is here?'

'Not tonight. And it's a waitress, not a waiter.'

'How do I find her? This woman?'

'You don't. If you wish, I can make contact. The decision to meet you is hers, not mine.' Her eyes drifted down to the register. 'Have you changed your mind about a room? Only that might make things a little easier.'

Tam produced his wallet. He'd be happy to stay the night. She took his money and presented him with a key. Then she nodded towards the stairs.

'I hope you like the room better than Mr Kovač,' she said. 'For some reason he never used it.'

*

Tam ate alone that night, waiting long after the plates had been cleared away in the hope that the waitress might turn up. When nothing happened he left the empty restaurant and took the stairs to his room. He only saw the envelope once he'd closed the door. It was lying on the carpet, no name, no room number. Inside was a single sheet of lined paper. He recognised the receptionist's hand, the carefully formed capital letters. HER NAME IS VALENTA, it read. SHE WILL BE WAITING DOWNSTAIRS AT MIDNIGHT.

Tam checked his watch. It was already gone eleven. He returned to the note, then folded it back into the envelope. Thanks to Renata and her contacts, he'd had enough conversations to be wary of midnight assignments with a total stranger. He tore a page from a notebook in his bag and scribbled a couple of lines about what little he knew: that Edvard Kovač had met an American the previous evening at the Hotel Kavalerie, that he'd never used the room he'd paid for, and that he – Tam – was about to meet the waitress who'd served them both on the hotel's terrace restaurant. He sealed the envelope and addressed it to Stronge in Prague, hoping that even without a stamp it would still get through.

Ten past eleven. Tam needed to get the envelope in the post. Normally he'd leave it with the receptionist but he wasn't prepared to trust her. Neither did he want to step blindly into this surprise rendezvous without some prior checks. Time spent in reconnaissance, he told himself, is seldom wasted. Rule One if you want to survive on any battlefield.

In the street outside the hotel, a full moon cast long shadows over the potholed asphalt. Tam paused for a long moment at the foot of the hotel steps, letting his eyes accustom themselves to the half-darkness. A cat emerged from beneath a parked car. In the distance, audible above the bubble of the nearby spring, the hoot of a solitary owl.

Tam set off in the direction of the town, searching for a postbox. He'd seen them in Karlovy Vary and Prague. They were yellow, relics from the old days, reminders – according to Renata – of the Austro-Hungarian Empire the war had destroyed. He thought of her now, and of Edvard. Had she managed to find him? Had he made it back to Prague from whatever had brought him here?

In truth, Tam hadn't a clue. He was new to this world of bluff and counter-bluff, of nothing being quite what it seemed, of cleverly sauced lies masquerading as the truth. To prosper amongst these people you needed to learn their language and ape their ways. That was something wholly foreign, something for which he was ill-prepared, but he was becoming uncomfortably aware that he no longer had any choice in the matter. If he was to do the job properly, to make any kind of contribution, he had to be as devious as everyone else.

He found a postbox on the well-lit corner where the road to the hotel joined the main avenue that led down to the middle of town. Half-past eleven. As he turned to make his way back to the hotel a car swept by. It was black, moving at speed, but he had time to register three figures inside. It slowed briefly at the junction of the two roads before heading up towards the Kavalerie.

Tam watched the tail lights disappearing into the darkness, feeling the first stirrings of something deep in his belly. The car and its occupants might have nothing to do with the message slipped under his door. On the other hand he'd seen no other traffic since leaving the hotel. He was unarmed. He was alone in a country he barely knew, in a town he'd never visited. He could call on no one for support. Was it sensible to be offering himself as a possible target? A hostage, maybe? A callow novice there for the taking? Was it these same questions that had led Edvard to abandon his room?

He set off up the road again, keeping to the shadows, alert for every movement. Beyond the first bend, the houses on either side thinned and then disappeared completely until the road was flanked by nothing but bare stone walls and stands of pine. In the moonlight he could make out the looming bulk of the mountains pricked by an occasional light. What would it be like to live up here? Tam wondered. How much difference would an army of Germans make if your world began and ended with a flock of sheep, rough pasture and the scouring wind? The thought took him briefly back to Scotland and long summer days on the bareness of the Cairngorms, but then – halfway round the next bend – he froze. The car that had passed him minutes ago was parked barely yards away, tucked neatly into the side of the road, the long bonnet pointing back towards the town. It appeared to be empty.

Tam steadied himself, looked carefully around. Nothing. No one. He judged the hotel to be at least half a mile away. They've gone ahead on foot, he told himself, to prepare a little surprise. He began to approach the car, still hugging the side of the road. It was an Opel, old, poor condition. The radiator was still warm and something was dripping slowly on to the asphalt beneath the boot. He bent to the driver's door, peering in. On the floor beside the passenger seat he could make out a discarded bottle. Then, from nowhere, came a sudden, firm pressure in the small of his back and a voice, male, low, just inches from his ear. German, again. And a message that left little room for ambiguity.

'Any tricks, I'll kill you. Put your hands on the car roof.'

Stupid, he thought. Stupid, stupid, stupid. Stupid and careless and entirely your own fault.

Tam feigned incomprehension. Best play the innocent Britisher.

'Do you mind telling me what's going on, laddie?' Thick Scots accent. Lost on his new friend.

The gun wavered. There was a rustle of clothing. Tam steeled himself, waiting for the right moment, knowing that he'd have a single chance to level the odds.

The moment came when the figure behind tried to turn him round. Tam lunged backwards, chopping sideways with his elbow. He felt the point of his elbow connect with bone and the stranger gasped with pain, reeling away, one hand holding his face. Tam didn't take his eyes off the gun. It was a small revolver, dangling uselessly from his other hand. Tam bent the arm double, hearing the gun clatter onto the road, and then he applied a chokehold around the scrawny neck, squeezing and squeezing until the body was limp in his arms.

The man was smaller than he'd somehow expected: broad, sallow face, bloodied nose, three-day growth of stubble. Open-mouthed, he was struggling for air. Tam dragged him to the rear of the car and then let him sprawl in the damp grass at the side of the road. One eye flicked open and he stared up at Tam, uncomprehending. From a trouser pocket Tam retrieved a pair of keys. The revolver was still lying in the road. Tam broke the barrel and checked the cylinder. Three bullets. Moments later, he was behind the wheel. The engine fired on the third tug on the starter. Releasing the handbrake, he trod on the accelerator, surprised by the car's response. Only when he reached the main road, his eyes still glued to the rear-view mirror, did he stop to find the switch that worked the lights.

There were no maps in the car. Tam drove through Jáchymov, searching for a signpost. On the other side of the town he found what he was looking for: Praha, 142 kms. He drove carefully, keeping his speed down, hauling the car round corner after corner, following the road down the mountain. With luck, he'd be in Prague within a couple of hours. Then he glanced down at the fuel gauge. The needle was hovering on empty.

He pulled over and stopped. The second key opened the boot. Hoping for a spare can of petrol, he found nothing but sacking and the sweet stench of excreta. Something or someone had been in this tiny space only recently. He stared at the rumpled sacking a moment longer then gathered an armful, trying to hold it at a distance length, and dumped it at the side of the road. He was right. Shit, very possibly human. What kind of people transported live bodies in a space like this? And didn't bother to clean up afterwards?

Driving slowly now, he motored on, praying for a town big enough to offer a petrol station. Minutes later, his prayers were answered. At a crossroads stood a café and a line of pumps. Both were closed, and when he pulled to a halt and tried one of the pumps he found it padlocked. He approached the café and peered in, hoping for some sign of life. Nothing. A glance at his watch told him it was barely one in the morning. He had six hours to kill. At the very least.

Abandoning the car and walking would leave him at the mercy of any passer-by. He had no idea where he was and little faith that a knock at some stranger's door would produce the offer of help. Salvation, he knew, lay at the embassy in Prague. Stronge would know what to do, who to talk to. Tam had no option but to wait.

He started the car again and parked in the shadows beside the café. A blanket of cloud hid the full moon and there was still a little warmth in the night air. He pushed the seat back as far as it would go, cursing himself for setting out from the hotel without his greatcoat, and tried to fit his long body to the sagging upholstery. For a while he tried to fight off memories that swam out of the darkness: the glimpse of faces as the car swept past back in Jáchymov, the moment he felt the gun in his back, and the eternity of waiting as he steeled himself to respond. Had he really signed up for this? A near-death encounter with a bunch of homicidal strangers in a faraway country of which he knew very little? The stench from the boot still lay heavy in the car. He shifted the weight of his body again and turned his face to the open window. Seconds later, a tribute to his days in the military, he was asleep.

*

A voice awoke him, hours later. The car was flooded with sunshine. A face swam into focus, peering in through the open window. He was young, freshly shaved. He was wearing a uniform.

'*Policie*,' he grunted.

He gestured for Tam to get out of the car. Tam struggled to open the door, then stood beside the Opel in the cool of the dawn and stamped the stiffness out of his limbs. A blue van was parked in front of the Opel, barring the way back to the main road. Two other policemen were staring down at the boot.

Tam retrieved the keys from the dashboard.

'You need the smallest one,' he said, nodding towards the boot.

'You're German?'

'English.' Tam's hand went to his jacket pocket. Thank God he was carrying his passport.

The movement had alarmed the young policeman. Tam found himself looking at a gun.

'This car is yours?'

'No.'

'A friend's, maybe?'

'Definitely not.'

'You stole it?'

'Borrowed it.'

There was an exchange in Czech between the policemen. The younger one motioned Tam towards the rear of the car.

'Come,' he said in German.

Tam found himself staring down at the open boot. Last night, in the dark, he hadn't noticed the long strip of torn sheet. It was knotted the way you'd tie a gag and it was heavily bloodstained. The smell of shit was overwhelming.

'Well?'

'I don't know. This is nothing to do with me.' Tam began to explain about last night, what had happened beside the parked car, but the young policeman wasn't listening. He told Tam to put his hands up. The stranger's revolver was in the pocket of his jacket. The policeman found it in seconds, extracting the three bullets, weighing them thoughtfully in his gloved hand. Then he looked at Tam.

'Well?' he said again.

11

BERLIN, 17 MAY 1938

The summons to meet *Generalfeldmarschall* Hermann Goering was delivered by Georg. It was early, not yet eight in the morning, and Dieter was half-naked in the kitchen of his apartment. At first he thought it was a joke, a light-hearted prelude to a planned night on the town ahead of the wedding at the weekend. Only when Georg tapped his watch and told Dieter to make himself look respectable did it dawn on him that he meant it. Half-past nine at the Air Ministry. And, if he was lucky, every prospect of one of *Der Eiserne*'s looted cigars.

Der Eiserne meant The Iron One. Dieter had laid eyes on Goering only once, at a passing-out ceremony after the final year of his flight training, but the more he heard about the father of the *Luftwaffe*, the more he'd grown to hold him in some regard. For one thing, he was a pilot's pilot, a combat veteran from the war of the trenches, a gladiator with a sizeable tally of enemy kills to his credit. He'd fought with the Brownshirts in Munich, sustaining a serious injury during the July putsch. This, so the gossip went, probably accounted for his rumoured appetite for narcotics but more to the point was the fact that he'd somehow kept the party hacks and the party apparatus at arm's length. *Der Eiserne* might not have the guile of a

Goebbels, or the fanatical attention to detail of a Himmler, but he'd managed to stake out impressive territory of his own amongst the warring chieftains at the top of the Reich, and that – for Goering and his young pilots – was a victory worth applauding.

Georg drove Dieter to the Air Ministry. He'd had the pleasure of piloting Goering on a number of occasions and described him as a man who'd never quite left his childhood behind. He loved the show of high office – medals, honours, fancy uniforms – and he never tired of helping himself to whatever caught his eye as the Reich began to expand. Only last month, Georg had flown him back from Vienna with the rear of the aircraft crammed with antique furniture and works of art, priceless objects which would doubtless end up in one or other of Goering's many properties. To Georg this hunger for other people's possessions was theft, pure and simple, yet he still warmed to the man's spirit and the way he never bothered to hide the sheer scale of his many appetites. A lot of these people are putty in Hitler's hands, Georg told Dieter. You can see it in the way they behave when he's around, in the way they bow to his every whim, laugh at his every joke. But Goering is never like that. He respects Hitler, of course he does. But in the end *Der Eiserne* is always his own man.

The Air Ministry was in Wilhelmstrasse, a stone's throw from Hitler's Chancellery. Unlike its Prussian neighbours, it was a modern, six-storey building with clean lines and even a spacious underground garage.

An aide from Goering's office was waiting for Dieter in the huge reception area. To survive at the top of the Berlin dunghill you had to make sure that your headquarters were at least as grand as everyone else's and in this never-ending battle for floor space and sheer effect Goering was already a seasoned veteran. Dieter followed the aide towards a huge staircase, pausing to admire a stuffed elk guarding a corridor that seemed to disappear into the far distance.

'The *Generalfeldmarschall* shot it last year at Carinhall.' The aide gave the elk a pat. 'It takes two men to lift it.'

Goering's first floor office was no less impressive: a desk the size of a small aircraft, more stuffed trophies on the wall, and the soft rumble of trams from the boulevard beyond the tall windows. Behind the desk hung a vast oil painting depicting a dogfight over the trenches during the last war. A single triplane with German markings was locked in a tight spiral dive, chasing some luckless English pilot to his death while brown-uniformed Tommies tried to shoot the Fokker down with small-arms fire. Goering happened to be on the phone. Noting his guest's interest in the painting, he offered a broad smile and nodded at the waiting chair, and Dieter let himself be enveloped by the velvet upholstery while he tried to identify the helmeted figure in the Fokker's cockpit. According to Georg, *Der Eiserne* had notched up twenty-two kills before the war came to an end, and this was doubtless one of them.

'Many of the English were children in the air. Some of them asked to get shot down.'

Goering had at last brought his phone call to an end. He was a big man in every way: big face, big handshake, his massive body barely contained by the bulging uniform. He appeared to be in the rudest of spirits. In a moment he wanted Dieter to tell him about Japan. But first he had to know more about Keiko.

'Is this woman of yours as wonderful as everyone's telling me? I thought Japanese women weren't supposed to be tall? How come someone your size can hook a beauty like that?'

Dieter didn't know whether to take this as a compliment. Goering came at you like a tidal wave, exactly as Georg had warned. Dieter had no right to be surprised but barely minutes of interrogation left him feeling like a dog on the beach after a thorough dousing. He wanted to shake himself dry, catch his breath, prepare for the next breaker.

'Well? You're in love with the woman? Is that it?' Goering slapped a meaty thigh. The thought clearly delighted him. Then his mood changed. He leaned forward over the desk. His face suddenly darkened. A ringed finger was inches from Dieter's face.

'Ribbentrop,' he snarled. 'The man's a fool. Make sure she understands that. You hear me, young man? Tell her. Sit her down and make sure she's listening. Spell it out. *Von* Ribbentrop is all show. There's nothing inside. He bought his title and married his money. He's an empty house. He should be demolished, put out of his misery. You've met the man?'

'Yes.'

'When?'

'Earlier this week. We attended a party for one of his children.'

'We?'

'Myself and Keiko.'

'As I thought. And the lady? What did she think of Mr Ribbentrop?'

'She said he was very polite.'

'And what else?'

'He seemed very interested in her.'

'That's a lie. Ribbentrop is interested in no one but himself. Himself and his own prospects. If we could teach a monkey to speak a couple of languages, he'd make a better Foreign Minister.' He glared at Dieter a moment longer and then composed himself. The squall had come and gone. Now he wanted to know about Japan. Was it good out there? Had they treated him well? Were they as crazy in the air as everyone said?

Dieter coped with the volley of questions as best he could. At first acquaintance, the Japanese were guarded and over-formal and hard to get to know but in the end they could be fun. Their hospitality was second to none. And yes, they flew like lunatics.

'Excellent.' Goering was beaming now. 'So what do *you* want to do, young man? Be honest.'

Dieter had anticipated the question. A return to operational flying would take him away from Berlin, away from Keiko, and just now he didn't want that. A recent conversation with one of the test pilots over at Johannistahl had suggested an alternative.

'Maybe a flying job on one of the research programmes?'

'That's a possibility. What about the *Regierungsstaffel*? Like your pal Georg?' The *Regierungsstaffel* was Hitler's private squadron at Tempelhof.

'I'm not multi-rated.'

'We could attend to that.'

'But I'd miss single-seat flying.'

'I'm not surprised. It's an addiction. Only fighter pilots understand that. Make the cockpit your own and you make the sky your own. Make the sky your own and you'll live for ever.' He paused for a moment, eyeing the phone. 'You've been having a try-out with the new Emils. Am I right?'

'Yes.'

'And?'

'Wonderful. A different aeroplane.'

'Good. I was talking to the *Kommandant* over at Johannistahl. He's been watching you from his office. A natural showman, he said, but safe, too. That's not an easy trick to pull off. Any fool can fly for the girls but it's surviving that matters. The *Kommandant* was impressed.'

Dieter felt himself blushing. It wasn't every day that the Head of the *Luftwaffe*, probably the most powerful airman in the world, offered a compliment like this.

Goering was brooding again, his big head lowered, his carefully manicured hands toying with a paperknife. Dieter wondered for a moment whether he'd lost the thread of the conversation. Then the huge head came up.

'Display aviator,' he said, smacking the flat of his hand on the desk. 'You did well in Japan. People liked you, especially the pilots. Put you in an Emil and you can fly your heart out. You'll be displaying solo all over the Reich. I'll have someone draw up a programme. Summer's coming. People have money in their pockets. I've never known this city so happy, so contented. The crowds will love you. Meet them. Shake their hands. Kiss the babies. Make eyes at the pretty women. Just keep them sweet, *ja*?'

Dieter nodded. It sounded the dream posting. From as far away as Munich, or even Vienna, it was only a couple of hours back to Berlin. Thanks to the new Emil.

'Thank you, Herr *Generalfeldmarschall*.'

'A pleasure, young man. One other thing.'

'Sir?'

'That fool Ribbentrop. Put an end to the man's fantasies, you hear me? Lock your lady up.'

*

The man's fantasies? In the tram back to his apartment, Dieter wondered what the phrase meant. At the birthday party in Dahlem he'd had the opportunity to talk to the new *Reichsminister* for Foreign Affairs. First had come a couple of perfunctory questions about Dieter's months in Japan. Then had followed a long monologue about his own diplomatic triumph in signing some pact or other, and how his standing with the Führer was unmatched by any other of the regime's leading figures. He alone understood the world beyond the German frontiers, and he alone had brought the Italians and the Japanese to the negotiating table.

Dieter had tried to listen to this speech with the kind of enraptured attention he imagined his host was used to but it was hard not to agree with Goering that the man was an embarrassment. He never looked you in the eye. His real attention was always elsewhere. He was pompous and over-loud and extremely pleased with himself, and when he abruptly broke off to stride self-importantly from the drawing room to answer yet another phone call, Dieter was swamped with relief. Reporting back to Berlin, Eugen Ott had doubtless done his best to blacken *Oberleutnant* Merz's performance in Japan but Ribbentrop would have been too busy to have given the matter the slightest attention.

And Keiko? Dieter found it hard to believe that she would ever be attracted to a windbag like this. Wrong.

Back at the apartment, he found her stretched on the chaise longue, the phone to her ear. The conversation was in Japanese. Dieter waited in the kitchen for it to end and then made a reappearance. The news that he was to become a display pilot at the behest of no less a figure than *Generalfeldmarschall* Goering sparked the ghost of a smile.

'You'll like that,' she said.

'You're right. I will. And it means we can stay here.'

'In the apartment?'

'In Berlin. They'll want this place back soon. I'll find us somewhere else.'

Us? She didn't say the word, but she didn't have to. Dieter was looking down at the chaise longue. At length Keiko made room for him.

'What's the matter?' he asked.

She shook her head. Didn't want to answer. Dieter nodded at the telephone.

'Who were you talking to?'

'Someone at the embassy. He's been in contact with my father.'

'News from home?'

'More government contracts. My father works so hard he'll explode. I need to write to him. I need to slow him down. These days that's hard. There's a madness in the air. I saw it in Seiji, too.' She finally reached for him. 'Maybe it's good you had the accident.'

She wanted to know about display flying. Dieter tried to reduce the job to its essentials. After months in Spain trying to kill Russians, he'd be there to please the crowds.

'You're joining a circus?'

'I *am* the circus. Just me.'

'It's dangerous?'

'As dangerous as I want to make it.' He moved a little closer. 'But why would I want to hurt myself again?'

She looked at him for a long moment and then traced the shape of his lips with her finger. Over the last few days, to Dieter's intense relief, they'd at last begun to make love. It was sex as he'd never experienced it before, lingering, prolonged, full of surprises. In some ways it felt like an extension of *reiki*, his therapist always in charge, always hanging over him, showing him new ways, new pleasures. Making love like this was intoxicating but Keiko's degree of control raised a question or two. Was she fully committed? Was her surrender as complete as his own? In truth he didn't know because she was a stranger to the world of endearments. The fact that she said so little either before or after their love-making had at first been an added excitement but after the conversation with Goering it was beginning to make him anxious.

She gestured for him to get out of his suit. Dieter didn't move.

'Tell me about Ribbentrop,' he said. 'What did you really think of him?'

The question seemed to amuse her.

'Ribbentrop worries you? You think,' she frowned, 'he matters?'

'I don't know. That's why I'm asking. Goering says he's sweet on you.'

'Goering's right. But Joachim only sees what he wants to see.'

'Joachim?'

'Joachim. I'm something new in his life, something exotic. Men are all the same. They think they know everything until it occurs to them that they don't. You understand what I'm trying to say?'

'Of course. You did it to me, too.'

'Wrong. What I did to you was different. You had a problem. I tried to help.'

'You cured it.'

'Good. And now?'

'I have another problem.'

'Joachim?'

'Ribbentrop.'

She withdrew a little into the corner of the chaise longue and tucked her legs in. She said she was good with men, especially men who couldn't help themselves, men who'd let their ambition get out of control, men who refused to listen to their bodies.

'Would that include me?'

'You fell out of an aeroplane. That's different.'

'And Ribbentrop?'

'That man's in pain. A different kind of pain. He knows already about the *reiki*. He thinks I can help and he's right, I can.'

'How does he know about the *reiki*?'

'Hiroshi Oshima told him. At the embassy.' Oshima was the Japanese military attaché in Berlin. Dieter had met him twice, a small, squat figure with a passion for kirsch. He, too, didn't bother to hide his appreciation of Keiko.

'So you'll be treating Ribbentrop?'

'Yes.'

'At his home?'

'At the ministry. He's ordered his staff to make time in his schedule. I told him that's where his trouble begins. Time.

Always time. He's just like my father. He never listens. So that's another challenge.'

'You'll teach him how to *listen*?'

'I'll teach him how to become a human being.' He was frowning now. 'Have I upset you?'

Dieter didn't answer. He could picture the scene only too well. The door locked. Phone calls blocked. Ribbentrop flat on his back, offering himself to Keiko's ministrations. Dieter saw no point in dressing up the truth.

'He wants to fuck you,' he said. 'Whatever way he puts it, that's where it begins and ends.'

'And me? Do I get a say?'

'Probably not.'

For a moment, Dieter thought he'd gone too far. But then Keiko put her hand over her mouth and started to giggle, something she'd never done before. For a brief moment she looked like the young girl she must once have been. Then she was in control again. She nodded towards the bedroom. She wanted an end to this conversation. Dieter was right about Joachim. The man was stupid beyond words. And pompous, too.

'One question you haven't asked me.' She cupped Dieter's face in her hands. 'You know how much money he wants to pay me?'

Dieter shook his head. No idea.

'Fifty *Reichsmarks* a session.' She gestured around the apartment. 'We can live wherever we want.'

12

PRAGUE, 18 MAY 1938

Tam had been in the cell for nearly ten hours before anyone came to see him. The cell was three paces by eight paces, roughly plastered walls, concrete floor, and a single barred window that didn't open. The mattress on the iron bedstead was heavily stained and leaked horsehair where the thin fabric had ripped. Face to the wall, lying down, Tam could hear the faraway clanking of trains in a goods yard and just occasionally the rumble of a tram. His eyes open, he tallied the names scratched in the rough plaster: *Duček*, *Kubik*, *Petr.*

On the drive to Prague, none of the policemen had said a word. Police headquarters was guarded by armed soldiers. The uniformed officers at the front desk had booked him in without much visible interest. They'd put his passport in a drawer and made him sign a form he didn't understand. He still had his own clothes but his stomach was empty and he badly needed something to drink. At the front desk he'd asked them to contact the military attaché at the British Embassy but the request had met with no response. Locked in the cell, he'd banged twice on the scabbed steel door and called for water but on neither occasion had anything happened. Being under arrest was the first shock. Finding himself adrift in this strange half-world was probably worse.

'Herr Moncrieff?'

Tam jerked awake and rolled over. The plain-clothes figure by the door muttered something to the uniformed policeman and then gestured for Tam to sit up. He was an older man, bony-faced, thinning hair. The domed forehead and the carefully tended fingernails suggested a different occupation, an academic perhaps, or even a musician, but what impressed Tam most was an overwhelming sense of exhaustion. This man appeared to be fighting battles on countless fronts and to be losing them all.

The policeman was back with a chair. Then he stepped out of the cell again and Tam heard the door lock behind him.

'This story of yours, Herr Moncrieff. Tell me again.'

His German was perfect. Tam repeated the account he'd offered to the policemen who'd arrested him. His visitor followed Tam's story with his eyes half-closed. Finally, Tam got to the end. The revolver belonged to the man who'd held him up at gunpoint. As did the car. He had nothing to do with the bloodstained gag in the boot. Neither could he account for the smell.

Tam's inquisitor wasn't impressed.

'We think you're a spy,' he said carefully.

To Tam, this sounded about right. He shook his head, denied it completely. Foreign, yes. A visitor to this delightful country. . . undoubtedly. But a *spy*? Good Lord, no.

'We've talked to the woman at the hotel where you were staying. You asked her lots of questions, mainly about Edvard Kovač. Why the interest?'

'He's a friend of mine.'

'You know what he does? How much trouble he makes for us?'

'I'm afraid I've no idea. I met him through another friend. Edvard knows the local area well. He offered to show me round.'

'So why the questions about the American?'

'Because that's the way the woman at the hotel might have remembered him. I couldn't give her a family name. I didn't even know one. But I knew he'd met an American the previous evening.'

'How? How did you know that?'

'My other friend,' Tam said lamely.

'He? She?'

'He.'

'Name?' A stub of pencil had appeared, along with a battered notebook.

Tam held his gaze. Then he shook his head.

'You've forgotten the name? Of this friend of yours?'

'Yes.'

'I don't believe you.'

'That's your choice.'

The inquisitor nodded, half-closed his eyes again, sucked the end of the pencil. At length he stirred.

'Might her name be Renata Nováková?'

Tam blinked. The name came as a shock. These people were good, far better than he'd expected, and his own performance so far had been woeful. Proper spies were born liars. They had carefully prepared stories, trenches dug behind them in case they needed to retreat. Tam had taken none of these precautions but he was still determined to protect Renata.

'I've never heard of her,' he said.

The inquisitor smiled and scribbled something in his notebook before slipping it back in the pocket of his jacket. He didn't believe Tam's denial for a moment but the Britisher's steadfastness appeared to have won him a moment of reprieve. Without a hint of a threat, or even any serious pressure, the pecking order had been established. Now what?

'You were arrested near Terezín. That happens to be in our part of the country. Just. That makes you a very lucky man, Herr Moncrieff, because the Sudeten police have no patience at all. By now, my friend, you'd be heading for another beating. That's if they hadn't decided to dispose of you completely.'

'Dispose?'

'Put a bullet in your head.' He sighed, picking at a cuticle on one of his nails. 'We live in ugly times. The Germans are on the move across the border. That makes our Sudeten friends very excited. They're expecting the Panzers in Karlovy Vary by the weekend. Just one reason why our President has been stirred into taking action.'

'He's mobilising?'

'He's called up the reserves. Put the Army on a war footing. Reinforced the frontier fortifications. Hitler isn't amused, but that, I assume, is the point of the exercise. We're not Austrians and we never will be. Slavs fight.'

'And the French? The British?' Tam was frowning. 'The Russians?'

'All parties will stand by their treaties. Should we be grateful? Of course we should. Will it be enough to stay the wretched man's hand? We'll have to see. In the meantime I understand you need a little water and maybe even something to eat.'

He pushed the chair back and stood up. Moments later, after calling for one of the guards to open the door, he'd gone.

Within minutes, Tam was looking at a bowl of something grey and hot, and a chipped mug brimming with water. He drank the water, sampled the soup, then left the bowl on the floor. Over the next hour or so the wail of air-raid sirens penetrated the thick walls. It was nearly dark by now and Tam sat in the airless warmth, braced for the first bombs. May, he thought, was the perfect time of year for any invading army: plenty of daylight, the ground dry and firm underfoot, the plump, spring-fed animals on every farm there for the taking. From what he'd seen on the frontier the Czechs would certainly make a fight of it but in the new world of fast-moving Panzer divisions, led by bold commanders, it would be child's play to bypass the fixed fortifications.

Would the western Allies really stand by the orphaned Czechs? And if they did, would the war be over before they'd organised themselves? Hitler, after all, had become master of the lightning thrust, the killer blow. At whatever level you chose to kick over the order of things, simple possession was all it took to win the arguments that followed. The logic was brutal. What I have, I hold. If you want it back, come and get it.

Depressed by his own small part in this unfolding drama, Tam sat on the bed, his back against the wall, wondering what would happen if and when the Germans made it to Prague. Would they throw the cell doors open and let the prisoners run free? Or would they shoot the lot?

The latter proposition, he suspected, was all too likely but what would be worse was the failure of his own mission. Maybe he should have been frank with his inquisitor. Maybe he should have owned up to Ballentyne's orders. Maybe he should have taken a liberty or two and painted himself as a friend of the Czechs, dedicated to somehow saving this little country before the grey hordes appeared in the west and broke it in half. That, at least, would have left him with a little self-respect. He stared down at the soup, tiny nameless particles swimming in the grey broth. Then he shook his head and lay full length on the bed again, still wondering about the bombers.

*

Stronge, the military attaché from the embassy, arrived at first light. A different policeman let him into the cell. Stronge had cut himself shaving and the wisp of cotton wool on the squareness of his chin gave him a strange vulnerability that added to Tam's conviction that he'd stepped into a world he no longer recognised.

Tam started to tell Stronge what had happened but the military attaché wasn't much interested. The main railway station, he said, was choked with reservists and the roads out of the city were full of trucks and light armour heading for the western frontier. Stronge had made representations on Tam's behalf at the highest levels in the Foreign Ministry and was pleased to report that the Czechs had sensibly arrived at a decision. They accepted most of Herr Moncrieff's story and were disinclined to pursue matters any further. His passport was now in Stronge's safe keeping and he had twelve hours to leave the country. In return for this largesse, the First Secretary at the Czech Foreign Office trusted that Herr Moncrieff would have good things to say about the Czechs on his return to the West.

'They're quite prepared to fight for their country,' Stronge said. 'They have the means and they have the will. All they want from us is the courtesy of meeting our treaty obligations, a point you might make when circumstances permit.'

Overnight, Stronge said, the crisis had reached flashpoint. London and Paris expected war at any moment but he'd just read a Whitehall cable suggesting that Hitler – faced with the probability of real opposition – might decide to back off.

'That's speculation, of course. We can but hope.'

Tam tried to digest the news. Maybe, after all, he shouldn't expect German bayonets at the end of the corridor. Then he remembered the moment when he lifted the boot of the Opel in search of a can of petrol, the moment when he realised something terrible might have happened.

'You dropped me at Jáchymov,' he reminded Stronge.

'I did.'

'I was looking for a man called Edvard. A Czech.'

'Edvard Kovač.'

'You know him?'

'No. But the people downstairs have been more than helpful. The man's gone missing. As you obviously know.'

'And?'

'He's still missing. But there's a woman he appears to be close to, a girlfriend. The Sudeten police have reported finding her body. That could mean anything. That could mean they killed her. Either way she ended up dead. Raped. Beaten. And then shot three times. You'll be glad to know you're in the clear. The good folk downstairs don't think you did it.'

In the clear. Tam was staring at the wall beyond Stronge. The smell, he thought. The bloodstained scrap of sheet to gag her screams. Had Renata made her way back to Jáchymov? Found the hotel? Asked the same questions of the same woman? Been lured into the same lethal trap? He closed his eyes, shook his head. The news was incomprehensible. So young. So committed. So *alive*. And now gone.

Stronge was on his feet. Time, he said, was moving on. He'd booked Moncrieff on the morning flight to Vienna, and then onward to Paris. He had just one more question to get things a little clearer in his thick head.

'That chap who jumped you? I understand you laid him out? Is that true?'

Tam barely heard the question. Just nodded.

'Excellent.' Stronge nodded towards the door. 'Shall we...?'

13

BERLIN, 19 MAY 1938

On the morning that Tam Moncrieff was expelled from Czechoslovakia, Dieter Merz made his way to the *Luftwaffe* research centre at the Johannesstahl airfield from where he'd been flying the new Bf-109-E. Weekends were normally quiet on most *Luftwaffe* bases and he was surprised to find himself stepping into a gathering of test pilots in the spacious downstairs area that served as a briefing room.

The centre's *Kommandant*, a quietly spoken veteran with a post-war degree in aeronautics, was standing beside a map of Czechoslovakia. The Sudetenland had been cross-hatched in red crayon but there was nothing on the map to indicate likely axes of advance. Instead, heavy blue circles indicated the most important of the airfields serving the Czech Air Force.

The briefing, it turned out, was highly provisional. In all probability, said the *Kommandant*, the so-called crisis was over. True, *Wehrmacht* divisions were still on manoeuvres close to the border, alarming the Czechs and triggering mobilisation, but there had never been any intent to turn a training exercise into a full-scale invasion.

This claim raised a hollow laugh amongst the listening airman and even the *Kommandant* had the grace to permit himself a smile. Hitler's plans for the Sudetenland were an open secret. The current upsets, suggested the *Kommandant*, might be viewed as a rehearsal for the real thing. There followed a base-by-base analysis of the strengths and weaknesses of the Czech Air Force with a reminder that this intelligence must remain strictly confidential.

The briefing over, Dieter intercepted the *Kommandant* on his way to the door. Dieter knew that one of the new 109-Es had been made available for Georg's wedding and that Goering himself had authorised the display as a fitting gift for one of his personal pilots. All Dieter needed now was confirmation that the aircraft was still serviceable.

'Of course.' The *Kommandant* paused to look Dieter in the eye. 'And one day soon you'll be showing it off over Prague.'

*

Tam Moncrieff's flight landed in Paris shortly after two in the afternoon.

Stronge had warned him to expect to be met on his arrival but the familiar face beyond the wooden passport control booth came as a surprise. His own departure from Czechoslovakia had been in some haste and he wondered how Ballentyne had managed to respond so quickly to the news from Prague.

Facilities at the terminal building were surprisingly lavish. A sizeable restaurant adjoined the ticketing desks and Tam eyed the waiters gliding from table to table, realising how hungry he was. Ballentyne guided him towards the doors marked *Sortie*.

'We're expecting a car from the BCR,' he said. 'Time waits for no man.'

'BCR?'

'It's an arm of French Intelligence. Good people. And friends of the Czechs.'

Ballentyne and Tam sat in the back of the big Citroën for the drive into the city centre. Ballentyne, it appeared, had already been talking to Stronge about Tam's arrest but now he wanted to know more. When Tam mentioned the American Edvard had met at the hotel in Jáchymov, he half-turned in his seat.

'You have a name for this chap?'

'Sadly not.'

'Description?'

'No.'

'Pity.'

By now they were in central Paris. Kiosks selling newspapers had attracted sizeable crowds, and as they approached the Seine Tam spotted the beginnings of what could only be a peace march. The bulk of the demonstrators were middle-aged men. Many of them carried visible injuries, a missing arm, a limp, hideous facial scarring, and Tam began to wonder how any government could reignite an appetite for war after so recent a bloodletting. *À bas la guerre!* declared one placard. *Jamais plus!* another.

BCR headquarters was on the Left Bank, a stone's throw from Napoleon's tomb. Ballentyne led the way into the building, pausing at the nondescript reception desk to offer his passport. An aide appeared to take them to a sunny, spacious office on the first floor. Tam sensed real warmth when Ballentyne shook the hand of the official behind the big desk. His name was François Aubert and he was in charge of the BCR's operations in Central Europe. He and Ballentyne were evidently old friends.

The Frenchman wanted a full account of the Czechs' readiness for war. Tam obliged as best he could, pressed by Ballentyne for more details when it came to his visit to the western fortifications. Aubert had a winning courtliness in English and at the mention of Colonel Maček he looked up from the pad on which he was scribbling notes.

'I know this man. He's the best. The very best. He showed you the photos of his daughters?'

'He did.'

'Charming. Fighters like Maček give patriotism a good name. I dare say he's out there as we speak, waiting for the Boche. You think he's got a chance?'

'I think he'll fight like a lion. To the death if necessary.'

'But you think he's prepared? You think he's ready? You think he'll teach the Germans to watch their manners?'

'I do.'

Aubert nodded, and then returned to his pad and made another note. After this meeting, he murmured, he was due to brief the Minister for War, who – in turn – would be attending an emergency cabinet meeting called for this afternoon. Politicians, he seemed to imply, were like a certain kind of woman. They needed constant reassurance and in this respect Tam's report might stiffen their resolve.

'We have one of the biggest armies in the world.' He glanced across at Ballentyne. 'All we need to do is use it.'

Ballentyne nodded. He was looking at Tam.

'Jáchymov?' he said.

Tam described his visit to the Hotel Kavalerie and his attempts to trace Edvard Kovač. Mention of Jáchymov had already sparked Aubert's interest.

'You know about the mine, Monsieur Moncrieff? The mine in Jáchymov? You know about uranium?'

Tam nodded. He'd picked up the essentials, he said. Nothing more.

'The mine is precious. Precious to the Czechs and precious also to customers who come knocking on their door.' He reached for his pen again. 'An American, you say?'

'Yes.'

'You have details? A name, perhaps?'

'Sadly not.'

'I see.' Aubert checked his watch and then muttered something in French to Ballentyne before getting to his feet. From a filing cabinet beside the door he produced a thick file and returned to the desk. Seconds later, Tam found himself looking at a photo. It showed a smallish man with a greying goatee beard, hurrying across a crowded pavement into what looked like an upmarket hotel. The fur-trimmed coat and silver-topped cane lent him a slightly Edwardian air, a well-heeled refugee from a different epoch, but what concentrated Tam's attention was the figure beside him.

'That's Edvard.' He looked up. 'Edvard Kovač.'

'You're sure?'

'Absolutely certain.' Tam was still staring at the photo. From God knows where, Edvard had acquired a suit and tie. He looked freshly barbered and was plainly eager to sample whatever lay beyond the revolving door but there was no mistaking the toothy, slightly lopsided grin.

'Where was this taken?'

'New York. Last month. The gentleman with Kovač has been of interest to us for a while. He normally travels under an alias, Seymour Willson, but his real name is Thomas Kreisky. We see a lot of our Mr Kreisky. He has an affection for French ocean liners, in particular the *Normandie*. Some months he's back and forth all the time, Le Havre–New York. One of our agents believes he keeps a permanent cabin on board. He also retains a suite at that hotel, the Beresford on Central Park West.' He tapped the photo. 'Kovač, as far as we know, was accommodated elsewhere.'

'But why? What was he doing in America?'

'Mr Kreisky shipped him over. We gather he was a prize specimen, much admired in certain circles. To most Americans, Central Europe is as remote as the moon. No one understands it. No one *bothers* to understand it. Your friend Kovač was invited to change a little of that. That was his purpose. To shine a light into darkness. As you may know, this man is at home in the Czech underground. He speaks their language. He shares many of their ideals. And most importantly he never wants to bend the knee to the Germans. Kovač was brought to New York so Kreisky could share him with his friends, fellow businessmen, fellow investors.'

'To what purpose?'

'To make more money. And to protect their investment.'

'In what?'

'The Jáchymov mine.'

Kreisky, Aubert said, had organised a syndicate to buy the mine. They'd tabled a lowish offer and were happily anticipating completion on the deal when a counter-bid arrived.

'American?'

'German. And for a great deal more money. Kreisky thought the sum ludicrous. At first he didn't believe it. The mine owners naturally came back to him. Did he care to increase his initial offer? No, he emphatically didn't, because a bidding war could end anywhere and recklessness of that type has never been Kreisky's style.'

'So he conceded? Is that what you're telling me? He lost the deal?'

'In a way, yes. In another, no. For dealers like Kreisky there are always options, alternatives, short cuts. American capitalism, Monsieur Moncrieff, is very supple, very fleet of foot. To put it bluntly, money attracts money. The German economy is booming. People at every level have jobs. The country feels prosperous. If you can't beat them, you join them. And that's exactly what our Mr Kreisky has done.'

'How?'

'His syndicate has decided to acquire a sizeable stake in their German rival. That way they keep the price of the mine down while still sharing in the profits. Neat, *n'est-ce pas*?'

Tam nodded. Neat, indeed. Renata, he thought. Had she ever known any of this? He looked at the photo, tried to imagine Edvard dining with a table of New York bankers.

'Did Kovač know about the deal with the Germans when this was taken?'

'Definitely not. He was there to guarantee the support of his people, his trouble-makers, *against* the German bid.'

'And did Kreisky's bid succeed?'

'Of course. Get the offer right and nothing speaks louder than money.'

'And did Kovač know that? Was he aware of the offer?'

'We think not.'

'So what was his purpose in meeting Kreisky? In the hotel? Just a couple of days ago?'

Aubert smiled, his gaze moving from face to face, enjoying this small moment of drama.

'We think he planned to blow up the quarry operation,' he said. 'To spike the German guns.'

Tam ducked his head. The logic of the deal was all too obvious. Aubert was right. Money nested where money would make more money. It was as simple and elegant and pitiless as that. Naïve, outmanoeuvred, the victim of their own idealism, Edvard and Renata had walked into a trap. Neither Kreisky nor his new German partners could afford to have production disrupted and so these callow Czech patriots had paid the real price with their lives. Renata's body had already been recovered. Doubtless Edvard's remains would be next.

Tam leaned forward, returning the photo to Aubert.

'*Dommage*,' he said.

*

Dieter took off from Johannesstahl at ten past three. Flying time to the Wansee was barely five minutes and he'd been on the phone to Georg twice in the last hour. The wedding ceremony in the big Catholic church where Beata worshipped every Sunday had gone without a hitch. The guests were gathering in the big garden behind the summer house. The champagne was on ice. The roast suckling pig was attracting a great deal of attention. All Georg wanted now was twenty minutes of *Der Kleine*'s best. Three fifteen start. Three thirty-five finish. Then, doubtless well-earned, a chance to join the party.

It was a beautiful day, cloudless, warm, with just a hint of wind from the south-east. Dieter pushed the throttle forward and fed in a bootful of right rudder to keep the little fighter on the runway centre line. Moments later he was airborne, the aircraft silky under his fingertips, the meadows that bordered the airfield disappearing under the nose. At two hundred metres he eased the 109 into a climbing turn, the city centre visible in the distance under a thin blanket of haze. One eye on the compass, he levelled out, searching for the gleam of sunshine on the broadness of the lake.

Earlier, Georg had laid a series of yellow buoys a hundred metres off the waterside property to mark the display line. Now Dieter would use the line of buoys as a reference point, the stave on which he'd compose and orchestrate the next twenty minutes. Against the sun it was hard to spot them and when they finally appeared, a neat line of six a little to the right, he was too late to dip the nose and make the low run he'd planned to open the display.

Cursing himself for not taking a wider turn and appoaching with the sun behind him, he climbed again, pouring on the power and rolling at the top of the loop to bring himself in line with the tiny yellow dots within touching distance of the wedding venue. He was diving now, keeping the nose steady as the lakeside property grew bigger by the second. Eighteen months earlier, over Northern Spain, his thumb would have been settling gently on the firing button as he arrowed down on some enemy position. Now he was concentrating fiercely on exactly the moment when he should pull hard on the control column, flatten the angle of approach and then head once again for the blue of the sky above.

The altimeter was unwinding fast. Watching guests had acquired heads, faces. Hands were raised against the glare of the sun. Someone – Georg? – was circulating with a bottle in one hand and a tray of something delicious in the other. Then came the moment when Dieter hauled back on the control column and his belly threatened to come out of his arse and the world went momentarily grey as the blood drained from his head. In combat, in a manoeuvre this vicious, he'd have left most enemy pilots for dead. In the heat of the chase, they'd miss their one chance of pulling out of the dive. He'd seen it happen a million times. Greed overcame them, and simple bloodlust, and something even more primitive that briefly turned you into a god before gravity intervened and put the record straight.

He was climbing now, colour returning to his vision, the world acquiring the blues and golds he loved most. A loop, he thought. A loop so perfect, so beautiful, so worthy of the occasion, that Georg would want to preserve it for ever in aspic and serve it to his guests years later when their first child appeared. He kept pulling on the joystick, feeding in the power, waiting for that moment when he was hanging briefly in his harness, the world upside down, then slowly righting itself as he completed the loop and levelled out again. A glance at the altimeter confirmed he'd judged it perfectly. At fifty metres above the blur of water that was the lake he was plumb on the display line. He glanced left as the wedding party flashed by. The men raising glasses. The women madly waving. And Georg, taller than the rest, standing a little to one side, his trusty wingman.

*

'You were damn good. . .'

Dieter had never seen Georg drunk before. His eyes were moist and his handshake was much warmer than usual. The extravagance of the bow owed more to alcohol than anything in the display but Dieter didn't care.

He'd made it back from the airfield after leaving the 109 in the capable hands of one of the ground engineers at Johannesstahl and now he was nursing his first glass of champagne. The engineer had extracted a pine frond from a recess in the belly of the aircraft and held it at arm's length without comment. Dieter had ended the display with a low departing pass over the trees on the other side of the lake and knew that he'd cut it extremely fine. The knowledge, oddly enough, came as something of a comfort. He'd taken a calculated risk without fear of the consequences. And survived.

'She's lovely.' Georg again.

'Who?'

'Your Japanese friend. Shame about the company she keeps, eh?'

Dieter had already seen Keiko. She'd arrived with Ribbentrop, and now the pair of them were deep in conversation at the water's edge. It seemed the presence of the *Reichsminister* had caused a stir amongst the guests and even now one or two of the men were casting curious looks in his direction. For the second time in less than a week, Keiko was wearing a kimono.

Dieter asked after Beata. How had she coped at the ceremony? And where was she now?

Georg lifted another glass of champagne from a passing tray. Beata, he said, had insisted on making her own wedding dress. She was the busiest, cleverest, most talented woman he'd ever met in his life but her mother had sewn her own dress, and so had her grandmother, and both marriages had survived in the rudest of health and so there was absolutely no way Beata was going to trust her wedding gown to anyone else.

'So how did she look?'

'Like an angel, *compadre*.' Georg was studying his glass against the glare of the sun. 'A gift from God.'

Compadre was an endearment Georg had picked up in Spain. He used it very sparingly.

'You've been drinking,' Dieter said.

'I have.'

'It suits you.'

Georg was grinning. Another first. 'She's over there,' he said. 'Beside the roses.'

Dieter followed his pointing finger. He'd met Beata twice since her non-appearance at the restaurant beside the Spree, and both times he'd understood exactly why she and Georg were the perfect match. She was tall, a little on the plain side, with a fall of lank brown hair and a passion for serious conversation that put most men on their guard. According to Georg, she loathed gossip, declined to share intimacies and was always the last to join a drinking song. On the other hand, much to Georg's astonishment, she had a huge repertoire of jokes, most of them unrepeatable.

'Who's she talking to?' Dieter was still watching her.

Georg tried to focus.

'Sol,' he said at length. 'Sol Fiedler.'

'Who's he?'

'Chap from the Institute. Nearly as bright as my wife. Lovely man. We see a lot of him. Come. . .'

He led the way across the crowded lawn. At Georg's insistence, Dieter was still wearing his flying suit. Women wanted to kiss him, to tell him how great he'd been. Men blocked his path, gave him a playful punch on the arm. One of them, a fellow aviator from the Legion, even ruffled his hair. He, too, was drunk.

'*Der Kleine*,' he said, 'once you stole only the women. Now you steal the whole fucking show.'

Dieter ignored him. The person he wanted to meet was Sol Fiedler. The last time he'd been alone with Beata she'd talked about some of the fellow physicists she was working with. These people, she'd said, had been a pleasure to get to know. Many of them came from humble backgrounds, making their mark by sheer force of intellect, but what defined them as a group was a wit and a civility increasingly hard to find in the rough clamour of Hitler's Berlin. As one of the few women on the quantum physics group, she made an easy target for certain kinds of men but so far she'd encountered nothing but respect. In short, her colleagues at the Institute were a breed apart. At the time, Dieter had made a mental note of the phrase. 'A breed apart' was often code for Jewish.

At a nod from Beata, Sol Fiedler turned to meet Dieter as he approached. Fiedler was a slight man, probably younger than he looked. In contrast to the dressier guests, he was wearing a pair of flannel trousers and a plain white shirt, open at the neck. His hair was beginning to thin and Dieter detected the flutter of a tiny nerve under one eye. He stood awkwardly, one leg crossed over the other, but what attracted Dieter at once were his hands. They were beautiful hands, long fingers, deeply expressive, and he used them all the time to make a point or shape a thought. The sight of Dieter's flying suit put a smile on his face. Like a child, he wanted to touch it.

'May I?'

'Of course.'

'Up there,' he raised his eyes to the sky, 'how do you feel?'

'Free.'

'Free how? Like a bird? Like a cloud? Like a puff of wind?' He bent towards Dieter, a hint of concern in his deep brown eyes. He wanted an answer. He wanted to *know*. Very Jewish, Dieter thought. And very charming.

'Flying takes you places you least expect,' Dieter told him. 'It's always full of surprises.'

'And the soul?' Fiedler's hand closed softly on his chest. 'What does it do for the soul?'

'I wish I could tell you. You should come up one day. It would be a pleasure.'

'For you, maybe. That's kind. But me? I get nervous on a ladder. As my friend Beata knows. Doing what you do? Way up there? I die even thinking about it. Let's drink to Beata. Long life and no aeroplanes. *Prosit*. . .' He clinked glasses, said he was very happy to make Dieter's acquaintance. A real flier. *Mein Gott*.

Dieter was curious about the KWI. He wanted to know what was happening there, what the regime's sharpest brains were getting up to, but so far Beata had proved less than helpful. The first time he'd asked she'd mumbled something about taking apart the smallest particles of life. When he'd tried to raise the subject again, she'd quickly changed the subject.

Now, he put the same question to Sol. What gets you people excited over at the Institute? What makes it a pleasure to go to work?

Sol responded at once. He loved the directness of the question. And, more to the point, he appeared to take it seriously.

'We're kids in the playground,' he said. 'We're kids in the classroom of your dreams. There are no limits. We can ask any question, take ourselves in any direction. You wake up with a crazy idea? Like a woodpecker inside your head? Something going tap-tap in the very middle of your brain? Then go with it, run with it, explore it, see where it fits, see what might be possible. Most times it doesn't work out, it's a dead end. But the beautiful thing is no one minds.' He circled Beata with his thin arm. 'We're kids, *ja*? And very spoiled.'

'You've told me nothing.' Dieter was grinning. 'That's a talent I admire.'

'But what do you want to know? You want to know exactly what I did yesterday? What Beata did the day before? That would be very boring. That would be pages and pages of calculations, of sums, of figures and symbols and mumbo jumbo that would mean nothing. Better I tell you that it matters and it works and it makes us very happy. You know something? I haven't seen champagne for years. Let's celebrate.'

The approaching figure carrying a tray of glasses turned out to be Beata's father. His affection for Sol Fiedler was obvious. He seemed to treat him like a child.

'I put your jacket over there,' he told Fiedler, 'out of the way.' He nodded towards a bicycle propped beside the fence. Folded over the crossbar was a grey jacket.

'You *cycled* here?' Dieter turned back to Fiedler. Beata's father had moved on.

'Of course. I cycle everywhere.'

'You've come far?'

'Prenzlauer Berg.' PB was on the other side of the city, a working-class area of factories, cheap walk-up apartments and noisy bars much favoured by students.

'You live there?'

'We do. My wife loves it. The woman at the end of the street makes strudel you've never tasted in your life and there's a park round the corner for the dog.'

'Is your wife here?'

'No.' He shook his head. 'She doesn't go out much. Apart from the strudel and the dog.'

'Is there a reason for that?'

'Of course there's a reason for that. There's a reason for everything. That's what people like us do for a living. Cause and effect. Why things happen the way they happen. How dangerous and exciting things might get if you gave them a little push. Isn't that true, Beata?'

How dangerous and exciting things might get if you gave them a little push. This was more code and all three of them knew it. Fiedler's wife was probably Jewish as well. Life in any city if you were a Jew was getting increasingly difficult. Numberless laws prohibiting the smallest pleasures. Restrictions on where you shopped or where you stood on the tram. Brutal house searches and random confiscations. For a Jew to hang on at somewhere as prestigious as the KWI was highly unusual, doubtless a tribute to Fiedler's ability, but a decent job and a bicycle, Dieter suspected, would only take him only so far.

'Your wife is happy here?'

'My wife is safe. She eats well. Most nights she sleeps OK. Happiness is an absurd proposition. Unless you happen to work with someone as wonderful as this lady.'

'Enough.' Beata had stepped in, her hand on Fiedler's arm. Her father was about to make a speech. He clapped his hands, called for attention, then summoned Beata and Georg to his side. Heads turned. Conversations died. Georg, to Dieter's relief, appeared to have sobered up.

The speech was brief. Beata's father had been a widower for years after the loss of his wife to breast cancer. Hanni, he said, would have loved her new son-in-law but for all the wrong reasons. The boy was taller than his father-in-law. More handsome than his father-in-law. And a great deal more sensible. But his little baby girl had always had a gift for choosing the perfect present and in the shape of Georg Messner, she'd done it again. According to Beata, her new husband also knew a thing or two about cooking. This, he said, was truly excellent news because the years to come were going to offer all kinds of surprises. Not just the patter of tiny feet. Not only the chance of male company and a proper conversation. But even – from time to time – a new presence in the kitchen.

'To Beata and Georg,' he raised his glass, 'and the prospect of a decent meal.'

With the laughter and applause came the echoed toast. Georg stepped forward to respond. Dieter watched him for a moment, then his attention was caught by a figure making his way around the edges of the crowd on the lawn. It was Ribbentrop. He was heading for Sol Fiedler. Fiedler, alone now, saw him coming.

There followed the briefest conversation, Ribbentrop doing all the talking. Then he broke off and pointed towards the bicycle.

By now Georg had the guests in the palm of his hand. He was telling a story about Beata's cooking. It involved a jelly that refused to set and a quart of thick cream, and the crowd were still awaiting the punchline when Fiedler got to his bicycle.

Dieter was already edging around the crowd, trying to intercept him. Fiedler's grey jacket still lay folded over the crossbar. Without a backward look at the watching Ribbentrop, Fiedler shook out the creases and slipped it on. The yellow star on the left-hand side carried the single letter: *J*.

'You don't have to do this. You don't have to leave.' Dieter was outraged.

'I do, my friend. But I appreciate your concern.'

'Stay. It's not his party. It's none of his fucking business.'

'You're right, of course. But it's not my job to make a scene. Beata says you fly people like him.'

'That's Georg. That's what he does. Me? I'm the entertainment.'

There was a roar and then applause from the crowd. Georg had finished his story. Dieter made one last attempt to head Fiedler off.

'This is what these people do all the time.' He nodded towards Ribbentrop. 'They want you gone. They want you out. Why make it so easy for him?'

'Easy?' The word seemed to amuse Fiedler. 'You think any of this is *easy*? A confidence, my friend. A secret, if you like.' He bent towards Dieter, a finger to his lips. 'Quantum physics will turn the world upside down. You have my absolute guarantee.'

'What's that got to do with Ribbentrop?'

'Nothing. Everything. Quantum physics will fry him alive. And probably us, too. A deep pleasure, my friend.' He extended a hand and then mounted the bicycle. 'Kiss Beata for me. And tell her thank you.'

He rode off without a backward glance, a thin figure wobbling into the gathering dusk. Dieter felt a presence at his elbow. It was Keiko. He studied her for a moment, still fighting his anger.

'Your friend Joachim belongs in the zoo,' Dieter said at length. 'One day you might tell him that.'

14

PARIS, 20 MAY 1938

Le Café des Capuches lay in the 14th arrondissement, a rundown bar that served imported Belgian lager in German steins and had a decade-long reputation amongst the rougher elements of the French extreme right. Blackshirted paramilitaries from the Croix-de-Feu and Le Faisceau had flocked here for years and if you were after somewhere reliable for bellowing thugs, fascist anthems, and the near-guarantee of violence in the street afterwards then the Café des Capuches was well worth the price of the metro ticket. The quickest way from the nearest station happened to pass one of the city's biggest hospitals, a geographical irony not lost on Tam Moncrieff.

He'd arrived on the instructions of Ballentyne, having spent much of his second day at the British embassy sharing the spoils of his Czech outing with a series of carefully chosen French politicians. Mainly men of the Left, these were voices raised in defence of the Czechs and most of them were only too eager to seize on Tam's report to bolster the internal fight against the appeasers. In Ballentyne's phrase, these seasoned politicians had no illusions about Hitler's direction of travel. First, Prague. Then Warsaw. And finally, in all probability, Paris.

Tam was more than happy to table his impressions of the beleagured Czechs, not least because it made him feel that his days in Prague and the Sudetenland had been well spent. Still numbed by the news about Renata and Edvard, Tam had sought reassurances from Ballentyne about the safety of other Czechs who'd featured in his report but none had been forthcoming. For the likes of Renata and Edvard, Ballentyne seemed to be suggesting, the war had started early. People would continue to get hurt, some badly. Renata had been a credit to the infant democracy she so obviously cherished. Best not to dwell too much on the smaller details of what might have happened.

The woman's dead, Tam thought. Abused, beaten, scared half out of her life and then driven to some nameless destination and finally killed. Curled in the boot, knees to her battered face, she'd have lost all control, all dignity. No one deserved an end like that, least of all someone as committed and vividly alive as the woman he'd so briefly got to know. Was it Edvard's fault for putting her in bad company in Jáchymov? Or was it his own in abetting the fantasy that mere amateurs, bit-part players, could somehow head off the coming conflagration? If he was honest, there was no way he'd ever know for sure but what he recognised in his heart was a deep anger fuelled by his own undoubted guilt. They'd been a team. He'd been there to keep her safe. And he'd failed.

Le Café des Capuches was packed, drinkers spilling out into the street. Tam spoke a little French, enough for his immediate purposes. Two men were stationed at the door. Tam chose the one with the leather shirt and the Croix-de-Feu tattoo.

'Wilhelm Schultz? A German? You know him?'

The man looked Tam up and down. His eyes were bloodshot and the remains of a cigarette still hung from a corner of his mouth.

'Who are you?'

'A friend of his. From London.'

'You're English?'

'Yes.'

The man spat on the pavement. He wanted to know about the Czechs. He wanted to know whether the English were ready to march.

'I've no idea. I doubt it.'

'That makes you a wise man. The Germans will kick your arse.' A jerk of his head directed Tam into the café. 'Stocky little *mec* in the corner. If you're a friend he'll know you.'

The closest Tam had ever got to Wilhelm Friedrich Schultz was the photo he'd seen in the embassy just hours before. The likeness with the face in the photo was poor.

Tam squeezed himself into a space between Schultz and a hatstand. The atmosphere in the bar was heavy with sweat and cigarette smoke. Schultz had lost weight but the folklore that attended him – the teenage soldier in the last war, the twenties street brawler who knew no fear – was still evident in the look he shot Tam. He had a good face – strong jaw, steady eyes – and when he swung round on the bar stool Tam glimpsed the butt of an automatic thrust into the waistband of his leather trousers.

'You're who?'

'Moncrieff. From London. Does the name Ballentyne mean anything to you?'

'Yes. You've got something for me?'

Tam handed over an envelope. It was full of money, American dollars. Schultz counted out the notes, licking his finger and thumb, keeping score under his breath.

'Five hundred,' he grunted. 'We agreed six.'

'I know nothing about that.'

'Ballentyne's a friend of yours?'

'Yes.'

'Tell him he owes me. A hundred today. Two hundred by next week. Three hundred by June. That's called inflation, by the way. We're experts because we invented it. You can tell him that, too.'

Tam nodded, said nothing. This conversation was going nowhere. At the other end of the bar, three men were arguing about yesterday's peace march. Tam picked up enough to realise that one of them might have killed somebody.

'You want to go somewhere else? Somewhere quieter?' He was back with Schultz.

'You're going to feed me? Pour wine down my throat? Find me someone clean to fuck? *Ja?* You can do that?'

Tam studied him a moment, realising he'd been put to the test. Ballentyne, after all, had some knowledge of this man. Never take him at face value, he'd warned. He'll be coarse. He'll play the hooligan. He'll try to wrong-foot you. But don't be fooled. Schultz hasn't made it to the top by accident. He's razor-sharp. His connections back home are second to none. And without him, we're dead in the water.

'Let's go and find something to eat,' Tam said. 'Mr Ballentyne will pay.'

*

The hotel was a ten-minute walk away, a small, discreet establishment half-hidden behind a line of plane trees. The man on the door told him the table was ready any time he wanted it. Schultz checked in his leather coat at reception and asked for his gun to be stored in the hotel safe. The receptionist, who obviously knew him, produced a handful of mail and a key.

'You're staying here?' Tam was eyeing the key.

'Yes. They keep an excellent table and they know how to leave a man in peace. These days, believe me, that's rare.'

They were halfway along a corridor in the depths of the hotel. Schultz paused at a door near the end and used the key to unlock it. Ballentyne had been right. The man was an actor. Back in the bar, Tam had walked into a charade.

'You'd like a drink?'

The room served as a private dining suite. Prints of eighteenth-century Paris lined the walls and the big antique table was laid for two. Tam lingered for a moment by the window, which offered a view of a tiny courtyard. A child was squatting in the dust, making pictures with the end of a twig.

'Pernod, please. With just a splash of water.'

Tam was still at the window. The child had been joined by a woman who seemed to be his mother. She studied the cartoon face in the dust and then bent to the child, easing the twig from his pudgy little hand.

'You're sure that's enough?'

Tam turned to take the drink. Schultz had already poured himself a glass of something amber from the array of bottles on the trolley behind the door.

'I knew another Scotsman once.' Schultz raised his glass. 'I was with him in Spain. He came from Glasgow. He was the toughest little man I ever met. Drank this stuff neat. Even the Communists were terrified of him.'

'You were fighting with the *Republicans*?'

'No. I met him after he was captured. He never told us anything.'

Outside, the child was howling but Schultz took no notice. Tam remembered Ballentyne's last word of advice. Let him settle down, he'd said. He'll take a look at you. He'll make a judgement. If he doesn't like what he sees, too bad. But don't rush the man.

'You come to Paris often?' Tam enquired.

'Only on business. This city can be a man's worst enemy. If I spent any real time in this place I'd never leave. Why fight for a better world when it's here already?'

Schultz gestured him into a seat at the table. A buzzer on the wall summoned a waiter. He gave Schultz two menus in soft leather bindings and left.

'We have all evening,' Schultz said. 'Tell me about your Czechs.'

'You know about my Czechs?'

'A little. Enough. What happened to that woman of yours was regrettable. The Sudetens need a lesson in manners. They're primitive. They're out of control. Henlein thinks he can control them and it turns out he's wrong. Murder is the least of their sins.'

'You've seen the body?'

'I've seen photos. They even botched the post-mortem.' He got to his feet and fetched a bottle from the trolley. Scotch. Tam watched him pouring himself a refill. 'You were close to her? This woman?'

'I spent time with her. She had a boyfriend, Edvard. But you'd know that.'

'Edvard's a good man. They tried to kill him, too.'

'And?'

'He gave them the slip.'

'You know where he is?'

'Yes.'

'Is he safe?'

'Yes. You know about Kreisky? The American? The man's a snake. If anyone deserves a dose of Sudeten justice, it's him. One day it will happen. He's like all kikes. He thinks wealth will spare him. Happily, he's wrong. I'm sorry about the woman. It should never have happened.'

The confirmation that Kreisky was Jewish came as no surprise. The name itself was all you'd need. Tam would have liked to find out more about the American businessman but Schultz was already moving on. The subject had been laid to rest and Tam sensed the beginnings of a rapport with this strange envoy. There was a hint of warmth in his eyes and when he asked how Tam was coping in his new role, he appeared to mean it.

'How much do you know about me?' Tam asked.

'Enough. My organisation has excellent connections in London, far better than Herr Ribbentrop's. Putting someone like you into play is a brave thing to do. The risk is substantial. You should be flattered.'

'Because?'

'Because you've come from nowhere. Because you carry so little baggage. Because your German is excellent. And because your experience in these matters is exactly this.' He narrowed the space between his thumb and his forefinger until it didn't exist. 'You were a serving soldier, am I right?'

'Yes.'

'A volunteer. Am I correct?'

'Yes. I was in the Royal Marines.'

There was a hint of pride in Tam's voice and Schultz caught it at once. For the first time, he smiled.

'The little Scotsman from Glasgow had been a Marine,' he said. 'They threw him out after some row or other. I think he hit one of the officers.'

'So what happened to him? In Spain?'

'We interrogated him. I just told you.'

'And then?'

'We handed him over to Franco's people.'

'And?'

'They shot him.'

Tam reached for his glass. Then came footsteps along the corridor and the softest knock at the door. The waiter was back to take an order. Tam's appetite had suddenly vanished.

Schultz was watching him across the table.

'I suggest the veal,' he grunted. 'You'll feel better in a minute.'

*

They talked throughout the meal. Two dishes came and went. Tam knew from Ballentyne that Schultz, after recovering from a serious war wound, had fought with various Nationalist groups hatched by the rise of the Nazis. He was rumoured to have had a hand in a number of killings but also cultivated an interest in poetry and journalism which gave him a special cachet amongst the brown-shirted thugs in Ernst Rohm's *Sturmabteilung*.

This combination of street warrior and poet was deeply unusual and probably accounted for his break with Hitler.

The Führer, Schultz decided, had turned leadership into megalomania. Enough was enough. This decision had nearly cost him his life when Hitler ordered the slaughter of the SA's top chieftains but he'd then found a perch with the Reich organisation charged with military intelligence.

According to Ballentyne, it was indeed the *Abwehr* had offered Schultz a safe haven from the attentions of the Gestapo. In return, Schultz was only too willing to maintain his links to the netherworld of disgruntled paramilitaries who'd also fallen out of love with Hitler's leadership. After years of service with the *Abwehr*, Schultz had now become one of their trusted envoys. Hence his presence in Paris.

The dessert plates lay empty. Schultz had lit a small cigar.

'The Czech thing's over,' he said. 'And you know why?'

'Tell me.'

'Hitler assumed the Czechs wouldn't fight. That's lazy on his part. There were plenty of people who knew otherwise.'

'Abwehr people?'

'Certainly. And others. But the man never listens. He thinks history's on his side. He plays to the street. He loves an audience. He gives the people Vienna and they howl for more. Or that's the way he chooses to think.'

'You're telling me he's wrong?'

'I'm telling you he's pulled back from the border. I'm telling you the Czechs have seen him off. And you know why? Because it turns out we were right all along. Toe-to-toe, they'd have made a fight of it. Maybe for a week. Maybe for longer. But that's all they needed to do. Hitler's a bully. He shouts a great deal. He thumps the table. He bites the carpet. He carries a big stick. He acts the maniac. He frightens people. But it's all bluff. Bend the knee and it's over. Do what the Czechs have just done and the man can be stopped.' Schultz tapped ash on to the side of his plate. 'He'll be back for more. I guarantee it.' He looked up. 'So what happens then?'

Tam shook his head. He was out of his depth and he knew it. He began to talk about how good the Czech Army looked in the field, about the strength of the fortifications, about Prague's determination to fight, but Schultz dismissed it all with a wave of his hand. This was common knowledge. This the *Abwehr* knew already. It shaped the contents of countless memoranda despatched to the Berlin Chancellery, only to be ignored. Hitler lived in a world of his own. He had no interest in either advice or moderation. Just now, the only person he listened to was Ribbentrop and that's because Ribbentrop knew exactly what his beloved Führer wanted to hear.

'Brickendrop,' Tam murmured. 'In London they called him Brickendrop.'

He explained the phrase. Schultz wasn't amused.

'The man's dangerous,' he said. 'We all know he fucked up in England. A year in London and he'd made an enemy of everyone who mattered. That's why he's turned against you English. That's why he's making eyes at the Japanese. And when he tells Hitler that you'll never fight, that the Czechs are there for the taking, Hitler believes him. Why? Because it's what he *wants* to believe. He thinks the French and the English have turned their backs on the Czechs. Somehow we have to change that.'

'By convincing Hitler?'

'By getting rid of him.' At last a smile. 'Don't tell me you're surprised.'

Part Two

15

MAY–JULY 1938

Tam Moncrieff returned to London from Paris. He spent two days in the Mayfair flat with Ballentyne and from time to time they were joined by others, all strangers to Tam, who were interested in specific elements of his report from Czechoslovakia. One of them was an American who appeared to be attached to the Embassy. He was disappointed that Tam hadn't met Thomas Kreisky personally but confirmed the businessman's interest in the Jáchymov uranium mine. When Tam asked him about Edvard Kovač he said he'd never heard of him. After he'd left, Ballentyne admitted this might be somewhat wide of the truth but when Tam pressed him about Edvard's whereabouts he simply shrugged. If Schultz said the man was still alive, then so be it. Lucky Edvard.

At the end of the second day Tam was alone in the flat when Ballentyne arrived. Tam heard him humming a piece of light opera as he let himself in. Schultz, he said, had been in touch from Berlin. The good news was that he'd enjoyed the meal he'd shared with Tam at the Paris hotel and was happy to discuss the possibility of further meetings. Reports from his contacts in the Sudentenland suggested that Tam had done well to avoid the fate of Renata. The ex-Marine certainly knew how to handle himself. He was resourceful. He could think on his feet. More to the point, he spoke German like a native and appeared to be undaunted in his new role.

Tam listened to the string of compliments from Schultz without comment. This was like being at school, he thought. He'd just sat some kind of exam and this was the verdict. Ballentyne's own congratulations were more than welcome but simply added to the mystery. Was his role over? Or was there something else these people wanted him to do?

He put the question to Ballentyne. Tam had been in touch with both his sister and with the housekeeper up in Scotland. There were pressing reasons why he needed to step back into his former life. His father's move to London wasn't going well, and neither were the bookings at The Glebe House. On both counts, something needed to be done.

Ballentyne was sympathetic but Tam sensed at once that his days as an apprentice spy were far from over. Schultz's approval appeared to be the key to whatever might happen next. Tam had indeed passed an important test and Ballentyne's assumption, for which he was careful to apologise, was that Tam might have an appetite for more.

'But what does *more* mean? More what?'

'More operational engagement. In the field.'

'That means nothing to me. So far I've done your bidding. To be frank, a lot of it was far from pleasant and what makes it worse is that I've no idea where I fit, no real notion of who you people are. The need for secrecy I understand. But if operational engagement means what I think it means, then you have to start to trust me. Does that sound reasonable?'

Tam's bluntness made no visible impression on Ballentyne. On the contrary, he seemed to be expecting it.

'We're the orphan child in the world of Intelligence,' he said. 'If you ask yourself what might happen if certain people are at their wit's end with this government of ours, then you might end up with an outfit like ours.'

'Are you official?'

'We are. Most of the time. Oliver is a businessman. He made a fortune in Malaya and he still attends to his interests there but unlike most businessmen he sees a great deal further than his balance sheet. He knows trouble's coming and he wants to head it off. Just now he's in Singapore. He worries about the German tie-up with the Japs and so he should. Me? I work in Whitehall. If you're going to press me for details I'm afraid I'll have to regretfully decline but you wouldn't be wrong to suspect that I, along with a number of other like-minded players in this game, would like to see an end to Mr Hitler.'

'Is that why you sent me to meet Schultz?'

'Yes. We've known about him for a while. We're impressed by what we've heard about the man. And now, thanks to you, we find we share a common interest.'

'In getting rid of Hitler?'

'Indeed. Diplomacy's hopeless and Schultz knows it. Only a bullet will do.'

Tam nodded. He'd worked much of this out for himself in the days and nights since leaving Schultz at his hotel but it was somehow different hearing it from Ballentyne's lips.

'And you're telling me we're going along with this? Assuming it happens?'

'Quietly, yes.'

'So it's official government policy? Having a hand in the murder of a head of state?'

'God forbid. Oliver and I and a number of other folk are simply there to chuck a log or two on the fire. And even that, we'd deny.'

'I don't understand.'

'About the denial?'

'About the logs. Why does Schultz need you?'

'Because he and his colleagues need to be certain that Hitler is leading them to disaster. And to make that credible they have to believe that we will fight.'

'For Czechoslovakia?'

'Of course. The current little upset is only a prelude. In the end Hitler will march. Regardless of whatever threats we make. The man himself believes our threats are empty. This is the world of bluff and counter-bluff – *our* world, if you want the truth. So our job is to persuade the likes of Mr Schultz that we mean to stand by our treaty with the French. That would take us to war. And that's the threat that will push Schultz and his friends to attend to Mr Hitler.'

'Friends?'

'Top generals. People in the *Abwehr*. Businessmen. The old Germany, if you like.'

'This is fact? Not wishful thinking?'

'Fact, Tam. We know about these people. So far their minds aren't made up and by mobilising just now the Czechs have let them off the hook. But the thing to remember is that these men, these generals, these intelligence chiefs, see themselves as patriots. They'd love to help themselves to Czechoslovakia.

They'd love to own the entire bloody world. But not at the cost of a war they're convinced they'd lose.'

'In the short term?'

'Of course. One day, in their judgement, they'll be ready. But not now. And not in a couple of months when Hitler will march again.'

'Regardless?'

'Indeed. That's the one thing we can depend on. In fact, that's the one thing that underpins this entire little operation of ours. Hitler is a glutton. He eats countries for breakfast. The marching season ends in October. The man can't help himself.'

'So he needs to be stopped.'

'That would be extremely helpful.'

'By Schultz and his friends?'

'Yes.'

'With our help?'

'I'm afraid so.' Ballentyne offered a thin smile. 'Or yours, to be precise.'

*

Tam spent the night at his sister's house in Belgravia, trying not to think too hard about the implications of his conversation with Ballentyne. On the phone from the Mayfair flat he'd had the impression that Vanessa had tucked his father away in the basement but it turned out that she and her husband had taken a joint decision to parcel him up and lodge him in a nursing home north of King's Cross. Having him on the premises, she said, had proved both tiresome and distressing. He hadn't got a clue who she was and appeared to believe that Alec had once played cricket for the Australians. Far better, under these circumstances, to leave him in the care of people who knew what they were doing.

That night, Tam ate at the kitchen table with his sister and her husband. Conversation was fitful and revolved around what Alec termed 'the happy resolution of the Sudeten nonsense'. Close friends of theirs, one a Tory MP, the other a journalist on *The Times*, commended Mr Chamberlain and his government for keeping their nerve, and looked forward to the day when Hitler's manners would improve. Neighbours, said Vanessa, had started to stockpile food in the belief that war was imminent but she viewed this reaction as unseemly. The fact that neither his sister nor Alec made any effort to ask Tam what he'd been up to over the last couple of weeks, came as a profound relief. Only Vanessa's choice of reading matter, left casually on the coverlet of his bed, offered any evidence that she'd even remembered their conversation before he'd left. Erskine Childers. *The Riddle of the Sands.*

*

Next morning Tam took a bus to King's Cross railway station. He booked himself a ticket on the night sleeper through to Aberdeen and then returned to the street. His father's nursing home was a five-minute walk away. It stood at the end of a rundown Georgian terrace beside a church but inside it was both clean and well appointed. It was also on the small side, which came as a bit of a relief. Half a dozen patients, all old, all male, were under the care of two women who'd spent most of their lives as missionaries in equatorial Africa.

One of them, who termed herself the Matron, sat Tam down with a cup of tea and a plate of rock buns still warm from the oven. Mr Moncrieff, she admitted, could be a challenge on occasions but he'd settled in well and had made best friends with a parson from Rotherhithe. Their games of chess, she said, could last for over a week and no move from either party appeared to comply with any of the known rules. Tam spent most of the afternoon beside these two men as they peered down at the five remaining pieces on the chessboard, and on three occasions his father lifted his head to enquire whether Tam had come to deal with the new gas boiler.

Before he left, gone seven in the evening, Tam escorted the old man to his room. In contrast with downstairs it was sparsely furnished, with few of the keepsakes that Tam had been careful to leave with his sister, but his father seemed happy enough. The tall window faced west. The view was dominated by a cemetery, a maze of crooked headstones, and when the clouds parted to reveal the beginnings of an impressive sunset, Tam thought he detected just a glimmer of recognition in his father's rheumy eyes when the old man glanced across at him. His nose was running and Tam lent him his handkerchief.

'Take care of that cold, Dad.' He bent to kiss him lightly on his forehead. 'I'll be back.'

Downstairs, before he left to find a restaurant, Tam paused to say goodbye to the Matron. She'd just emerged from a room at the back of the entrance hall and she smelled of bleach. She escorted Tam to the door and then suddenly asked him to wait while she fetched something. Moments later she was back with an envelope.

'Take your time.' She nodded at the envelope. 'There's no hurry.'

*

It was an hour or so before Tam opened the envelope. He'd found a decent hotel near the station and settled down with a copy of the *Daily Telegraph* to await the arrival of the food. A report on the front page confirmed that Czech President Beneš had ordered the bulk of his army back to barracks. The crisis, it seemed, was over. Tam sat in the hotel's restaurant, wondering what the people in this teeming city had made of the last few weeks. Unpronounceable names. Unfathomable political groupings. A hotchpotch of strangers bent on doing each other immeasurable harm. Did any of it matter? Was there any real possibility that this faraway quarrel would come to a proper war?

Tam permitted himself the faintest smile, knowing now that the answer was yes, then he reached for the envelope. Inside was an account for the first month of his father's stay. Four pounds ten shillings and sixpence was a sum he couldn't possibly afford. He gazed at the bill for a moment longer. Then he folded it into his pocket.

*

Over the weeks that followed, back at The Glebe House, Tam buried himself in tasks that needed addressing before he could think of opening the shoot again. Parts of the garden were a wilderness. Fencing needed attention. Long days of hard physical labour brightened his mood and gradually memories of the Sudetenland, of Renata and Edvard, began to recede. By the end of June The Glebe House was finally ready to accept more shooting parties when a letter arrived from his father's nursing home.

Tam opened it in some trepidation. By raiding a fund set by for estate emergencies, he'd managed to settle the first bill but he'd still no idea how to keep meeting sums as large as he knew he should expect. This problem had been compounded by a brief phone call with the Matron. His father, she said, was beginning to deteriorate physically. While he was still at peace with himself and his surroundings, he was having gastric and urinary problems and required a great deal of attention. This was bad news. Over the recent days Tam had toyed with getting his dad back to Scotland but under these circumstances he knew the move would be impossible. The Glebe House was a business, not a hospital.

The contents of the letter from the nursing home took him by surprise. Instead of a demand for yet more money, Tam found himself looking at a cheque. It was drawn on the account of the nursing home itself and represented repayment in full for his first month's fees. His father's account, it appeared, was being settled by a third party. Tam thought at once of Vanessa, his sister, but when he offered his thanks on the phone she denied any knowledge of the payment. There was a vague possibility, she said, that Alec may have put some kind of arrangement in place but he'd been very busy just recently helping host a trade delegation from Germany and in any case he'd never taken much interest in her family's affairs.

For several days Tam let the matter rest. He'd never believed in the Good Fairy but just now, with the shoot about to reopen, he was too busy to pay much attention to anything else. Then a telegram arrived. It came from Ballentyne. *Regret short notice but would appreciate an hour of your time. Very glad that your father is still in good spirits.* There followed a London phone number. Tam stared at the message. The key word was *still.* These people were in touch with his father. The funds to keep him in good hands must be coming from them.

And so it proved. Ballentyne appeared the following afternoon in a taxi from Laurencekirk station. For whatever reason, Ballentyne insisted that they talk away from the house and Tam was only too happy to turn his back on yet more painting and take the path that tracked across the estate towards the bareness of the mountains beyond.

It was July and high summer had settled on the bright yellows of the gorse. The path was steep in places but Ballentyne was a great deal fitter than he looked. Halfway up the mountain was a hollow amongst the rocks, a favourite spot for Tam when he needed to think. It hadn't rained for nearly a week and the moss was soft and dry underfoot. The view to the south extended for miles across the Dee Valley and in the far distance Tam caught the gleam of sunshine on a bend in the river.

Ballentyne settled on the moss, his back against a rock. So far, neither men had mentioned the nursing home.

'Your father's in good hands,' Ballentyne said. 'That must come as a bit of a relief.'

'You've *seen* him?'

'Twice. You'll have met the missionary ladies. Impressive, I must say, and comforting, too. Religion appears to be a blessing in the right hands.'

'So how is he?'

'Mad as a coot... but you'll know that. They look after him well. You should have no qualms on that score.'

Tam nodded, said he was grateful.

'I rather assumed you'd finished with me,' he said carefully.

'Assumed or hoped?'

'Probably both.'

'May I ask why?'

'Because of this,' Tam nodded at the view. 'Spend a little time away and you realise what you're missing.'

Ballentyne had produced a pipe. He began to stuff it with tobacco from a rubber pouch. Then he fumbled for some matches before gesturing towards a lone deer that had broken cover below.

'You'd prefer all this belonged to Berlin?'

'Of course not. But it can't be that bad.'

'It is, Tam. In fact, it's probably worse. Our leaders are trapped on the wrong side of history. They show no signs of understanding the phenomenon that is Hitler. These are people who belong to a different world. In a way it's not their fault. They think their world is Hitler's world and they couldn't be more wrong. We see no prospect that any of this will change. But change it must. Otherwise you won't be the only one round here speaking German.' He paused to light his pipe, then looked up. 'You're telling me this comes as some kind of surprise?'

Tam shook his head. In his heart he knew that Ballentyne was right. Listen to Henlein, watch the faces of the crowds in Karlovy Vary, picture the Jew Spielmann with his picture book and his flensing knife, and you realised the sheer reach of the darkness that was beginning to envelop the Continent.

He lay back in the sunshine, his eyes closed. He loved the sweetness of Ballentyne's tobacco. His father had once smoked something very similar.

'So what happens next?' he asked.

'The Germans are working on a plan. *Fall Grün*.'

'Case Green?'

'Indeed. It's a blueprint for the invasion of Czechoslovakia. The generals are happy to march in a couple of years' time, once they're ready. Hitler thinks September more appropriate or maybe, at the very latest, October. We were right about what happened in May when you were there. It was exploratory, an opening move.'

'Where does this stuff come from?'

'Berlin. Unimpeachable sources.'

'For instance?'

'The generals themselves. They think it's folly. They think he's mad. As I believe I explained the last time we met.' He paused. 'We need to get you into Germany. There are doors we need to unlock and the key to those doors is Schultz.'

'And me?'

'You're the key to Schultz. He sends his regards, by the way. Says he's looking forward to meeting you again.'

'Do I have any choice in this?'

'Of course you do. This is still a free country. Which is rather the point.'

Ballentyne fell silent, gazing out at the heather. Insects were busy in the no-man's-land where the rocks were lapped by the softness of the moss. At length Tam said he needed a day or two to make a proper decision.

'Of course. I imagine you must have a great deal to do. We wouldn't need you for at least a couple of weeks, if that helps.'

Tam nodded, picking at a scab of yellow lichen on the rock.

'What about my father? If I say no?'

'Then you'll have to fund his stay yourself.'

'And afterwards? If I say yes?'

'We'll look after him until. . .' he looked briefly pained, '. . . he no longer needs those wonderful ladies. We'll pay you, of course, in addition to all this, thanks to Oliver's largesse. It won't be a fortune but it might be handy nonetheless.'

Tam smiled to himself. His father held hostage. The promise of extra funds. And that subtle appeal to something he could only describe as patriotism. People like Ballentyne, when required, could be as quietly ruthless as anyone in a Nazi uniform.

Ballentyne glanced at his watch. If possible, he'd like to catch the 6.15 train back to London. Was there anything else Tam might like to ask?

'You haven't said what you want me to do. I might be missing something here but that strikes me as important.'

'Of course. A little group of generals have formed. Let's call it a conspiracy. They have the good of the nation at heart but they need reassurance.'

'About what?'

'About us. They need someone to tell them we'll fight. Someone in the position to know. Someone who speaks their language. And someone, ideally, who's also met the Czechs.'

'That's me.'

'Indeed.'

'An emissary?'

'Nicely put.'

'And *will* we fight?'

'Of course.' Tam felt a reassuring hand on his arm. 'Anything else is inconceivable.'

*

After Ballentyne's departure, Tam prowled the emptiness of the house, wrestling with the decision he knew he couldn't duck. Ballentyne's brief visit had revived his guilt about Renata. Staring out of an upstairs window, he imagined her stepping into view, whole, intact, undamaged, offering him a chance to make things right again. She was standing beside the trellis of roses he'd so recently pruned. She was looking up at him, a smile on her face. This happened often. Sometimes she was with Edvard. Sometimes not. Then, worst of all, she began to appear in his dreams, an accusation more than a presence, and he'd jerk awake in the darkness, one hand glued to the cold metal of the Opel's boot, terrified that he'd find her inside.

Tam had never been especially religious. His attendance at the small kirk in the village had been fitful, duty rather than belief, but he knew his father's respect for the priest back in the days when the two men would share a glass or two. The priest's name was MacBraine. Everyone called him Cally.

He lived in a draughty stone cottage down the lane beyond the kirk. Tam arrived unannounced. Cally tidied the paperwork on his desk and sat him down. He was tall and ageless, and rarely trimmed his beard. He wanted to know about Tam's father. Tam explained about the nursing home. More guilt.

'You're here about your father?'

'No. I think I've let someone else down, too. Badly.'

Badly sounded pathetic. The woman had died, for Christ's sake. Died because he'd taken his eye off the ball. Died because he should have understood about her and Edvard. Died because he should have gone with her to wherever she was going. Died because he hadn't cared enough.

Tam had disguised the real circumstances. He didn't mention Czechoslovakia or the Sudetenland or the way this friend of his had met her death. Only the fact that he was complicit. All he wanted from this man was a clue about what he should do next. Guilt exacted a savage price. It pestered him night and day. He wanted, needed, to get rid of it.

'By changing the past? By pretending it never happened? You can't do that, laddie. What's done is done. Every decision has a consequence. Live with it. Understand it.'

Every decision has a consequence. Indeed.

'I want a second chance.'

'To redeem yourself?'

'Of course.'

'Then take it. Do it.'

'As simple as that?'

'Not at all, laddie. Nothing is ever simple. Simplicity is a joke dreamed up by the devil.' He leaned forward, taking Tam's hand. 'When you were young, out every day, out on your own, your father was very proud of you. You know what he told me once? Of course you don't. He told me that you were the bravest wee boy he'd ever had the privilege of knowing. Some days he couldn't believe you were his son, that he'd fathered a giant like this. That was his phrase, the very word he used. A *giant*.' He paused, then gestured towards the paperwork piled on his desk. 'Give thanks to God you don't have to deal with all this nonsense. In your heart you know what to do.'

Tam stared at him. He'd come for advice, maybe a little comfort. Not this.

'Is that it?'

'It is, laddie. You need to set the record straight.' He smiled, getting to his feet. Then he stepped around the desk and extended a hand. 'Good hunting.'

Tam walked the mile and a half back to The Glebe House. From the lawn at the rear of the property the swell of the Cairngorms was framed by a huge elm. He'd always loved this view and when his mother was alive, and the weather was clement, she'd sometimes take afternoon tea here. Now Tam gazed at the browns and greens of the mountains shadowed by the racing clouds. Barely hours ago he'd been up there with Ballentyne. He could feel the soft mattress of the heather, smell the sweetness of the man's tobacco. *Every decision has a consequence*, the priest had said. And he was right.

Tam lingered for a moment longer, before returning to the house. The telephone was in the hall. He'd taken the precaution of memorising Ballentyne's number and he waited an age for the operator to get through.

Finally Ballentyne was on the line. Tam bent to the phone.

'It's me,' he said briefly. 'The answer's yes.'

*

In Berlin, in late May, Dieter Merz and Keiko Ayama had to surrender the apartment off Friedrichstrasse. With the help of the Ministry of Aviation, Dieter found alternative lodgings in a recently converted stable out near Potsdam. The stable lay behind a grand house that had once belonged to a Prussian nobleman. It was quiet and spacious and there was plenty of scope in the nearby woods for Dieter to run. Running, he knew, would be the real test of his injury. He was cautious at first, a gentle jog, alert for the slightest twinge, but as the days went past he picked up speed and pushed himself harder and harder until he was doing the kind of distances he'd managed in Spain.

Dieter was still under the supervision of a neurologist in the big military hospital that served the *Luftwaffe* and when he presented himself for the next of his periodic check-ups, the medic was astonished at his progress. He took Dieter through a series of exercises and then shook the post-operative X-rays from an envelope and held them up against the light. Dieter followed his finger as it darted around the bones at the bottom of his spine. The surgeon, he said, had done a fine job but even so Dieter had no right to be pain-free. It was, he concluded, a miracle. Dieter was tempted to tell him about the *reiki,* about the long evenings of surrender to his favourite therapist, but knew the relationship was beyond explanation. A miracle indeed, he agreed.

By now, Dieter was display-flying twice and sometimes three times a week. Word that he was to star in a programme that included a strapping wing walker called Brunhilda, plus three of the new Stuka dive bombers, spread quickly to every corner of the Reich. By early July, the holidays were fast approaching and the crowds grew and grew with families – especially the men and the young kids – eager to see what the heavily publicised Bf-109-E could do.

With the help of colleagues he respected, many of them Legion pilots with hundreds of hours combat time in Spain, Dieter developed a display that could showcase the little fighter, and more recently he'd tempted Georg back into the seat of a sister 109-E. Together, at weekends, they engaged in mock dogfights over enraptured crowds with Dieter always guaranteed victory. Special smoke canisters signalled a lethal hit and Georg began to excel at dead-stick landings, nursing the wounded fighter back to mother Earth as the prop windmilled and the sea of upturned faces held their breath.

Goebbels had long recognised the public hunger for authentic Reich heroes and in the shape of *Der Kleine* and his lanky, unsmiling wingman he'd found the perfect example. One of the Ministry's propaganda film units put together a thirty-minute profile of the two aviators, drawing on their shared experience of combat over Northern Spain. The movie went into cinemas all over the Reich, and to Beata's amusement her new husband became something of a film star.

Crowds at the flying displays grew and grew, especially at weekends, and Goering began to recognise that some of this celebrity would do the Nazi leadership no harm at all. The presence of Georg at some godforsaken airfield, ferrying his charges to a rally or a military parade, was attracting a bigger crowd than usual, but it was Ribbentrop who made the obvious suggestion. Star of the show was Dieter Merz. Why not enlist him in the Führer's special squadron?

Dieter was the first to point out once again that he'd need special training to join the *Regierungsstaffel*. He'd always flown single-seat fighters. That was his speciality, his trade. Piloting one of the bigger transports required expertise he didn't have. Map-reading. Navigation. Night-flying. Multi-engine operations. It had taken Georg more than a year to master all these skills. When – between flying displays – was he supposed to find the time for all this extra tuition?

Goering ignored these pleas. He knew that Ribbentrop was receiving intermittent treatment from Merz's Japanese girlfriend. Like others at the top of the Reich, he resented the way that the *Reichsminister* still had the ear of Hitler. Any chance to disrupt that relationship, to expose Ribbentrop for the bloated fool he'd always been, might be gold dust in the months to come as Hitler plunged ever closer to involving Germany in a war she couldn't win.

At Goering's request, *Abwehr* agents had planted microphones in Dieter Merz's converted stable in the search for confidences Ribbentrop might have shared with his *reiki* therapist. Goering had briefly listened to a handful of the recordings but so far Keiko hadn't said a word about her new patient. In the upper reaches of the *Abwehr*, Dieter Merz was already known as the luckiest man on God's earth, a tribute to Keiko's many talents, and so Goering wanted the young aviator exactly where he could keep an eye on him. No better a career move than joining Georg on the Führer's *Regierungsstaffel*.

Dieter battled against the posting but this, as he knew only too well, was one dogfight he'd never win. It was Georg who handed him the training schedule he'd have to accept over the coming months. When Dieter shook his head, said the whole thing was impossible, Georg pointed out that the display season would soon be coming to an end. With the onset of autumn and winter, Dieter would have more than enough time on his hands. Either he joined the *Regierungsstaffel* or he might end up back with an operational squadron, marking time in some godforsaken corner of the Reich. Did he really want that?

They were drinking coffee at an airfield outside Munich. The display over, the weekend crowds were filing past the window of the squadron mess.

'There's a war coming,' Dieter pointed out. 'You know there is.'

'Wrong.'

'Who says?'

'Goering. I fly these people. I know what they're thinking. No war. Not until we're ready.'

'And Hitler?' Georg shook his head, wouldn't be drawn. 'Well? Isn't he the guy in charge? Or am I missing something here?'

'Of course he's in charge.'

'Then it's his decision. His call. We jump on the Czechs.' Dieter shrugged. 'And the game's over.'

'You think so?'

'Yes, I do.' Dieter was frowning now. 'Unless you're telling me different.'

16

BERLIN, 27 AUGUST 1938

Tam Moncrieff flew to Berlin on the day that London was again alive with rumours about a coming war. Hitler had recently called up three quarters of a million men. Chamberlain had despatched an envoy to talk sense into the Czechs. And now the Chancellor of the Exchequer, no less, had warned about the possibility of imminent hostilities.

Tam had stayed overnight in the Mayfair flat, having met Ballentyne for a final briefing at lunchtime. Ballentyne had given him a contact at the embassy in Berlin. Her name was Isobel Menzies. She was resourceful, well-connected, and had won the approval of diplomats Ballentyne respected. He also gave Tam the number for a secure line in London if he needed to get in touch in a hurry. Tam had committed the number to memory and enquired about the possibility of a weapon. Carrying his own gun, at the very least, might give him an option or two if he ran into more trouble. To his surprise, Ballentyne had rejected the request.

'On balance I think not,' he'd said. 'You'll be in good hands.'

*

Wilhelm Schultz was at Tempelhof Airport to meet the incoming flight from London. With him was another man, younger, whom he didn't introduce. They were both wearing civilian clothes. Schultz, with his leather jacket and tight mouth, ignored Tam's extended hand and nodded at a nearby door marked *Privat*. Beyond the door, a maze of corridors led to a small, bare office. The colours were beginning to fade on a souvenir poster for the '36 Olympics and there was a waiting chair in front of the metal desk.

Schultz told Tam to sit down. The aide produced an ink pad and a folded sheet of white paper. Schultz opened the ink pad and took Tam's fingers, one by one, pressing the tips to the pad and then the paper. The index print, he said, would form part of his ID card, to be delivered later to the hotel where he'd be staying, while the rest of the prints would be put on file.

Tam wanted to know where the file would end up.

'That's not a question you need to ask,' Schultz said. 'You have to learn to trust me.'

*

The Hotel Altmark lay in a side street off Wilhelmstrasse, a narrow-fronted, four-storey building with ruched pink curtains and a menu displayed beside the entrance. *Abwehr* headquarters, where Schultz had an office, was a five-minute stroll away. He'd be in touch later, once he had time for a proper conversation.

Tam took the stairs to his room on the fourth floor. In keeping with the rest of the hotel, it was spotless, if modest: single bed, handbasin, wardrobe, telephone and a new-looking radio on the table beneath the window. The room felt airless in the July heat and Tam opened the window. From here, he could see the back of another building beyond the tiny courtyard, almost close enough to touch. In this area of the city it might have been government offices or perhaps another hotel. The figure of a woman bent over a table caught his attention on the third floor, but the moment she turned towards the window he stepped back and pulled the curtain.

The room already felt like a cell. Tam slipped off his jacket and stretched full length on the bed. Ten short weeks ago he'd found himself in similar circumstances, except on that occasion the cell had been real, and he'd relied on a Czech inquisitor to keep him fed and watered. Here in Berlin, he had the freedom of the city. He could speak the language. He had support in the shape of Wilhelm Schultz. And over the coming days and perhaps weeks he might make some small contribution to the storm brewing on the Czech border.

Over sandwiches at the flat in Mayfair, Tam had pressed Ballentyne for more details on the rebel German generals he was likely to meet. The word 'rebel' had made Ballentyne wince. These were patriots, he kept insisting, men for whom loyalty was a blood debt to the Fatherland. Treat them as rebels, let the word slip into the wrong conversation, and Tam's mission would be over. He was there to underwrite the gamble they were taking, not just with their careers but very possibly their lives. He was there to offer the reassurance that Paris and London stood four-square behind the Czechs.

This guarantee, Tam pointed out, might come more naturally from the lips of politicians but Ballentyne told him he was wrong. By the very nature of their calling, politicians became creatures of endless compromise. Ask a politician for a yes or a no and you got a maybe. What mattered infinitely more was the truth about British military resolve. And that would come with far more conviction from the lips of someone like Tam.

Even now, he wasn't convinced. It was the politicians, after all, who made the decision to go to war or not. Or so he'd always believed. At this point, watching the faintest breeze stir the curtains in his hotel room, Tam had a sudden thought. In corners of this very city, men with power and authority and a great deal to lose were plotting to change the leadership. That's why he was here. That's what he'd come to encourage. What if something similar was happening in London? What if a bunch of renegade politicians, backed by the Army, had come to despair about appeasement? About the country's elected leaders at the beck and call of Hitler and Mussolini? Wouldn't the likes of Ballentyne and Sanderson fit neatly into a conspiracy like this? And wouldn't they be looking for an envoy of their own, someone they'd schooled and tested, to go to Germany and grease the wheels of a bid to kill Hitler?

Tam closed his eyes, telling himself it was nonsense, but the more he thought about it, the more it made sense. He knew just enough about the workings of the intelligence world to understand that everyone was groping in the dark. That's how you preserved secrets. And that's how you minimised damage if parts of your organisation were compromised.

Even now, despite his best efforts, Tam knew very little about either Sanderson or Ballentyne. One was apparently a businessman. The other, it seemed, was a government servant. But where did they work from? And where, exactly, did they fit into the larger scheme of things? To both questions he had no answer and after his experiences in Czechoslovakia that realisation made him feel increasingly uncomfortable.

He got up on one elbow, eyeing the telephone. He had a Berlin number for his contact at the British Embassy but Ballentyne had been emphatic about use of the telephone. The Germans will be watching you, he said. And, more importantly, they'll be listening. Expect a microphone in the room and some remote presence monitoring your phone calls. Wherever possible, make every contact face to face, ideally *en plein air*, where no one can bother you. Think enemy. Even where Schultz and his chums are concerned.

*

The British Embassy was in Wilhelmstrasse, a handsome, three-storey building that had once belonged to a railway baron. Near-neighbours included Hitler at the Reich Chancellery and Ribbentrop at the Foreign Ministry. Tam paused on the other side of the road, waiting for a break in the traffic. He needed an ally, a secure point of contact, and just now he had only one name.

'Isobel Menzies?'

The suited functionary behind the reception desk had just come off the phone. He took Tam's particulars and asked to see his passport.

'Is Miss Menzies expecting you?'

'No.'

'May I ask in what connection you wish to see her?'

'I'm afraid it's personal. You might tell her that Andrew Ballentyne sends his regards.'

The name Ballentyne appeared to register. He spared Tam a second look and then disappeared into a side office, shutting the door behind him. A woman appeared from nowhere and took his place. She returned Tam's passport and suggested he take a seat.

Tam waited and waited. From the banquette he had an excellent view of the street outside. Letters arrived, delivered by hand. A woman in overalls carried in a huge floral bouquet, followed by a sturdy young man in SS uniform. After a long conversation in German, he leaned over the desk and kissed the receptionist's hand. Tam wasn't sure about the details but he gathered they'd met last week at an embassy function. He watched the young man take a step back from the desk, his cap tucked beneath his arm, and offer the Hitler salute before making for the door. Half-turning on the banquette, Tam followed his descent to the street. The city was alive. Tam could feel it. The trams rolling down the broad boulevard. Well-dressed women on the pavement, handsome, purposeful. And that same young man pausing to adjust his cap before striding across the road. We haven't got a prayer, he thought, against people like these.

'Mr Moncrieff?' The faintest Border accent.

Tam turned back. She was tall, almost as tall as he was. The dress, emerald green, barely covered her knees. Her eyes were startling blue beneath a fringe of blonde hair and there wasn't a line on her body that Tam would have changed. Mid-thirties? Older? Tam didn't know.

'Miss Menzies?' He got to his feet.

She nodded and indicated a staircase beyond the reception area. Her high heels clack-clacked on the polished marble. Tam followed her up to the first floor, wondering how she got the time to acquire such a perfect tan. Her office lay at the very end of the corridor. Just the single desk. Impressive.

There was a moment of silence after Tam shut the door. Then she slipped behind the desk and lifted the phone.

'We'll have some coffee,' she said. 'And you can tell me everything.'

*

Early the following morning, Georg Messner took off from Tempelhof to fly the Führer to inspect the Reich's defences. Hitler's personal pilot Hans Baur was fighting a savage attack of mid-summer flu and had ordered Georg to take his place. Dieter, in his first taste of VIP flying, occupied the co-pilot's seat.

The West Wall stretched from the Dutch border in the north to the town of Weil am Rein, within sight of the Swiss frontier, six hundred and thirty kilometres of concrete bunkers, smaller pillboxes, and a rich array of artfully designed tank traps. Lately, according to Georg, Hitler had been demanding improvements in depth against impossible deadlines and today's flight was designed to check up on progress so far. The Führer, it was rumoured, needed to protect the Reich's arse from dozens of French armoured divisions if Paris ever took up the cause of the Czechs in earnest. Otherwise the gate to the heartlands of industrial Germany would lie wide open.

Dieter had reported to the airfield at dawn. Georg was already out on the hardstanding, one of three long shadows deep in conversation beside the Führer's tri-motor. The Ju-52 had just emerged from four days in the maintenance hangar and Georg was cross-checking Baur's list of reported faults against the workshop's schedule of repairs. Happy to accept the engineer's assurance that the aircraft was as good as new, Georg did a final visual check before taking Dieter to the wooden hut that was serving as the squadron's temporary mess.

A woman in a *Luftwaffe* uniform was serving coffee and pastries. It seemed that Hitler liked to pause here if time permitted and Dieter spotted a ribboned box put carefully to one side.

'From the Café Flockner in Salzburg,' Georg told him. 'They fly them in specially overnight.'

Hitler and his party were due in less than an hour and from his table beside the window Dieter watched two women emerge from the Ju-52 and clamber carefully down the ladder to the hardstanding. Rain had cleared to the east, leaving near-perfect visibility, and a light wind ruffled a feather duster as the women hurried away.

Georg had spread a map of the western frontier on the table. Take-off was scheduled for 06.30 and the first leg of the journey would deliver them to a northern section of the fortifications. Georg had already pencilled in the aircraft's track, circling diversion airfields en route in case of emergencies. He was estimating just over an hour in the air before they landed at the *Luftwaffe* base near the border. From here it was a short drive to where General Adam would be waiting to offer the Führer a personal tour of one of the West Wall's strong points.

Dieter wanted to know whether Georg knew the general.

'No.' Georg shook his head. 'He's got an engineering background. That's why he's in charge of all this. . .' Georg's finger traced the line of the Wall as it headed south towards Switzerland. 'I just hope he's got a tongue in his head, as well, because there's buckets of shit coming his way.'

'How do you know?'

'Hans Baur told me. Hans knows everything. He's mad he's not in the cockpit today. He was looking forward to it.'

The Führer arrived in a convoy of vehicles slightly ahead of schedule. A uniformed officer sprang out of the first car and opened the passenger door of the big Mercedes, standing back to offer a salute as Hitler emerged into the rich yellow spill of sunshine. Dieter had seen this man in countless newsreels and press photos but never in the flesh. He was slightly smaller than he'd imagined but the moment he'd adjusted the cap and stamped the stiffness from his legs the sense of presence was obvious. The way he looked across to his aircraft, the faintest anticipatory smile on his lips. The way he took in the rest of the airfield, his hands briefly on his hips. The moment when a single murmured word to his adjutant was enough to head the entire party towards the squadron mess. This man owned everything he laid his eyes on, Dieter told himself. There was nothing in Germany that wasn't rightfully his.

The door of the shabby little hut opened to the adjutant's touch. Everyone inside was already on their feet. A forest of outstretched arms and a muted *Heil Hitler* in recognition that it was still very early. Hitler went straight to the counter. He evidently knew the woman who served the coffee and cakes and they shared a brief conversation. She showed no sign of being intimidated by his presence and when he asked about her scoundrel of a husband, she said something Dieter didn't catch and then laughed.

Hitler nodded, evidently pleased, but when she reached for the box of Salzburg pastries he shook his head.

'Enough.' He patted his belly beneath the raincoat. 'Don't tempt me.'

At this, the visit appeared to be over. Hitler offered the woman a courtly kiss on both cheeks, glanced in Georg's direction, and then led the way out. Dieter noticed the adjutant seizing the box of pastries as he left.

'He has them later?'

'No.' Georg was folding up his map. 'We do.'

Beside the aircraft, Dieter waited for Hitler's party to get settled. He'd yet to see the inside of the Ju-52 and when he finally stepped into the cabin he was struck by how similar it was to any other passenger aircraft: two rows of single seats either side of a central aisle. The only concession to Hitler's status was a fold-down table for his personal use, plus a line of dials fixed to the bulkhead in front of him.

Dieter was following Georg up the narrow aisle towards the cockpit. Hitler motioned for Georg to stop and muttered something in his ear. Georg nodded, then introduced his co-pilot.

'*Oberleutnant* Merz, *Mein Führer.*'

Dieter wondered whether he should salute. Instead, he shook the proffered hand, much softer than he'd anticipated. Hitler wanted to know about his air displays. One of his staff at the Berghof had recently been at an air show in Munich. She'd described Dieter as 'the acrobat'. Fair or unfair?

'Fair, *Mein Führer.* Maybe I should have joined a circus.'

'Like Richthofen?' Hitler smiled at his own joke, then hoped Dieter confined his circus tricks to weekends. They all had work to do. Straight and level, if you please.

It was Dieter's cue to move on. He glanced at the instrumentation fixed to the bulkhead: clock, altimeter, airspeed indicator. All the information Hitler would need to satisfy himself that everything was going to plan.

In the cockpit, once Dieter had buckled in, Georg shot him a look.

'You're blushing,' he said. 'You look like a girl.'

They took off. Georg kept low over the south-western suburbs of Berlin, because Baur had told him that Hitler enjoyed the view. These were the haunts of the old Prussian kings. Previous masters of an earlier Reich had ridden here, hunted here. Now a new Führer could shrink the remains of the forest to one of the windows in his personal aircraft.

Beyond Potsdam, Georg began to climb, levelling out at three thousand metres beneath a coverlet of high cloud. Moments later, he assigned control to Dieter. Already, over the past couple of weeks, he'd flown the Junkers on at least three occasions, always with Georg, and always without passengers. Hitler, as it turned out, was his first VIP. He smiled at the thought, one eye on his compass heading. Compared to a single-seater, flying the tri-motor was like making conversation with a maiden aunt. You had to watch your manners. You had to avoid any possibility of giving offence. Nonetheless, as he banked to port on Georg's instruction, the aircraft felt light and responsive to his touch. The only problem was the noise. The cackle of three piston engines was close to deafening.

'Down there!' Georg's shout drew Dieter's attention to a tiny line of grey dots in the rich green pastureland below. Dieter loosened his harness and leaned closer to the cockpit side window for a proper look. Georg was motioning for him to lose height and as he started to nose down the dots began to resemble pimples. They went on and on, straddling hills and valleys, blemishing the landscape.

'*Der Westwall*,' Georg confirmed. 'I have control.'

Dieter was looking for signs of an airfield but Georg, who'd been here before, found it first. He dipped a wing and began a silky turn to starboard. Flying from the airfield had already been suspended in expectation of the Führer's arrival but Georg radioed ahead nonetheless. He expected to be on the ground within a couple of minutes. There'd be no need for any refuelling.

The landing was perfect, Georg nursing the Junkers to within metres of the grass runway and then lifting the nose and letting the aircraft settle gently on the racing turf. Delicate jabs on the pedals finally brought the plane to a halt in front of a line of biplanes.

Dieter recognised them at once. He hadn't seen an He-51 since leaving Spain and he found himself watching a young-looking cadet perched in a front cockpit, listening to the instructor crouched on the wing beside him. That was me once, Dieter thought. Me learning about flying in the raw. About plunging into combat without a radio. About trying to figure out how to reload the machine gun one-handed while maintaining some kind of control. An age seemed to have passed since those days cheating death amongst the Asturian mountains and he was still trying to remember how to find the boost control when a uniformed figure appeared in the cockpit.

'The Führer presents his compliments.' It was the adjutant Dieter had seen earlier in the squadron mess. He asked Georg if he and his young friend would like to accompany them to take a look at the fortifications.

Georg and Dieter exchanged glances. Why not?

The base commander had already provided enough vehicles for the Führer's party. Dieter and Georg rode in the third of three cars. The journey, through a succession of neat little villages, took less than half an hour. Finally the convoy swept through a checkpoint manned by soldiers in *Wehrmacht* grey and came to a halt in a clearing near the mouth of what looked like a tunnel.

Hitler was already exchanging salutes with a bent, ageing figure who'd stepped forward from the welcoming committee. His boots were highly polished and he wore the shoulder flashes of a General Staff Officer but building *Der Westwall* had written a different story on the paleness of his face. This was a man, Dieter thought, who must live the bulk of his life underground. And it shows.

'Wilhelm Adam,' Georg muttered. 'Poor bastard.'

Adam led the way into the tunnel. It was warmer in here after the chill of the early morning and there was a faint smell of kerosene. Thick cables hung from brackets on both sides of the tunnel and lights disappeared into the far distance.

Dieter was several paces behind the lead group but he sensed that Hitler's mood had already changed. He appeared to be half-listening to Adam's careful explanation of progress on the West Wall to date but his face was a mask. From time to time he'd pause for no particular reason, gazing at some detail on the tunnel wall while Adam droned on, then shake his head and mutter something to his adjutant. His adjutant had a notebook readied and by the time the group finally came to a halt the first page of the notebook was full. To Dieter it was obvious that this little routine had been perfected elsewhere, in other circumstances, but with the same intention in mind. Hitler stalked easy game. And this was part of the ritual.

A crude table had been set up at a junction where two tunnels met, a pair of wooden trestles planked with what looked like railway sleepers. A large map had been unrolled, the edges weighed down with clips of small-arms ammunition. Hitler's group gathered round the map. Hitler himself expressed a cursory interest, barely following Adam's finger as it tracked along the line of fortifications. The Führer's gloved hands were clasped in front of his raincoat and from time to time he seemed to stiffen, bracing his shoulders, throwing his head back, the actions of an actor waiting in the wings.

Dieter was watching his entourage, the adjutant in particular. Without attracting the slightest attention they were edging away from their leader, giving him the space he no doubt needed. Looking back, trying to remember, Dieter couldn't pinpoint the moment the hapless General Adam lit the fuse. It might have been his mention of the French Army should it come to a shooting war with the Czechs. It might have been something more mundane, like the ongoing shortage of raw materials on which the upgrade of the West Wall depended. Either way, Hitler exploded.

A gloved hand was pointing at the map. It was a gesture of contempt or perhaps dismissal. His voice, low to begin with, began to echo back from the four tunnels, distorting the mad torrent of statistics Hitler seemed to have memorised by heart. How Germany produced no less than twenty-three million tons of steel a year, *twenty-three million tons*. How the French could barely manage a quarter of that. How the famous British Army could call on no reserves, *none at all*, and how the French spent most of their time chasing enemies at home.

'Pitiful, General Adam. We deserve to be fighting against grown-ups, proper armies, not this rabble.'

He began to rant, his voice harsh, the Austrian accent unmistakeable. He wanted to know why progress underground was so slow, why deadlines were never met, why orders from Berlin were ignored, why a project as important as this should be so poorly managed. He rocked back and forth on his heels, the same gloved finger stabbing at the air, the wall lights painting his face a strange shade of yellow. His entourage stood to attention, waiting for the tirade to come to an end, and suddenly it was over, silence in the tunnels again, broken only by a distant drip-drip of water.

Hitler stepped towards the makeshift table. He put his hands on the edge of the map and rested his weight on his arms. To Dieter, he resembled an athlete at the end of a particularly gruelling race. Then his head came up.

'Well? You have anything to say to me?' He seemed to be staring into nowhere. The question was evidently meant for General Adam.

Adam stirred. So far his role had been to say nothing and he knew it. But from somewhere there appeared a flicker of courage or perhaps defiance.

'If our enemies are so weak, *Mein Führer*, why do we need a wall at all?'

The silence was absolute. Even the water had stopped dripping. Down here, in the bowels of a project that Hitler clearly viewed as a disaster, someone had dared to answer back.

Slowly he turned to Adam. There was nothing in his eyes. Absolutely nothing. Then he nodded towards the tunnel so far unexplored.

'Show me more,' he said.

17

BERLIN, 28 AUGUST 1938

An early evening dinner at the restaurant out on the Wannsee was Isobel Menzies' suggestion. To her regret, yesterday's coffee at the embassy had been cut short by the urgent need for her to confer with one of Herr Goebbels' aides. With profuse apologies she'd shepherded Tam to the door, the text of a message still in her hand, delivered by a lightly perspiring forty-something who'd stepped into her office without knocking. A place by the water called Der Hafen, she'd promised. Unforgettable views and brilliant food.

The restaurant was half-empty, a surprise in view of the glorious weather. The staff appeared to know Isobel well. They called her Fräulein Menzies with the kind of murmured politesse that suggested a long acquaintance but as far as Tam was concerned, she insisted on Bella. Already, in the taxi from Wilhelmstrasse, they'd swapped a clue or two about their separate life stories. Bella, as Tam had suspected, had Lowland Scottish roots. After a troubled adolescence at an Edinburgh boarding school for girls she'd spent three years at Oxford, reading German and Italian. University, she said, had been her salvation. The butterfly had emerged from the chrysalis and she'd settled greedily into a world she loved.

'So what's so loveable?'

'That. Amongst one or two other things.'

Tam followed her pointing finger. Out on the lake, a rowing eight were making good progress in the beginnings of the setting sun. They moved as one, with a smoothness and a power that could only come from endless training. Tam watched them with envy as well as admiration. Then it dawned on him what she was really saying.

'You do this? You row?'

'I do.'

'With them?'

'Yes. That's a men's crew. My ladies train tomorrow.'

'Germans?'

'Most of them. Not all. There's a French girl. She's really good. And an Italian lady from Verona. But the training routines are German. We race as often as we can. And we always win.'

Tam was impressed and said so. He'd been a rower himself at university and afterwards he'd missed it. The Royal Marines, he said, weren't slow to push you to your physical limits but there'd always been something about rowing that was special.

The fact that he'd been a Marine drew a nod from Bella which Tam took as approval. She said she'd once had a boyfriend who'd tried for selection. Totally mad but ludicrously brave and always good fun. Tam didn't respond. He was still watching the rowers out on the lake. Their timing was truly impressive.

'And is that why you're so brown?' He nodded at the fast-disappearing eight.

'Of course. The days are long this time of year and the weather's been beautiful. We wear as little as possible. But you'd know that.'

The comment was playful rather than flirtatious, but Tam sensed that some kind of relationship might be on offer. He wanted to know more about her life after Oxford.

'Was it difficult getting into the Security Services?'

'The what?'

'The Intelligence world. MI5. MI6. Whichever bit you belong to.'

'You think I'm a spy?' She was laughing. 'Here? In Berlin? Henderson can't stand Intelligence people. He thinks they're below the salt. He won't give them houseroom. Untrustworthy, he says. Snakes in the grass.'

'So what about me?'

'He thinks you're a journalist. That's what I told him. Not that he'll ever remember.'

Sir Nevile Henderson was the Ambassador in residence. According to Ballentyne, his closeness to the regime often amounted to fully paid-up membership.

Tam sat back for a moment, his eyes returning to the lake.

'So what do you do?' he said lightly. 'In that embassy of yours?'

'I meet people. I keep my eyes open. I make contacts across the city, often journalists, funnily enough. I try and keep my finger on the pulse of the place and I do my best to keep the Ambassador in the swim.'

'That sounds close to spying.'

'You're probably right. Except I don't carry a gun and lots of nice Germans make a fuss of me. If you want the truth, it's a lovely job and I'm lucky to have it. You're going to ask me next about all those entrance exams, how someone like me ever got into the Foreign Office in the first place, so here's where we come to the shameful bit. I got the job because of my German and because of my dad. He knew the right people. Believe me, that helps.'

'He's some kind of diplomat?'

'Never.' She was laughing again. 'Diplomacy and Dad were never best friends. He wouldn't know where to start. He's a businessman. He made a fortune in rubber and invested well. That buys you respect in certain quarters, believe me, and more than a little pull. He has friends in interesting places.'

Tam was gazing at her. Very slowly, the pieces were falling into place.

'I know him, don't I? Your father?'

'You do.'

'Oliver Sanderson.'

'Yes. Actually he's my stepfather. My real dad was killed at Mons. I barely remember him. Oliver came on the scene later. Swept my mum off her feet and dragged us all out East. I was in Malaya for the holidays. That hideous school in Edinburgh the rest of the time. As it happens, Dad's in Singapore right now.'

'You know Ballentyne as well?'

'Of course. Andrew and Dad go back years. In fact, he used to spend Christmas with us when I was a kid. He and his wife. Out on the plantation. Lovely man. Nice wife, too. When I was back at school it was Andrew and Daphne who kept an eye on me. They'd come up to Edinburgh at half-term and we'd go off to a place they had on Skye for a week. They were kind of honorary aunts and uncles. If you want the truth, they probably understood me better than my own folks.' She paused, aware of Tam's renewed interest in the view through the window. By now the rowing eight was a speck at the far end of the lake.

'You want me to get you a row? You've certainly got the build for it.'

'Yes, please.'

'How fit are you?'

'Try me.'

She held his gaze for a moment longer than strictly necessary and then ducked her head, reaching for the menu. The fish, she said, was divine. Especially the halibut. When the waiter arrived, Tam ordered a bottle of Gewürztraminer and wondered how best to move the conversation on. To his relief, Bella needed little prompting.

'You know about Runciman?' she asked.

Tam nodded. Lord Runciman, a Tory stalwart, had been despatched to Czechoslovakia by the Prime Minister to try and hold the ring between President Beneš and the Sudeten Germans. According to Ballentyne, his mission was a bid to buy a little time while London and Paris tried to prevent another German lunge at the Czech frontier.

'Am I right?' Tam was pouring the wine.

'That's a generous interpretation. He's there to twist arms and bang heads together. Chiefly Czech heads. London wants Beneš to give the Sudetens everything they're after. The Czechs still have their pride, if little else. Runciman's getting nowhere.'

It was a compelling if brisk analysis. Tam was impressed. He asked her about Henlein.

'I know nothing about Henlein. He's been in town recently to get his orders. There was talk of some private meeting at the embassy but I don't think it ever happened.'

'The Sudetens are lunatics,' Tam said quietly. 'You were probably spared.'

'You've been there? You know these people?'

'I do.'

'You want to tell me more?'

'Not really.' Tam ducked his head, sought a change of subject. 'What's it like here? What's the mood in the streets?' He nodded out towards the lake. 'What do your German friends really think?'

'My rowers, you mean? I'm not sure they pay much attention. Everyone's busy these days. There's no problem with jobs. In fact, there's too much to do. Most of the people I meet seem to assume the country's in good hands and even if it wasn't they wouldn't know what to do about it. It's summer. The sun shines. The Nazis have their fun but everyone knows they're idiots and *Untermensch* so nobody really cares.' She shrugged. 'These are the best of times. So why look for trouble?'

'The Jews?'

'You look the other way.'

'Vienna?'

'It was German anyway.'

'The Czechs?'

'Next on the list. Definitely.'

'As easy as that?'

'Of course.'

'And you? What do you think?'

'I keep quiet most of the time. I'm a foreigner. This isn't my country. But there are women in that boat out there who take Hitler at his word and it frightens them. If I was German he'd frighten me, too.'

'So what would you do about it?'

'*Do* about it?' The question sparked a sudden smile. 'Is that why you're here? To organise some kind of coup?'

The question, so direct, so perceptive, alarmed Tam. He'd spent the morning waiting at his hotel for word from Schultz but nothing had happened. In the end, sick of the limbo to which he seemed to have been assigned, he'd stepped out into the sunshine and spent a couple of hours walking, first along Unter den Linden and later in the Tiergarten. From a bench in the park he'd watched the Berliners in the warmth of the late afternoon and he knew that Bella was right. Young mums pushing prams. Old men playing chess. Children chasing squirrels. In no time at all, these people had seen their country transformed. They were happy. They were well-fed. They had money in their pockets and decent prospects for their kids.

Now, in the restaurant, Tam began to talk about the freedoms the Germans had lost, the ways in which the Nazi state had tightened its chokehold on any form of protest. A free press? Gone. Unions? Barely a memory. The right to oppose the Nazis at the next election, supposing one ever happened? A death sentence.

The restaurant had filled up and some of these people might be speaking English but Tam didn't much care. Individuals counted for nothing in this shiny new Reich and what had happened to Renata was only the start. He had no intention of sharing his experiences in Czechoslovakia but even now he couldn't hide the anger triggered by those memories.

Bella was gazing out at the lake. Then she leaned forward over the table and gestured him closer.

'Henderson flew home this morning,' she said. 'People much wiser than me think something's brewing in London. Our Mr

Chamberlain, God help us, may have a plan. Has that ruined your appetite?' She sat back as the waiter approached. 'Or can you still manage that wonderful fish?'

*

It was nearly dark by the time they left the restaurant. To Tam's relief, Bella appeared to have forgotten her little joke about a coup. Thanks to her father, she obviously knew he had connections to the Intelligence world but with some deftness she kept the conversation light. Berlin, she said, had turned out to be the sweetshop of her wildest dreams, full of mouth-watering treats and unexpected surprises. It might not have the chic of Paris or the mischief of Italy but if you looked hard enough there were clubs and bars and hidden corners of the city that definitely repaid a visit or two. If he was ever in the mood, she'd be very happy to show him around. Otherwise, she wished him good luck.

They took a taxi back. She lived in a block of apartments reserved for foreign personnel. Tam leaned across to open the door, then hesitated. He knew he'd talked too much, especially before the meal arrived.

'That was a lovely evening,' he said. 'If I sounded gloomy, I'm sorry.'

She studied him a moment, then she extracted a small notepad from her bag and scribbled a number. Her face was very close.

'Something's happened to you.' She tore off the sheet of paper and slipped it into his pocket. 'Anything I can do to help, you only have to phone that number.'

'You can get me into the rowing club?'

'That's not what I meant.' She kissed him lightly on the cheek. 'And you know it.'

Moments later she was out of the car. Tam watched her crossing the pavement towards the entrance to the apartment block. Two uniformed soldiers flanking the entrance gave her the Hitler salute. Then she was gone.

Tam's hotel was a two-minute drive away. He paid the driver, took a breath or two of the night air, and then climbed the stairs to his room. He could smell the presence of a stranger before he paused to insert the key. Cigar smoke. And a line of light beneath his door. For a moment he toyed with returning to reception. Then he inserted his key in the door and pushed it open. Half-expecting to find Schultz inside, the only person who knew his whereabouts, he found himself looking at a man who must have been in his sixties. He was fat. He was reading a newspaper, a copy of the *Völkischer Beobachter.* The cigar, still alight, lay in an ashtray on his lap.

He glanced up. He looked irritated by this sudden interruption. He had a thick Berlin accent.

'You're the Englishman?'

'Yes.'

'Come.' He struggled to his feet and carefully folded the newspaper. Twice Tam asked him who he was, what he was doing in the room, but he didn't seem to be listening.

At the old man's insistence, they took the lift down to the lobby. Once they were out of the hotel, Tam refused to move another step unless the old man told him where they were going. Traffic at this time of night was light and the pavement was empty apart from a handful of pedestrians hurrying home from the darkened offices along Wilhelmstrasse.

The old man looked him up and down in the cold throw of the street lights.

'Where are we going?' he repeated. 'You've met Wilhelm Friedrich and you're asking me a question like that?' He shook his head and began to waddle away down the pavement in the direction of the Reich Chancellery. He looked, if anything, disappointed.

Tam watched him for a moment and then set off in pursuit. Then he became aware of a car drawing up beside him. It was black, new-looking. The rear door opened and he had time to glimpse the face in the back. Schultz.

'Get in.' Schultz might have been smiling. 'The old man doesn't expect a tip.'

They drove for perhaps half an hour, maybe more. Schultz offered a gruff apology for what he called 'the comedy' at the Altmark. Like many of the hotels and *pension* that housed foreign nationals, it was under surveillance. The Gestapo had far too big a budget for their own good. How they ever found time to cross-file all their raw intelligence was beyond him. Maybe one day Uncle Heinrich would run out of shelf space and then Germany might breathe a little easier.

'You didn't want to come to the hotel yourself?' Tam asked.

'Of course not. Why make things any easier for those bastards?'

Schultz sat back on the plump leather seat, his legs crossed, his thick fingers drumming on his knees, musing on the way layer after layer of bureaucracy had turned Berlin into a swamp. We Germans are obsessed by paperwork, he said. Write something down, a name, a date, an accusation, *anything*, and we think we've done a good day's work. Not true. Not true *at all*. If you want the truth, he said, we're nothing but native bearers paying tribute to the scum in power.

The scum in power? Tam wanted more, a readier clue to whatever awaited him next, but when he took advantage of a moment of silence and enquired where they might be going, Schultz put a cautionary hand on his knee.

'Trust me,' he said again. 'Why are you English so impatient?'

Their destination lay in an area of woodland outside the city. The villa loomed in the darkness, no lights in any of the windows. Tam got out of the car. A dog on a chain stirred and began to bark. A wind had appeared from nowhere, sighing amongst the branches overhead, and beyond the trees he caught a glimpse of moonlight on water.

Schultz seemed to be waiting for someone. At length the front door opened and the figure of a woman appeared.

'Wilhelm?'

The woman stood aside and Schultz led Tam into the house. The interior had the stillness and the smell of a museum. An assortment of oils on the wall featured a mixture of battle scenes and formal military portraits. A grim-faced general looked sternly down from the landing at the top of a flight of stairs. In the painting he was flanked by twin regimental standards and a hunting dog lay curled at his feet. Beside the painting hung a pair of crossed swords with an inscribed brass plate below. No swastikas anywhere.

The door at the end of the corridor lay slightly ajar. Schultz knocked twice and waited. At length a voice ordered him to come in. Schultz stepped back and gestured for Tam to enter, closing the door behind them

'*Mein General*, Herr Moncrieff. From England.'

The figure behind the desk didn't move. Late middle-aged, Tam thought. A face hollowed out by too little sleep. Buttons loosened on his grey tunic. Watchful eyes.

'Beck.' He introduced himself, then nodded at the empty chair in front of the desk. 'Please sit down. You want something to drink?'

Tam shook his head, politely declined, but the General had already despatched Schultz in search of a bottle. His manicured finger was still anchored on a line of the document spread before him and he returned to whatever he'd been doing, reaching for a pen when he'd got to the bottom of the page.

Beck.

Tam recognised the name. Bella had mentioned it at the restaurant, one of the highlights of Embassy gossip over the past week or so. Until very recently, this man had been Chief of Staff of the German Army, a position of unrivalled power. Then, quite suddenly, he'd resigned and the shock was compounded by the fact that nobody appeared to know why. Old school, Bella had said. Ex-cavalry man but never had any problem with the Nazis. In fact, he was always pushing for an army even bigger than the one Hitler wanted. In short, a real warrior.

Schultz was back with a bottle of French brandy. Beck inspected it at arm's length and then told Schultz to find some glasses. This wasn't his house, he explained to Tam. It belonged to a friend who was sadly indisposed but just now it offered a little welcome privacy.

'You live where, Herr Moncrieff?'

'Scotland.'

'I like Scotland. I like the cold. Even your rain I can put up with.'

Schultz had charged the glasses. He passed them round. Then he proposed a toast.

'To our English friends, Herr General.'

Beck stared at the glass and muttered something Tam didn't catch. Then he was looking Tam in the eye.

'In London they called our Foreign Minister "Brickendrop". Is that true?'

'I'm afraid it is.'

'And what does Brickendrop mean?'

'It means that he offended people. In many ways he was an embarrassment.'

'Because he didn't understand the English?'

'Exactly.'

'But no one understands the English. Ever. Isn't that true? Isn't that what history tells us?'

Tam was fumbling for an answer. Beck spared him the effort.

'In this instance I grant you the English are right. Ribbentrop is a fool. Under the circumstances Brickendrop is kind. I've heard much worse.' He at last took a sip from his glass and then turned to Schultz. 'You've heard about Adam? The West Wall?' Schultz shook his head. 'There was some ruckus yesterday in one of the tunnels. He had words with our leader. The deadlines are impossible and Adam knows it. The triumph of the will is a pretty phrase but it doesn't pour concrete any quicker. You agree, Mr Moncrieff?'

'Of course.'

'Very wise. That puts you in the same camp as General Adam. That man is a fine soldier and probably an even better engineer. He faces two challenges, Mr Moncrieff. One is getting his damn wall in proper shape. The other is Hitler. As I understand it, his big mistake yesterday was voicing his doubts in public. In this regime you do that only once. But General Adam, God help him, takes no notice.'

Schultz asked what had happened. Beck's eye drifted back to the document on the desk. His finger found the quote he wanted.

'General Adam has expressed a personal opinion, once again, about his wall. If we march against the Czechs next month, and the French arrive in earnest, you know how long he thinks his sandcastle will keep them out?'

'No, *Mein General*.'

'No time at all. From this, gentlemen, we can deduce three things. One is that he's probably right. The second is that Hitler will take no notice. And the third is that dear General Adam's days in uniform are undoubtedly numbered. If he's lucky, Hitler will put him out to pasture like an old horse. Otherwise his children will be looking for a new papa by Christmas. Personally, I applaud the man. He has courage. We all have courage. But courage may not be enough. Why not? Because telling the truth in this regime has a habit of making a man an orphan. You awake one morning, and you look around, and quite suddenly there is no one. Absolutely no one.'

He tipped his head and gazed up at the ceiling. Schultz cleared his throat.

'Not quite true, *Mein General*. As we both know.'

Beck fixed him with a long stare. Finally, he nodded. This, he said dismissively, was a conversation for another time and place. Just now he wanted Herr Moncrieff to have no illusions about the difficulties that patriots, men of good faith, faced in Hitler's Germany. A Panzer tank ran on gasoline. The Fatherland ran on naked fear. Hence the Gestapo. Hence the concentration camps like Dachau. And hence the insane race to plunge Europe back into war.

'It can't happen, Herr Moncrieff. We have to put a stop to it.'

'War?'

'Of course.'

'Against the Czechs?'

'Yes.'

'Because the French will march?'

'Yes, and you too I daresay. Do you want that? Do the French want that? Can we afford that? At the moment? Here and now? No, no and again *no*.'

Tam watched his fist descending softly on to the desk. *Afford that* was the key. Beck wasn't taking some Quaker pledge against the very idea of war. On the contrary, he was simply postponing any invasion until the odds looked a great deal better.

'So when do you anticipate marching?' Tam enquired.

'I've no idea. The future looks after itself.'

'But you don't rule it out?'

'Of course not. We're not fools. We're not Ribbentrop. We rule out nothing.'

Beck pushed his chair away from the desk and then stood up. He was taller than Tam had anticipated and command was something he was plainly used to. He toyed with his glass for a moment, eyeing Tam.

'One question, Mr Moncrieff. Just one. And I'd be obliged for a simple answer. Wilhelm tells me you've been in the Sudetenland. I've seen intelligence that suggests you paid their fortifications a visit. You'll tell me that their army is first class and that their defences in the west will give us a very big headache. I know that already. Which is another reason our leader should be giving General Adam the benefit of the doubt.'

'And the question?'

'The question is this. It's very simple. If our leader has his way, if we move against the Czechs, will the English march?'

'I'm not a politician.'

'I understand that. I also understand that you have the ear of people who matter. Your answer, please. A yes or a no will be sufficient.'

Tam nodded. So simple, he thought. All this way, all this effort. Just for a single word. Was he qualified to provide any kind of answer? He didn't care. Would this martinet hold him to account if he got it wrong? He hadn't the slightest idea. But at last his small role in this huge drama was swimming into focus.

'Yes,' he said.

18

PRENZLAUER BERG, BERLIN, 29 AUGUST 1938

Dieter Merz had got Sol Fiedler's address from Beata. Take the tram to Prenzlauer Berg, she'd told him. Get off at Torstrasse. Cross the road by the traffic lights and look for a pastry shop on the corner. If you want to make a friend for life, then take Sol's wife one of their *Franzbrötchen*. If you want two friends for life, ask the woman who runs the shop for a couple of *Pfannkuchen*. Sol says he'll kill for a doughnut. Marta believes him and ties him to the bed when she's got some in the oven. That much cream isn't good for any man, she insists. What's so great about having a husband who dies on you?

The apartment block lay behind the arterial road that ran north-east out of the city. Dieter got off the tram and crossed at the lights. The pastry shop was closed, the blinds lowered. Dieter peered at the handwritten notice carefully taped to the door. Frau Blicken and her family were enjoying a well-earned holiday out on the Baltic Coast. Back for the start of September.

Dieter spotted a bar on the side road that led away from the traffic lights. Flurries of rain had been blowing in the wind, pebbling the windows of the tram, but now the sun was out again. According to Beata, Sol normally left the Institute at five. Allow half an hour for the journey home, and a little time to embrace his wife and take off his shoes, and Dieter would be wise not to appear until six. Dieter checked his watch. He had forty minutes in hand.

The bar was dark after the brightness of the street. Dieter asked for a glass of bock and found himself a table. The bar was filling up fast, a mix of students and workers from the nearby furniture factory. With the scent of newly sawn pinewood came the clack-clack of dominoes and the comforting conversational hum of a day's work put to bed.

Dieter sipped at his beer. Watching Hitler in the tunnel, being so close, had affected him in ways he'd never anticipated. In one sense, as he'd tried to explain to Keiko last night, the whole thing had felt so mundane. Hitler was an ordinary man, for God's sake. Not much to look at, odd haircut, receding chin, funny little moustache, two arms, two legs, the usual ration. Yet in spite of this there was something else lurking inside him, something the colour of the blackest night you could ever imagine, something an earlier age might have blamed on the devil. In front of Dieter's eyes, he'd changed, become possessed, become someone, some*thing* else.

Being in the tunnel hadn't helped. He remembered the dim lighting and the way the voice with its peasant Austrian vowels had bounced back and forth, echo on echo until it emptied itself of all meaning and left nothing but an overwhelming sense of rage.

Rage. Dieter recognised the actor in Hitler, understood the way he wound himself up like a spring, waiting for some internal curtain to rise, eager for the moment when he could launch himself on an audience of tens of thousands or on some luckless individual like General Adam. All this made perfect sense. This was the way Hitler could hold an entire nation in the palm of his hand, this was the stuff of spell-casting and magic. But what he'd seen yesterday, down in the tunnels beneath Hitler's fabled Wall, told him something else. That the magic was dark. And that the way ahead might not be quite what the bulk of his countrymen were so eagerly expecting. Which brought him to Sol Fiedler and the telling little incident, infinitely sad, at Beata's wedding.

Everyone knew about the Jews. You couldn't avoid realising how tough life had become for these people but he'd been shocked by how easy it was to look the other way. Some *Untermensch* of a storm trooper kicking the shit out of a couple of kikes who dared to answer back? The crudest insults daubed on the door of a tailor's shop? Yellow-starred kids, political innocents, hand in hand with their harassed mums? Images like these had become part of the streetscape of every German town but these people were on the very edges of the nation's life and until he'd met Sol at the wedding he hadn't realised how it must feel to be at the receiving end of one of the nastier consequences of Germany's rebirth.

Ribbentrop had been wrong, he'd told Keiko. It wasn't his wedding, his property, his day. He'd absolutely no right to lord it over other people, to play God with a fellow guest who happened to be Jewish. Keiko, for a while, had tried to defend her client. She said he wasn't very bright. She thought he never really understood the consequences of his actions. That's why he was in such trouble in his head, in his heart, in his soul. The man was a muddle, a mess, a tangle of contradictions that probably went back to his childhood. Keiko understood all that because she'd once found herself in a similar place. And that's why she was doing her best to put him right.

Last night, in bed, Dieter had laughed in her face. The gesture was unpardonable and he'd apologised at once, but the thought that *reiki* could turn Joachim von Ribbentrop into a human being was optimism of the richest kind. The man's twisted, he told her, just like so many of them. You're probably right. Life must have been unkind to them in one way or another but should an entire nation suffer the consequences? These people are midgets, he'd told her. Dwarfs. Grotesques. Gargoyles. Goering with his fancy uniforms. Himmler with his growing empire of concentration camps. Ribbentrop with his rich wife. And now the Führer himself. A collection of echoes with a terrifying void behind the blackness of his eyes.

Sol again, riding his bicycle into the same darkness, leaving the champagne and the laughter and the soft evening light behind him as he wobbled off on his ancient bike. God knows what would happen afterwards but these were the first people to suffer, the first victims to taste what probably lay in wait. Dieter reached for his glass and swallowed the last of the beer. At the very least, he owed the man an apology.

*

On the corner of the street where the Fiedlers lived, a gypsy was selling heather. She was old, slightly bent, claw fingers, milky eyes. She pressed three sprigs into Dieter's hand and helped herself to a one RM note when he got out his wallet. They'll bring you luck, she said, turning her back when he enquired about change.

The lobby of the apartment block was spotless. Dieter counted eighteen numbered boxes for mail and there was a wooden chair with a plump, new-looking cushion for anyone who wanted to rest before tackling the stairs. A recess at the back of the lobby contained four bicycles. Dieter gazed at them a moment, trying to remember which one was Sol's.

His apartment was on the third floor. The smell of cooking hung in the warm air and Dieter caught the murmur of wireless sets as he passed door after door. At this time of the evening, people appeared to listen to music rather than the interminable announcements from the Ministry of Propaganda, and Dieter was reminded of a conversation he'd half-overheard just now in the bar. The Czechs beating up those idiots in the Sudeten? How much do they pay Goebbels to invent this rubbish?

The Fiedlers' apartment lay at the end of the corridor. No music. Dieter tapped lightly on the door. At length it opened to reveal a woman in her early forties. She was small and thin, almost bird-like. She was wearing a grey cardigan that she might have knitted herself and her feet were enveloped in a pair of slippers that were far too big. The sight of a stranger at her door plainly alarmed her.

Dieter had started to explain about Beata and the wedding, when Sol appeared behind her. He recognised Dieter at once. He was very welcome. Supper was already on the table but there was plenty extra for a guest. Beef goulash the way the Magyars made it in Budapest. Marta's speciality.

Dieter was already on the point of leaving but Sol held the door wide open, insisting that he come in. The apartment was small and over-furnished, heavy walnut bookcases, a marble-topped dresser and a table laid for two. Dieter recognised a woman's touch in the careful arrangement of knick-knacks on the dresser but what struck him most of all was a wooden perch standing beside the window. On the perch, king of this tiny living room, was a stuffed parrot.

Sol had left to fetch another chair for the table. Dieter asked Marta about the parrot. The question drew a sorrowful shake of the head.

'Ask my crazy husband.' She settled at the table and resumed eating. 'The real one was called Moshe.'

'The real one? You mean this one? Before he died?'

'No. Another one. Ask him. Ask Sol.'

Sol was back with the chair. Dieter sat down while Sol disappeared again to the kitchen, returning with a bowl brimming with silky goulash.

'Eat,' he said.

Dieter reached for a chunk of bread. The goulash was delicious, the paprika not too fierce, the meat dissolving on his tongue. He wanted to know about Moshe the parrot. Moshe meant Moses.

Sol shot his wife a reproving look. Maybe I've happened on a family secret, Dieter thought. Maybe I'm intruding still deeper into this cosy little ménage. Sol took a mouthful of goulash, then another. Finally he nodded at the perch.

'We had a real parrot last year. It belonged to a friend from the Institute. He was leaving Germany and the parrot couldn't go with him and so he gave it to us.'

'This is Moshe?'

'Sure. Moshe was a character. He was very Yiddish, very bright, very outspoken. He also had lots to say. My friend was very patient with him. He'd taught him well.'

Marta interrupted. She'd never wanted the damn bird in the flat, having to clean up all the time, feed it, listen to it, but it was close to Sol's birthday so in the end she'd said yes.

'And?'

'It talked all the time. Talked and talked. Wouldn't stop. Night and day. On and on. Maybe it was missing its owner. I don't know. I told Sol we'd be in trouble with this parrot but Sol never listens, which is fine if you're away all day, but not if you're me, stuck here with nowhere to hide and that bird watching me all the time.'

'Next door,' Sol murmured. 'Tell our young friend about next door.'

'Next door live older people, even older than us. Party people. The walls here are thin. They listen to the radio all the time, all the rubbish they put out.'

'And Moshe. . .?' Another prompt from Sol.

'*Ja*. The damn bird is clever, very clever, but mainly he says just one thing, God help us.' She was looking at her husband, as if to seek permission for whatever came next in the story. Light from the window shone on her glasses, masking her eyes.

'*Heil Moshe!*' Sol was smiling. 'A real squawk, again and again. *Heil Moshe!* He could do it soft. He could do it loud. *Heil Moshe!* God knows how my friend managed it. Maybe he got the parrot to listen to the radio, just to get the accent right. It sounded perfect. Proper Austrian. Be in the next room and you'd think Hitler had moved in.'

'*Ja*.' Marta again. 'You think I want to share my whole life with that man? You think there's not enough of him in the papers? Out on the street?'

The people next door, she said, had complained to the block warden. They said their neighbours, *Jewish* neighbours, were daring to take the Führer's name in vain. The block warden came round to check on the parrot. Sol was out at work. She had to waste some of her precious coffee on the block warden while Moshe did his party piece and afterwards, before he left, he told Marta she had until that night to get rid of the parrot. Otherwise she and her husband were in real trouble.

'So what did you do?' Dieter's spoon hovered over the remains of the goulash.

'I opened the window and threw it out.'

'It flew away?'

'Yes. And then it flew back again. Maybe it was hungry. Maybe it was in love with us. I don't know. But it sat on that windowsill and still pretended to be Hitler. *Heil Moshe!* When Sol came back from work he was still there and the neighbours were banging on the wall and soon the block warden would be round again. In this city they send you to the camps for less.'

She shook her head, visibly distressed, and Sol leaned across the table and put a hand on her thin arm.

'Moshe's gone,' he said. 'We solved it, didn't we?'

Dieter was looking at the stuffed parrot. He wanted to know how.

'There's a shop in Pankow that sells stuffed animals. They do fish and birds too. Another friend of mine had a carp stuffed once, a huge thing. So I went to the shop and bought the parrot. Cost me a fortune but it did the trick because Moshe thought some other parrot had moved in and after that we never saw him again.'

'And the neighbours?'

'They were disappointed. They wanted us gone.'

'The block warden?'

'He was OK. You want the proof?' He gestured round at the living room. 'We're still here.'

Dieter finished the goulash. Then he fumbled in his jacket pocket and produced the sprigs of heather. He gave one to Marta, another to Sol, kept the third for himself.

'For Moshe,' he said. 'To bring him good luck.'

Marta left the heather beside her bowl. For some reason she didn't want to touch it. Sol thanked Dieter and tucked the little sprig into the breast pocket of his shirt. When Dieter said he'd come to apologise for the incident at the wedding, Sol told him it didn't matter. It was Ribbentrop's fault, not Dieter's, but it was foolish to expect anything else. Like so many others in his position, the man had lost touch with what really mattered. If he felt anything about Herr Ribbentrop, he felt pity.

'For him?'

'For his wife. For his children.' He paused. 'Beata tells me you have a Japanese friend.'

'I do. Her name's Keiko.'

'And she attends to Ribbentrop?'

'She tries to help him. You know about *reiki*?'

'No.'

'It's a way of curing people. A way of changing them.'

'Good. I hope she has a lot of patience.' He studied Dieter for a moment or two. 'Do you play chess at all?'

Without waiting for an answer, he fetched a board and a box of pieces and cleared a space on the table to set up the game. From the kitchen, he fetched a bottle of schnapps and poured two glasses. When Marta announced she was taking the dog next door to the bedroom he gave her a hug and said he'd be along later. Watching his eagerness to get back to the table, Dieter wondered how often this couple had visitors to their flat.

Sol gave Dieter first move. From the outset, Sol played the game with an intuitive brilliance that Dieter had never encountered before. He also played at breakneck speed, seeming to read Dieter's mind the moment he deployed a particular piece, blocking here, countering there, making life tougher and tougher while all the time preparing a final set of moves of such murderous elegance that Dieter was obliged to surrender his king with a muttered apology for his own naivety. Marta, thankfully, had closed the bedroom door.

'You play often?' Sol enquired after Dieter's third straight annihilation.

'I played a lot in Spain. It kept us out of the bars. Now it's harder to find the time.'

'Your lady doesn't play?'

'My lady plays a different kind of chess. She doesn't need a board.'

'What does that mean?'

'She lives up here.' Dieter tapped his head. 'She's very Japanese. She gives nothing away.'

'And you can live with that?'

'I depend on that. All my life I've been looking for someone...' He frowned, hunting for the right word.

'Someone what?'

'. . . someone who doesn't give all of themselves away. I fall in love too easily. I fall in love and the girl is all over me and months later, sometimes only weeks later, I'm bored to death because I know every inch of them. Then it happens all over again, another girl and another girl and pretty soon I'm knocking on Georg's door and begging him to come out and get drunk with me because I can't face the prospect of going home to whoever it might be. It gets to be like a book you've read before. Some people say there are only a dozen stories in the world. Maybe that's true.'

'And Keiko?'

'I still don't know her story. And that's exciting.'

'Will you ever know?'

'I hope not.'

'So will it ever end?'

'Ask Georg. He's much wiser than me.'

Sol smiled. Then he nodded at the board and suggested another game. Dieter shook his head. He enjoyed this man's company immensely. Sol had the gift of listening, of asking the right questions, of getting in close and unlocking secrets you'd rarely shared with anyone. In a dogfight, Dieter suspected he'd be close to unbeatable. He'd manoeuvre the way he talked, the way he played chess, taking advantage of the smallest opportunity, the merest glimpse of weakness, but just now, on the chessboard, Dieter had lost his taste for humiliation.

'Tell me about the Institute,' he said. 'Is what you do secret?'

'Yes. But it's complicated, too. We try and reduce matter to its essence. Do atoms and molecules mean anything to you?'

'No.'

'That's as it should be. Leave this stuff to us. Think of one of those spiral mazes. Get closer and closer to the middle and in the end you might be looking at a very big bang.'

'Literally? Some kind of explosion?'

'We hope so. That's what the science tells us. Split the atom in a certain way and you might blow up half the world.'

'And that's a good thing?'

'It might be. As long as you lived on the other half.'

Split the atom. Dieter hadn't a clue what this meant. Did you need a special atom? Or would any do?

'Uranium. That's where it begins and ends. Uranium's radioactive. It has special properties. Dig it out of the ground and it can do you harm. Enrich this stuff, make it really pure, and who knows what might be possible?'

'You've got lots of it?'

'Enough for our purposes. It's hard to lay hands on. Much rarer than gold.'

'We mine it here? In Germany?'

'No.'

'Where, then?'

'Czechoslovakia. Africa, too. There's lots in the Congo.'

Sol began to pack the chess pieces away, returning them carefully to their box. Dieter watched him for a moment or two. His next question, he knew, was only too obvious.

'And you think you may succeed one day?'

'Succeed in what?'

'Being able to blow up half the world.'

Sol put the lid on the box and stored it under the dresser. Then he turned round again.

'Are you religious? A man of God?'

'Not really.'

'But just sometimes? When things are really tough?'

'Then yes. Maybe I am.'

'Good. Then the answer is yes. One day someone will split the atom.' He reached out and cupped Dieter's face in his hands. 'Just pray it doesn't happen here.'

19

BERLIN, 30 AUGUST 1938

Next day, Tam Moncrieff awaited word from Wilhelm Schultz. Nothing happened. This, thought Tam, was odd. These people have taken a look at me. I appear to have been signed up for some role in what they plan to do next. Yet the detail – what they expect me to do – is as vague as ever.

At lunchtime he telephoned Bella. She was busy but said she could spare twenty minutes at her office in the embassy. He found her surrounded by a mountain of paperwork and a half-eaten orange. Twenty minutes had just become ten. He had to be quick. He gave her a name. Thomas Kreisky.

'Have you ever heard of him?'

She put the orange to one side, then nodded.

'Yes,' she said. 'Why do you ask?'

'Because I'd like to meet him.'

'Is this something private? Personal?'

'It might be.'

'I only ask because the man's a banker. He's an American, as you probably know, and I understand he's brilliant at what he does. He represents a number of interests in New York. I have it on very good authority that the regime loves him. Apparently he does them all kinds of favours.'

'Like?'

'Money, mainly. He puts together funding syndicates. There are also occasions when he can keep Germany's name off the table. In this city that can be a very big help. You're telling me you want to do business with him?'

'No.'

'Just as well. The man's a shark.' She glanced at her watch. Then she rummaged in a drawer for a file and extracted an address. 'The regime keeps an eye on Kreisky, as you might imagine, and so do we.' She gave Tam the address and then found a card and handed it over. 'He goes to this place a lot, early evenings. It's a club, the Kasbah. It's near where he lives. It seems the man has some fearsome appetites. If you really want to meet him, you might start there.'

Tam was looking at the address. He glanced up.

'What kind of club are we talking about?'

'Homosexuals, mainly. Kreisky is a man who likes risk. The regime frowns on his sort but he's useful enough to be left alone. The club is discreet. Friends in high places keep it open. They say Kreisky will fuck anything. And not just in business.'

*

Tam returned to his hotel to find still no word from Schultz. Several hours later, after another lengthy wait, he took a tram out to the suburb where Kreisky lived.

Workmen were hanging brand new swastika banners the length of Wilhelmstrasse and, sitting in the tram, Moncrieff wondered whether another of the interminable military parades that featured on the British newsreels might be in the offing. Hitler, as he now knew, had a habit of raising the nation's blood pressure ahead of the next military adventure, and now might be just the time to march a division or two through the city to impress the locals. Poor bloody Czechs, he thought.

Kreisky's apartment block was a five-minute walk from the tram stop. It was built in the Bauhaus style, emphatically modern, but a line of linden trees at the kerbside softened the harsher angles. A bench across the road offered a perfect view of the plate-glass doors at the building's entrance and Tam settled down in the sunshine to keep watch.

Over the next couple of hours, men and the occasional woman hurried down the street and disappeared into the apartment block across the road. None of them looked remotely like Kreisky. As far as he could judge, entry meant getting past the concierge on the door, a smartly uniformed figure whose watchful courtesies suggested a wealthy clientele, but what Tam had in mind for the American banker depended on Tam himself keeping a low profile. Kreisky might, or might not, make an appearance. But either way, Tam knew he had no choice but to wait.

Kreisky appeared towards eight o'clock in the evening, delivered to the apartment block by a taxi. He seemed shorter than Tam remembered from the surveillance photo he'd seen but there was no mistaking the face, especially the little goatee beard. He greeted the concierge with a nod and a passing touch on the arm and disappeared into the building. Barely minutes later he was out on the street again. Tam gave the portly figure a fifty-metre start and crossed the road to follow him.

Kreisky was walking slowly, pausing to light what looked like a small cigar. Tam caught a glimpse of his face as the match sparked and moments later, on the move again, he could smell the cigar. A park lay off to the left. Dusk was falling and Kreisky had stopped once more, this time beside a telephone box. Tam paused, watching him picking up the receiver and waiting to be connected. Twice Kreisky checked his watch, then he talked for no more than thirty seconds, replaced the receiver and walked on. Beyond the park, he stopped to check the traffic and then crossed the road. Tam followed, still comfortably behind.

Ahead, beyond what looked like a school, were a series of side streets. Kreisky had disappeared. Tam quickened his step, trying to remember the address of the club. A couple of hundred metres later he recognised the street name. He turned the corner. It looked residential. He stopped, confused. Then came a voice, very close, very soft, an American accent.

'You're looking for the Kasbah?'

Tam could feel the presence of the man behind him. He turned round. Kreisky.

'I am.' Tam smiled down at him. 'Is this the right street?'

'It is. You'll need a word or two at the door to get in. I don't recall your face.'

'You wouldn't. I'm a visitor. Passing through.'

Kreisky was wearing just a hint of perfume. His eyes were blue in the paleness of his face and his smile revealed a set of stained teeth, two of them capped in gold.

'You're Scots?'

'Yes.'

'You have business in the city? Friends maybe? Someone who told you about our little fuck palace?'

Tam didn't answer. He'd sparked Kreisky's interest. He could see it in the smile that played around the fleshiness of his lips. This lanky stranger was a prospect. He might merit a little investment. Maybe a drink or two. By which time it would be dark.

'You really know the place?' Tam looked him in the eye. 'Or am I wasting my time?'

*

The club was busy, couples everywhere, all men. Two young boys were at the door to hand out masks. There was a choice of a mask on a hand stick or a mask with a loop of elastic to keep it in place. Tam chose the elastic. His mask belonged on a woman: a flourish of eyebrows, wildly dramatic cheekbones and a mouth rimmed in scarlet lipstick. He modelled it for Kreisky, who extended a hand.

'Come meet some friends of mine. What do I call you?'

'Rory. You?'

'Seymour.' Kreisky gave his hand a squeeze. 'Be frank with me, Rory. How much time do we have?'

'Three hours. I have to be elsewhere by midnight.'

'Perfect. This is young Hans. Behind the mask he has the sweetest, softest mouth. Say hi to my new friend, Hans.'

Hans was shirtless below the mask. He'd oiled his upper body and it gleamed in the candlelight. He put his arms around both Kreisky and Tam. He smelled of recent sex.

'As you can probably gather, Rory, Hans is a busy boy. Special favours for the English. *Very* special favours if you happen to be Scots. Do I hear that right, *Liebling*?'

'Always.' Hans nodded towards a door beyond the tiny crescent of the bar, hung with fake-looking gemstones. 'Now? Or later?'

Tam shook his head. He said he was with Seymour. He didn't want jealousy to wreck a perfect evening.

'This man? Seymour? *Jealous*?' Hans was rocking with laughter. 'To be jealous you have to be human. Seymour's a machine. He eats people alive. Small extra charge but – hey – what's money *for*?'

Kreisky pulled Tam away. Bad company, he said. Bad, bad boy. They went to a booth beyond the dance floor, picking their way between couples moving slowly to a couple of jazz musicians on the raised stage. One after another, they each broke off to drape a languid hand over Kreisky and ask about his new friend. Nice and tall, one of them said. Interesting, purred another. Godlike, a third.

'Sure. And speaks better German than you guys. I like a man with a tongue in his mouth.'

From the booth, Kreisky summoned the waiter and ordered French champagne. He wanted to know more about Tam.

'You're in the military, a build like that. Lean. Mean. Spot guys like you a mile off.'

'You're right.' Tam went along with the fiction.

'Army?'

'Royal Marines.'

'On attachment?'

'On holiday. I have a sister who used to work in Berlin. She's the one who told me about this place.'

'That was nice of her. How come she knew about it?'

'Her ex-husband. He went missing for a day or two. The last place she looked was here, by which time it was too late. He was besotted with a young Italian guy. Luigi offered to sleep with them both but she'd only do it with him.'

'And?'

'The husband divorced her. She lives in Naples now with the handsome Luigi. Loves it.'

Kreisky had a mask on a stick. He dropped it briefly. His face wasn't built for smiling but he was doing his best.

'That was a very good story,' he said. 'Tell me you didn't make it up.'

'Of course I made it up.'

'A soldier with a sense of humour. Exciting. Did you make that up, too?'

'What?'

'About being a soldier?'

'Maybe. Maybe not. Life's a game, Seymour. Behind the mask we could be anyone.'

The champagne arrived. The waiter, a young Moroccan, popped the cork and blew Kreisky a kiss. Kreisky ignored him.

'*Prosit*,' he lifted his glass. 'I've got a place down the road or there's a park I know. Me, I'd prefer the great outdoors but I'm not a greedy man. Your call, my friend, not mine.'

*

It was dark by the time they left the club. Tam was lightly drunk. He let Kreisky link arms and they pursued their shadows down the pavement towards the main road. Back in the booth, over a second bottle of champagne, Tam had gently led the conversation to Czechoslovakia. When he said he'd never been to the place, Kreisky had advised him to not to leave it too late. Beautiful women, boys with a playful sense of humour, and some fine cuisine if you knew where to lay hands on it. Cross the border tomorrow, he said, and you'll have the week of your life. Leave it until October and the show will be over.

'You know that?'

'I do, my friend. Always trust an American. We travel often and we travel well and we always have an eye for a bargain. In Czech-land the low-hanging fruit is unbelievable. And I'm not just talking about the boys.'

'You're a businessman? You do business there?'

'I do. Did. It's over now but it was fun.'

It's over now but it was fun.

At the main road, they paused for a moment at the kerbside. The beckoning darkness of the park seemed to stretch for ever and when Kreisky's hand found his, Tam fought the urge to bring this charade to an early end. Renata, he thought. Renata at ease amongst her own people. Renata with Edvard. Renata leaving the bar in Prague and making her way back to the Sudetenland to try and find her lover. Renata curled in the boot of the Opel, her mouth gagged, her bowels exploding. It was Kreisky who'd put her in harm's way, Kreisky who'd manipulated the sale of the mine, Kreisky who'd traded a life for a fatter share of the profits. Since flying out of Prague, Tam had been waiting for an opportunity to hold this man to account. And now, on a warm evening in a quiet Berlin suburb, here it was.

Wait. Be patient.

They crossed the road. A hundred metres took them to the entrance of the park. Kreisky had drunk most of the last bottle of champagne. He held his drink well but he'd begun to lower his guard. If Tam had a day or two to spare, if his sister could bear to part with him, there might be a way he could show

Tam places in Prague, in Brno, even in goddam Karlovy Vary, he'd never forget.

'You'd like that? You'd like to come along with me? Take in some sights? Meet one or two people? Have a fine time?' He pulled Tam to a halt. They were deep in the park now, the lamp posts along the path shedding a soft, yellow light. Kreisky was gazing up at him, his eyes moist. 'You know something else? That mask of yours was just great. But the real thing? Even better. Kiss me. . .'

His hands reached up for Tam's face. Tam shook his head.

'Not here,' he said. 'Over there.'

He led Kreisky away from the path and on to the grass. As far as Tam could judge, the park was empty. Cloaked in darkness, he brought Kreisky to a halt. Nearby he could make out what looked like an ornamental pond, surrounded by a tumble of rocks. Back on the road, hundreds of metres away, a truck rumbled past.

Finally Tam stopped. Kreisky began to fumble with the waistband of his trousers, then swore as his fingers snagged on the buttons of his fly.

'On your knees,' Tam said.

Something in Tam's voice, a new note, brought Kreisky's head up.

'That's my line,' he said.

'Just do it.'

'Me first, you mean?'

'Yes.'

Kreisky nodded, uncertain. Then he reached for Tam's fly. 'OK, buddy. I guess this round's on me.'

'My pleasure.'

Tam's knee caught him under the chin. Kreisky's head jerked back and his mouth opened as he fought for air. His hands clutched at nothing, flailing in the darkness. He tried to scream but could manage nothing but a thin wheeze. Prone on the grass, he stared up at Tam. At last he managed to swallow a little of the pain.

'Shit,' he managed. 'You guys like it rough.'

Tam straddled his chest and drove his fist as hard as he could into the very middle of his face. First one fist, then the other. Then again. And again. The remains of Kreisky's nose was pumping blood.

Tam stopped. Waited. Kreisky was moaning, barely conscious. Finally his eyes fluttered open.

'You're going to kill me?'

'Not yet.'

Kreisky stared up at him, trying to make sense of the answer, of this abrupt shift in his fortunes, trying to understand. Then his hand went to his face, mopping at the blood.

'What does it take?' he whispered through his broken teeth. 'A thousand? Two thousand? We're talking US here. Dollars. Ten thousand?'

'Tell me about Edvard. Edvard Kovač.'

'I've never heard of him.'

'A woman called Renata?'

'I don't know what you're talking about.'

'Little town called Jáchymov? The Hotel Kavalerie?'

Silence this time. Tam asked the question again. Kreisky was terrified now and it showed in his eyes.

'Never,' he said. 'I never went there.'

'You're lying. You were at the hotel. You met Kovač. And afterwards there was Renata, too.'

'Never.' He shook his head. 'I've never set foot in the Sudetenland.'

'Then how do you know about Karlovy Vary?'

'Rumour. Hearsay. Call it a guess. Call it any fucking thing you like. I'm a businessman. I make an honest living. People rely on me. Sure, I earn good money but why the hell shouldn't I?' He paused for breath. He'd begun to hyperventilate. Finally, he was back in control of himself. 'Twenty-five thousand and we'll call it quits. How does that sound?'

'You had the woman killed. Either that or you shot her yourself.'

'You're crazy.'

'And probably Kovač, too. For what? For money. You know what that woman must have suffered before she died? Have you any idea?'

Kreisky shook his head. He was whimpering now, small animal noises that seemed to lodge in his throat. Tam told him to turn over.

'Why?'

'Just do it.'

'You're gonna kill me?'

'Turn over.'

When nothing happened, Tam hauled him to his feet then pushed him roughly to his knees, facing out towards the darkness. Then he made a gun from his two fingers and put them behind Kreisky's ear, very light, very gentle, just tickling the hairs on the nape of his neck. 'This is a gun. It happens to be a Czech gun. I don't suppose you even knew her name, did you?'

Kreisky shook his head. 'Don't,' he said. 'Don't kill me. Please don't kill me.'

Tam was staring down at him.

'All I want is the truth,' he said. 'About Renata.'

'And you won't kill me?'

'I won't shoot you.'

'She was there. You're right. I met her. The rest I don't know about. You're telling me she's dead? I never knew that. On my word, I never knew that.'

'You're lying.'

'God help me, I'm not.'

Tam heard a dog in the distance. He looked round. There was a figure on the path, close to one of the lamp posts. From a distance it looked like a woman. She had a dog on a lead. The dog had started to bark and she was peering into the darkness in Tam's direction.

Tam froze. Then he put Kreisky in a chokehold, settled one knee in the small of his back, tensed for a moment and then jerked hard. The body beneath him went suddenly limp. Tam thought his neck was broken but he couldn't be sure. His hands were covered in blood.

Tam got to his feet, grunting with the effort. The woman on the path had spotted movement in the darkness. The dog was off the lead, bounding across the grass. Tam took a final look at Kreisky, then stirred his body with his foot. Was he dead? He didn't know. The dog had arrived, some kind of terrier. It was panting with excitement. Tam was good with dogs. He knelt beside it, fondling it, gentling it as the animal licked the blood from his hands. With luck, he thought, it might eat what was left of Kreisky's face.

Tam looked up for a moment, checking to make sure the woman was still on the path. Then he headed deeper into the darkness of the park. After a while he found a stream and knelt beside it and did his best to clean himself. The water was colder than he expected and he splashed it on his face, watching the tiny figures in the far distance, silhouetted against the street lamps. Torch beams told him that the police must have arrived in force. He watched them for a moment and then he spotted a footbridge that led across the stream. On the far side of the park was an unlocked gate beside another main road. Minutes later he'd found a public phone. He'd committed Bella's number to memory.

'Who is this, please?'

'It's me. Tam.' He read her the location of the phone from the placard in the box. 'I need a little help.'

She was there within half an hour, driving – of all cars – an Opel. Tam had been hiding in a recess beside a garage. He hurried across the pavement and ducked into the car. Bella saw the blood at once, thinly diluted by the water.

'Have you hurt yourself?'

'No.'

'What happened?'

'Just drive. Please.'

She put the car in gear and headed back into the city. Twice they passed police cars speeding out towards the park.

'I'm afraid I can't go back to the hotel. Not like this.'

'You're right. Come back to my place. But be careful what you say.'

'Why?'

'Listening ears. We need another story. You've been out late. You're drunk. I've brought you home. You lucky, lucky man.'

Tam spared her a glance. He could still picture Kreisky kneeling on the damp grass, still feel his neck pinioned in the angle of Tam's arm, still remember the moment his body went limp.

'I think I killed a man tonight,' he said softly. 'I think that's something you should know.'

'Was it Kreisky?'

'Yes.'

'That could be a problem.' She might have been smiling. 'But nothing we can't resolve.'

Part Three

20

POTSDAM, BERLIN, 31 AUGUST 1938

It was still dark when Dieter jerked awake. Someone was hammering at the door downstairs. He rolled over, feeling for Keiko. She was still asleep, her mouth barely open, her face a mask.

Dieter got out of bed, reaching for Keiko's dressing gown. He could hear shouting now, two voices, both male.

'Merz!' one yelled. '*Raus!*'

Downstairs, the stone floor of the old stable was cold underfoot. Thieves, Dieter told himself, were masters of silence. These people weren't thieves.

He opened the door. Not two men but three, all uniformed, all Gestapo. The leader pushed past him without a word, then gestured for the others to follow. Dieter half-turned, the door still open behind him, aware of the thunder of boots on the wooden staircase.

He could hear Keiko now. She was calling his name. Then came the slap of flesh on flesh and she began to scream.

Dieter was already halfway up the stairs. The tiny passage to the bedroom was blocked by one of the men. Dieter tried to push past, glimpsing Keiko. The leader had pinned her against the bedroom wall, naked, while the other man tore a blanket off the bed. Seconds later, they wrapped her in the blanket and hustled her towards the door.

Dieter tried to fight but it was hopeless. He landed a couple of blows on the third policeman but found himself looking at a Luger automatic. The leader had wrestled Keiko past and was heading for the stairs.

'If Merz is trouble,' he yelled over his shoulder, 'shoot the little bastard.'

Dieter demanded to know what was going on. Where was the paperwork? On whose authority had these people even arrived?

'Ask your poxy friend Ribbentrop.' It was the leader again. '*Heil Hitler!*'

The two policemen left the house with Keiko. Moments later, Dieter heard the cough of an engine and a grinding of gears as the car nosed away. Dieter was still facing the gun. The remaining policeman gestured towards the bedroom and told him to get changed. Something warm. Something suitable.

'Suitable for what?'

'More visitors,' the man was close to apologetic. 'They're on their way, I'm afraid.'

They arrived within minutes in a black van. There were four of them, all in plain clothes. Dieter sat downstairs in the tiny kitchen, still facing the policeman with the gun while they tore the house apart. Not a word of explanation or apology, just a grim-faced determination not to leave a single object intact. Cupboards were emptied, drawers ransacked, Keiko's personal bag, in scarlet and yellow silks, seized and carried out into the darkness. Upstairs, the floor joists trembled as the bed was upended and subject to detailed inspection. One of the search party descended with something black and metallic in his hand, festooned with tape. He put it on the kitchen table in front of Dieter.

'It's a listening device,' he announced. 'Yours?'

'Of course not.'

'Then whose?'

'I've no idea. I thought you people knew everything. Where's my girl gone? What's all this about?'

The searcher shook his head. These weren't questions for him. He was simply here to do his job. And now it was over. He led his men back to the van without a backward glance at the chaos he'd left behind. Shortly afterwards, the policeman holstered his Luger, bade Dieter a solemn farewell and stepped into the thin light of dawn. He must have arrived on two wheels because Dieter heard the roar of a powerful motorbike before silence descended once again.

An hour, he thought. Maybe less. An hour for your entire life to be demolished in the hands of strangers. Who had sent these animals? And why? Dieter shook his head, mounting the stairs, approaching the open bedroom door, viewing the wreckage inside. A book of haiku he recognised as a treasure of Keiko's had been destroyed, the pages ripped from the binding. A favourite print from Nagasaki, mounted and framed, had been smashed to pieces, and beside it, torn to shreds, lay a clutch of souvenir photos he'd brought back from Japan.

Dieter stared down at the remains of the life he'd shared with Keiko. This was wanton, violence for the sake of violence, a shove in the chest writ large. He felt utterly helpless, but angry, too. This is the way it must happen to the Sol Fiedlers of this world, he told himself. No logic. No apology. No hint of explanation. Just the glorious certainty that other people – their possessions, their loved ones, their very lives – were there for the taking.

He wondered about the time. He always slept with his watch under his pillow. It was a special watch, a Stowa Marine based on an old naval pocket watch, and it had been a presentation trophy from the happy days in Northern Spain. It marked his twenty-fifth kill in the war against the Reds. He began to lift sheets and blankets and the splintered remains of the wooden bedframe until finally he found it, the case stamped on and wrecked, the broken hands frozen at 04.17.

*

Georg was preparing breakfast for Beata when Dieter arrived. They were still living in the house by the lake while Georg tried to find a place of their own. Dieter knocked on the door and then walked in. He could hear Beata upstairs in the bathroom. She was singing.

Georg turned round to find Dieter behind him. Georg swam every morning in the lake. He'd wound a towel around his midriff and his hair was still plastered to his scalp.

'It's barely seven.' Georg tapped his watch. 'We're not flying until midday.'

Dieter told him what had happened. Keiko had been arrested, the house turned over. He was determined to find out why but he didn't know where to start. Georg, still laying out gherkins and thin slices of cheese to go with the black bread, listened without comment. Dieter came to the end of the story. In all, he said, there'd been seven of them. And he hadn't got a single name to put to a face.

'Gestapo?'

'Yes.'

'Himmler's lot, then.' Georg fetched eggs from a cupboard and plunged them into boiling water. 'Any reason you can think of?'

'None.'

'Honestly?' Georg turned to face Dieter. Since their earliest days together in Spain there'd been an unspoken acceptance that they'd be straight with each other. This respect for the truth, for the order of things, had always come naturally to Georg, less so to Dieter.

'She's done nothing,' Dieter said.

'Meaning you trust her.'

'Of course.'

'But you don't actually *know*.'

'It's the same thing. I know her well enough to trust her.'

'But you keep telling me how mysterious she can be. How she keeps bits of herself to herself. I hate to say it but Himmler's boys just love a challenge like that. Maybe you should go to Prinz-Albrecht-Strasse and join the queue at the front desk, just like everyone else. The Gestapo never listen but if you play the boyfriend it might just make a difference.'

Prinz-Albrecht-Strasse housed Gestapo headquarters. The interrogation cells were in the basement, poorly soundproofed. Georg's bluntness offended Dieter. He'd come for advice and perhaps just a little sympathy.

'Ever thought of the Gestapo yourself?' he said. 'I hear the overtime rates are more than generous.'

The sarcasm was wasted on Georg. He was grinding beans for fresh coffee.

'So what did they find?' he asked.

Dieter mentioned the microphone. Georg looked up from the grinder.

'Where was it?'

'Hidden in the bed frame.'

'And you didn't know?'

'Of course not. We had better things to do. There was a transmitter, too, up in the roof space.'

Georg nodded. He wanted to know what might have been of interest to listening ears.

'Nothing. I just told you.'

'She's still seeing Ribbentrop?'

'She's still treating him.'

'You think there's a difference?'

'I know there is.'

'That may be true. Or it may not. But the difference will be lost on lots of other people. If you want a list you'll need a very big sheet of paper. Ribbentrop's only talent is for making enemies.'

'You really think this is to do with Ribbentrop?'

'Of course it is. There's a war going on just now and every bullet has his name on it. Your lady's caught in the crossfire. Anything that might hurt him. *Anything*.'

'Thanks.' Dieter was reeling. This was worse than this morning. He sat down at the kitchen table, closed his eyes, asked the one question that mattered. 'How do you know all this?'

'I fly these people. They're wolves, most of them. The slightest opportunity, the slightest hint of weakness, they're at your throat. Just now, most of them are shitting their pants about the Czech thing. They think Hitler's gone insane and they blame Ribbentrop for feeding him what he wants to hear. I get it from Goering. From Goebbels. From the senior army generals, those that are left. They talk amongst themselves. Sometimes they even talk to me. All I have to do is listen.'

'And Himmler?'

'Himmler's different. Himmler won't jump until he's absolutely sure where he's going to land. That's why he needs all those microphones, all that intelligence.'

'All those cells.'

'Indeed. Not a pretty thought. I'm sorry for your lady. I'm sorry for you, *compadre*. But maybe it's better to understand the way things are. We live in a zoo. Beware of the animals.'

Dieter nodded. Georg, as ever, was right.

'So what do I do?' Dieter asked.

'I'm flying Ribbentrop tomorrow. You should come along, try and talk to the man. It's either that or Prinz-Albrecht-Strasse. Ribbentrop is a fool but he'll do you no harm. Himmler's someone you should avoid at all costs.'

'Dieter! At this hour?'

It was Beata. She was standing in the open doorway, dressed for another day at the Institute. Dieter struggled to his feet and embraced her. She sensed at once that something was wrong but when Dieter began to explain, Georg cut him short. He'd tell Beata the full story later. In the meantime she needed a proper breakfast.

'All this is for her?' Dieter nodded at the table.

'She's eating for two,' Georg grunted. 'And it's for you and me as well.'

'Two?' Dieter was staring at Beata. 'You're telling me you're pregnant? Already?'

'I'm afraid so.' Beata was beaming. 'I'd blame my husband but that would be unkind. Make a note in your diary. Twentieth of April. Next year.'

'That's the Führer's birthday.'

'I know. But she's bound to be late.'

'She?' Georg was looking horrified.

'She,' Beata confirmed. 'I made a wish.'

*

Tam awoke to find the bed empty. For a moment, uncertain where he was, he lay motionless, replaying the events of last night. For years, in the hands of experts, he'd been trained in the applications of extreme violence. He knew how to shoot someone at implausible range with pinpoint accuracy. He knew how to use a grenade and a knife. He could plot ambushes, lay booby traps, and bring someone down at close quarters with his bare hands. That was what his years in the Marines had taught him. That was his trade. Yet he'd never tried to kill anyone before. Not for real.

From next door came the fall of water into a shower tray. A minute or two later, Bella was back in the bedroom, enveloped in an enormous dressing gown. She began to dry her hair with a towel, standing beside the bed.

'Tell me exactly what happened,' she said.

Tam gazed up at her. Last night, she'd insisted they slept together for the benefit of the hidden microphones. Now, they didn't appear to matter. He asked her why.

'The whole block has been checked,' she said. 'We shipped people across from London.'

'And?'

'They found microphones everywhere. Snip the right wires and you send the message you hope these people understand.'

'So last night. . .?'

'Was good. A girl deserves a little attention. You?' She sat on the side of the bed and kissed him softly on the mouth. 'I have a girlfriend back in London. She works for Oliver. She met you at the flat in Mayfair. Evidently you made quite an impact. You should be proud of yourself.'

Tam frowned. He remembered the woman. She'd arrived with a couple of files for her boss. He thought her name might have been Jenny.

'She was only there for fifteen minutes.'

'Fifteen minutes can be enough.' Bella kissed him again. 'Though longer might be better.' She lingered on the bed a moment, then shook her hair out and stood up.

'Do you sleep with strange men a lot?' Tam was watching her getting dressed. She was expected at the embassy in less than half an hour and the woman responsible for timekeeping was evidently merciless.

'You mean with every man who comes along?' She was wrestling with a garter belt.

'Yes.'

'Then the answer's no. But it happens maybe more than it should. That would certainly be my mother's view, though probably not my step-dad's. Women in this country have a very different attitude. Though I'm not sure I should be telling you that.'

'Maybe I know already.'

'Maybe you do. Most men I've met view women as the enemy. You're different. We might even end up friends. Bit of a find really. Clever old me, eh?'

Tam asked again about Kreisky. On balance he thought he was probably dead. Bella said she'd make some discreet enquiries. She had a reliable contact in the Kripo who owed her a favour.

'Is that a confession?' Tam gestured at the bed.

She gazed at him a moment, then turned to the mirror and ran her fingers through her hair. She wore no make-up.

'It's a she, if you were wondering. We compare notes. It's very liberating.' She stepped back from the mirror for a final check, then stooped low over the bed.

'So what exactly happened? Last night? Are you going to tell me?'

'No.'

'Shame.' She kissed him on the lips. 'One favour? Please?'

'Anything.'

'Try not to kill anyone else,' she said lightly. 'Otherwise the game's probably up.'

*

Tam left Bella's apartment a couple of hours later. She'd phoned from the embassy and told him to expect a courier with a new shirt. Tam, trying it on, was impressed. The lightest blue stripe on white cotton and a perfect fit across the chest. With the shirt came a plain brown paper bag and a scribbled note telling him to leave the old shirt in a waste bin on the street. *Remember to take the tags out just in case*, she'd written. *It's got to look German, not English.* Good advice, he thought. Commendable attention to detail.

He dumped the paper bag in a half-empty bin midway between the apartment block and the hotel. As he entered the hotel the woman behind the reception desk presented him with an envelope. Tam waited until he was back in his room before opening it. It came from Schultz. It was handwritten in German and it sounded urgent. *We need to meet. The entrance to the Tiergarten by Pariser Platz. Find a street phone. Call this number and just say yes or no. If yes, give me a time as close to midday as possible.*

Tam knew there was a phone on Wilhelmstrasse, a two-minute walk away. He checked his watch. It was already nearly eleven. He left the hotel and waited in a three-man queue for the phone, scanning the boulevard for signs that he was being watched. The image of Kreisky's face wouldn't leave him. The way he clutched his throat. The fear in his eyes. And that final moment when his neck snapped and his body went limp. When the operator at last made the connection there was no voice on the line, just a cavernous silence. Tam paused a moment. Then hung up.

He found the church by accident. He'd walked the length of Wilhelmstrasse, stopping from time to time to check behind him. It was lunchtime by now and the pavements were crowded with office workers hurrying to join the queues outside the cheaper cafés. A handwritten placard at a street corner was advertising an organ recital in the Deutscher Dom, pieces by Handel and J. S. Bach. Tam followed the arrow. The church was barely yards away, the big oak door an inch or two ajar. Tam mounted the steps, checking behind him yet again, and then slipped inside.

The church was dark and cool after the brightness of the street and he stopped for a moment to let his eyes adjust. A scatter of listeners had settled in the body of the church, mainly older men, most of them alone. Tam found an unoccupied pew and did his best to make himself comfortable. He needed, above all, to think.

He didn't regret killing Thomas Kreisky. Far from it. But he recognised that he'd crossed a line and he needed to anticipate what might lie in wait on the other side. This, after all, was a society wedded to violence. The price of a life, even an entire country, was alarmingly cheap. And so the old rules and restraints he'd so recently taken for granted no longer applied. To survive in a place like this you had to be quick and you had to be ruthless. Otherwise, in Bella's words, the game was probably up.

The concert over, Tam was last out of the church. He followed the organist towards the door and stood in the sunshine for a while, enjoying the warmth on his upturned face. The music had worked in ways his poor mad father had always promised. Peace was a big word but he felt quieter inside himself, more settled. He'd done what he'd done, and now he must deal with the consequences.

Back on Wilhelmstrasse, he returned to the telephone. He gave the operator the same number and waited for her to make the connection. Across the boulevard he could see arms pointing skywards. He could hear the steady growl of an aircraft, the beat of the engine getting closer and closer, and he looked up to find the brief silhouette of one of the new fighters against the glare of the sun. It was directly overhead now, the engine howling as the pilot hauled the little plane into the beginnings of a loop, and pedestrians stopped to watch. At the top of the loop, a tiny silver fish in the blueness of the sky, the aircraft seemed to hang motionless for a moment before the pilot dipped the nose and began the long graceful dive back to earth.

So easy, Tam thought. So graceful. So perfectly under control. Then came the operator's voice in his ear and that same eerie silence. This time he left a message.

'Half-past three,' he said, still looking skywards. 'That's the best I can manage.'

*

Dieter powered down the engine and released the canopy, grateful for his first lungful of fresh air. The Chief Engineer at Johannistahl was already squatting on the wing beside the cockpit. He wanted to know about the oil temperature and the aircraft's behaviour on the more extreme of the inverted turns. Next week Dieter was to display the Emil at the start of this year's Nuremberg Rally, Goering's chance to showcase the aircraft that had caught the imagination of the entire nation. The engineer was determined to avoid any surprises.

'Was it OK going into the turn?'

'Perfect.'

'No negative G problems?'

'None.'

'And the oil?'

'One hundred and two degrees. Rock steady.'

The Chief Engineer grunted his approval. Tonight some of the boys were having a drink. Dieter was welcome to come along.

'Some kind of celebration?'

'A birthday.'

'Whose?'

'Mine. Fifty.' The engineer pulled a face. 'Who'd have thought it?'

Georg was waiting for Dieter in the squadron mess. It turned out that Beata had been to a clairvoyant, something she'd never done before. She wanted to know whether her child would be a boy or a girl and the clairvoyant had no hesitation in predicting what would happen. Come April next year, God willing, Georg was to be presented with a little girl.

'And you believe this?' Dieter asked.

'Of course not.'

'But you're telling me a daughter would be unacceptable?'

'I'm expecting a boy,' Georg said stiffly.

'Then look on the bright side. Think of a name. Heinrich. Adolf. Joachim. Buy him a little pair of lederhosen and a nice fat swastika. Tempt him out to join the Party. The music goes on. *Alles gut, ja?*'

Georg shot him a look. He was uncomfortable. He wanted to change the subject. He said he'd been making some enquiries about Keiko.

'Me, too,' Dieter said.

'And?'

'I tried the Japanese embassy. They didn't even know she'd been arrested but they're going to lodge a protest. Diplomatic immunity? Have I got that right?'

'She needs to be employed,' Georg pointed out. 'She needs to be working for them. Was she?'

'I think so.'

'*Think* so?'

'That's what she always told me.'

'And you believed her?'

Dieter didn't answer. Georg studied him for a moment and then changed the subject. He'd been with an aide of Goering's this morning, going over the transport schedules for the coming week. *Der Eiserne* was evidently in the best of moods.

'What's that got to do with Keiko?'

'I've no idea. Except her arrest seems to have put Ribbentrop in the shit. In this town, rumour is all you need. Nothing has to be true any more. Just as long as it raises a laugh. Ribbentrop can't cope with that. The man has absolutely no sense of humour and Goering knows it.'

'So what's the joke?'

'Apparently Goering thinks that girl of yours is a spy. That's why she spends so much time with Ribbentrop. All Goering had to do was whisper in Himmler's ear and everything else follows. That's why they arrested her. And that's why you got the treatment.'

'A spy for who?'

'The Japanese.'

'But we're friends with the Japanese. We're allies. You're talking to someone who spent four months being nice to them. I *know* about the Japanese.'

'You only know about the young bloods at the sharp end, the pilots, the aviators. From where I sit there *are* no friends, only opportunities. In politics you trust no one and with this lot it's even worse. Loyalty's a mark of weakness. This is a war of all against all.'

Dieter shook his head. *A war of all against all.* Perfect. From the rubble, he thought, there might one day emerge a victor. And this is before the war proper, the shooting war, the war with France and England and – God help us – Russia, has even begun.

Georg hadn't finished. He wanted to talk about Keiko again.

'Well. . .?' he said. 'You think it might be true? Her being some kind of spy?'

'I've no idea. She said nothing to me but whoever was listening would have known that. So maybe they were listening to Ribbentrop, too.'

'You'd need a lot of patience to listen. All that man ever talks about is himself.'

Dieter nodded. For the first time he began to fathom the darker implications of what was happening.

'So what do they do to spies?' he enquired.

'Most times they kill them. Someone like Keiko, maybe they just send her home.'

'Deportation?'

'Yes. Hopefully undamaged.'

'And in the meantime?'

'They'll talk to her. They'll be looking for a confession.'

'To what?'

'Spying. That's how this story has to end. Regardless.'

'But say she's not a spy.'

'That's irrelevant. All that matters is the confession. The moment she admits it is the moment life gets easier for her. Deportation would really hurt Ribbentrop. That's another reason they might not kill her.'

Dieter sat back. Georg rarely saw the point of softening bad news. In three bleak minutes he'd forced his *compadre* to contemplate a brutal truth about the regime. It might be fear or greed or ambition or spite or just vanity, but whatever the motivation, mere individuals counted for nothing. In the war of all against all, no one was safe.

'So I might never see her again,' Dieter said softly. 'Can you imagine that?'

*

Schultz was waiting for Tam a hundred metres beyond the Pariser Platz entrance to the Tiergarten. A pair of dark glasses did nothing to hide his anger.

'We walk,' he nodded towards the distant lake, 'while you explain yourself.'

'In what respect?'

'We tried to find you last night. You weren't at the hotel. We tried again this morning. Nothing. We leave you a message and expect a prompt response. Again, nothing. The owner of the hotel is a friend of mine. Your bed wasn't slept in. Why might that be?'

'I have a life to lead,' Tam said. 'With great respect, you're not my keeper.'

'But I am, my friend. I am. For as long as you're here with us, that's exactly what I am. We keep you close. We keep you safe. And in return we expect to be taken seriously.'

'Of course. My apologies.'

Schultz stared at him, suddenly uncertain. No decent quarrel ended as abruptly as this.

'So where were you?'

'With a woman.'

'A German?'

'No. She's a friend and she has nothing to do with any of this. You've talked to Beck at all? Since our meeting?'

'Of course. You told him the English will march. You remember that?'

'I do.'

'Well, he doesn't believe you. We had an envoy in London last week, a man who knows a great deal about the Hitler plans. He had a number of meetings, a number of conversations. People in power, people who *matter.* None of them believes that Hitler will move against the Czechs. And so none of them will give us the assurance we need. Without that assurance, nothing can happen from our end. *Nothing.*'

He spat the word out and Tam felt a brief jolt of sympathy. After all, Schultz and his fellow conspirators were putting their very lives on the line. To bring Hitler to his senses they had to make him realise that a move against Czechoslovakia would have catastrophic consequences. Yet the English would say nothing.

'I'm not a politician,' Tam said mildly. 'I believe I made that point last night.'

'But you have connections. That's what you also said. And that's what we *know.* It takes a spy to know a spy and you, my friend, are one of us.'

'Does that make me reliable?'

'It makes you useful. We speak the same language. Sometimes I suspect we have the same ends in view. In this case, that couldn't be plainer. Your people don't want a war, not a proper war, and neither do mine.'

'So what are you suggesting?'

'I'm suggesting you return to England. Tonight if necessary. I'm suggesting you talk to your people. I'm suggesting you tell them that you have the ear of someone important, truly important, and I'm not talking about Beck. You'll be meeting this person at Nuremberg next week. We'll get you down there from Berlin. And we expect you to bring a message of support. Is that clear?'

Tam came to a halt. The prospect of leaving a murder investigation behind him was more than welcome. He asked Schultz who this important person might be. Schultz ignored the question. Instead, he beckoned Tam closer.

'A word in your ear, my friend. Call it a favour.'

'What kind of favour?'

'Kreisky is dead. As you probably know. A loss to his family and a loss to the Reich. As it happens, the Gestapo have made an arrest already. A Czech patriot. A man blinded by his own folly. Naturally he had nothing to do with Kreisky's death, but happily he fits the bill. Not my bill, Herr Moncrieff, but theirs. The evidence is conclusive, as it would be. The man will stand trial tomorrow morning. He'll be dead before nightfall. His name? Would you care to hazard a guess?'

Tam was staring at him. He felt physically sick.

'Kovač,' he said. 'Edvard Kovač.'

'Indeed.' He offered Tam a cold smile. 'Just one more bullet for Goebbels' gun when it comes to justifying the invasion.'

21

BERLIN, 31 AUGUST 1938

Dieter got very drunk that night. The Chief Engineer's name was Stefan, a hard-featured wisp of a man. At work he was stern and unforgiving, insisting on the tightest standards of accuracy and attention to detail, but off-duty – especially when any kind of celebration was involved – he could shed one personality and become someone entirely different.

Stefan also had a second wife of whom he was inordinately proud. Her name was Ines. She was a big woman, much bigger than Stefan, with a smoky laugh and faraway eyes. Stefan had met her in the Pankow jazz club where she'd occasionally appeared as a guest singer. Her father had come from Saxony and her mother was Creole, a combination that sat uneasily with certain elements in the Reich, but the maintenance crews loved her and she – in turn – had recently acquired a passion for *Der Kleine*.

She loved anyone who took risks. She'd watched him in the air and on the ground and concluded that he belonged in some faraway corner of outer space denied to ordinary mortals. In the Middle Ages, she said, you'd probably have found the little imp embellishing a stained-glass window in one of the bigger cathedrals. With his perfect features and his ready grin he had something of the divine about him. Dieter, who'd first heard some of this from the lips of her husband, didn't pretend to understand but Ines cooked a legendary strudel and you'd be foolish to argue with that.

Ines had brought a couple of musicians from the jazz club to enliven the party. Dieter, increasingly unsteady, had been dancing with Beata. Ines's version of 'Happy Birthday', wildly suggestive, had just won a huge round of applause from engineers and pilots alike, but when she stepped down from the tiny makeshift stage Dieter had trouble keeping her in focus. To more cheers, she was embracing her husband. Then she broke off and made her way through the crowd towards Dieter. This afternoon, returning from a display over central Berlin, he'd performed a low roll over her neighbourhood in honour of Stefan. Now she wanted to say thank you.

Dieter was still clinging on to Beata. He seemed to have a problem understanding what Ines was trying to say.

'This afternoon,' she repeated. 'I heard you coming. I always hear you coming. That was me in the garden. Waving.'

'At me?'

'At you.'

'Why?'

The two women exchanged glances. Men were starting to move away. This wasn't the Dieter they'd got to know. Even Stefan, locked in conversation with Georg, had started to take an interest.

Beata beckoned Ines closer, whispered in her ear. Dieter understood only one word. *Keiko.*

'They will,' he said. 'They're going to.' The words came out wrong and he knew it. Slurred. Mangled. Damaged.

'Will what?' Ines was looking concerned.

'Kill her.' Dieter was crouching now, his eyes moist, one hand locked on some imaginary control column, his thumb feeling for the fire button. 'Brrr. . . brrr. . .' He tried to mimic the chatter of a machine gun, failed completely.

Ines put her arms round him, her face very close. Dieter peered up at her. She smelled wonderful. She smelled of Keiko.

'Not you,' he muttered. 'They won't kill you. No one will ever kill you.'

'No one will kill anyone. You're dreaming. Imagining things. This is a happy time. We love you. Come.'

Gently, she led him from the room. Down the corridor was her husband's office. Dieter found himself sitting in Stefan's leather chair. It swivelled left and right. He wanted to throw up.

'Here. . .' It was Ines. She'd found the waste-paper basket. She slipped behind him and cradled his forehead while he began to retch. His father had done something similar, when he was a child. He reached for her other hand, held it tight.

'Thank you.' At last he'd finished.

'You want to stay here? Just for a while? Then maybe come back to the party when you're ready?'

Dieter gazed up at her and nodded, more grateful than he could possibly explain.

'Yes,' he said.

There was a lavatory across the corridor. She emptied the waste-paper basket and returned with a dampened flannel. She bathed Dieter's face and then kissed him. Maybe a little coffee?

Dieter was gazing up at her. He shook his head. No coffee.

Ines left the office, closing the door behind her. At first Dieter shut his eyes, still slumped in the chair, but sleep wouldn't come. All he could think of was the chaos that awaited him at home in Potsdam. That's where they'd made a life for themselves. That's where they'd started to plan for some kind of future once things had settled down.

He knew places up on the Baltic Coast that Keiko would adore. They could save for a little chalet where the pine woods met the sea, a broken-down old place they could make their own. They could hammer and saw and cook and swim, and make as many babies as they wanted. The world would be at peace and no one would dream of killing anyone else, and in the early mornings there'd be no footprints on the sand but their own. He smiled at the thought, gazing sightlessly at the office walls, trying to tell himself that it could still happen, that the last twenty-four hours had been some kind of nightmare, or maybe just a simple mistake. He'd find his way home and the place would be untouched and the face waiting on the pillow would be hers.

Wrong. Beside the door there was a row of hooks. Dieter tried to count them, gave up. Each hook held a key. Some belonged to cupboards in the big maintenance hangar. The one at the end he'd seen only hours ago. It unlocked the canopy on his beloved Emil.

He struggled to his feet, steadying himself on the edge of the desk, and then made it to the door. The key nestled sweetly in the palm of his hand. Out in the corridor he could hear laughter. The music had started again, the first in a round of drinking songs, and for a moment he toyed with rejoining the party. Then he shook his head, telling himself he had a much better idea.

At the other end of the corridor was a side entrance that led on to the grass, and thence to the maintenance hangar. Dieter leaned back on the door to close it, staring out at the darkness. Far away to the north he could see the yellow glow of the city's lights. Above, when he looked up, a thousand stars. He began to walk again, weaving left and right, making for the dark shapes of aircraft parked in front of the hangar. Landings, he told himself. Life is all about landings. Losing height. Maintaining speed. Shedding a little more altitude. Having faith in your judgement, in your machine. Resisting gravity until that last sweet moment when you felt the wheels touch.

He paused to be sick again, staring at the puddle of vomit at his feet. Ines had served *Blutwurst* earlier. Stefan loved *Blutwurst.* Dieter wiped his mouth on the back of his hand, looking up. The little Messerschmitt was dwarfed by the bigger planes, Hitler's Ju-52 and the other tri-motors in the fleet. Compared to these monsters, the Emil was an orphan. It seemed a thousand miles away. It seemed beyond reach.

He started to walk again, his head a little clearer. He could do this. The plane was the brother he'd never had, the one sure thing he could rely on, his last best hope. Finally he made it. To his faint surprise he was still clutching the key. He reached up for the grab-holds on the fuselage, cold under his touch, and somehow levered himself up on to the wing. There was a small element of miracle in this. It was as if his body belonged to somebody else, under their control and not his own.

He wavered, fighting to stay upright, and then his fingers found the lock that secured the canopy.

He couldn't get the key to fit. He tried and he tried. He held it very close to his eye, frowning with concentration, trying to spot what might be wrong, maybe dirt, maybe something else. He gave it a wipe on his trousers and this time it worked. He turned it slowly, feeling the lock give, and then opened the canopy.

The cockpit yawned before him. Home, he thought. He got in like a blind man, using his hands to ward off obstacles. The joystick. The throttle control. The undercarriage lever. Finally, he settled in the seat, automatically slipping the harness over his shoulders and buckling himself in. No life jacket, he thought. Who cares?

He sat back, savouring this moment of silence. The canopy was still open and he could smell summer on the wind. He reached for the master switch. Prime first, he told himself. Then see if she fires. He smiled, peering out of the cockpit, trying to map his way between the surrounding aircraft, then plotting a track towards the runway. The dashboard was lit now. Full fuel tank. Perfect.

'*Compadre?*' It was Georg. His face hung over the cockpit, pale in the darkness. He'd appeared from nowhere.

Dieter stared up at him, wondering whether he was real or not. He looked real enough.

'News?' He wiped his eyes. 'Keiko?'

'No.'

Dieter nodded, stared at the controls. No news.

'What were you going to do?' Georg was squatting on the wing.

'I was going to fly it.'

'That's what I thought.'

'Bad idea?'

'Terrible idea. You'd never fly again. Assuming you survived.'

'You mean they wouldn't let me?'

'No. And neither would I.'

Dieter let the news sink in. Very sensible, he thought. Very Georg. His fingers found the harness and he unbuckled himself.

'I'd like to go home,' Dieter said.

'No.' Another shake of the head. 'You're coming home with us. Here. This is from Beata. Sol Fiedler gave it to her this afternoon. It's for you.'

'What is it?'

'I don't know. Sol said it's a gift from Jewish science.'

'Jewish science?'

'Goebbels' word for anything he doesn't understand. Open it. Take a look.'

He gave Dieter the parcel. Dieter examined it, felt it, shook his head. Finally he managed to get the paper off. He could feel the waxiness beneath his fingers.

'It's a candle,' he said. 'What do I do with a fucking candle?'

*

Bella was able to confirm that Kreisky was dead. Her friend in the Kripo was involved in the ongoing investigation. A post-mortem had found a break between the second and third vertebrae but what appeared to have killed him had been a massive heart attack.

'You scared him to death,' she said. 'The broken neck didn't help but it didn't kill him.'

They were talking in the bar at Tempelhof Airport. Hours earlier, she'd booked Tam on the day's last flight to London but there was a technical problem with the aircraft and he was still waiting for the call to board.

He wanted to know more about Edvard Kovač. Was it true he'd been arrested?

'Yes. He's been in prison in Karlovy Vary for a couple of weeks. The Sudetens handed him over at the border and the Kripo brought him to Berlin. Someone at the top wants a Czech to take the fall and Kovač is perfect. There's no evidence, of course, but that won't matter. The Kripo can be very creative. They'll just invent it.' She paused. 'You know this man?'

'Yes.'

'How? Do you mind me asking?'

'Not at all.'

At last Tam told her about his visit to the Sudetenland. It turned out she knew about the mine outside Jáchymov that Kovač had planned to sabotage.

'This is delicate territory,' she said. 'I don't understand the science but nothing happens without the stuff they dig out of that place.'

'It's called uranium.'

'I know. I gather we're in the queue as well.' She looked Tam in the eye. 'Is that why you killed Kreisky?'

'Not exactly. I met Kovač through another woman. Her name was Renata.'

'Was?'

'She died. She was killed. Kreisky was part of that.'

'And she mattered to you? This woman?'

'She did. She does. She was my introduction, if you like. I was never part of this game until I met her.'

'That sounds like an accusation.'

'On the contrary, it was me who let her down.'

'Guilt, then? Is that it? Is that why Kreisky's dead?'

Tam didn't answer. From the bar he had a clear view of the London plane through the windows of the departure lounge. Handlers were offloading bags from the cargo hold. Not a good sign.

Bella had taken Tam's hand. She turned it over, began to trace the lines on his palm.

'A girl's allowed to be superstitious.' She glanced up. 'Do you mind?'

'Help yourself.'

'I see a journey.'

'Very clever.'

'And a meeting.' She was frowning. 'Someone old. Somewhere in the country. This person builds walls. He also tears them down. He's a rebel. A free spirit. No one trusts him. Neither should you.' She looked up at him. 'You're so new to this, aren't you? And so unprepared? I find that rather touching.'

The flight was cancelled. The Lufthansa manager arrived in the bar, offered his apologies and asked Tam to report back to the airport at seven o'clock tomorrow morning. He guaranteed a serviceable aircraft and a clear run to London. In the meantime, he was more than happy to offer him a room at a nearby hotel.

'Is that for two?' Bella had abandoned Tam's lifelines.

'Of course, madame. It's the least we can do.'

Tam appeared to have little say in this arrangement. She'd driven him to the airport and now they took her car to the hotel. The restaurant was about to close but Bella managed to conjure a table. One of her many chores at the embassy was to meet incoming visitors above a certain rank and she'd used this same hotel on a number of occasions.

Waiting for the meal, she pressed him a little harder about Renata. Tam was beginning to find her curiosity uncomfortable.

'Why do you want to know?'

'Because you interest me. That doesn't happen as often as it should. Grateful is a word I've never had much time for but just now it sounds about right.'

'Grateful for what?'

'For you. For this. People tell me I'm the luckiest girl in the world. Travel. Foreign cities. An interesting job. Believe me, it doesn't always feel so wonderful.'

'Nothing does. Life deals you a hand. You play it the best way you can. We had an instructor once, back in the Corps. You're expecting thirty hard miles. It's raining. Everything hurts. The hills get steeper and steeper. Then night falls and you know that's where the real pain begins. The next step, he always said. That's the one that counts. The next step. Just do it. Just get through it. Because one day it will stop.'

'For a while.'

'Of course. Otherwise you're probably dead.'

'Like your Renata?'

'She wasn't my Renata. As a matter of fact she was Edvard's Renata. Which makes me twice as guilty. If I hadn't let her down, if I'd been a bit smarter, she'd still be alive. And if I'd never touched Kreisky, then Edvard would still be tucked up in his little cell in Karlovy Vary.'

'What if it was you they arrested?'

'Then at least we'd still be talking about justice.'

'So are you going to phone someone? My Kripo friend? Tell her you did it?'

'Of course not. And you know why? Because it wouldn't make the slightest difference. These people live in a world of their own making. A man is beaten in a park. He dies. The question isn't who did it, the question is how best we take advantage. The truth doesn't matter any more. The truth is for the little people. The bigger the lie, the better they like it.'

Bella mimed applause. Tam stared at her.

'You think I'm naive?'

'I think you're honest. In this city that can be the same thing.'

'So you think I should get on that plane tomorrow? Go back to England? To Scotland? Tell our people I've had enough? Try and forget any of this happened? Is that what I should do?'

'Yes.'

'Why?'

'Because otherwise you're going to get hurt. And that's if you're lucky.' She checked whether the restaurant was still empty, and then leaned forward. 'As it happens I know why you're here. Oliver told me. If you want the truth, I had a hand in setting this whole thing up. Schultz. Beck. Half a dozen others. They're in it up to their necks. They're brave and they're sincere, and they might even be honest. They'll still take the Czechs when it suits them but that time's not quite now and so we owe them our support. The politicians won't do it. Not Halifax. Not Chamberlain. Not the people at the top of government. But there are others at the margins and if you're passionate enough you might just make a difference. That's why Schultz is sending you back. And that's why we're sitting here.'

'You know Schultz?'

'Of course I know Schultz. I was the man's first point of contact. He's an old bruiser and you wouldn't show him to your maiden aunt but he tells a good story.'

Tam sat back. He was trying to get his bearings.

'So if you know so much, how come you didn't know about me in the Sudetenland? About Edvard? Renata?'

'Because none of that was my business. They tell me what I need to know. Not a *Pfennig* more. I'm on the ground here. That's my job. I'm close to the likes of Schultz. I report back to my father. He talks to Uncle Andrew and doubtless one or two other folk. They put my tiny part of the jigsaw with all the other bits and in no time at all I'm opening my office door to this tall stranger with a wonderful Scots accent who plans to settle his scores with an American banker. The latter, to be frank, we could have done without but at least you're still alive.' She smiled at him. 'Does that help?'

The food arrived, plates of lukewarm goulash from a kitchen that had closed half an hour ago. Tam took a forkful and pushed his plate aside. The taste of paprika on his tongue took him back to the evening in Karlovy Vary when he'd first met Edvard's mother. Renata had been alive then. Another life.

'So you think I should creep back to Scotland? Stay there? Shut my door on the world? Have I got that right?'

'I think that's what you ought to do, yes. Under the circumstances that would be more than sensible.'

'But?'

'That won't happen. You know it and I know it. And you know something else? That makes me very happy.'

*

Hours later, in the middle of the night, Tam awoke to find Bella hanging over him. They'd gone to sleep without making love, arms wrapped round each other, comfort rather than sex. Now she dipped her head and kissed him.

'You're beautiful,' she said. 'I just wanted you to know that.'

'Really?'

'Yes. Take a compliment. It doesn't happen often.'

Tam turned his head on the pillow. The curtains were open and he thought he could detect a blush of light in the darkness where the city should be. He thought of Edvard in some cell and of what he must be thinking. Then he remembered Kreisky sprawled on the damp grass, his lifeless body, his ruined face. Nothing connected the two images except Tam's own complicity. He'd killed one man. And now he was responsible for two more deaths.

'Easy,' he murmured. 'So easy.'

'What is?'

'Killing. That's the real surprise.'

'But you were a soldier. A Marine. A tough guy.'

'I know. It's inexplicable.' He peered up at her. 'You really want me back in Berlin?'

'Yes.'

'You can't find this somewhere else?'

'What's this?'

'Sex? Company?'

'I can find both. That's never a problem. What's different is you.'

Tam smiled. Pretty, he thought. And immensely beguiling.

'I'd like to believe that,' he said. 'I really would.'

'But?'

'I'm not sure I believe anything any more.'

'Do you mean that?'

'Yes.' Tam found her hand under the sheet. 'Why do you ask?'

'Because of something a good friend once told me. We were up at Oxford. The exams were over. We'd been drinking most of the night.'

'So what did he say? This friend?'

'He said everyone had to have something they totally believed in. It could be religion. It could be some other calling. It might even be another human being. But without it – without that total commitment, that total otherness – you were lost.'

'That total otherness?'

'That's the way he put it. It's a kind of surrender. You have to give up part of yourself.'

'And was he right? Did you believe him? Have you done it?'

'Yes, I have.' She was smiling now. 'Hard? God, yes. Something I'd ever regret?' She kissed his hand. 'Never.'

Tam was tempted to enquire further but sensed this wasn't the time. After a while, Bella stirred. Her face was very close in the darkness.

'So what do we do?' she said.

22

LONDON, 1 SEPTEMBER 1938

Ballentyne was waiting for Tam at Heston Airport in the back of a new-looking black Humber Super Snipe. In the front passenger seat, next to the driver, sat a portly man in his late fifties. Ballentyne introduced him as Freddie and said he worked for the *Daily Telegraph.*

Tam got into the back beside Ballentyne. The car smelled of stale cigar smoke.

'Berlin?' Ballentyne said at once. 'All well?'

'Far from it.'

'Excellent. We have someone in mind you ought to meet.'

They skirted the southern suburbs and then motored south, deep into rural Surrey. Ballentyne wanted to tell Tam about his father. The old boy, he said, was in good spirits. His vicar friend had sadly passed on but he was now playing chess with a younger fellow he appeared to like a great deal. His new friend, according to the Matron, had lost his wits in a plane accident in which he'd suffered a brain injury. Otherwise unhurt, he spent most mornings in the back garden, sawing a consignment of logs in preparation for the coming winter, a commitment which had won unqualified respect from Tam's father. Tam nodded and thanked Ballentyne for making the effort to keep an eye on his dad.

'Not at all, young man.' Ballentyne patted his knee. 'We always protect our investments.'

They were in Kent now, glorious landscape and a succession of sleepy villages where even the dogs sought shadow in the heat of the day. This, thought Tam, was the picture-book England the politicians were so desperate to preserve from the likes of Hitler and Mussolini. No one could possibly fault their intentions. The harder question was whether or not they could possibly succeed.

Ballentyne was quizzing the journalist about yesterday's emergency meeting of ministers in Downing Street. Freddie, it seemed, had a source inside the Cabinet and reported that Chamberlain had won a convincing majority for his determination to keep Hitler guessing.

'Guessing about what?' Tam asked.

'About whether or not we'd go to war.'

'But Hitler doesn't believe us,' Tam said. 'That's why his generals are running for cover.'

Ballentyne shot Tam a look and then put his finger to his lips. The journalist caught the gesture and wanted to know more.

'There is no more,' Tam said. 'Hitler's a madman. That isn't a secret either, least of all in Berlin. How much faith does Chamberlain have in this guessing game?'

'Faith?' Freddie laughed. 'He has faith in himself, in his own judgement. That's where it begins and ends. He believes in the personal touch. He thinks he can play the peacemaker by being inscrutable. But he's a realist, too, which is why he's looking so ill. The truth is he can't make Hitler out but he won't admit it.

Not even to himself. He's gone to Balmoral this weekend for the shooting. He thinks a day on the moors might relax him. Either way, he's up against a deadline.'

'Deadline?' Ballentyne was staring out of the window.

'The party rally begins in a week's time. Hitler makes the final speech. People I respect tell me we could be at war the following day.'

Tam made a mental note. The annual party rallies took place at Nuremberg. Schultz had promised to fly him down for a discreet meeting. Someone at the very top, he'd said. Someone waiting for a message.

Freddie hadn't finished. He'd half-turned in his seat, looking back at Ballentyne.

'A favour, Andrew? Do you mind?'

'Name it.'

'I'm hearing about a Plan Z. This is Downing Street again, something the PM's dreamed up. Ring any bells with your lot?'

Ballentyne shook his head. His face was a mask.

'Can't help you, I'm afraid. Never heard of it.'

*

Twenty minutes later, past the town of Oxted, the driver slowed for the turn off the main road. The lane wound through neat hedgerows and stands of oak in full leaf with glimpses of fat cattle in the meadows beyond. This was a landscape tamed by history and wealth, thought Tam. The contrast to the wildness of his native Cairngorms could scarcely be more marked. What would it be like to grow up here, he wondered. What kind of person would you become?

In the distance, looming above a frieze of trees, he caught a glimpse of a manor house, the bricks a soft ochre against the curtains of green, splinters of sunshine caught in the mullioned windows. Then came a lake overlooked by more trees, cupped by the soft rise of the surrounding hills.

Tam turned to Ballentyne. He wanted to know who lived here.

'Winston Churchill.' He was looking at his watch. 'I'm afraid we're early.'

Tam knew a little about Churchill. One or two of the officers had talked about him when Tam was serving in the Royal Marines, mostly with a kind of guarded affection. As a politician, one of them had said, the man was a maverick, loyal to a fault when it suited him but never a team player. He'd served the Navy's needs well, and the lower deck had always loved his readiness for a fight, but he'd somehow become sidelined during the thirties, a brooding and often grumpy presence on the backbenches. When he chose to, he could rise to the occasion and Tam remembered listening to a couple of speeches on the radio that had won his admiration, but Churchill was an old man now, well past his prime, and the current crisis, Tam suspected, called for younger, more nimble politicians.

They parked behind the main house. Freddie, who'd plainly been here before, led the way round the building towards the front of the property. Chartwell, he said, had long been a personal favourite. To his eyes, the architectural style shouted Tudor. Who'd have thought it was built by the Victorians?

They found Churchill slumped in the sunshine beside a table on the terrace. He was dressed like a gardener – soft patterned shirt, work trousers, straw hat – and at first Tam thought he might be asleep. Then he caught sight of the pile of manuscript on his lap, and a fountain pen that raced from page to page. At the approaching footsteps, the old man looked up, frowning at the disturbance.

'Freddie,' he growled.

Freddie extended a hand. Churchill made no effort to get up. Freddie introduced Ballentyne but had to check Tam's name. Tam was aware of Churchill's eyes on his face.

'Moncrieff? The Argyll Moncrieffs? From Lochgilphead?'

'I'm afraid not, sir. We started in the Lowlands.'

'And now?'

'We have a place near Crathie.'

'The Cairngorms?' The big face lit up. 'Wonderful light. And people who leave you alone. You're a lucky man, Mr Moncrieff. I can't begin to think what you're doing here.'

There was a small handbell on the table. Churchill summoned a thin, slightly swarthy retainer from the depths of the house. It was too late for morning tea and too early for lunch. They would therefore have something a little more robust to drink.

The retainer was back within minutes with a silver tray laden with glasses and two bottles of champagne. Freddie and Churchill were deep in a conversation about the old man's current project. The *Daily Telegraph,* it seemed, was interested in publishing extracts from this new book and Freddie was here to enquire how it was going.

'Like the wind, Freddie.' Churchill gestured at the pages still on his lap. He was glad to report that the muse was blowing at gale force and that he had every prospect of meeting his publisher's deadline. Writing a history of the English-speaking people had opened doors he was ashamed to acknowledge he'd never been aware of. Choose any period and you found yourself in the company of a remarkable tribe. Romans? Saxons? Those magnificent Tudors? It made no difference. A mongrel race blessed by history, favoured by geography, and prisoners of their own insatiable appetites. A pleasure to make their acquaintance.

'That makes me privileged, Freddie. I hope my readers will feel something of the same.' He half-turned and stared out across the estate. The hills to the south dissolved into a soft blue haze. 'I was privy to a conversation last week. Most disturbing. If the Germans come they'll head directly for London. Bound to. And you know one of the first steps our lords and masters plan to take? Evacuation. Not just down on the coast. Not just here. But the whole of Sussex and Kent. Can you imagine that? Can you imagine millions of people on the move with their tails between their legs?' At last he turned back to the table and his gaze settled on Tam. 'Will you have room, Mr Moncrieff? In those mountains of yours? Will we all be eating venison and fighting midges?'

He left the questions unanswered while the retainer opened the champagne. Churchill had gestured Ballantyne to his side. He understood he worked for Military Intelligence.

'Something of an oxymoron, is it not?' There was a sparkle in his eyes and when Ballentyne showed signs of taking offence he put a hand on his arm. 'A joke, Mr Ballentyne. You people man the ramparts. We'd be even more naked without your sort. Every democracy has truth at its heart. And you know what we need to protect that truth? A bodyguard of lies. You have my full attention.' He at last reached for his glass of champagne. 'Tell me about Czechoslovakia.'

This was Tam's cue and he did his best. He talked about the state of the western defences, about the excellence of the Czech Army's kit, about the mood in Prague. At the mention of Konrad Henlein, Churchill leaned forward.

'That man is a symptom, not a cause,' he said. 'Henlein is someone we should take extremely seriously. We had a dear friend to lunch the other day. She's English. She's working as a journalist. She has excellent contacts in Prague and one of those contacts is a Junker of the old school at the German embassy, a man of some refinement. They've always enjoyed each other's company. But she tells me something has changed, even in the soul of this Junker friend of hers. After *Anschluss*, the Germans have forgotten their manners. She taxed this friend of hers about what happened in Vienna. The arrests and the suicides and all the other atrocities after the Nazis arrived. And you know what he said? This fine Junker gentleman? He told her, *Wir lachen nur darüber.* Mr Moncrieff? If you please?'

Tam realised he was being asked for a translation.

'We just laugh about it.'

'Exactly. This is the world we have to cope with. Alas, it's a world that suits the likes of Mr Henlein only too well. Except that he, too, will be eaten alive.'

Churchill glowered at the faces around the table. Tam wasn't sure what he was expected to say next but Churchill, as it turned out, hadn't finished.

'We are dilatory and profoundly remiss, Mr Moncrieff. We ignore every signal that we should be on our guard for. We belong to the nation of Ethelred and we have never been more unready.' One hand settled on the manuscript on his lap. 'You know the worst fate for any politician, Mr Moncrieff? It's the curse of opposition. You've no doubt come to warn me of terrible things about to happen. I hear it all the time. Here, in London, in Paris, even in the south of France. Naturally, I do what I can. I get to my feet and I raise my voice but sadly no one listens. Men like Freddie here do their best. Our newspapers aren't entirely supine. One can write the odd article, bang the odd table, but it makes pitifully little difference. More and more, Mr Moncrieff, I feel like an old horse put out to pasture, my time done, my oats eaten. On occasions, it's even worse than that. I feel *gelded*.'

He let the word settle. Then he wanted to know about General Beck.

'You think he means it?'

'Means what, sir?'

'Means to oppose Hitler? I understand he's resigned. And I understand you've had the pleasure of meeting the man.'

Tam shot a glance at Ballentyne and then nodded. Beck, in his judgement, was a patriot who now saw no alternative to getting rid of Hitler.

'And how, pray, will he do that?'

'To be frank, I've no idea. But I suspect he means it. And I suspect he's not alone.'

'Mr Ballentyne?'

'That's right, sir. I can give you a handful of names, but not in this company.'

Churchill nodded, then invited Freddie to take a turn around the distant lake. Freddie got up and left without a word. Tam wondered whether he shouldn't be doing the same.

'Well, Mr Ballentyne?'

Ballentyne tallied the names. Hans Oster, number two in the *Abwehr*. The Kordt brothers, senior diplomats. Hjalmar Schact, a leading businessman. Hans Bernd Gisevius, a senior Gestapo figure. Ewald von Kleist-Schmenzin, a Prussian aristocrat. The list went on.

Churchill listened attentively, nodding at each of the names. When Ballentyne had finished he sat back for a moment and closed his eyes, the action of a man who had just enjoyed a good meal. His hands were clasped over the swell of his belly. He seemed replete.

'So what do you want me to do?' he asked at last. 'For this brave little platoon?'

'They need an assurance that we'll help the Czechs.'

'By marching?'

'Yes. And they have to believe it. That's the message we want to send. And Moncrieff here is in a unique position to deliver it.'

'I believe it, Mr Ballentyne. And Mr Moncrieff, I wish you nothing but good fortune. I, too, am a messenger. I am only too happy to pass the word on, to try and do justice to these men's courage, but I fear the message, *my* message, *your* message, will fall on deaf ears.' He fell silent a moment, his eyes closing again. But then he stirred. 'Our Foreign Secretary is a man of unswerving moral purpose. He cannot deal with evil because he lacks the ability, or perhaps the inclination, to recognise it. Halifax, alas, is a sheep. And that is deeply unfortunate because we live in the age of the wolf. Therein lies the problem.'

Tam felt like applauding. *The age of the wolf*. Perfect.

Churchill reached for the bell. When the retainer appeared from the house Churchill gestured at the other bottle. Tam heard the cork pop.

'Courage is right,' he said softly. 'Step out of line in Berlin and you pay with your life.'

'I believe you, Mr Moncrieff. These people are playing with us. Have you ever noticed how Herr Hitler specialises in weekend crises? The Rhineland adventure? The morning he chose to crush Austria? Always a Sunday. I sometimes wonder whether this isn't personal. The last upset happened back in May when the Czechs mobilised. That was a weekend, too, and Mr Chamberlain had to be summoned back from his trout fishing. Is that any way to treat a serving Prime Minister?'

He was grinning now and Tam glimpsed the child he must once have been: impish, mischievous, ungovernable. Then, from nowhere, came a sudden gust of wind, scattering page after page of manuscript from the pile on the table. Tam was on his feet at once, while Ballentyne secured the rest of the pile. One by one, Tam retrieved the vagrant pages and returned to his seat.

Churchill, with that same grin, thanked him for his services to literature. Then he beckoned him closer.

'You know the secret about Mr Chamberlain?'

'No, sir.'

'He wants to fight the Gods of War single-handed. Which is why he will lose.'

23

POTSDAM, BERLIN, 2 SEPTEMBER 1938

It took Dieter many hours to dispose of the damage to the converted stables at Potsdam. Georg talked to the squadron commander and won him time off. Dieter, sleeping on a borrowed mattress on the floor of the living room on his first night back home, rose early. By midday, the pile of discarded wreckage in the stable yard outside the back door was at waist height: the remains of the bed frame, a smashed chest of drawers, shelving torn from the wall, cupboards ripped apart, floorboards splintered by frenzied work with a crowbar.

Back in the kitchen, on the single table that had survived the carnage, Dieter had amassed a smaller, more intimate collection of objects: presents he and Keiko had swapped over the brief weeks of their relationship: a drawing of an eagle she'd penned to celebrate his birthday; an insect trapped in amber Dieter had acquired from a market stall in Pankow. He'd had this tiny keepsake attached to a delicate silver chain. Keiko had worn it only once, and now – stepping into the blaze of sunshine outside to examine it more closely – Dieter thought he understood why. The tree resin, aeons before it hardened into amber, had robbed this tiny insect of its life. Was hanging it around your neck a celebration of that moment? Or were there darker implications?

These were questions of a kind that had never troubled Dieter before but times were changing fast and with bewilderment came something else that was hardening into anger. Strangers had arrived in the middle of the night and torn his life apart. The woman he loved had disappeared into the bowels of a regime that would answer to no one. The best party tricks, as he was beginning to recognise, defied explanation. So just how was he supposed to get Keiko back?

There was another item of Keiko's he'd so far failed to find. It was a sash she wore around her waist when a special occasion called for a kimono. The last time he'd seen it was the afternoon they'd paid a visit to the Ribbentrops' villa out at Dahlem. The embroidery was intricate. The work of many months, it had been made by a great aunt of Keiko's whom she'd always treasured. But search as he might, Dieter couldn't find it.

By midday, the house was cleared of wreckage. Dieter, stripped to the waist in the hot sun, sipped a glass of water from the well in the courtyard. In the corner of the yard was a stable stall that had survived the attentions of the Gestapo. When they'd first moved in it had been full of old tools, mainly implements for the garden, and Keiko had begun to add other junk. He'd seen her cross the yard from time to time and disappear inside.

He finished the water and made for the stall. The door was hung in two parts. The latch on the upper section was stiff and he had to pull hard to get it open. Sunshine revealed a tableau of spades and forks and rusting buckets, heavily cobwebbed. Dieter wrestled open the lower half of the door and stepped inside. Very faintly, he thought he caught the smell of hay, of horses. At the back of the stall was an old chest of drawers piled high with more rubbish: broken flower pots, empty paint tins, packets of seeds. Dieter gazed at the debris for a moment, knowing that Keiko would never leave her beloved sash in a place like this. Then his attention was caught by one of the drawers. It was an inch or so open.

He stepped closer, then pulled out the drawer. Inside was more debris: tobacco tins full of screws and nails, binder twine, paint brushes that had never been washed properly, stiff with neglect. The drawer was deep. He began to poke about. At the very bottom, hidden from any casual inspection, was a biggish envelope. Beside it, carefully wrapped in a grubby towel, an object he could hold in the palm of his hand.

Dieter glanced over his shoulder, then peeled away the towel. It was a camera, very small. He stared at it. A metal cap protected the lens and there were Japanese ideograms on the reverse. Dieter took a tiny step backwards, wondering whether he wanted to take this search any further. Already, the implications were uncomfortable. A miniature camera in the hands of a foreign national.

The clinching evidence, he knew, would be the contents of the envelope. They felt knobbly beneath his touch. The flap wasn't gummed down. There was no writing of any kind, no address. He opened the flap and reached inside. His fingers counted four, then five, of the little cylindrical objects. He took one out, held it up. It was a roll of film, much smaller than the normal 35 mm, and it had been exposed.

Dieter returned the film to the envelope and sealed the flap. He had to find somewhere else for this, and for the camera too. All it would take was another visit from the Gestapo, another day's grim demolition of everything they could find, and Keiko's fate would be sealed, because the camera and the exposed film told only one story. That Goering had been right. That Ribbentrop had opened his office, his files and perhaps his heart to a spy.

Dieter took the envelope and the camera back to the house. His abandoned shirt lay on the floor. He put it on, tucked it into the waistband of his trousers and then slipped the envelope and the camera inside. Back in the sunshine, he returned to the stables. The best of the spades had seen better days but it would have to do. Later, he'd return to the stall for a more thorough search but now he had to make it out to the woods.

His running circuit crossed the farmer's meadow behind the stable block. Dieter ambled towards the distant treeline. He was whistling. He was enjoying the sunshine. For anyone who happened to be watching, he hadn't a care in the world. There were rumours of truffles in the woods. He loved truffles. And so now was the time to put those rumours to the test.

It was cooler once he'd left the meadow. For several hundred yards he followed the path he knew. Then, after a check behind him, he plunged into the trees. The ground was soft underfoot and sloped away towards the gleam of sunshine on a pond. Dieter was looking for something he'd recognise later, a particular tree, a landmark of some kind, and he found it in the shape of an old stone trough, half-hidden beneath a thicket of brambles.

He knelt quickly beside it, carving a tiny notch in one end with the blade of the spade. Then he measured seventeen paces along the face of the hill. Seventeen was his lucky number and it brought him to the bole of a huge oak tree. He studied it for a moment, memorising the spread of the tree as it sent its roots deep into the earth. Then he began to dig, spading the cool earth into a neat pile beside him. A spy, he kept telling himself, I fell in love with a spy. Minutes later, the camera and film safely hidden, he shovelled the last of the earth back into the hole and stepped back before covering it with a layer of vegetation. It looked, he thought, like a grave.

*

That same afternoon Tam Moncrieff landed at Tempelhof Airport. Bella was there to meet him. The area beyond the passport control booth was crowded with friends and relatives awaiting arrivals. A little to his surprise, Bella threw her arms around him and kissed him on the mouth.

'Cover story.' She kissed him again. 'It's a spy thing.'

They drove into the centre of the city. Tam described the visit to Chartwell and his meeting with Churchill.

'Didn't I tell you that? When I read your palm?'

'You did.' It was the first time Tam had made the connection. 'So you knew all along?'

'Either that or I'm psychic. What do you think?'

Tam smiled. He realised how much he'd missed this woman. She had a buoyancy and a disregard for the normal rules that verged on the reckless.

'So whose idea was Churchill?' he asked.

'Uncle Andrew's. He's got family connections with Blenheim Palace. He got you in.'

Tam nodded. He gave her other names, mainly diplomats and journalists he'd met over the last couple of days.

'Uncle Andrew again. He's a free spirit when it comes to the Establishment line. But he's a believer, too.'

'In what?'

'In you. Any use? These people you met?'

Tam shook his head. In every conversation, he'd been talking to the converted. To a man, and in one case a woman, they believed that Britain was best defended on the Czech frontier. If we caved in on this occasion, then no London bomb shelter would be deep enough to cope with the consequences.

'They know what's coming,' he said. 'And we all know we have to stop it. The question is how.'

Bella nodded. The Czechs in Prague, she said, had just given in to Henlein's demands, a development that had come as a nasty surprise to Hitler and Ribbentrop.

'They had a meeting in the Chancellery a couple of days ago,' she said. 'They summoned Henlein and told him to make yet more demands, the more extreme the better. What they can't afford is any kind of reasonable settlement. They want trouble, too, in the Sudetenland. Czechs beating up the locals. Blood on the paving stones. They call them *incidents*. If you think that's code for lying, you'd be right.'

Tam nodded, staring out of the window. The lines of huge swastika banners appeared to have thickened over the last few days. Set-dressing, he thought. For the start of the next act.

'And Edvard?'

'He's gone, I'm afraid.' Tam felt her hand close on his.

'Hanged?'

'Shot.'

Tam absorbed the news. He'd expected no less but it still made his belly heave. These people are psychotic, he thought. Tell the same lies for long enough and the entire world will believe you. First Edvard, blindfolded, on his knees before some pitted brick wall. Then a series of confected atrocities from the heartlands of the Sudetenland, yet more compelling reasons why Hitler owed the locals a helping hand.

'Any word from Schultz?' He glanced across at Bella.

'He wants to see you this evening. Six o'clock. The Hauptbahnhof. Platform 7. The western end.'

*

Tam was at the station with minutes to spare. Of Schultz there was no sign. The platform was crowded with city workers waiting for a train home and Tam watched them, wondering what these people made of the latest developments. Were they aware of what really went on behind the closed doors along Wilhelmstrasse? And if so, did they care?

'Moncrieff.'

Tam spun round. It was Schultz. He was in civilian clothes – black leather jacket, black leather trousers, black boots – and the strain on the whiteness of his face told its own story. Too much time indoors, too many crises, resolved or otherwise.

'You look awful,' Tam said.

Schultz shrugged. You did what you had to do. None of it was easy but he'd be a fool to expect anything different. He'd no idea rebellion was such hard work, paying visits, stiffening resolves, feeding egos, keeping a bunch of wilting flowers at least half-watered.

'Look on the bright side,' Tam said. 'One day they'll give you a medal.'

'They?'

'Whoever's left.'

'You think it's that easy?'

'I'm sure it's not.'

A train was approaching, the locomotive wreathed in steam. The crowd retreated a step or two from the edge of the platform. Tam wanted to know whether the train was for them.

'No. Some of these people will get on. The rest are waiting for the next train. It's a place to meet, that's all.'

Hitler, he said, had now issued the order for the invasion of Czechoslovakia. The first divisions were to cross the frontier on the first of October.

'When did this happen?'

'Yesterday. The generals are shitting in their pants. Goering, too. Only Ribbentrop opened a bottle.'

'The generals told you?'

'Of course. When they need their arses wiping they come running. Playing Nanny was never a role I wanted.' He paused to let the steam train come to a halt. 'And you?'

'I'm back. Isn't that the news you want?'

He nodded, then took Tam by the arm and steered him away from the hiss of the locomotive. He needed to be sure about the forthcoming visit to Nuremberg.

'The person you'll be meeting. You've brought a message? Some kind of assurance?'

'Of course.'

'Well. . .? What is it?'

Tam held his gaze. The last of the carriage doors were banging shut and a piercing whistle announced the departure of the train. Tam waited for the final carriage to clear the platform and then turned back to Schultz.

'The British will fight,' he said. 'If that helps.'

'I'm sure it will. Is that a guarantee?'

'It's whatever you make of it.'

'Then it might be worthless.'

'In which case I won't bother even going to Nuremberg. It's your decision, not mine.'

Schultz was frowning. This wasn't the conversation he'd anticipated.

'It's Kovač, isn't it?' he said at last. 'You can't forget him. You can't lay the fucking man to rest. Don't bother denying it. Just say yes.'

'Yes.'

'Then I don't understand what you're doing here. Who'd come back to Germany feeling the way you're feeling? After what we've done to that friend of yours?'

'Me,' Tam said. 'And precisely for that reason. When do you want me in Nuremberg?'

'Tomorrow night.'

'I take the train?' Tam nodded down the platform.

'No. We'll be flying you down there. The Führer's special squadron.' Schultz at last managed what might have been a smile. 'That makes you honoured, my friend, as well as lucky.'

*

Dieter had searched for hours for the tiny notebook where Keiko had kept addresses and telephone numbers that were important to her. The cover was black leather, embossed in gold, and he knew that the information inside included a telephone number that would take her directly to Ribbentrop's office. Empty-handed by the end of the search, he could only conclude that the Gestapo had seized the notebook as evidence. Which meant that he'd have to ask for the Foreign Ministry's main number, just like any other member of the public.

When the operator connected him to the Foreign Ministry switchboard, the voice on the other end laughed.

'*Reichsminister* Ribbentrop? You want a personal conversation, Herr Merz?'

Dieter bent to the telephone. Mention of Keiko Ayama sparked an abrupt change of tone.

'Of course, Herr Merz. A moment, please.'

The line went dead, then Dieter found himself talking to an aide. He gave his name and mentioned Keiko again. He'd appreciate a little of the *Reichsminister*'s time. The matter in hand, he said, was personal. In the background there was a brief exchange of conversation, then the aide was back on the line.

'The *Reichsminister* presents his compliments. He asks you to be at 73 Wilhelmstrasse at half-past six this evening. At the street door you are to ask for Herr Schiff.'

Dieter thanked the aide and hung up. He knew from Keiko that 73 Wilhelmstrasse was to be the new Foreign Ministry, once Ribbentrop's alterations had all been completed. Georg, too, had mentioned the project. The sheer scale of Ribbentrop's plans, he'd told Dieter, had made the *Reichsminister* a laughing stock the length of Wilhelmstrasse. Even Hitler had scoffed at the poor man's pretensions.

Dieter drove into the centre of Berlin. He'd acquired the loan of a rather tired BMW from one of the squadron engineers who'd been posted away and it was nearly six when he presented his ID to the *Luftwaffe* sentry and headed down the ramp into the parking lot in the bowels of the Air Ministry. The Foreign Ministry was a five-minute walk away. Already, the moment he set foot on the pavement, he spotted a couple of heavy trucks parked at the kerbside.

Herr Schiff was a brisk thirty-something with the practised smile of a career diplomat. He gestured for Dieter to stand aside as two labourers manhandled a slab of marble between the glass double doors, and then followed them inside. The *Reichsminister*, he said, was undertaking one of his regular tours of inspection. By now, he should be on the upper floor.

Dieter gazed around. He was no architect but a first glance was enough to confirm that the space available was too small, too restricted, to permit the kinds of effects that Ribbentrop was bent on achieving. Everything gleamed and twinkled: the half-completed marble floor, the huge suspended chandelier, the over-wide steps ascending to the floor above. The tang of fresh plaster hung in the dusty air and a stack of framed paintings were propped against what Dieter imagined to be the reception desk, waiting to be hung. The biggest canvas was a recent-looking portrait of Hitler.

'You approve, Herr Merz?'

Dieter recognised the bark at once. Ribbentrop had appeared on the upper landing. He was leaning on the balustrade, his arms folded, the pose of a proud proprietor. His Ministry, his taste, his vision, his Führer.

'It's wonderful,' Dieter said. He had no idea whether Ribbentrop meant the building or the painting but in either case his response would have been the same. By simply appearing, Ribbentrop had taken Dieter by surprise. According to Georg, the *Reichsminister* made a habit of keeping people waiting, often for hours.

'*Komm. . .*' Ribbentrop beckoned him up.

Dieter took the stairs two at a time, wondering whether Ribbentrop would notice his agility. He did.

'Remarkable.' He nodded in approval. 'I suspect we know who to thank for that.'

He led the way down the corridor towards an open door at the end, pausing to berate a suited individual who'd been checking a detail on the skirting board. The man got to his feet, embarrassed by Dieter's presence, assuring the *Reichsminister* that everything would be attended to. Ribbentrop dismissed him with an imperious wave and showed Dieter into the nearby office.

'It doesn't belong to me, obviously. Mine is still under construction. As you might imagine, it's somewhat bigger than this rathole.'

Dieter was looking round. The room was empty, the floor bare. From the window he could peer down into the courtyard that occupied the space behind the building. He regularly attended meetings in offices half this size.

'I gather this is about our young Japanese friend.' Ribbentrop might have been addressing some kind of public meeting. Clad in a beautifully cut three-piece suit, he was standing to attention, chest out, his hands clasped behind his back.

'Keiko,' Dieter confirmed. 'You're right.'

'And you're doubtless concerned.'

'Of course I am.' Dieter briefly described the pre-dawn bellow beneath their bedroom window, the way the Gestapo had behaved the moment they were inside the door, the lack of respect they'd shown.

Ribbentrop seemed to be half-following this account, his eyes straying to the view from the window.

'They can be rough fellows,' he said at last. 'Best avoided.'

'So why were they there? Do you mind me asking?'

'Of course not. As you might imagine, I've made some enquiries of my own. That young lady has some remarkable gifts. You're a lucky man, Herr Merz.'

'I'm glad you think so.'

'I do. I do. As I was saying to my wife last night, I miss her already. She's made such a difference to this. . . and to this. . .' His manicured hands fell briefly on his shoulder and the nape of his neck. 'Life at my level in the Reich is never kind on the body. We must sustain the pace, all of us. And thanks to the likes of Miss Ayama, that might just be possible. To be frank, as I explained to Annalies, she's irreplaceable. And you know something else? Three times a week might not be enough.'

'They're releasing her?'

'Of course. Today? I doubt it. Tomorrow? Perhaps not. Our Gestapo friends need to be thorough. I understand that and doubtless you will too. But we need, all of us, to understand something equally important. That I have the unqualified backing of the Führer. As it happens, he's met Miss Ayama on a number of occasions. And, dare I say it, he's as impressed as I was.'

Dieter blinked. This was news to him. Keiko had never mentioned meeting Hitler. Did he have problems, too? Little knots of discomfort, or even pain, that only she could tease out? And had her little camera accompanied her visits to the Chancellery?

'She's at Prinz-Albrecht-Strasse?'

'She is.'

'And she's well?'

'So they say. To be frank, Herr Merz, there is absolutely no cause for concern. I have the Führer's fullest backing in whatever I choose to do. Should the Führer no longer be in a position to help, of course, that might cease to be the case but as long as he leads our nation, Miss Ayama will be safe. I'm sure this whole business is a misunderstanding and I can assure you that the Führer shares my view. Might that ease your concerns?' He glared at Dieter, then made a great show of checking his watch. Dieter took the hint.

'I'm grateful, Herr *Reichsminister*,' he said. 'Will you be seeing her at all?'

'I might. *Reichsführer* Himmler has been kind enough to allow us use of a room over on Prinz-Albrecht-Strasse. I fly to Nuremberg tomorrow afternoon with the Führer. If the current madness permits, I may find time in the morning for your good lady to administer a little more relief. I certainly hope so.'

'And you'll give her my best?'

'I will. You have my word. Permit me to show you the way out.'

Ribbentrop left the office. At the head of the staircase he briefly surveyed the floor below. Progress, he said, had been much slower than he'd have liked but he'd had a word with the architect and now there was every prospect of his wife's designs being completed on time.

'Your wife was responsible for all this?'

'Of course, Herr Merz. We owe our women everything. Don't you agree?'

A formal bow, and Dieter was dismissed.

*

Tam spent the evening at Bella's flat near the embassy. At the Ambassador's insistence, the building had been examined yet again for hidden microphones by the specialist team from London, but the search had revealed no attempt to reinstall the surveillance system. For the time being, at least, he and Bella were free to talk.

Bella was in the tiny kitchen, preparing a veal dish soaked in milk. Tam stood in the open doorway, telling her about the plan to fly him south to Nuremberg for the Party Rally. He was to report to a Georg Messner at the *Regierungsstaffel* base at Tempelhof.

'You're flying Air Hitler? Who says?'

'Schultz.'

'Schultz doesn't have that kind of clout. The *Abwehr* have their own set-up. Steerage all the way. Air Hitler?' She shook her head in wonderment. 'Who'd have thought?'

She reached for the shelf where she kept the spices. Tam watched how deft she was and how confident. No sign of a recipe.

'I'll be in Nuremberg myself,' she said. 'We go down every year to see who's doing what to whom. On one level it's grotesque but on another it's rather wonderful. Say what you like about Goebbels, he'd make a fortune in Hollywood.'

'You approve?'

'Approval doesn't come into it. You never get the time to make any kind of judgement. It's like one of those huge tsunami waves you get in Japan. It's music and searchlights and millions of marching soldiers and speeches that go on for ever. Mainly about motherhood and death. You just get swamped.'

'And that's good?'

'That's fun. That's different. Is it dangerous? Well, yes. Do I buy any of this nonsense? Definitely not. But a girl can have a good time and still face herself in the mirror next morning. Where are you staying?'

'I've no idea.'

'They'll put you somewhere ritzy. Maybe even the Deutscher Hof, though I doubt it.'

'Deutscher Hof?'

'Hitler's favourite hotel. It's small, though. And they always book the whole place.' She sprinkled paprika on to the warming milk and checked the potatoes. 'You really don't know who you're supposed to be seeing?'

'No.'

'Does that worry you?'

'Not at all. I'm strictly the messenger. Whether these people take any notice is their affair. If you want the truth, I'm doing this for Edvard and for Renata. If we can keep Hitler out of the Sudetenland, so much the better.'

'We won't,' she said, stirring the milk.

'How do you know?'

'We're just not up to it. I've been in this city for long enough to know what's possible. You haven't met our Ambassador but he's absolutely key to everything. He's where Whitehall meets Wilhelmstrasse. He's London's eyes and ears. They must have put him in post for a reason but none of us can fathom what that reason might be. And you know why?'

'Tell me.'

'The poor man's absolutely terrified of Hitler. Worse still, Hitler knows it. These people can sniff weakness at a hundred paces. And they're seldom wrong.'

'The age of the wolf,' Tam said softly. 'That's what Churchill said when we met last week. He's got Chamberlain down as a sheep. Maybe that applies to Henderson, too.'

'That would be unkind, my love.' Bella licked her finger. 'On the sheep.'

*

After the meal, still mid-evening, they went to bed. They made love twice, the second time at some length. Bella moved sweetly on top of him and Tam let his mind wander back to special times in his life when the world, just for an hour or so, appeared to have stopped spinning on its axis. These moments of suspension, of surrender, of hanging motionless in deepest space, were rare as well as precious and afterwards he told her about crossing the dam in the middle of the night in the company of a bunch of hobbling recruits too exhausted to care what happened next.

'Where was this?' She was propped on one elbow, gazing down at him.

'Scotland. Where else?'

'You love it, don't you?'

'The dam? All that stuff?'

'Scotland. It speaks to you. I can see it. Feel it. It's nothing to be ashamed of. On the contrary. Close your eyes. Just relax.'

She began to explore his body, mapping the hollows, running her tongue across the flatness of his belly. If he'd been born a country, she decided, it would be Italy. Long and quite skinny, but blessed with the most wonderful bones. A body, in short, that could cope with anything.

Tam smiled at the thought. 'You really think I'm like that?'

'I do. You have really low blood pressure. It's probably nothing you can measure on those silly instruments. It just is. You take things in your stride. You're never moody. You know what's important and what isn't. That's rare, believe me.' She sat back a moment, looking thoughtful. Then she smiled. 'You know something, Herr Moncrieff? One day I'm going to take you somewhere hot and sunny where no one wears a uniform. We'll eat like kings and fuck like rabbits and if we're really lucky, we'll never see the point in coming back. You think you might be able to cope with that?'

24

BERLIN, 5 SEPTEMBER 1938

'Hitler weather.' Georg was on the hardstanding beneath the wing of his Ju-52, squatting beside a tyre that had drawn his attention. 'How does the man do it?'

Dieter had just arrived from Potsdam. High summer this year seemed never-ending. Here at Tempelhof, even at eight in the morning, it felt like the middle of July.

Georg was fingering what looked like a small tear on the edge of the tyre tread. Changing a landing wheel on the big Ju-52s was the work of a couple of hours. If he commissioned the job now he could still meet his take-off time of 11.00. At least four of today's passengers had important pre-Congress lunch appointments in Nuremberg.

'I'd take the risk.' Dieter was examining the tyre. 'It's superficial.'

George said nothing for a moment. Then he glanced at his watch.

'There's an Englishman on the passenger list and he needs a lift.' He gave Dieter the address of a hotel off Wilhelmstrasse. 'He's expecting you around nine. Ask for Herr Moncrieff.'

Dieter drove into the city. The traffic coming the other way was already heavy for a Sunday, mainly families heading to the beaches around the Wannsee. Berliners were determined to enjoy what might be left of this glorious summer, to top up their sun tans and give their kids one last treat before the weather cooled and the Führer's armies headed east.

Yesterday Dieter had seen Ribbentrop arrive at Tempelhof for his flight down to Nuremberg. He'd done his best to attract the man's attention, to maybe raise some small indication that Keiko's days with the Gestapo might be over, but the *Reichsminister* had simply looked through him. His concerns about Dieter's private life, if they ever existed in the first place, had plainly gone. In the gallop to war, all he could hear was the thunder of hooves.

Back in the city centre Dieter found the hotel without difficulty. He'd stayed here himself before setting off to Japan, and he'd obviously made an impression on the woman behind the reception desk because she recognised him at once.

'Herr Merz!' Her face lit up. 'So famous now!'

She got to her feet and stepped around the desk to accept a kiss on both cheeks. Beside her was a tall, lean figure taking an amused interest in the exchange. The receptionist turned to him and did the introductions. Dieter had lipstick on his cheek.

'Dieter Merz, Herr Moncrieff. Dieter is our favourite pilot. He's a film star. Women love him. If Dieter takes you to Nuremberg, I wish you luck. You like flying upside down?'

Dieter smiled. In the air, at least, life was still simple. He shook Tam's hand and enquired about bags. Just the one? Perfect.

They left the hotel and got into the car. Seated, Tam's head brushed the roof. Dieter eyed him for a moment. Strong, bony face, lightly freckled. Receding hair. Laugh lines around his eyes and an interesting scar along the line of his jaw. Late thirties? Early forties? Hard to judge.

'You like flying?' Dieter asked.

'I love flying.'

'Good.'

The traffic out of the city was even heavier now. Tam wanted to know whether Dieter had been performing over Berlin a couple of days ago. Early afternoon. Single aircraft. One of the new Messerschmitts.

'*Ja*. That was me.'

'Superb, if I may say so. Half the world was watching. You do this for a living?'

'Sort of. I used to be a fighter pilot.'

Tam wanted to know more. Dieter told him about his days with Georg in the Asturian Mountains, freezing his arse off in a leaky tent while fighting someone else's war. The mention of mountains sparked a story or two from Tam and by the time they joined the queue for the security check at the aerodrome gate, Dieter knew he had a friend in the making.

The flight was nearly ready by the time Dieter and Tam arrived at the squadron mess. Beside the waiting Ju-52, an engineer was making the final adjustments to a new tyre. Dieter, who was flying as co-pilot with Georg, had already had a look at the passenger list.

'There's normally a scramble for the best seats,' he told Tam. 'The man you want to avoid is Julius Streicher. He looks like Mussolini and everyone hates him. Georg thinks he's the conscience of the Party, which is good news because it means Georg still has a sense of humour. What are you doing in Nuremberg, by the way? I never asked.'

'I've come for the show,' Tam said lightly. 'Will that do?'

*

Half an hour later Tam was in the air. Julius Streicher, who was sitting across the aisle, spent most of the flight scribbling notes and pestering the uniformed adjutant for more coffee. On the descent towards Nuremberg, sudden turbulence spilled most of the third cup in his lap and he called loudly for a towel. The rest of the passengers were a mix of *Wehrmacht* and SS. One or two lowered their newspapers and watched Streicher's efforts to clean himself up with quiet satisfaction.

Schultz was waiting at the airfield at Nuremberg, part of a gaggle of uniformed adjutants awaiting their superiors from Berlin. Passengers from the plane, after an exchange of Hitler salutes, disappeared into a fleet of limousines and headed for the city. Schultz and Tam were the last to leave.

'I was hoping for tonight.' Schultz seldom wasted time on small talk. 'But it's not going to happen. The man has other appointments. I told him you could wait at your hotel in case things changed but he said that was pointless. Later in the week, I'm afraid.'

'The man?'

Schultz shook his head. One of the conditions on meeting at all was the preservation of anonymity until the last possible moment.

'Then he's waiting,' Tam pointed out. 'On events.'

'Of course he is.'

'In case anything changes.'

'Yes.'

'And then what?'

'It depends. Things can happen in Prague, in Karlovy Vary, and they probably will. But things can also happen in London and Paris.'

'Which is where I come in.'

'Indeed.' He put a meaty hand on Tam's sleeve. 'Let's just hope you're right, eh?'

He drove Tam into the city centre and dropped him off at a modest pension in the warren of alleys behind the Hauptmarkt. He'd be in touch later but didn't specify how or when. Tam booked in, left his bag at reception and returned at once to the street.

He'd never been to Nuremberg before and already he was impressed. Centuries of wealth had settled on the Altstadt and within the city walls it was easy to half-close your eyes, block out the traffic and imagine the way life must have been. This, after all, was the ancient treasure chest of the old German Empire, the city of Dürer, and of generation after generation of traders and artists and clerics whose fierce pride had given rise to churches and monuments and the soaring, half-timbered civic buildings it was still possible to glimpse behind the curtain of Nazi banners.

Wherever you walked there were new streets to explore, more cobblestones underfoot, yet another café where the pastries looked sumptuous and the coffee smelled irresistible. It was lunchtime now, the hour for serious eating, and the restaurants were packed with party functionaries bent over plates of *Schnitzel mit Kartoffelsalat*, poring over their schedules for the coming week. The place oozed self-confidence. Germany was on the move. Germany was pleased with itself. No wonder

Nuremberg, with its beguiling mix of quaintness and raw, Nazi energy, had become the cradle of the new regime.

Tam ate alone at a shadowed café within touching distance of the Hauptmarkt. Before he'd stepped out of the aircraft Dieter had pressed a folded note into his hand. It contained the name and address of a *Bierhalle* where he and Georg planned to share a beer or two in the early evening. Tam was very welcome to join them.

Tam left the café in the early afternoon and plotted a long, circuitous route back to his hotel. This was a city preparing for the carnival of parades, speeches, concerts, meetings and celebrations that would fill the week to come, and the place was already tuning up. There was music everywhere – from brass bands to a lone singer in a long cotton skirt performing outside a café bursting with Nazi uniforms. She was dark and Italian-looking with a face that might have belonged to a gypsy, and she sang excerpts from Bizet arias with a deep brio that drew waves of applause from the watching crowd. Tam loved *Carmen*, always had done, and he was mouthing the words from the 'Habanera' when he first became aware that he was being followed.

He'd seen the man before. Twice. He was thin, sallow-faced. He was wearing a dark suit with a white shirt open at the neck. There were stains on the shirt and his shoes badly needed a clean. He was carrying a copy of *Völkischer Beobachter*. He might have been a clerk in an enterprise that had seen better days. Or a Gestapo stooge, semi-submerged in the swirl of a busy afternoon.

Tam left the singer and headed back towards the hotel. Twice he paused at a street corner and on both occasions he turned quickly enough to spot his new friend ducking into a shop or a nearby café. Approaching the hotel, the man was still there, still in attendance, still watching, and Tam toyed with sauntering back and offering a formal introduction but decided there was no point. This was something he should expect, he told himself.

Up in his room, lying full length on the narrow bed, he shared the thought with Bella, who was still in Berlin. Last night, anticipating telephone conversations like these, they'd agreed a number of crude code words. *Thunder* would indicate a problem of some sort. *Rain* was the moment when the problem became serious. *Hans-Christian* was the mystery person he'd been despatched to see.

'Strange weather,' he told her. 'Everywhere I go there's thunder.'

'You should be flattered.' She was laughing. 'It doesn't happen to everyone. It's a sign of importance. Rain, too?'

'Not so far.'

'Have you got your coat?'

'Of course. But I doubt I'll need it.'

'And Hans-Christian?'

'Busy, I'm afraid.'

'So what do you do with yourself?'

He described the singer outside the café and began to sing to her down the phone.

'L'amour est un oiseau rebelle
Que nul ne peut apprivoiser,
Et c'est bien en vain qu'on l'appelle,
S'il lui convient de refuser.'

He came to a halt, forgetting the next line, and heard Bella clapping.

'Seville,' she said. 'For sure. We'll spend Christmas there. We'll go to Granada. We'll visit the Alhambra. No thunder. No rain. I promise.'

Seconds later she was gone, leaving Tam with the sun on his face through the open window. He napped for a while and then woke up, wondering whether this meeting of his would have happened before he saw her next. She was due to take the train south with embassy colleagues on Friday, leaving plenty of time to get organised before Hitler's big winding-up speech on Sunday. This was the moment, according to Bella, when the rest of the world would know whether or not to reach for their gas masks. In the light of what Tam had just seen in the streets, this was a difficult thought to comprehend. The city was bursting. So much laughter. So much music. But if the days of peace were truly numbered, then maybe Bella should take an earlier train. Like tonight. Or, at the latest, tomorrow morning.

*

Tam left the hotel at six. To his relief, the Watcher seemed to have disappeared. Following directions from the woman at the reception, he found the *Bierhalle* without difficulty. Stone steps led from the street to a basement. There was a poster for a Bruckner concert on the door and the promise of a ten per cent discount on production of a party membership card. It was dark inside and it took a moment or two for Tam to get his bearings. Faces swam out of a gloom laden with the heady fug of beer and cigar smoke. For once, there wasn't a uniform to be seen.

He found Dieter at a table near the back. So far, he hadn't laid eyes on Georg. At first glance he was nearly as tall as Tam himself.

'So you're this morning's pilot?'

Georg nodded but didn't say anything. Tam noticed that Dieter hadn't got a drink.

'You want a beer?' Tam had signalled a woman with fistfuls of the big steins, busying from table to table.

'He's flying tomorrow,' Georg grunted. 'If you think I'm his keeper you'd be right. Fall out of an aeroplane once and you never want to do it again. True, *compadre*? Or am I making this stuff up?'

'Never.' Dieter was swaying gently on his bar stool, as if the entire bar was afloat. 'Tomorrow we'll have a proper night of it, I promise. We think you're a spy, by the way. Please don't disappoint us.'

'*He* thinks you're a spy.' Georg reached for his beer. 'Me? I was reserving judgement.'

'And now?'

'A spy. For sure. Every other nation on earth tries to make their spies hard to spot. Only the English save you the trouble of working it out for yourself.'

Tam's gaze went from face to face. Dieter was drunk. That much was obvious. Under the circumstances, Tam's best defence was to play along with the joke.

'You're right,' he said. 'I am a spy.'

'And you've come for the big show?' Dieter asked. 'The animals? The clowns? One half of the nation thinking they've seen God? The other half with its trousers down?'

'Of course.'

'Then welcome.'

Tam stopped the woman with the steins. He passed one beer to Georg and took another for himself before proposing a toast.

'To God,' he said. 'And the Czechs.'

'More bloody trouble than they're worth.' Dieter again, his head lowered. 'The good guys are the Sudetens. Why? Because they speak German. The bad guys are the Czechs. Why? Because they don't. Blacks and whites. Your face fits or it doesn't. I think I want to throw up.'

Dieter put a hand on Tam's arm, the lightest touch, and then slipped off the stool and made his way towards the lavatory. Georg and Tam exchanged looks.

'He's really flying tomorrow?' Tam asked.

'Mid-afternoon. Over the Zeppelinfeld. After the opening ceremony.' He began to count the fingers of his left hand. 'That's twenty hours, give or take. Lots of water. A night's sleep. He should be OK.'

Tam was staring at him. He couldn't get the memory of the little fighter over Berlin out of his head. The tiny silver fish in the blueness of the sky.

'Does this stuff go with that kind of flying?' Tam nodded at Georg's stein.

'Only once. Unless you're lucky.'

'And your friend?'

'He's lucky.'

'So it happens a lot?'

'No. Only recently. Very recently. You want to take notes? Or you have a spy's memory?'

'I remember the important stuff. Always. In perfect detail. The rest I put out with the rubbish.'

'Very wise. Your German is excellent, better than most of my friends. But then everyone will tell you that.'

'You're kind. And it's not true.' Tam held his gaze. 'So why is your friend drinking so much?'

'That's not a question I should be answering. Not to you.'

'Because I'm an Englishman?'

'Because you're not family. Merz has no one. That should be obvious enough.'

'I don't believe it.'

'Suit yourself. He happens to like you, which is a very considerable compliment. Merz is a man who lives on his nerve ends. He has excellent reflexes, which is no surprise at all, but he also relies on his instincts. Those instincts rarely let him down, especially where other people are concerned. He can smell a phoney like a dog can smell a fox, and he can do it from many metres downwind. He doesn't work it out. He doesn't put all the clues together and draw the appropriate conclusions. He just *knows*.'

'Is that why he thinks I'm a spy?'

'In a way, yes. But he knows something else as well. The man's a spy, he told me. And he's shit at it. For Merz, that's a mark in your favour. He thinks you're miscast. And he's intrigued to know why you let that happen.'

It was a very good question. Tam had asked it himself on a number of occasions.

'Maybe I'm a patriot,' he said. 'Would that help?'

'We're all patriots. Every country is a mother and we all have one. But in the end, thank God, there are closer ties. I've known Merz for years, which has been a pleasure as well as a privilege, and there have been moments when we saved each other's lives.'

'His more than yours?'

'Yes. But mine, also.'

'And is now one of those times?'

'It is, yes. Tomorrow will be no problem. Shortly, I will take him back to where we sleep. I shall stand guard like the trusty dog I am and make sure he drinks only water. He has a strong body, strong guts. The problem is up here,' he tapped his head, 'and in here,' a hand cupped his heart. 'Merz is a very emotional man and just now that puts him in a very dangerous place. The fact that he likes you, trusts you, suggests to me that you, too, have some of this instinct, this awareness, that can make life so tough.' His eyes strayed to the corner of the bar where the lavatories lay. Dieter had emerged. His face was pale and he was wiping his mouth with the back of his hand. Georg watched him for a moment and then returned to Tam. 'This conversation never happened. We agree on that?'

*

Tam was in the huge crowd out at the Zeppelinfeld when he next laid eyes on Dieter. The arena was the one display area to have been completed, a gigantic stage where the Reich could mount spectacular parades of martial prowess, and Tam had found himself a seat on one of the banked stone terraces amongst tens of thousands of others. Below him, column after column of uniformed infantry seemed to stretch for ever, untold divisions of Germany's finest, hundreds of thousands of shock troops. Helmets gleamed in the sun. Hundreds of swastika flags rippled in the soft wind. Arms rose, palm down, at the faintest mention of the Führer. *Sieg Heil!* yelled the distant figure behind the bank of microphones. *Heil Hitler!* came the answering roar from half a million men.

Tam had just sat through a series of interminable speeches about martyrdom and motherhood, about the nation's birthright and the nation's destiny, about the sacrifices and the glory that lay ahead. Everywhere there were huge black loudspeakers and the voices from the tiny figures on the tribune in the far distance echoed and re-echoed across the vast arena. After the speeches came marching bands, a cavalry charge, and finally a parade of tanks, each commander standing upright in his turret. The dust was settling when a stir went through the arena and faces looked skywards as the growl of the lone 109 stilled the crowd.

The display, to Tam, was magnificent. It was hard to associate the succession of dives and rolls and dizzying loops with the hunched figure in last night's bar. This was a plane in the hands of someone of rare genius, of someone who'd broken the fragile ties that bound normal beings to Mother Earth. The plane, with its bold swastika on the tail, soared into yet another climb, rolled off the top of the loop and then headed south-west in what many mistook for the end of the display. Wrong. Seconds later, out of the sun, it was back again, passing low over the arena, maximum speed, its little pilot clearly visible, lifting the nose an inch or two to clear the oncoming saluting tribune. The tribune was white with upturned faces and Tam watched the shadow of the plane race over the crowd before the beat of the engine began to fade.

There was a moment's silence before a portly new figure steadied himself behind the microphones. Tam recognised the voice at once. The father of the Air Force. The *Luftwaffe*'s patron saint. The one-time commander of the Richthofen Squadron. Herman Goering.

He asked for the crowd's support and he got it. The *Luftwaffe* had taken the first of the Reich's young warriors into action, he reminded them. They'd shown the Communists just what Germany could do. Over Spain, in the shape of young pilots like Dieter Merz, they were giving the Reds a spanking they'd never forget. Millions of foreigners from London to Paris to New York to Tokyo were witnessing an epic battle that could, in the end, have only one outcome. The likes of Dieter Merz were sweeping the enemy from the skies and in so doing cleansing the soul of Spain. This was what was possible. And this is what the rest of the world should expect.

The crowd loved it. Thanks to German engineering, German daring and German courage, Goering roared, there would be no escape, no quarter. Hands on hips, he thrust out his chest. In the air, he said, the Reich spoke only the language of conquest. At the heart of the *Luftwaffe*, the long arm of the bomber force. Protecting those brave men, fliers like Dieter Merz. What other nation on the face of the earth could resist a power like that? He glared out at the ocean of faces, letting the question hang in the heat of the afternoon, then he thrust a uniformed arm towards the crowd. *Heil Hitler!* came the answering incantation. *Heil Hitler! Heil Hitler!*

Afterwards, Tam badly needed a drink. This week's events marked the tenth anniversary of the Nuremberg Rally. He already knew from Bella that each one had been themed. That was the way that Goebbels liked to play it, tossing sixty million Germans fresh chunks of propaganda to whet their appetite for what lay ahead. The theme to this year's rally was

Grossdeutschland, Greater Germany, a week-long homage to the guile and sheer guts of a leader who'd already delivered Austria without firing a single bullet, and as Tam fought to keep his place in the flood of spectators pouring out of the Zeppelinfeld, he wondered what surprises next year's rally might offer. Would the Czechs have folded? Would the Poles? The French? The English? Where did it end? And what new stunts might *Der Kleine* pull to celebrate yet more victories?

He found him hours later, sitting alone at a table at the very back of the same *Bierhalle*. After the display there'd been plans to whisk him away for a reception at the Deutsche Hof, Hitler's hotel, but he had no taste, he said, for Goebbels' brand of celebrity. The movie that had won him a national following had been fine in its way but the worship of millions of *Mädchen* was a joke, a fantasy. These women knew absolutely nothing about him. The darkness and the anonymity of the *Bierhalle* was therefore more than welcome, a place of sanctuary and of solace, somewhere he could briefly call his own.

When Tam offered, he said yes to a drink. His next flying display was two days away and there was no Georg to keep an eye on him.

'Where is he?'

'Back in Berlin. He flew a full load this afternoon. Georg is a lucky man. He likes sleeping in his own bed.'

'He's married?'

'Very. And she's perfect for him.'

Dieter began to talk about Beata. Then he described the wedding celebrations and the Jew Sol Fiedler and the dark presence of the *Reichsminister* for Foreign Affairs.

'Brickendrop was there?'

'Who?'

Tam explained the term. Dieter was delighted.

'Brickendrop.' He tried the word out in his mouth, the way you'd taste something you didn't entirely trust. 'It means idiot, you say?'

'Fool. Buffoon. The man made lots of enemies in London. People laughed at him.'

'Here, too. Except he lives in the pocket of the Führer, which puts him beyond reach. Without Hitler, he'd be nothing. Maybe less than nothing.'

Tam nodded. He wanted to know what it felt like to be doing what Dieter had done this afternoon over a crowd that large. Speaking personally, he couldn't begin to imagine it.

'It had to be half a million people,' he said. 'At least.'

'You counted them?'

'I read it in the paper.'

'The *Beobachter*? Believe nothing.'

'Of course. But you're up there. Bird's-eye view. Just you. So what's it like?'

The question put a smile on Dieter's face. Georg was right, Tam thought, he really likes me. Dieter was studying a tiny cuticle of nail on his thumb. He picked at it, then looked up.

'You want the truth? You make a high pass first, a really high pass. You don't want anyone to see you, to hear you. You want to settle yourself down, nice and easy, take a look around, taste the wind, fill your lungs, clear your throat. . .'

'Literally?'

'God no, the cockpit opens sideways. You'd never get the thing closed again. It's in here,' he tapped his head, 'you have to be *ready*.'

'And then?'

'And then you start. You have a routine. One thing follows another. It's like dancing in a way. Except you *are* the music.'

You are the music. Perfect.

Dieter hadn't finished. There was something else he wanted to say. Not about the flying or the various elements in the display, or that mysterious kinship between his fingertips and the machine that every flier recognised. No. It was about Nuremberg, the city itself, the way it looked from ten thousand feet, and the difference the regime had made in five short years.

'I came here the last year my father was alive,' he said. 'He told me it was the finest city in Germany and maybe he was right. It felt very old and very beautiful. I could see that. Even as a kid, even then.'

'So what happened?'

'The Nazis.'

'You're a party member?'

'No.'

'Your father, maybe?'

'Never. He thought they were thugs, gangsters, and he was right. But what none of us knew, none of us *realised*, was how clever they were. And how ambitious.'

He began to talk about the new cluster of monumental buildings to the south-east of the town, away beyond the Hauptbahnhof. Albert Speer's Luitpoldarena. The Congresshalle. The fat arrow-thrust of Grossestrasse. And, grandest of all, the Zeppelinfeld. Tam had walked round these sites earlier. Most were promissory notes hidden behind scaffolding but collectively Dieter was right. They were real. They were enormous. They were totally different in scale to anything else that had ever been built, huge down payments in granite and reinforced concrete on a thousand year future only one man had glimpsed.

'A thousand years,' Dieter mused. 'Will it ever happen? *Should* it ever happen? Who knows? But it exists. You can see it, touch it, feel it, be part of it. That's the cleverness. That's what my father never took into account. He thought they'd never last. He thought they'd be gone. And he was wrong.'

'And from ten thousand feet?'

'It looks like a cancer, a tumour, a growth, something that doesn't *belong.* Get enough height and you can see exactly what they're doing. That whole complex, it feeds off something that was once a thing of beauty. It's so obvious. So clear. You needn't be a surgeon. You just have to *look*. These people do terrible things. They're sucking the life out of the old Germany. And in the end they'll kill it.' He stared at his empty glass and then glanced up at Tam. His eyes were moist. 'More beer?'

25

NUREMBERG, 8 SEPTEMBER 1938

Bella arrived midweek, the Wednesday, two days early. She'd phoned Tam at the hotel when he was still in bed. She was taking the train and would be in Nuremberg by late afternoon. It was important they met. Still half-asleep, Tam gave her the name of the café where he'd listened to the lone singer. He'd be there from four o'clock. He might be in the company of a friend.

Bella arrived half an hour late, directly from the station. A taxi dropped her at the kerbside and it was Dieter who was first to his feet to carry her suitcase back to the table. She looked at him the way most strangers did. A face familiar from God knows where. Of the Watcher, for once, there was no sign.

Tam had a chair ready on the tiny terrace. After yesterday's rain it was sunny again and unseasonably warm. Hitler weather.

'Dieter Merz,' Tam said. 'My guide and protector.'

Dieter offered a courtly bow and extended a hand. Bella was still staring at the face.

'You're the flier,' she said at last.

'I am.'

'Wonderful.'

'What does that mean?'

'I've seen the film. Twice as it happens. What a job.'

Dieter nodded, said nothing. Then he bent quickly to whisper something in Tam's ear, smiled at Bella and stepped out on to the street. Seconds later, he'd disappeared.

'A pressing engagement,' Tam explained. 'Either that or he wants to leave us alone. Shame. I wanted you to meet him properly.'

'Another time, maybe.' Bella was already hunting through the contents of her bag. 'You need to read this.'

She produced a copy of *The Times*. Copies had been flown across from London on yesterday's morning flight to Berlin.

'Page seven,' she said. 'You can't miss it.'

Tam found himself looking at a leader addressing the subject of Czechoslovakia. He scanned it quickly. It expressed impatience with the slow progress of talks about Henlein's demands for Sudeten independence and ended with a long-winded plea on behalf of 'that fringe of alien population who are contiguous to the nation to which they are united by race'.

'This is an argument for break-up.' Tam was frowning. 'Who wrote it?'

'Geoffrey Dawson. He's the editor.'

'He's doing Hitler's work for him. This is the stuff of Henlein's dreams. Independence on a plate.'

'Exactly. The Russians are up in arms. Prague are demanding an explanation. Even the French want to know whether this represents the official view.'

'And does it?'

'The Foreign Office says no.'

'And Halifax?'

'Halifax had a couple of meetings yesterday with Masaryk. The man's a Czech. He's very emotional, a real patriot. He's outraged, of course, and we understand there was a great deal of table-thumping. In the end Halifax had the grace to disown the piece. That means nothing, of course, and Masaryk knows it. As do this lot.'

Tam sat back, folding the paper. Two streets away he could hear the blare of a band and the thump-thump of jackboots on the cobblestones as yet another parade swung through the Hauptmarkt. Hitler might be there, standing beside his gleaming Mercedes, ready to take the salute, or it might be any of the other chieftains who'd arrived in the city with their separate courts.

Bella hadn't finished.

'Something else.' She reached for the paper. 'Hitler's upped his demands. He wants Prague as well as the Sudeten. The Dutch and the Belgians have called up their reserves. And so have we.'

'A good sign?'

'Possibly. Maybe the penny's beginning to drop.' She smiled. 'Maybe that trip to Chartwell wasn't wasted. We can but hope.'

Tam nodded. His conversation with Churchill seemed to belong to another life. After three days in this city, under constant bombardment from every quarter of the party machine, he was beginning to think like a Nazi, not a pleasant experience.

'These people are frightening,' he murmured. 'Even Dieter Merz says so.'

*

The summons to meet *Reichsführer* Himmler had arrived at noon. For the last three days, through a variety of back channels, Dieter had been trying to secure ten minutes of the SS leader's time. The overlord tasked with keeping the Reich safe had a suite in a grand hotel near the Castle. Merz was to report to reception at five o'clock and ask for *Standartenführer* Lindt.

Lindt, to Dieter's surprise, was waiting for him inside the big double doors. He offered a formal bow and the Hitler salute and complimented Dieter on Sunday's display over the Zeppelinfeld. He'd lost count, he said, of the compliments from friends and comrades. Even the *Reichsführer* regarded the appearance of the 109 as the highlight of the afternoon. One could, he said with the suspicion of a smile, have just a little too much of horse-drawn artillery and massed armour.

Himmler's suite, heavily guarded, was on the hotel's first floor. Pausing beside the sentries at the door, Lindt warned Dieter that the *Reichsführer* was in his bath. This evening he was hosting a reception for the domestic and clerical staff from Wewelsburg Castle, a social occasion that had become an important feature of the SS calendar, and the first guests would be arriving in less than an hour.

Dieter nodded. Wewelsburg Castle was in the north of Germany and it had become a shrine for the SS. On *Luftwaffe* bases the length of the country mere mention of the place sparked the blackest of jokes but for true believers it had an almost religious pull.

Lindt opened the door and stood aside to let Dieter in. The sitting room was huge and over-furnished – reproduction furniture, heavy drapes at the window, and a vast conference table with room for a dozen chairs. Through an open door at one end, Dieter had a glimpse of a bedroom.

'Please,' Lindt gestured towards the bedroom, 'the *Reichsführer* is expecting you.'

Dieter stepped inside. Yet another door, also open, led to the bathroom. Dieter could hear the splash of water and an occasional grunt.

'You want me to go in?' Dieter nodded at the open door.

'No. Here, please.' Lindt patted the coverlet on the bed. 'The *Reichsführer* would like to conduct the interview from his bath but it would show respect to grant him a little privacy.'

Lindt closed the door to the sitting room and settled himself at the table beneath the window. A pad had been readied. Two pencils, both newly sharpened, both black.

'Merz?' It was Himmler calling from the bathroom. 'Are you there? Are you ready?'

Dieter muttered his assent. All he could see through the open door was a pair of pink feet. One of them toyed with the hot tap, on-off, on-off. Bizarre, he thought.

Himmler made a laboured joke about the presence of so famous a film star in his bedroom and then wanted to know his business. Unfortunately, he could give young Merz only a little of his time.

'You have my full attention, Merz. An explanation, if you please.'

Dieter tried to keep it simple. He was here to play the lovelorn victim, the patriot-flier who awoke one morning to find Himmler's policemen at his door. For reasons he still couldn't fathom, they'd arrested the woman with whom he intended to share his life. All he wanted to know was why this had happened and when Keiko Ayama might be released.

From next door, there was silence. Then a big toe found the tap and more steam arose from the bath.

'Ayama,' Himmler mused at length. 'You know about the family?'

'Of course. They're very successful.'

'And rich, we understand.'

'Indeed.'

Another silence. Then the toe turned off the tap and Himmler called for shampoo. Lindt got to his feet and disappeared into the bathroom. Moments later he was back.

'Ribbentrop.' It was Himmler again. 'It appears he reported a number of missing documents. Might you know anything about that?'

'No, Herr *Reichsführer*.'

'And Miss Ayama? She knew?'

'Not to my knowledge.'

'But you're aware the two of them used to meet a great deal?'

'Yes.'

'And you're aware of the gravity of a charge like that? Assuming she had something to do with the missing documents?'

'Of course.'

'She's a foreign national, Herr Merz. I hardly need to point that out. She comes to our country as a guest. Guests are expected to behave themselves. If they don't, their lives could become difficult. Regrettable, I agree. But necessary.'

Dieter said nothing. Behind him, Lindt was making notes. Then came a splash of water and a sigh. He's washing his hair, Dieter thought, while a woman's life hangs in the balance. Very SS.

Dieter swallowed hard. He'd been toying with this question for days, aware that the answer might shape the rest of his life.

'You really think she's a spy, Herr *Reichsführer*? Please be frank with me.'

There was no reply. Dieter stared at the open door. Then the feet disappeared and he caught a thump as Himmler struggled to his feet in the bath. Lindt fetched a dressing gown from a wardrobe in the corner of the bedroom and laid it carefully on the bed beside Dieter. Moments later, Himmler was standing in the open doorway, wiping the condensation from his glasses, his little pot belly and thin legs enveloped in a towel.

He gazed down at Dieter. He was evidently in a good mood.

'I understand you're keeping interesting company, Herr Merz.'

'Where?'

'Here. The Englishman. The tall one.'

Dieter nodded, said nothing. Himmler took another towel from Lindt and began to dry his hair. He wanted to know more about the Englishman.

'His name's Moncrieff, Herr *Reichsführer.* We flew him down from Berlin on Sunday.'

'And he's become a friend?'

'Yes. In a way he has.'

'You like him?'

'Yes.'

'Trust him?'

'Yes.'

'Good.' He paused to put on his watch. Then he looked up. 'You know about Prinz-Albrecht-Strasse? SS and Gestapo headquarters?'

'Of course.'

'Your Miss Ayama's been there for nearly a week now. Down in the basement.' He smiled. 'Good luck with your new friend, Herr Merz. Keep talking. And keep listening. We understand each other, *ja*?' The pink ankles came to attention on the wet carpet, a gesture of dismissal. '*Heil Hitler!*'

*

Tam met Bella for the second time in mid-evening. Embassy staff had been summoned by the Ambassador, Nevile Henderson, after a longish meeting with Goering. The *Luftwaffe* chief's patience with the diplomatic comings and goings over Czechoslovakia was exhausted and he was now broaching the possibility of direct face-to-face negotiations to sort the matter out. As a gesture of good intent, he was trying to tempt Halifax to the table with the offer of a hunting expedition at the end of the month, with four of the best stags in Germany guaranteed. This conversation was the subject of a detailed note dictated by Henderson and despatched by private plane barely an hour ago.

'Has Goering read *The Times*?' asked Tam.

'Of course he has. They all have. They assume it's written in Downing Street and in some respects they're right.'

'So where does that leave the Czechs?'

Bella said she didn't know. The feeling was growing that Hitler's speech, now just days away, would offer the key to everything that might follow but just now that was the least of her problems.

'It gets worse?'

'It does. Hitler's on again tomorrow. This time he's talking about art. The great man's thoughts. Where Michelangelo and Rembrandt and Picasso and the rest of them went wrong. Me? I made the big mistake of expressing an interest in some of this stuff and as a result I've got a ticket as a delegate. Front row. High visibility. Showing the flag for my beloved country. Believe me, it doesn't get much worse.'

'Sekt?'

'Afterwards. They're not fools, these people. We'll all be asleep by then. And you?'

They were sitting in the front window of a restaurant down by the river. There was a terrace at the back that overlooked the river Pegnitz but on the street side the view was restricted to a row of half-timbered houses rented out to top party officials for the duration of the rally.

'Over there,' Tam said. 'Second lamp post on the left. Don't make it too obvious.'

'What am I looking for?'

'Thunder.'

'Description?'

'Old grey suit. White shirt. All very shabby. I think he probably sleeps in this stuff.'

Bella took her time before stealing a look over her shoulder. Then she was back with Tam.

'This is the same one you mentioned on the phone?'

'Yes. There was a day when he didn't turn up at all, but since then it's like having a dog. He follows me everywhere. He's very faithful. We've started nodding to each other. Yesterday he smiled at me. Tomorrow we might even get to talk.'

'Schultz? Has he seen you and Schultz together?'

'No. That's probably why Schultz is keeping his distance.'

'No contact at all?'

'None. I'm starting to feel a bit of a fraud.'

'I bet.' Bella glanced out of the window again and then her hand stole across the table cloth and she leaned forward for a kiss. 'Why don't we give him something to keep him interested?'

*

Bella was staying at a hotel beyond the railway station, on the road out towards the Zeppelinfeld. Tam walked her home. It was true about Schultz. Without his one and only link to the conspiracy, Tam felt himself marooned in a strange limbo. Should he treat his week in this carnival city as some kind of holiday? Or should he be thinking day and night about the meeting which still might transpire? His single chance to stiffen these people's resolve and point them in the direction that Schultz wanted them to go?

He didn't know and, worse still, he was fast losing faith in being able to make any kind of difference. Only now, in the very cradle of the regime, was he beginning to understand the sheer reach of Hitler's Reich. Everything was listened to, monitored, noted, cross-referenced, and the thought of someone unseen trying to make sense of all this information was deeply unsettling. To find yourself under the gaze of a permanent Watcher, on the other hand, was almost a solace. In this instance the regime at least had a face and a physical presence.

Tam said goodbye to Bella at the hotel door, promising to make contact in the morning, and set off back towards the railway station. The city was still alive, still busy, people everywhere, and twice he spotted what he assumed to be the Watcher but on both occasions he was wrong. Beyond the railway station the main road made a sharp turn to the right before penetrating the walls of the Altstadt. Tam assumed the car behind him was slowing for the bend but it came to a halt beside him. He glanced down, glimpsing the face in the back. Schultz.

The rear door opened. Tam climbed in.

'We're going now?' he said to Schultz. 'This is it?'

'Ja.'

Nothing else. No name. No clues. Just a blur of faces on the pavement as the driver hauled the car into a U-turn and accelerated away from the city centre.

Tam sat back, oddly content, knowing that this encounter would mark the end of his assignment. He'd try and do himself justice. He'd try his level best to convince whoever wanted to listen that the conspirators had allies in England who'd call Hitler's bluff. Beyond that, as he knew only too well, he was helpless.

They were en route through the suburbs towards the complex of new buildings where the rally's main events were being held. A late-night tram clattered past, heading back into the city. Ahead lay the entrance to the Zeppelinfeld.

The car was slowing now, Schultz leaning forward, talking to the driver. He was to look for a mobile field headquarters. He described it as a big caravan, an office on wheels. The driver was circling the outside of the Zeppelinfeld. Ahead, looming out of the darkness, Tam could see vehicles parked nose to nose across the paved roadway. Then came a soldier, stepping out of nowhere, his carbine readied, and another, and finally a third. The last one was the officer. He bent to the driver's window, checked his papers, shone a torch into the back of the car. The beam of the torch lingered on Tam, and he thought he heard the click of a camera, but he couldn't be certain. Then Schultz was telling him to get out of the car.

Tam stood in the darkness. The bulk of the caravan loomed ahead of him. Abruptly an oblong of light appeared as someone opened a door. Silhouetted against the light was a portly figure he'd seen only recently. The big barrel chest. The hands planted on the hips. The hint of an outstretched hand as Tam got closer.

'Herr Moncrieff.' The voice – laden with the beginnings of a cold – was still unmistakeable. Hermann Goering.

Tam shook hands, glad to be spared the Hitler salute. The caravan was bare and functional: a desk with a bank of telephones, a map of the Zeppelinfeld with various sectors carefully edged in different colours, and three clocks, each set to a different hour.

Goering was watching Tam's every movement. His visitor's interest in the clocks seemed to amuse him. The middle one, he said, was Berlin time. On the left, two hours ahead, Moscow.

'And this one, Herr Moncrieff?' He stepped forward and tapped the clock on the right.

Tam studied it for a moment. It was an hour behind. The answer, he knew, was all too obvious.

'London?' he enquired. 'Is this some kind of clue?'

The word *clue* produced a roar of laughter.

'You think you're next, Herr Moncrieff? You think that's all it takes? You think we have an army of watchmakers? Vienna time? Prague time? Paris time? *London* time? If only it was so simple.'

An aide in *Luftwaffe* uniform had joined them. He had a bottle of brandy and two glasses. Tam watched while the Field Marshal lowered his bulk into the bigger of two chairs readied in the far corner. At Goering's invitation, Tam took the other one.

'It's Spanish, I'm afraid. The Civil War has done us many favours and this is one of them.' Goering was examining the bottle. 'A Gran Reserva Imperial. If you like it, the others in the box are yours.'

He dismissed the aide and told him to lock the door. He wanted no interruptions and no one anywhere near the door or the windows.

'If you see anyone taking an interest, shoot them. Understood?'

The aide saluted and Tam heard the turn of a key in the lock seconds after he shut the door. Goering spread his legs and plucked at the creases in his uniform trousers before unstopping the bottle and pouring two generous measures. Tam couldn't help counting the rings on his fingers. There were four.

'It pays to be frank, Herr Moncrieff.' He passed one of the glasses to Tam and then patted him on the thigh. 'I have many friends in England and they all tell me the same thing. What do you think that same thing might be?'

'This is to do with the Czechs?'

'Of course.' One finger drew a large circle in the air. 'Everything has to do with the Czechs.'

'Then I don't know. I too have friends, contacts, colleagues. That's why I'm here.'

'These people are in Downing Street?'

'No.'

'Who, then? I need names.'

Tam had anticipated this question, as had Ballentyne. 'Winston Churchill,' he said carefully.

'Churchill is an old man. Churchill counts for nothing. Brave in his day, a real warhorse, but now he belongs in the meadow. Who else?'

'You won't have heard of them.'

'That's an assumption. Just tell me.'

'Anthony Eden. Duff Cooper. Harold Nicolson.'

Goering said nothing. From the nearby Zeppelinfeld he could hear a roll of drums. Tam held his gaze. Then Goering lifted his glass.

'To Churchill,' he said. 'In that meadow of his.'

The brandy torched Tam's throat. He felt his eyes beginning to water. Goering swallowed half the glass and wiped his mouth with the back of his hand.

'So these people of yours say what?'

'Two things. They say that we should fight. And they say that we will fight.'

'And if you don't?'

'Then the Government will fall.'

'Governments only fall because they lose the support of the people. You're telling me the English want another war? So soon?'

'The English recognise evil when they see it.'

'*Evil?*' The word appeared to amuse him. 'We're that bad?'

'Not you, Herr *Feldmarschall*. Hitler.'

'Ah. . . an Englishman who tells the truth. Very rare, if I may say so.'

'I'm from north of the border, Herr *Feldmarschall*. When it comes to the truth, we Scots have no time for anything else.'

'Touché.' He appeared to be delighted. Another mouthful of brandy and the glass was empty. 'Did you hear about Ribbentrop today? He received a deputation of ambassadors this morning, our people from London, Paris, Rome and Washington, the four corners of the known world. And you know what they all told him? They told him exactly what you've just said. That France and England and maybe even Russia mean to stand by their treaty commitments. That they have the stomach for a proper fight. And you know what Ribbentrop did? He sent them all packing. He told them to take leave. Compulsory leave. They are not to trouble him with news like this and they are absolutely forbidden to approach the Führer. Why? Because Hitler wants a fight and Ribbentrop is determined that he shall have it. My friends in England tell me that Chamberlain thinks Hitler is beset by monsters. He couldn't be more wrong. Because Hitler *is* the monster. The biggest monster. The Führer-Monster. And in a country like this, a regime like this, he needs to be.'

Tam nodded. It made perfect sense.

'Get rid of Hitler,' he said. 'And peace stands a fighting chance.'

'I could have you shot for that.'

'I know you could.'

'You don't care?'

'I'm a Scot. I told you. I care a great deal. But not about Hitler.'

Goering smiled. He seemed, if anything, to be impressed. He nodded at Tam's glass and proffered the bottle. Tam shook his head, watching Goering fill his own. This man, after all, was Hitler's designated successor. Should Hitler die, the office of Chancellor would be his.

'Who says we want that kind of peace?' Goering was gazing at the brandy. 'The peace of the landowners? The peace of the aristocrats? In Germany we fight a people's war. Everything comes from the people. You heard the Führer say it only a couple of days ago. So it must be true, *ja*?' He raised his glass and this time the smile was wider.

'That's insolence,' Tam said. 'He could have you shot for that.'

'The Führer holds me in high regard. I bring him nothing but good news.'

'And Ribbentrop?'

'Ribbentrop brings him fantasies.' He paused. 'How many other people have you talked to in Germany?'

'One.'

'Schultz? He's a good man, his own man, that's rare.' He was frowning now. 'No one else?'

'No one.'

'I don't believe you.'

Tam shrugged. He had no intention of mentioning General Beck, but the brandy had warmed him. He felt bigger, bolder, more secure. He knew he'd become an object of curiosity for this man, an opportunity for Goering to try out a theory or two in the privacy of their own company, and he had no objection to playing along. A game, he thought. Like so much else in the merciless upper reaches of the Reich.

'What would you do, Herr Moncrieff? If you were me?'

'I'd get rid of Hitler.'

'Why?'

'Because he doesn't know when to stop. Because he'll go on and on until someone arrives with a bigger stick.'

'And you think that will happen?'

'Of course it will. In a thousand years? I doubt it. In a hundred? Maybe.'

'In a hundred years we'll all be dead, Mr Moncrieff. Even Hitler.'

'Then the question is academic.' Tam nodded at the bottle. 'Yes, please.'

*

The phone in Tam's hotel room rang at half-past eight. Tam rolled over and groped for the phone. It was Bella.

'Schultz tells me you saw Goering last night.'

'That's right."

'And?'

'We got very drunk.'

'And?'

'I failed completely. He's got the measure of us. They all have.'

Tam put the phone down. His head was splitting and he felt ill. He made himself throw up in the bathroom and did it again ten minutes later. The water in Nuremberg tasted slightly sweet. He'd noticed it before. He drank a full glass, then another, then a third. Back in bed he drifted off to sleep, trying to keep the worst of the nightmares at bay, but the same two faces swam up through the murkiness of the swamp in which he was desperately trying to stay afloat. Renata. Edvard. People he'd failed. People who'd died.

By the time he awoke again it was late morning. He could hear the distant rattle of trams from the Hauptmarkt. Much closer, a woman was singing something he didn't recognise in German. He lay motionless, marvelling at the way the water appeared to have purged his system, not wanting his head to split in half again. Last night Goering had bested him in every department: he'd drunk more, told better jokes and surfed the wave of bonhomie that had carried them through to dawn. How on earth the man could cope with yet another day of back-to-back engagements after a night like that was beyond him. Maybe all the Nietzschean tosh about a race of Supermen wasn't so crazy after all. The Third Reich's best-kept secret? Spanish brandy.

Someone must have driven Tam back to the hotel. He didn't remember who. He rolled over and stepped carefully out of bed. He'd kept Ballentyne's London number in his wallet. He fetched it out and reached for the phone. Dimly, he remembered the three clocks on the wall in the caravan last night and he wondered whether there was anything symbolic in London being an hour behind the rest of the continent. Was that the time it took for the penny to drop? Was Britain fated to be for ever at the mercy of developments across the Channel?

The moment Ballentyne recognised Tam's voice he wanted to know whether the line was secure.

'It's not,' Tam said. 'But it doesn't matter. It's over. I'm coming home.'

'We understand your meeting wasn't a success.'

'That's not true. It was deeply pleasurable.'

'That's not what I meant.'

'Then you're right.' Tam, naked, was staring out of the window. Bella, he thought. She's briefed him about Goering already. Just who could you trust in this world?

Ballentyne was telling him to stay put in Nuremberg. There was an edge to his voice that Tam hadn't heard before. The suggestion had the force of an order.

'Why?' Tam asked. 'What good can I do?'

'The situation is very fluid. It's changing from day to day, sometimes hour by hour. Stay in touch with Miss Menzies. And well done for last night.'

'I beg your pardon?' Tam was staring at the phone.

'We understand Goering wasn't at his best this morning.' At last Ballentyne managed a chuckle. 'You too, I suspect.'

*

That night Tam returned to the Zeppelinfeld, his head beginning to throb again. This time he was here to watch the *son et lumière*, an extravagant light show that had become a traditional midweek feature of the rally. Dieter had contacted him at the hotel and they met in the street outside before joining the crowds that were streaming out of the city towards the immense oval of vertical searchlights that prefaced the evening's entertainments. The Watcher, once again, had failed to turn up.

Inside the Zeppelinfeld the crowd was huge, gazing in awe at the white columns against the night sky, but the moment the speeches began they stilled, a sea of attentive faces. Dieter listened to the *Reichsminister* for Propaganda for no more than a minute or two. Then he turned to Tam.

'I can't take any more of this shit,' he said. 'We need a drink.'

Tam nodded in agreement, glad to be spared another dose of propaganda. Goering was next after Goebbels, doubtless recovered from his hangover. That meant at least a couple of hours of ceaseless haranguing. Tam and Dieter left the arena, threading their way past family after family, ignoring the disapproving frowns and muttered comments. Back out beyond Grossestrasse, Dieter hailed a passing taxi. Georg had introduced him to a bar on the other side of town. This time of night, with the fireworks due later, it should be half-empty.

It was. After a second beer Tam felt normal again. He wanted to know about Goering. Had Dieter ever met him?

'I have. A couple of times. He's a good boss and he's a big man. He fights our corner. He could also handle himself in the air. Pilots like to know that. It makes them feel more secure.'

'So how does he get on with Hitler?'

It was a direct question. Dieter looked up, surprised.

'Why do you ask?'

'I'm curious, that's all. Last night we had a few drinks.'

'We?'

'Me and your boss.'

'*Goering?*'

'Yes. I'd never met him before, never had the pleasure. He struck me as a real human being. Not someone you'd associate with the likes of Hitler.'

'You were alone, the pair of you?'

'Yes.'

'So what did you talk about? You mind me asking?'

'Not at all. We talked about Hitler. And then we talked about Czechoslovakia. And once we'd had enough of politics we talked about each other.'

Dieter nodded. He was still trying to work it all out.

'You're some kind of diplomat?'

'Hardly.'

'Then what are you?'

Tam shook his head. The fireworks out at the Zeppelinfeld had begun and beyond the window the night sky was blooming with golden flowers. A shorter dose of speeches than usual, he thought. Maybe, after all, Goering had failed to appear.

Tam gestured at Dieter's empty stein. For someone so slight, he seemed to have a bottomless capacity for alcohol. The woman behind the counter caught Tam's eye and pulled more beers. Dieter watched her approaching with the foaming steins, his eyes bright with anticipation.

'You find this helps?' Tam gestured at the beer.

'With what?'

'With whatever's happened to you.'

'Who says anything's happened?'

'Georg.'

'Georg is my friend. He shouldn't be saying things like that.'

'Maybe that's why he said it. That's what friends are supposed to be for. He cares about you. I'd take it as a compliment. It's a tough old world. Especially here.'

Dieter nodded, toying with his beer. Then he took another swallow or two.

'What else did he tell you?'

'Nothing. Except that you were drunk and you were due to fly next day and I thought that was odd. Georg said it wasn't. Not under the circumstances.'

'Georg thinks there's a reason for everything. If there isn't then he has to find one. He's that kind of guy.'

'But maybe he's right.'

'Yeah,' Dieter was gazing sightlessly into nowhere, 'maybe he is.'

Tam said nothing. After a long silence, Dieter beckoned him closer and described the accident that had nearly killed him. Months of hospital care had left him with a chronic pain he'd have to live with for the rest of his life. Then had come Keiko. In ways he still didn't understand, she'd made him whole again. Not only physically but in his head, and in his heart. They'd come back from Japan together. They'd lived together. She'd become irreplaceable.

'Lucky man,' Tam said.

'You think so?'

'I do.'

Dieter nodded, then reached for his glass. 'Have you ever heard of Prinz-Albrecht-Strasse?' he asked.

'No.'

'It's Gestapo headquarters. In Berlin. It's where you never want to end up.'

'And Keiko's there?'

'Yes.'

'So what has she done?'

'I've no idea. She's Japanese. That could be enough. It doesn't pay to be different any more, not in this country, not the way things are.'

'Then maybe you should change them.'

'Me? How do I do that? How does anyone?'

Tam sat back for a moment. He'd been anticipating this conversation for most of the week, ever since he'd watched Dieter displaying over the Zeppelinfeld. It was happening far more quickly than he'd expected but helplessness, as he recognised only too readily, could breed anger. And Dieter Merz was very angry indeed.

'You fly a fighter plane,' Tam pointed out. 'And you seem to belong to the squadron that flies the VIPs around.'

'That's true.'

'And those VIPs include Hitler?'

'Of course.'

'Then shoot him down.'

Dieter stared him. His hand found the stein again.

'Shoot him down?' he whispered. '*Hitler?*'

'Yes. It can't be hard. Not if they trust you. Not if you have access.'

'And Keiko?'

'You'd trigger a revolution. A coup. Everything would change. In some people's eyes you'd be a hero. And those same people would have the keys to Gestapo headquarters.'

'Who says?'

'Me.'

'How do I know I can trust you?'

'You don't.'

'But you know these people?'

'Yes.'

'You have their names? Their confidence?'

'Yes.'

'And they really want Hitler dead?'

'Yes.' Tam leaned forward, his hand on Dieter's arm. 'These people exist, believe me. And I can arrange for you to land at a foreign airfield. France? Belgium? Denmark? Your choice. But it has to be done quickly. Before something happens to that lady of yours.' He found a scrap of paper and scribbled the address of his hotel. 'Take your time. Think about it. Then let me know. You'll do that?'

Dieter looked up. The ghost of a smile came and went. Then he nodded.

'Yes,' he said.

*

Tam spent the following two days awaiting word from Dieter. The phone never rang, neither was there any sign of any message at reception. Maybe he's been called away, Tam thought. Or maybe he's got cold feet and decided to forget their conversation ever happened. Shooting the Führer down was a very big step for any *Luftwaffe* pilot, especially someone as feted as Dieter Merz, but Tam had glimpsed the desperation in his eyes when he talked about Keiko and suspected that there was a great deal more to Dieter's story. Life in Hitler's Reich could be undeniably brutal. Maybe there were other reasons why the Führer plunging to earth might be the answer to a young flier's dreams.

Bella made contact at the end of the Friday afternoon and appeared at the hotel shortly afterwards. Her colleagues from the embassy, she said, were doing the best to handle the developing crisis. After the fireworks at the Zeppelinfeld, Hitler had held an all-night conference with three of his top generals. No one was privy to the details but everyone knew that there was only one subject on the agenda. Hitler had already demanded uprisings in the Sudeten, needing a pretext to march his armies east. Now, it seemed, he needed to be certain the *Wehrmacht* invasion plans were sound.

'It gets worse,' Bella said. They were sitting in the small courtyard behind the hotel, enjoying the last of the sunshine. 'The Cabinet have mobilised the fleet, which is a good thing, but they've also asked Henderson to deliver a verbal warning to both Ribbentrop and Hitler.'

'Saying what?'

'Telling them we'll support France.'

'You mean go to war?'

'Yes.'

'And?'

'Henderson never delivered his little message. He thinks it's bad tactics. He says he knows Hitler. He insists he knows what'll happen. The man will just blow up. If you want a war tomorrow, then Hitler will gladly oblige. That's his thinking and God knows he might be right. Better to wait until Sunday's speech, Henderson says. After which things might be clearer.' She checked her watch and got to her feet, her coffee barely touched. 'There's another meeting at six. I had to lie to get out of the last one.'

Tam looked up at her. He was still thinking about Dieter Merz.

'We'll meet later?'

'I doubt it.'

'Tomorrow?'

'Maybe.' She bent quickly and kissed him on the forehead. 'One day we'll make it to Seville,' she said. 'God willing.'

*

Tam spent the evening alone, half-hoping Dieter might turn up at the hotel but there was no sign of him. He went to bed early and slept dreamlessly until dawn. On Saturday the city was full of Hitler Youth, fit-looking adolescents with brutal haircuts and a hunger for the big occasion. Tam watched them marching and counter-marching across the Hauptmarkt, while various Nazi luminaries – fatter, older – looked on. When the display was finally over, an elderly man hobbled slowly across the cobblestones. He settled himself at Tam's café table with a sigh, his gnarled old hands resting on top of his stick, and ordered a bock. At length he turned his gaze on Tam.

'You must be the only man in Nuremberg without a uniform,' he said. 'Apart from me.'

That night, back in his hotel room, Tam began to worry about Dieter. They'd been discreet over the beers they'd shared. The bar was virtually empty and there was no chance that they'd been overheard. Conversationally, Tam had certainly taken a risk or two but he'd sensed that he was pushing at an open door. Georg had been right. Dieter Merz wore his heart on his sleeve and that heart belonged to his Japanese lover.

Tam was half-asleep over a copy of *Völkischer Beobachter* when he heard footsteps outside his door. He stiffened for a moment, then checked his watch. Nearly half-past ten. The knock, when it finally came, was light. Tam got to his feet. It was Dieter. He slipped past Tam and told him to close the door. He was clearly nervous.

'What is it?'

Dieter put his finger to his lips and then looked up at the ceiling.

'*Mikro?*' he mouthed.

Tam nodded, said he understood. He tore a leaf from the writing pad beside the bed. Dieter scribbled a note. It was very short. A single sentence. *I'll do it.*

Tam nodded, took the pen.

Hitler? Kill him? he wrote.

Dieter looked at the note and then folded it into his pocket.

'*Ja*,' he said, making for the door.

Tam caught him before he left the room. There were a thousand questions he needed to ask. They could find somewhere quiet, somewhere outside. They could discuss this thing in detail, plot times and opportunities, spot flaws in the plan, make sure there was provision for Dieter's escape afterwards, but Dieter was adamant. He to go. He had to be somewhere else. Tomorrow maybe, back here at the hotel after the Hitler speech. Then they could find somewhere suitable.

In the end, Tam looked him in the eyes, patted him on the arm and said goodnight. Only later did he realise that Dieter still had the note they'd exchanged.

26

NUREMBERG, 12 SEPTEMBER 1938

Bella had invited Tam to the Diplomats' Enclosure at the Zeppelinfeld for the Hitler speech that would close the Party Rally. Tam arrived at noon, as instructed, joining the swirl of suited guests. With Bella's help, he spotted Henderson at once. He was sharing a table with Goebbels, making cheerful small talk with a long line of spectators queueing for his signature on a pile of cards. Pretty girls in Austrian dirndl dresses mingled with the crowd, carrying plates of sweetmeats and pastries. This could be a giant picnic, Tam thought. Not the prelude to a speech that might plunge Europe into war.

He asked Bella about the cards. She made her way through the eager press of excited men and women and returned with an example.

'A souvenir,' she said. 'Cherish it.'

Tam was looking at the card. It was a sepia study of the Hauptmarkt with ranks of Hitler Youth beaming at the camera. *Strength Through Joy City, September 1938*, read the inscription across the bottom. He turned the card over. Two signatures, one of them Henderson's.

'And this one?' He showed the other signature to Bella. It was indecipherable.

'Goebbels,' she said. 'They're brothers-in-arms.'

*

Hitler mounted the tribune in mid-afternoon. The huge crowd responded with a roar of welcome and a forest of eagerly raised arms. Hitler beamed out across the giant arena, his legs slightly apart, his right arm raised in an answering salute, his sheer presence stilling the crowd. There followed a moment of complete silence, a moment of anticipation and deep respect, and Tam gazed at him, knowing that the memory of this moment would stay with him for ever. The press of the diplomats around him. The faces in the crowd below. A light wind stirring the flags around the Zeppelinfeld.

Hitler nodded, a gesture – Tam thought – of quiet satisfaction, and then stepped towards the microphone.

'Soldiers of the German *Wehrmacht*! For the first time you stand here as soldiers of the Greater German Reich. . .!'

Loudspeaker towers carried his voice to the far corners of the arena. Half a million people strained to catch every word, every nuance, every bellowed clue to the nation's destiny. Hitler was picking up speed now, his fist pummelling the air, his voice rising, warning his people, his *Volk*, of the blood-soaked alliance between the Jews and the Bolsheviks. Germany, he warned, could be imperilled by enemies like these. They need to be confronted, challenged, soundly beaten. Otherwise the nation faced ravishment and rape. Minutes of racial abuse followed, glistening hunks of red meat tossed to the crowd, and watching the faces below Tam wondered how many of these people really felt that badly about the Jews and the Communists. In the end, he thought, you simply went along with it. Which is probably where the real dangers lay.

After a while, the sun still hot, Hitler paused to clear his throat and address a new set of demons. Mention of the Versailles Treaty and the bastard child it had fathered on the Greater Reich's eastern border had a number of nearby diplomats reaching for their notepads. This was the heart of the speech. This was what they'd come to hear and transcribe and report back to their masters.

'We Germans have an obligation,' roared the Führer. 'And we will never take that obligation lightly.'

Three and a half a million Germans, he said, lived in the Sudetenland. But with them, over them, loomed seven million Czechs. And those Czechs had business with the Sudetens. They were hunting them down like animals. They were beating them until they bled. They were creating a situation, a crisis, that Germany could no longer ignore.

Hitler turned briefly to glare down towards the Diplomats' Enclosure. Work on the West Wall, he announced, was nearly complete. He began to stab the air, unloosing a torrent of statistics. Half a million labourers. A hundred thousand tons of gravel a day. Four lines of fortified defence works fifty kilometres deep. Germany, he roared, was impregnable.

Tam glanced at his neighbours. Some were still scribbling notes. Others, staring up at the figure behind the microphones, were visibly uncomfortable, understanding only too well the implications of this diatribe. Other nations are provoking Germany at their peril. The Greater Reich will have her way in the Sudetenland and doubtless in the rest of Czechoslovakia.

Not for the love of war, nor of conquest. But in the name of justice.

'We shall stand by our *Volksgenossen*,' Hitler's fist drove into his open palm. 'We shall come to the aid of our comrades, our brothers. Let there be no mistake. Because Germans must be *free*!'

The crowd erupted. Tam closed his eyes. Thunder, he thought. Followed by a great deal of rain.

*

Estocada. Dieter Merz sat in the cockpit of the Bf-109, the canopy still open, his ground crew making a final round of checks to ready the aircraft for take-off. Flying time between the airfield outside Nuremberg and the Zeppelinfeld was a handful of minutes. The controller who would wave him towards the grass runway was bent over a radio. In contact with the Zeppelinfeld, he was awaiting a signal that Hitler's speech was heading for its climax. Dieter's orders called for a single pass over the heads of the crowd as they saluted their Führer once the speech was over. This was a tribute scored for half a million delirious spectators and the wider world beyond, dreamed up as an end-of-rally surprise by Goebbels and Goering. Even Hitler himself didn't know.

Estocada. For days and nights since the evening in the bar, Dieter had been putting Moncrieff's proposal to the test. In theory, the Englishman was right. Dieter had the motive and the means, and in the shape of Hitler's many aerial excursions to the four corners of the Reich, untold opportunities. Through Georg, or perhaps even Hans Baur, he could lay hands on the Führer's flight schedule. Loading live ammunition wouldn't be a problem because he regularly visited the firing range to polish his gunnery skills. All it would take, therefore, was the kill itself. An unarmed, undefended Ju-52 was a target even a child couldn't miss. Get the approach right, come in really close, and it would take a matter of seconds to cripple the aircraft and kill everyone on board.

He sat back in the sunshine, trying to imagine the tri-motor steadying in his sights. He'd attack from beneath, probably the port quarter. He'd open fire at a hundred metres, maybe less. He'd shoot for the engines on the wings. That way, with full fuel tanks early in the flight, there was every chance the aircraft would dive away, rolling on its back, a ball of flame. A single burst, he thought. The thrust of the true matador. *Estocada.*

And afterwards? Moncrieff had talked about fleeing to Belgium or France or even Denmark. With a full fuel load and careful preparation he could be out of German air space within the hour. Doubtless controllers would send aircraft to intercept him but with the new Emil and his box of Spanish Civil War tricks, he'd simply outrun and outgun them. He smiled to himself, aware of one of the engineers approaching. He was thinking about the afternoon he'd played with Ribbentrop's son, staging mock dogfights in the child's bedroom. Easy, he thought. So easy.

The aircraft rocked as the engineer climbed on to the wing. Then his face was beside the open cockpit. The Zeppelinfeld had signalled ten minutes to the end of the speech. Time to fire up.

Dieter nodded and reached for the master switch. As hard as he tried, he couldn't resolve the only question that remained. With Hitler dead, could the Englishman really guarantee Keiko's release?

*

Taller than everyone else, Tam gazed up at the tribune stand. Hitler was addressing his soldiers now, just the way he'd begun the speech. The *Wehrmacht*, he said, had a sacred duty to defend the Volk. And the Volk, in turn, owed a debt of national gratitude to the everlasting courage of the brave guardians pledged to defend them.

The crowd, once again, roared their approval. They'd spent a whole week in the fantasy world that was Nuremberg. They'd celebrated the Greater Reich day and night. They'd attended folk festivals, gymnastic displays, concerts, picnics and countless march pasts. Every event was calculated to cement their collective conviction that Germany was on the move and that nothing could stop her, and here in the early autumn sunshine, was the final proof that the Reich was destined for even greater glory. *Heil Hitler!* they bellowed. *Heil Hitler!*

*

Dieter was at a thousand feet when the controller ordered him to begin the run-in. Dieter acknowledged the message and dropped the nose. Through the shimmering heat haze he could see the arena ahead, the fat oval of flagpoles, the bowl of the Zeppelinfeld black with hundreds of thousands of the faithful.

He pushed the throttle to its limits and held it there as the huge crowd grew larger and larger. At the far end of the arena, flanked by endless columns, was the tribune stand familiar from a thousand newsreels. Black against the whiteness of the stonework stood the lone figure of the Führer.

Dieter's eye swept over the instruments. Airspeed 670 kph. Altitude 143 metres and unspooling fast. He looked up again, the mouth of the area lunging towards him, faces beginning to turn, fingers pointing, Hitler growing bigger and bigger. For a second Dieter held the gunsight steady on the tribune stand then, almost too late, he lifted the nose and coaxed the aircraft into the sweetest of rolls as it soared towards the blueness of the sky. In the privacy of the cockpit, he was grinning. Rolls denoted victory. You performed a roll when you'd killed someone.

Estocada.

*

'Jesus!' It was an English diplomat, one of Henderson's team. 'That was bloody close.'

Tam eyed him for a moment, struck by how suddenly the little plane had come and gone. Dieter, he thought. As elusive and quicksilver as ever.

Bella was talking to the diplomat. Henderson had called a meeting for an hour's time to dissect and analyse the Hitler speech before composing a report for the Cabinet Office but already a consensus was emerging. He hadn't declared war, which was something of a relief, but his direction of travel was unmistakeable. Within weeks, maybe days, the put-together little country that was Czechoslovakia would be part of Hitler's Reich.

'You want to come with us? I could maybe smuggle you in.'

Bella appeared to be inviting him back to the embassy team's hotel. Tam shook his head. He'd have nothing to contribute except the now obvious fact that Hitler meant what he said.

How the Cabinet, the French, the whole world chose to react was their affair. For now, he had one last card to play.

Tam shook his head and made his apologies. Then came a pressure on his elbow and a grunt in his ear. He half-turned, sensing already who it might be.

Schultz.

*

He had a car parked on Grossestrasse and a driver Tam had never seen before. Crowds were already flooding out of the Zeppelinfeld. Schultz told the driver to move. He and Tam were sitting in the back.

'Goering enjoyed your company,' he grunted.

'I'm glad to hear it. His liver must be made of iron.'

'Just like the rest of him. He doesn't believe the English will lift a finger, by the way. He's with Ribbentrop now. And Hitler. He thinks the Czechs are there for the taking.'

'I'm sure he's right.'

'You, too?' He sounded slightly shocked.

Tam still had the signed card from the Diplomats' Enclosure. Schultz recognised Goebbels' signature at once.

'Who's the other one?'

'Henderson. Our ambassador. They were handing these out to German Sudetens who'd come to listen to Hitler. They made a good team, Goebbels and our ambassador. First you get the card. Then you get the country.'

Schultz offered the card back. Tam told him to keep it.

'You were right about Hitler,' Tam said. 'The only way to stop him is to kill him. What if that were to happen?'

'I don't understand.'

'Who would take over?'

'The generals, in the first place.' He was frowning. 'Are we talking about a coup?'

'No.'

'Something else?'

'Obviously.'

'Some*one* else?'

'Yes. And I need to know he'd be safe.' He frowned. 'Afterwards.'

*

Goering threw a party that night at the Altes Rathaus. Dieter didn't want to go but Georg made it plain that he didn't have a choice. His performances over the Zeppelinfeld, opening and closing the Party Rally, had won glowing plaudits from every corner of the party machine and Goering himself had murmured that *Der Kleine*'s absence was unthinkable.

The Town Hall dominated a square in the northern quarter of the Altstadt. Dieter, again at Georg's insistence, had borrowed a *Luftwaffe* dress uniform but the trousers and the jacket were half a size too big and simply added to his growing sense of dislocation. He shouldn't be here, in this city, in this company. After the victory roll over the Zeppelinfeld he should have kept going north, hopscotching from airfield to airfield until he was safely back in Berlin. Shooting Hitler down wasn't something you'd ever do lightly. Before making a real commitment, he needed to pause and take stock.

Goering's party occupied a suite of rooms on the ground floor. Tall doors had been folded back, revealing a handful of musicians on a raised stage. Beside them were tables laden with plates of local wurst, piles of glistening sauerkraut, endless breads, and huge tureens of something that looked like goulash. This was the food that Goering adored, food that you'd fall upon after a good day's hunting, and he expected his hundreds of guests to do it justice.

Dieter gazed round. Already he was on his fourth glass of Sekt and he'd lost touch of the sheer number of compliments he'd been offered. His face ached with having to smile and respond, and add a little joke or two about the perils of spending half your working life upside down. The newsreels had turned him into public property, an experience he was beginning to resent.

The centrepiece of Goering's party was an eagle with the globe in its claws, sculpted in ice. Every time Dieter eyed it afresh, it was melting a little faster. Holding court nearby was the unmistakeable figure of Julius Streicher. He was dressed in a uniform Dieter didn't recognise, his trousers tucked into high leather boots. He had a woman on each arm and beads of sweat glistened on the bareness of his shaven scalp.

As *Gauleiter* for Franconia, Streicher had been the top Nazi in the region for years and he revelled in making life impossible for the Jews. The paper he'd founded, *Die Stürmer*, was a cesspit of obscene cartoons. Jews, Streicher insisted, were no better than vermin. They were filth, responsible for everything from inflation to prostitution and ritual murders. Dieter had once viewed Streicher as a bad joke. Now, on closer inspection, he loathed him.

Both men were drunk. Georg tried to head off the confrontation, but failed. One of Streicher's women, a blonde beginning to run to fat, didn't bother to hide her interest in Goering's young display pilot. A space had been cleared in the middle of the room. The woman extended a hand and suggested they dance. She was taller than Dieter, a fact that appeared to amuse Streicher.

'You want to borrow my boots, little man? And maybe get yourself a uniform that fits?'

Streicher slapped his thigh at his own joke. Ignoring the woman, Dieter stepped a little closer. All he could think of was Sol Fiedler and the stuffy apartment in Pankow.

'I've known parrots that were funnier than you,' he said.

Streicher blinked, trying to work out whether he'd just been insulted. He had a reputation for violence, as many of his opponents had discovered to their cost.

'I own this fucking city,' he said at length. 'If you don't like a good party, you know what to do.'

Dieter stood his ground. 'Shit always sticks,' he said softly. 'And you're the living proof.'

The woman stared at Dieter a moment and then began to laugh. Streicher slapped her hard, then turned on Dieter. He wanted to kick this little pansy's arse. He wanted to teach him a lesson he'd never forget. Dieter said he was happy for him to try. Either here or outside. Then came a pressure on his arm. Georg.

'Leave me alone.' Dieter tried to push him off.

'This way, *compadre*.'

Georg was strong. Still protesting, aware of the stir he'd caused, Dieter found himself beside the tables of food, where Hans Baur was wolfing a plate of grey-looking fish.

'You like eels?' Baur was oblivious of the incident with Streicher.

'Not for me.'

At Georg's request a waiter was spooning something hot on to a plate. Moments later, Dieter was looking at a huge helping of goulash.

'Eat,' Georg told him. 'You drink too much.'

They stayed with Baur while the party resumed. Tomorrow, Hans said, he was flying the Führer back to Berlin. Take-off, mercifully, wasn't until noon. For once he was looking forward to a proper night's sleep.

Georg asked about Hitler. Surely this party had been for him, another of *Der Eiserne*'s surprise presents?

'He's busy,' Baur grunted. 'Always busy, always in conference, always talking. God never taught him how to relax. Maybe that's the secret for getting on in life. How's the goulash?'

Dieter shrugged. Already he was looking for another drink. Georg intercepted him as he made for the nearest waiter. A turn to the left took them into the vast entrance hall. Footsteps echoed on the polished marble floor.

'What's the matter with you?' Georg was angry.

'Nothing you'd understand.'

'Try me.'

'I can't.'

'Why not? You drink like a fish. Another scene like that and you're done. It's over.'

'It's over anyway.'

'This is about Keiko?'

'Everything's about Keiko. Is that something else you want to hold against me?'

'I hold nothing against you. She's gone. You're trying to get her back. In the end it will happen. Believe me.'

'You know that?'

'Of course I don't. I'd be lying if I said I did. But I know something for sure and when one day you wake up sober, you'll know it too.'

'Like what?'

'Like stop tormenting yourself. Like stop pretending it's you against the world.'

'You're telling me it isn't?'

'I'm telling you it will be if you don't take things in hand.'

Take things in hand.

Dieter stared up at Georg.

'You're right,' he said at last. 'That's exactly what I should do.'

*

Tam watched the city beginning to empty. He'd been sitting at this café table for over an hour, waiting for Bella, but so far she hadn't turned up. At the far end of the square he could hear the sound of dance music. It came from the Alte Rathaus, rising and falling in volume as a door opened and closed.

Tam glanced at his watch. Nearly ten o'clock. Soon the restaurant kitchens would be closing and in any case it was beginning to get cold. The rising wind was stirring the banners hanging from the Rathaus and couples hurrying across the square were wearing coats.

Earlier, in the car with Schultz, Tam had resisted pressure to reveal details of the operation to kill the Führer. Schultz wanted a name and some indication that this wasn't a fairy tale on Tam's part, a fiction to compensate for his failure to tempt Goering into the conspirator's camp, but Tam had shaken his head and insisted that secrecy, imparting nothing, was the key to whatever might follow. All that mattered was that Tam had faith in the contact he'd made. All he needed now was Schultz's assurance that this mysterious figure would be looked after, should Hitler be killed.

Schultz, once again, had demanded more detail but Tam was unmoved. He'd learned a trick or two these last few weeks. Discretion, he'd murmured, was what kept you alive in Hitler's Reich.

Now Tam decided to give up on Bella, settle his bill and go back to his hotel. He finished his drink and got to his feet. As he turned his back on the square to step into the bar a diminutive figure in full dress *Luftwaffe* uniform emerged from the Rathaus and ghosted away.

27

NUREMBERG, 13 SEPTEMBER 1938

Dieter rose at dawn. To his surprise, he'd slept well. His flying suit was hanging in the cheap wardrobe behind the door. He rinsed his face in the tiny sink, ran a brush over his teeth and packed the bag he'd brought from Berlin. He knew the engineers on the base started early, tackling the backlog of repairs that never seemed to get shorter. He made his way downstairs and then stepped into the first rays of the chill autumn sunshine. The maintenance hangar lay beyond the line of parked aircraft. His own 109, his precious Emil, was closest to the huge double doors.

Access to the hangar at this time in the morning was through a side entrance. Inside, a lone engineer was deep in an engine on one of the Ju-52s. He looked up, a spanner in his hand, hearing footsteps. The fact that it was Dieter put a smile on his face. The little flier had brought this corner of the Reich nothing but the best of news. To work on an aircraft flown by a genius like this was a privilege.

Dieter had a favour to ask. He was back to Berlin this morning but he wanted to make a detour to the firing ranges near Paderborn to keep his logbook up to date. Might the engineer have access to the base armoury?

'What are you after? Shells or bullets?'

The Emil had two wing-mounted cannon and a pair of machine guns in the nose. The Oerlikon cannon shells, especially at short range, could tear a target aircraft apart.

'Both,' Dieter said. 'And I want fuel, too.'

The engineer nodded, then checked his watch. He needed another hour at least to finish working on the engine, maybe two. And in any case the keys to the armoury were held by the Maintenance Chief who rarely turned up before nine.

'There's fuel over there if you've got time on your hands and you want to make a start.' He nodded at a line of jerrycans beside the door. 'But I'm afraid the ammunition has to wait. It's not just the key. It needs the Chief's signature as well.'

'What if there's a war?' Dieter was smiling.

'There won't be. Not until Hitler says so.'

'Next week, then. Make sure the Chief's up in time.'

Dieter spent the next forty minutes hauling fuel out of the hangar. Normally he'd be using a bowser but under the circumstances he told himself he didn't have a choice. He wanted the plane at least half-fuelled in case Hitler's plans changed. His weeks on the Führer squadron had taught him never to rely on anything that appeared on a schedule.

Each jerrycan held twenty litres of fuel. The Emil, barely a quarter full, would need hundreds of litres to top up the tanks. It was hard work. Each full can weighed nearly twenty kilos and Dieter was sweating heavily by the time the gauge in the cockpit had even begun to move. Emptying the last can, he heard the trill of a phone from the hangar.

The engineer had finished the conversation by the time Dieter appeared at the open door. He was shaking his head.

'Unbelievable,' he said. 'The *Führermaschine*'s leaving early.'

The *Führermaschine* was Hitler's personal aircraft, a specially modified Ju-52 that was parked at the other end of the line.

'When is it off?'

'Soon. Thank Christ we prepped it last night.'

'And the Chief?'

'He won't be here for at least an hour.' He was checking his watch. 'You'll just have to wait.'

'Right.' Dieter nodded. He was thinking fast. Aware of the engineer watching him, he did his best to muster a shrug.

'Forget the ammunition,' he said. 'I have to roll with the *Führermaschine*.'

Dieter needed to know exactly when Baur planned to take off. The squadron mess was five hundred metres away. When Dieter got there, it was locked and empty. Confused, he set out again for the hangar. A hundred metres short, he became aware of a convoy of cars moving at speed towards the *Führermaschine*. Then came the cough of an engine, then another, then a third. Dieter began to run. When he got to the hangar, the engineer was wiping his hands on a rag.

'You'll help me outside? They're here already.'

The engineer followed him into the sunshine. He was an older man, forty at least, but he ran as fast as Dieter. Dieter had already opened the canopy earlier, leaving his helmet on top of the dashboard, and now he scrambled on to the wing and lowered himself into the cockpit. The engineer was doing a lightning exterior check – prop, flaps, wheels, rudder – and then appeared on the wing beside the cockpit. He reached in, making sure Dieter's harness was fast, then helped him on with the helmet. Dieter plugged in the radio lead, aware of the engineer probing into the depths of the cockpit.

'No parachute,' he said. 'Where is it?'

'Shit. I forgot.'

'It's a scrub, then. You can't fly without a chute.'

Dieter looked up at him. Then he put his hand on the engineer's arm.

'Trust me.'

The engineer didn't want to. Dieter could see it in his eyes. Yet Dieter Merz was Dieter Merz, the closest this man had ever been to a legend, and what kind of engineer argued with a god?

'You're sure?' he said.

'Absolutely. *Kein Problem*.'

The engineer hesitated a moment longer. At the other end of the line, Baur was running up the *Führermaschine*'s engines, a prelude to departure. Dieter glimpsed two of the cars returning to the perimeter track that would take them out of the airfield.

'I have to go,' he said. 'Now.'

*

The *Führermaschine* had appeared from behind the line of parked aircraft, bumping over the grass towards the threshold of the runway. Turning into the wind, Baur paused for a moment, running up the engines again and holding them at maximum power against the brakes. Dieter had fired up the 109, checked that the prop was set to fine pitch for take-off, and was now signalling for the engineer to pull the parking chocks away. A burst of throttle turned the aircraft to starboard before it began to move forward, Dieter keeping the *Führermaschine* in sight through the canopy's side window. It was still early, barely nine o'clock, and the tail of the big Junkers threw a long shadow over the shimmering grass.

Hitler normally occupied the seat at the back of the cabin on the right-hand side. That's where Dieter had briefly paused to be introduced on the flight to the West Wall. He remembered the flabby handshake and the pasty upturned face and a spark of recognition in the piercing blue eyes. Hitler's a creature of habit, he told himself. Same seat. Same restless hands. Same impatience to have the journey over and done.

Baur slipped the brakes and the Ju-52 began to move. On the ground it looked ungainly, the three big piston engines disfiguring the clean lines of the monoplane, but the moment the tail lifted and the main undercarriage parted company with the runway, it became a thing of grace. Dieter watched Baur climbing away before wheeling the 109 on to the runway. A last check – controls fully free, flaps set, brakes off – and he pushed the throttle lever to the limits. The beat of the engine deepened at once and the aircraft began to surge forward.

The ride on the Emil was stiff. Taking off and landing you felt every bump on the runway but Dieter enjoyed moments like these: the groan of the airframe, the quickening blur of the markers that edged the runway, a split-second glimpse of a hare, a brown dot bounding away towards the distant hangar.

Dieter pushed the control column, lifting the tail. Beyond the end of the runway, suddenly visible, lay a farmer's meadow and then a line of houses. As ever, the 109 was pulling to the left but a bootful of right rudder was enough to keep the oncoming meadow on the nose. This take-off, Dieter told himself, might be his last. Best to make it perfect.

He eased the control stick back and abruptly the bumping stopped. The aircraft felt weightless now. It had argued with gravity and won and every second that passed, the houses and fields below became a little smaller. Ahead, Hans Baur had begun a graceful turn to starboard. Last night, in his room, Dieter had pencilled the track that would take the *Führermaschine* north, back to Berlin. He'd thought 147 degrees should do it. And so it proved.

Still climbing, carefully throttled back, Dieter hugged the inside of the turn, keeping behind and beneath the Ju-52. Earlier, bent over his maps in the hangar, Dieter had done the key calculations about his precious fuel load and the likely reserve he'd need to make it safely to a foreign airstrip. This computation had given him a window of just seventeen minutes within which he had to shoot down the *Führermaschine*. After that he'd have to risk a landing at some *Luftwaffe* base kilometres short of the border, or simply wait until he ran out of fuel. Both options were grim but now his situation was infinitely worse.

Dieter was eyeing the fuel gauge. The chaos of the sudden departure had wrecked his plans. No parachute. No ammunition. Nothing to attack the *Führermaschine* and send Hitler to his doom. The silver tri-motor was above him now, maybe three hundred metres ahead, still climbing. Dieter watched it carefully as it wallowed upwards through the quickening wind, aware that his options were narrowing fast. The 109, with its tanks barely half-full, would never make Berlin. Either they could maintain formation until Dieter was forced to peel off and hunt for fuel or he'd have to find another way of bringing down the *Führermaschine*.

The latter challenge grew clearer and clearer, taking shape and body in his mind, resolving itself into the simplest of propositions. If he wanted to kill Hitler, he'd have to destroy the aircraft above him. And to do that would mean taking his own life.

Baur had reached his cruising height now, slightly under seven thousand feet, and the big Ju-52 had levelled off. Dieter's left hand found the throttle lever and he reduced speed to maintain perfect formation. From the cockpit of the *Führermaschine* there was no way that Baur could see the 109. The lurking Emil, with the Reich's favourite display pilot at the controls, was invisible.

The thought pleased Dieter. In his own life he'd always believed that the angels of death would strike unannounced. That's what his father had always told him. That they were ever-present in every dogfight, in every take-off, in every crosswind landing. Some small mistake, he'd said, some tiny oversight, some faraway misalignment of the stars, and the game would be over. Older now and wiser, Dieter knew that his father had been right. Would you see your own death coming? Probably not. Would you have time – maybe just milliseconds – to realise that this was the end? Sadly, yes. Only now was different. Because ending his life this way would be a conscious decision, an act of will.

He checked the fuel gauge again and then peered up through the Perspex canopy, trying to work out exactly where he'd hit the big silver bird. As he'd anticipated, the deadliest impact would be a metre out from the wing root. That way he'd smash one of the engines, puncture the fuel tank and probably rip the entire wing from the body of the fuselage. Retaining any kind of control under those circumstances would be impossible. Probably on fire, the aircraft would plunge earthwards.

And the Emil? Dieter thought quite suddenly of Seiji and the conversations they'd had out in Japan about the Ivans. These were the craziest pilots in the world. Over Spain, and now over China, they'd cheerfully expend every last bullet trying to bring down the enemy, and if that didn't work then they'd turn the aircraft itself into the crudest of projectiles, smashing the target aircraft to pieces. Was there some strange satisfaction in ramming another aeroplane? In watching it grow fatter and fatter in your windscreen until nothing on earth could prevent a collision? In knowing that this next heartbeat, a second before impact, would be your last?

Dieter shook his head, knowing that questions like these were beyond resolution. Even asking them, even acknowledging their existence, was an act of madness.

And yet. And yet.

The needle on the fuel gauge gave him another thirty minutes in the air. If this thing was to happen, it had to happen soon. If not, then his only other choice – getting back to the airfield intact – would vanish.

Dieter closed his eyes a moment, aware that he was contemplating his own death. Then he shook his head. Keiko, he told himself. This is about Keiko. If I bring down the aircraft, if I kill the Führer, then whoever takes his place may spare her. Otherwise, I and she and maybe millions of others are in the hands of Hitler and Himmler and evil *Untermensch* like Julius Streicher.

Dieter eased the throttle again. He needed a little space to accelerate properly, to hold the *Führermaschine* at arm's length, to toy with it for a moment or two, to savour that brutal moment of violence that might, God willing, make a difference to Germany and to the wider world. He was half a kilometre behind now, still slightly lower than the Junker. Then Baur dipped a wing, a sudden turn to starboard that took Dieter by surprise and wrecked his angle of approach. He banked the 109, trying to reposition the aircraft, but he was closing far too fast and the angle was completely wrong. He overshot, cursing himself, and instinctively pulled the 109 into a steep climb, realising the moment he'd started the manoeuvre that Baur would see him.

Seconds later the radio cracked into life.

'*Compadre?*'

Dieter stared down at the *Führermaschine*. Already it was a silver speck against the greens and browns of the Franconian forests, readjusting its course, still heading north.

'Georg?' Dieter's finger had found the transmit button.

'Me.'

'Where's Baur?'

'Food poisoning. Too much bloody eel.'

'And Hitler?'

'He's gone to the Berghof.' Dieter heard Georg laughing. 'Change of plan.'

*

That same morning Tam Moncrieff booked out of his hotel and walked the half mile to the Hauptbahnhof. He left no message for Bella, neither did he make contact. Last night he'd asked Schultz whether there might be a place for him in one of the aircraft returning to Berlin but the answer from Goering's office had been no. The implications were plain. Regardless of whatever plot he'd dreamed up, Tam had failed.

The next train for Berlin left at eleven o'clock. The platform was thick with uniforms, party apparatchiks returning to work after their week in the Bavarian sun. Tam found a window seat in a compartment towards the front of the train. The journey felt interminable, conversation returning again and again to what might happen next in Czechoslovakia. The mood was buoyant. Victory – *justice* – was already assured because the Führer had said so. The only calculation that mattered was whether or not the French and the British would ruin the party. Most thought not. France was full of children and old men. The last war had robbed them of an entire generation of serving soldiers and there'd be no appetite for more slaughter.

And the British? Tam closed his eyes and swayed with the motion of the train, listening to opinion after opinion. The British were fickle. You'd never trust them. The British cared only about themselves and their empire. The British were happy to hide behind their Navy and their damned English Channel. Then came a lone dissenting voice. Tam opened his eyes. He was a small man, alert, with a pockmarked face and a thin black moustache. Unusually, he wasn't wearing a uniform.

'The British are just like us.' He was looking directly at Tam. 'We're brothers, we're family. The real mystery is why they don't accept it.'

Maybe they do, thought Tam, closing his eyes again.

*

Berlin. Early evening, back in his hotel off Wilhelmstrasse, Tam was packing his bag when the phone rang. It was Bella.

She wanted – needed – to see him. She gave him a time and the name of a restaurant and rang off. No debate. No small talk. Just be there.

Tam walked the half-mile to the restaurant. At Tam's request, Ballentyne had booked a ticket on tomorrow morning's flight to London. In twelve hours, God willing, he'd be leaving this place. For the first time in days, he didn't bother to check to see whether he was being followed.

Bella was already at the restaurant. She'd found a table tucked discreetly beside a tank full of ornamental fish. She gave Tam a wave and beckoned him over. She looked exhausted.

'I've ordered already,' she said. 'I hope you like pork belly.'

Tam shrugged. The last thing on his mind was food.

'Why the rush?'

'Time waits for no woman. Least of all me. Someone told me last night that this was history in the making and I was lucky to be here. I think he was trying to help but it doesn't feel that way.'

'So what's happened?'

'It's over. It's finished. The French panicked this morning. Yesterday's speech alarmed them. As far as the Sudeten is concerned they think Hitler means it and they're right. They're on the hook for the Czechs and they don't like it. The least you deserve is a peek at this. It came in this afternoon from London. Henderson took it to Ribbentrop.'

She produced a single sheet of paper from her bag. The typed note, a carbon copy, ran to six lines. Having regard to the increasingly critical situation, Prime Minister Neville Chamberlain was proposing a personal visit to Germany to meet with the Führer. He would be coming by air and he asked, with some urgency, for Hitler's thoughts about a time and a place.

'Is this usual?' Tam looked up.

'Far from it. The game's called diplomacy and you're talking to an expert. It normally involves hundreds of people and squillions of meetings and aeons of time. This is one man thinking he can make peace by himself. Alas, our friends here won't play ball. All they'll see is the rabbit bolting from the hole. They can't wait to pounce.'

'And Hitler? He's back in Berlin?'

'No.' She shook her head. 'He's gone to the Berghof. That's his hideaway in the mountains.'

'Why?'

'To prepare himself for the meeting.' She smiled at last, nodding down at the note. 'To light the stove and sharpen the knife and get the saucepan ready.'

Bella was certain that Hitler would eat Chamberlain alive, that he'd bang the table and play the madman, that he'd blow hot and cold, muddy the waters, agree a timetable, then change it, then tear the whole thing up. People at the embassy, she said, *good* people, *bright* people, had been watching this circus for years. They were familiar with the routines. They knew the script by heart. In the end, comforted by some meaningless concession or other, Chamberlain would trail back to London and proclaim victory or at least peace.

'At what cost?'

'Czechoslovakia. Obviously. That's where all this begins and ends. For now.'

'And later?'

'Later it will happen all over again. Open the map. Close your eyes. Stick a pin in. It doesn't matter. In the end Hitler will own the lot. This shouldn't be a surprise, by the way. He told us years ago.'

'And the conspiracy? Schultz's lot? The plotters?'

'I'm told they're running around Berlin trying to work out whether this is the time to strike. It's far too late, of course. Hitler wants the Sudetenland on a plate and Chamberlain will be happy to oblige. When it comes to negotiation, it'll be no contest. Whatever the cost, the Führer always gets his way. There'll be no war with France, no Royal Navy blockade. How many Germans out there are going to argue with that? And how many of our own people for that matter? The plotters have nothing left to plot. They'll fold their tents and steal away.'

Tam could only nod. He was thinking of the civilian in the train compartment. *The British are just like us. The mystery is why they don't accept it.* Tam put the thought to Bella.

'Perfectly reasonable,' she said wearily. 'Nobody wants to get bombed.'

*

At Bella's suggestion they abandoned the meal and returned to Tam's hotel. She anticipated nothing but chaos in the days and weeks ahead and wanted to make the most of the briefest lull before the going got really tough. In the restaurant Tam had mentioned tomorrow morning's flight but it turned out she hadn't really been listening. The sight of his open suitcase on the bed came as a surprise.

'You're leaving me?'

'I'm going home.'

'Why?'

'Because I'm not needed any more.'

'No Seville?'

'Seville will always be there. It's part of its charm.'

'No us?'

Tam didn't answer. He took her in his arms and looked down at her face and then kissed her forehead the way you might kiss a child before turning out the lights.

He felt her body stiffen. She resented this. She really did.

'No?' She was looking at the bed.

'No.'

'Care to tell me why?'

'Because you're right. Because the game's over.'

'And that's what it was? A game?'

Tam didn't answer. He felt empty, sickened. Hitler was stronger than ever. The Czechs were doomed. Nothing had worked. Not even this.

Tam was looking at the door. Bella, after a moment's uncertainty, reached up and cupped his face in her hands.

'Life is all negotiation,' she said softly. 'And you know what? I thought I was close to a deal.'

28

BERLIN, 14 SEPTEMBER 1938

Tam was late getting to the airport. He'd woken at seven, after a restless night. He washed, shaved, vacated his room in a hurry and came downstairs to find a large parcel with his name on it in the care of the receptionist. It had been dropped off, she said, by a courier from the embassy. Slightly irked, he'd retreated to a corner and opened it on the spot. Inside was a black bear, slightly overweight but beautifully made. With it came a note. It was from Bella. *A souvenir from Berlin*, she'd written. *At least something gets to share your bed.*

Some*thing*? Was he that tough? That impersonal? He showed the present to the receptionist and when she said it was lovely and explained that the bear was the city's official mascot, he told her to keep it. Pocketing Bella's note, he left the hotel and made for the waiting taxi.

At the airport he had minutes to spare before they closed the gate to London-bound passengers. At first he took no notice of the two men flanking the Lufthansa desk. Only when one of them blocked the path to the departures door and demanded to see his passport did he give him a proper look. Medium height. Belted raincoat. Impassive expression. Dead eyes.

'I'm late.' Tam nodded at the waiting plane. 'Who are you?'

The man produced an ID card, discoloured from heavy use. *Kriminalpolizei.*

'Your papers?'

There was no hint of aggression in the demand but the implication was clear. Without a look at his passport, Tam was going nowhere.

Tam surrendered his passport. The man took his time, leafing carefully through. At length he nodded at his colleague and then his eyes settled once again on Tam.

'You speak German, yes?'

'Yes.'

'*Sie sind festgenommen.*'

'I'm under arrest?' Tam stared at him. 'Why?'

The policeman didn't answer. His colleague had produced a pair of handcuffs. The girl behind the Lufthansa desk watched them heading across the concourse towards a suite of offices. Then she glanced over her shoulder at the waiting plane and lifted a telephone.

Tam had been in these offices only recently when he'd arrived from London to be met by Schultz. He recognised the carefully framed Hitler portrait on the wall and the souvenir poster for the '36 Olympics. At the end of the corridor was an exit to a parking space. Amongst the marked *Polizei* cars was a black van. The policemen brought Tam to a halt beside the van. At length the passenger door opened and another figure got out. Medium height. Skinny. Pockmarked face. Poor-quality suit. He looked Tam up and down and then nodded.

'*Ja*,' he said.

It was the civilian from yesterday's train journey. Tam held his gaze until he turned away and got back into the van. Judging by the reactions of the two policemen, he seemed to be in charge.

They put Tam in the back of the van. There was a faint smell of disinfectant, with a hint of exhaust fumes from a hole in the floor. Once the doors had been slammed shut it was dark and claustrophobic. Tam felt his way around, wedging his back against the bare panels as the van began to move. His suitcase was still at the Lufthansa desk, his passport still with one of the two policemen. Already he felt helpless, stripped bare by whoever these people might be. It was so easy, he thought, to disappear in this country.

They seemed to be out of the airport now. Tam had no idea about the destination or even the direction of travel. He did his best to anticipate the sharper bends and the moments when the driver hit the brake but twice he was sent sprawling, fighting the fumes and the darkness and a growing sense of dread.

Finally the journey came to an end. He heard the passenger door open. Then came a muttered curse, much closer, and suddenly the rear doors were wrenched open. Two guards, uniformed this time, SS. One of them reached in and the moment Tam took the extended hand he found himself hauled out of the van and dumped on the paving stones. The other guard kicked him hard in the belly, then stamped on his hand. He heard himself screaming, more in anger than pain, and then he was suddenly upright between the two guards, still fighting for breath. They were in a parking area behind a sizeable building that towered above them. Tam could hear the bell of a tram slowing for a junction. Prinz-Albrecht-Strasse, he told himself. Gestapo headquarters.

It had started to rain. The guards half-carried, half-dragged him towards a door that was already open. Inside stood the man he'd seen earlier, the figure from the train. One of the guards addressed him as *Kriminaldirektor.* He peered at Tam for a moment, the way you might assess cattle before bidding at an auction. Evidently satisfied, he nodded towards a flight of steps that descended to the basement below.

It was colder here and Tam recognised the smell again. Definitely bleach. The country runs on it, he thought. Bleach to wash away your sins. Bleach to make some brief chemical peace with all the shit that's gone before. Everywhere, bleach. Would he find Dieter's Keiko down here? As bleached as everything else?

At the bottom of the stairs, corridors extended in both directions. Every few paces were cell doors, steel-faced, with heavy glass inserts. From somewhere close came the screams of someone begging for his life. The guards were pushing Tam now. Then, on some hidden signal, they stopped him dead. The *Kriminaldirektor* stepped past and turned to look up at Tam.

'Watch,' he said simply.

The guards hauled Tam round and pressed his face against the heavy glass. The glass gave everything a yellowish tinge. Inside the cell a man was strapped in what looked like a dentist's chair. His chest and lower torso were bound with thick leather straps and there were more ties around his legs and ankles. Beside the chair stood a figure in a white coat. He might have been a doctor. He might have been some other kind of medic. But his real specialisation was pain.

He had a small electric drill in his hand, the lead snaking away to a point on the wall near the floor. On the other side of the chair was a bigger man in an SS uniform. He was sitting on a stool and as Tam watched, he stifled a yawn. Then came a nod to the man with the drill. He bent to the figure in the dentist's chair. Blood was already running down his face from puncture wounds around his eyes. The drill began to whirr, high-pitched, unmistakeable, and the man in the chair began to scream again, trying to convulse as the drill bit into the flesh around his eyes, and into the ridges of bone beneath. The man in the white coat worked the drill carefully, taking his time, looking for fresh bundles of nerves, and the body heaved in one final spasm before everything went suddenly still.

'OK?' The *Kriminaldirektor*'s gaze was locked on Tam. It was a meaningless question and both men knew it. All that mattered was the helplessness and agony of the man in the dentist's chair. We can do anything we like, went the message. OK?

A cell at the end of the corridor was empty. The guards pushed Tam inside and locked the door behind him. Still handcuffed, he gazed around. No bed. No chair. No primitive lavatory. Nothing except bare concrete. He looked up, half expecting a camera or some evidence of a microphone. Again, nothing.

He sank to the floor, his knees drawn up, his back against the coldness of the wall, trying not to think too hard. In the Marines they prepared you for capture and interrogation. They taught you ways of shutting out the enemy, of closing doors in the deepest parts of your brain, of defending yourself against the gut-loosening effect of the most basic fears. They can mess with you all they like, went the standard line, but your silence will defeat them. Fine, he thought. As long as you never ended up in a place as malevolent as this.

Tam shut his eyes. Try as he might, there were questions he had to answer, if only to prepare himself for what might happen next. How much did they know about him? Where did Schultz figure in all this? What about Beck, the retired general with his borrowed villa in the woods? And, most important of all, what about Dieter Merz?

*

They came for him later, Tam had no idea when. The interrogation room was on a different corridor: a bare desk, three chairs and a single window high on the wall. It looked dark outside. Mercifully, the screaming had stopped.

Tam was handcuffed to one of the chairs. It was made for a much smaller man. He wriggled for a while, trying to get himself comfortable, then lifted his head in time to see the *Kriminaldirektor* slip behind the desk. It was colder now and he was wearing a waistcoat under the suit jacket.

He asked Tam to confirm his name. He said he spoke good English but he'd be happier to conduct the interview in German. Tam obliged on both counts. The notion of an interview, under different circumstances, would have amused him. So urbane. So sweetly civilised.

'We think you're a spy, Herr Moncrieff. In fact, we know you are.'

Tam forced a smile and enquired whether they were at war.

'Why do you ask?'

'Name, rank and number. That's all I have to give you.'

'Spies have a rank and a number?' The thought sparked a smile. 'Excellent.'

The parrying went on, neither man giving an inch. Tam insisted he was in Berlin on private business. The details needn't concern the *Kriminaldirektor*.

'The American? Kreisky? He was private business?'

'Yes.'

'You admit you killed him?'

'Yes.'

'Why?'

'He tried to assault me.'

'Sexually, you mean?'

'Yes.'

'After that club you went to? The pair of you? You're telling me what happened in the park came as some kind of surprise?'

'Yes.'

'I see. And do you treat all your partners like that? Miss Menzies, for instance? Is she lucky to be still alive?'

Tam didn't answer. This exchange was only the warm-up. The Reich had no interest in who really killed Kreisky. On the contrary, they were more than happy with the version they'd invented. What really mattered was just how much they already knew about Herr Moncrieff.

The *Kriminaldirektor* was toying with a pencil. So far the pad at his elbow was blank. He looked at his watch.

'You could be back in England by now, Herr Moncrieff. In fact, you might have been wiser never to leave.'

'You think so?'

'I do. But life is life. We all make mistakes. In your case, alas, far too many. Some people you should listen to. Some you should ignore. Alas, you chose the wrong people.'

Tam badly wanted to know who. Instead he said nothing.

'You want Hitler dead. Am I right?'

Tam didn't react.

'I don't want motive, Herr Moncrieff. I'm not interested in who fucked with your brain. All I want are names.'

Tam shrugged. He had no names.

'Then let me be a little more specific. You came here as the messenger. You arrived with good news. You told certain people that the British would fight to keep Hitler out of Czechoslovakia. And you did that so they could get on with their own little war in peace. Isn't that true, Herr Moncrieff? Weren't you interfering in someone else's family quarrel? A quarrel that should have been no concern of yours?'

Tam gazed at him. So far, this man appeared to know everything. So why did he need names?

'I'm afraid I don't know what you're talking about,' Tam said.

'But you do, Herr Moncrieff, and what I'm offering you now is the chance to share those names. Otherwise this might get difficult.'

This? The space between them? The beginnings of some kind of relationship? The puppet-master and the dummy? The firing squad and the man on his knees?

'I'd love to help you,' Tam said, 'but I can't.'

'Won't?'

'Can't.'

'Then you understand what will happen next?'

'I have no idea. We're civilised people. We're not at war. I've told you what little I know. And now I imagine you'll release me.'

'Alas, no.'

'Why not?'

'Because you're a spy, Herr Moncrieff. And worse than that you want to see the Führer dead.'

The *Kriminaldirektor* studied him a moment longer and then the door opened. He's got a buzzer under the desk, thought Tam. Otherwise the timing is too perfect.

The same two guards he'd met earlier in the courtyard stepped into the room. They unlocked his handcuffs from the chair and hauled him roughly to his feet. Tam made no attempt to resist, not a single backward glance at his inquisitor. Within a minute they were back in the corridor that housed the torture cell. The door was already open. This time the dentist's chair was almost horizontal.

Tam heard the door closing behind him. The guards manhandled him on to the chair, pushing his head back and then securing the strap around his chest. More ties bound his legs and ankles. Tam was trying to still his racing pulse, trying to empty his mind of the image of the drill and the blood coursing down the face in the chair. Then the *Kriminaldirektor* stepped into view. He knelt low, the way a priest might talk to a dying patient in hospital. Calm reassurance about the afterlife. An apology or two for how painful dying could be.

Tam tried not to listen. He had no full list of names. Only Schultz and Beck and Dieter Merz. Could the drill deliver these three? And if so, might it not be best to get the whole business over with?

He shook his head, hunting for a way to resist, some means of survival, and far too late he realised the opportunity that was offering itself. This was the path to redemption. This, long overdue, was the moment when he could atone for Renata and for Edvard. Whatever they did to him now would be nothing compared with the suffering he'd inflicted on the two Czechs.

He looked up at the *Kriminaldirektor*. There was still no sign of the man in the white coat, nor the drill.

'Names?' It had come down to a single word.

'No.'

'You're quite sure?'

'Yes.'

'You have a fear of drowning, Herr Moncrieff?'

'Everyone has a fear of drowning.'

'Good. The record, if you're interested, is one minute, sixteen seconds. You're a big man. You must have big lungs. We wish you luck. All you have to do is this.' He raised his thumb. 'And the drowning will stop. Then you will tell us the names. Otherwise, I'm afraid you will die.'

There was a movement in the background and the man in the white coat finally appeared. Instead of the drill he was carrying a metal watering can and two towels.

He came to a halt beside Tam. Bending low, he cranked the chair flat until Tam was lying horizontal, his head tipped back. Moments later the man in the white coat plunged both towels in the watering can and then laid them on Tam's face. The water was ice cold. Already he was having trouble breathing.

'Are you ready, Herr Moncrieff?' It was the *Kriminaldirektor*.

Tam didn't move, didn't answer. He didn't want to dignify this obscenity with any kind of compliance. They were going to drown him. In cold blood.

He heard the scrape of the watering can on the concrete floor and then came the first trickle of water on to the towels. There was pressure on the towels, maybe from one of the guards, keeping them in place. Tam was holding his breath the way he'd always been taught, just the lightest lungful of air, nothing dramatic, nothing that would quicken his pulse and set off all the other alarm systems.

'More. Not too much.' The *Kriminaldirektor* again.

Tam tried to relax. So far so good, he told himself. He had a picture of Renata and Edvard in his mind. They were at Edvard's mother's table, that first night in Karlovy Vary. They were laughing. They were alive.

'More. He's good.'

The pressure on his face increased for a moment, then relaxed as more water found its way through the sodden towels. He could feel the coldness of the water creeping down his throat but the nose was the worst. His body was beginning to strain against the leather straps. As the water trickled deeper and deeper it was triggering reflexes he couldn't control. Renata, he thought. Concentrate on Renata. Remember what happened to her. Remember that moment you lifted the boot of the Opel, and that moment rather later when you realised just who had been responsible for her death. You. You, who didn't care enough. You, flat on your back in the bowels of this foul regime. You, earning the pain and maybe the exit you so fully deserve. Death in Jáchymov. Death in Berlin. Death everywhere. An entire regime, an entire *Volk*, distilled in a single word. *Tod*. Death.

He began to choke. He was aware of nothing but darkness and an overwhelming desire to breathe again. The water had reached even deeper. He tried to imagine it pooling in his lungs, but all control had gone. He was suffocating. He was losing consciousness. People who'd nearly drowned always talked about those moments before the lights went out, how suddenly peaceful you were, how resigned, even how thankful. They were wrong, wrong, wrong. Drowning was foul. Drowning was terrifying. Drowning was a place you'd never want to visit again.

Then, abruptly, it stopped.

The towels were removed from his face. Someone altered the pitch of the chair, returning it to the upright position. Even the straps were undone. Tam was on his side on the chair, retching on to the floor. The thin pale liquid from his lungs bubbled on the grey concrete. He stared at it, trying to work out whether he was still alive.

The *Kriminaldirektor* cleared his throat. His tone had changed. He was checking his watch. There was a hint of admiration in his voice.

'Very good, Herr Moncrieff. One minute, twenty-one. Our congratulations. Before we start again, perhaps you'd like to take a look at this.'

He was holding a scrap of paper. He gave it to Tam. Tam wiped his eyes on the back of his hand, then tried to focus. Slowly it dawned on him that he'd seen this piece of paper before. It came from a pad beside the bed at the hotel in Nuremberg. Their name at the top. Their address. And beneath, in two hands, the briefest dialogue.

I'll do it, Dieter had scribbled.

Hitler? Tam had queried. *Kill him?*

*

The guards took him back to the office. His shirt was soaking. He felt sick. The thought of another session with the wet towels made him tremble. The *Kriminaldirektor* settled himself behind the desk.

Tam wanted to know where the note had come from.

'Dieter Merz. He gave it to us. The man is a patriot. You'd expect nothing more.'

'He's alive?'

'Of course he's alive. In fact, they both are. He and that lady of his.'

'She's released? She's back with him?'

'I have no idea. Our enquiries are at an end.'

'And Merz?'

'Merz has been promoted. Services to the glorious Reich. And I don't mean his flying.'

Tam tried to take in the news. At least, he thought, just the hint of a happy ending. Even now, in the age of the wolf, death sometimes knew its place.

'Merz tells us that you wanted him to shoot down the Führer. Is that true?'

'Yes.'

'Why? Am I allowed to ask?'

'Of course. You're right. I was sent on a mission. To Czechoslovakia. Two people died. I hold myself responsible. Along with Kreisky, the banker.'

'Whom you also killed?'

'Yes.'

'And the Führer?'

'He's responsible for everything. For my friends who died. For whatever happens next in Czechoslovakia. Everything.'

'And so he must die, too?'

'Of course.'

'But that makes you crazy, doesn't it? Thinking life's that simple? Thinking you can make a friend of this flier, this Dieter Merz, take advantage of him, use his access to the Führer. . .?'

'He didn't do it,' Tam pointed out. 'He came to you.'

'Do you blame him for that?'

'Not at all. I'm sure the Japanese lady was more important than me.'

'Indeed. Unless you gave him assurances about those friends of yours.'

'Which friends?'

'The ones who were to secure her release. After the Führer had perished.'

Tam held his gaze. This, he knew, was the crux, the end of the road. These were the names they wanted. Schultz. Beck. And whoever else was plotting to settle their own debts with the Führer.

'I lied to Merz,' Tam said. 'There were no friends.'

'That's nonsense, Herr Moncrieff. And you know it.'

He paused to check his watch. Then he looked up. Tam braced himself for another trip downstairs, another session with the wet towels, another cupful of cold water bubbling in his lungs, but the *Kriminaldirektor* hadn't finished. He pointed out that there wasn't a mark on Tam's body. He'd been arrested at the airport on a technical charge that had proved groundless. There'd been no torture, no duress. He'd been rebooked on this morning's flight to London and it would be in his interests never to enter Germany again.

'You're releasing me?' Tam blinked.

'We are.'

'As long as I keep quiet?'

'Exactly.'

'And if I don't?'

'Then *Oberleutnant* Merz won't be quite so lucky a second time. He sends his compliments, by the way. And he hopes you'll understand.'

'Understand what?'

'That you owe him your life. He only talked to us on the condition we spared you. *Schön, ja?*'

The *Kriminaldirektor* got to his feet. Tam stared up at him.

'You said this morning's flight.'

'I did, Herr Moncrieff.' He checked his watch. 'It's a quarter to three in the morning. There's a woman downstairs who will look after you. *Heil Hitler!*'

*

Bella was waiting in an office inside the main entrance. She was sitting alone, staring into nowhere. Tam, accompanied now by a plain-clothes clerk, lingered for a moment in the open doorway. The clerk had a form for Bella to sign. Herr Moncrieff was being released into her care. She studied the form briefly.

'This is to attest the goods are in an acceptable condition.' She looked up at Tam. 'They didn't drop you at all? No damage round the edges?'

'I'm fine. Let's go.'

She looked at him a moment longer, then scribbled a signature on the bottom of the form and returned it to the guard. The clerk separated the copy beneath and gave it to Tam.

Outside, the broadness of the street was empty. Tam sucked in a lungful of the cool night air.

'Where are we going?'

'My place. I have to get you to the airport first thing. Pain of death if I don't.'

They began to walk. Tam wanted to know about his luggage.

'It's still at the airport. The woman at Lufthansa is looking after it. She's the one who phoned us when they arrested you. We were making representations all day. I suspect you owe our Ambassador a drink.'

'Who did he talk to?'

'A flunkey at the Foreign Ministry in the first place. Then Ribbentrop. To be honest we never expected to get you out so soon. Chamberlain's flying over this afternoon. Maybe releasing you is a gesture of good intent.'

Tam nodded. The thought that he might have become a pawn in the wider negotiations over the Sudetenland was richly ironic.

They turned off Wilhelmstrasse and made their way towards the building that housed Bella's apartment. Tam was walking slowly, his head up. She asked whether they'd hurt him or not.

He nodded, said nothing.

'How?'

He shook his head. He wouldn't say. They crossed the road. Bella had produced the key to the outside door. She paused to insert the key, then pushed the door open with a little mock-curtsey.

'Full service,' she said. 'After you.'

Tam gazed inside. Opening the door had triggered the light in the lobby. Freshly painted green walls. Newish carpet. And the faintest scent of bleach.

He shook his head. He knew he couldn't go in, couldn't risk another enclosed space.

'How do I get to Tempelhof?' he said.

'Now? At this time of night?'

'Yes.'

'I can drive you there. If it's that important.'

'I want to walk.'

'Alone?'

'Yes.'

She studied him for a long moment. Then she stepped closer.

'Be honest,' she said. 'What did they do to you?'

Another shake of the head. The last thing he wanted just now was to revisit that hideous basement room.

'Just give me directions,' he said. 'Please.'

He wouldn't meet her gaze. At length, she shrugged. She was under orders to make sure he got to the airport in good time to make the flight. Could she trust him not to get lost on the way to Tempelhof? Or simply disappear?

'Why would I want to do that?'

'I've no idea. I thought I knew you. Now I'm not so sure.'

For the first time he smiled. She hesitated for a moment, then described the route. First bridge across the Spree. Then keep going south. The airport was five miles away. Two hours at the very most.

'You're sure you'll be OK? You're sure you don't need me?'

Tam was already looking down the road. He might have been imagining it but he thought he caught the first pale light of dawn away to the east.

'You'll need this.' She was holding out his passport. 'It'll get you out OK but they'll never let you in again. Persona non grata. In some quarters that stamp is a badge of honour. Cherish it. Show it to your grandchildren. Are you married, by the way? I never asked.'

Tam shook his head. No wife. No children. He opened the passport and flicked through to the page that held his entry stamps. She was right. *Wiedereintritt verboten.* Re-entry forbidden.

He pocketed the passport and bent to kiss her goodbye but she took a step back, keeping her distance. He knew he'd hurt her. It was there in her eyes. She held his gaze for a long moment and then forced a smile.

'We were going to Spain,' she said. 'Remember?'

'I do,' Tam nodded.

There was a long silence. Then a car whined past. Bella's face was pale in the throw of the headlights.

'You think you've failed?' she said. 'Is that it?'

'Yes.'

'Then you may be right. But we all failed. Every single one of us. You know what the Czechs are carrying to work now? In Prague?'

Tam shook his head. She'd stepped a little closer. There were tears in her eyes.

'Gas masks,' she said. 'They're carrying gas masks.'

29

BERLIN, 15 SEPTEMBER 1938

First light. Dieter Merz was about to leave for Prinz-Albrecht-Strasse when Georg arrived at the Potsdam stables. The call had come minutes earlier. The voice at the other end of the phone, a *Kriminaldirektor*, presented his compliments and requested Merz's presence at Gestapo headquarters at his earliest convenience. Pressed by Dieter for details, the *Kriminaldirektor* confirmed that the matter was in connection with a Miss Ayama. The sooner Merz appeared at Prinz-Albrecht-Strasse, the better.

Dieter was hand-cranking his borrowed BMW when Georg drove in. He got out of his car and gestured towards the house. Georg had always been an early riser but turning up at this hour promised nothing but bad news.

'We need to talk,' Georg grunted.

Dieter began to explain about the conversation with the Gestapo but Georg cut him short. He'd taken a call himself, unpardonably early.

'From who?'

'One of Goering's aides. *Der Eiserne* sends his compliments, by the way. He thought your run-in with Streicher at Nuremberg was the high point of the evening. Maybe that's why you got the promotion.'

'Promotion?'

'*Major.* Backdated to when you got back from Japan.'

Dieter stared at him, then returned to the house and unlocked the door. Georg wanted coffee.

'I'm not going to Prinz-Albrecht-Strasse?' Dieter couldn't make sense of the news.

'No.'

'Why not?'

Georg had found the coffee. He filled a saucepan with water and put it on the stove. Then he turned round and gestured for Dieter to sit down. Dieter shook his head. He was getting angry again. Georg was making a habit of treating him like a child.

'Keiko's been released,' Georg said.

'When?'

'Yesterday. They delivered her to the Japanese Embassy.'

'So when do I get to see her?'

'You don't, *compadre*. She's a spy. Apparently Goering's seen the evidence, so it must be true.' He spooned the coffee into a jug and checked on the saucepan. Then he turned back to Dieter. 'The Japanese are taking her to Hamburg this morning. There's a boat to Yokohama leaving tonight. They're calling it reassignment but what it boils down to is deportation.'

'So this is against her will?'

'Far from it. It seems she's happy to go. And after a week with the Gestapo, nobody would blame her. They shaved off her hair, by the way. The aide said Ribbentrop barely recognised her.'

'She said goodbye? To *Ribbentrop*?'

'She did. Maybe there was more to all that than we know. Don't torment yourself. It's over. Finished.'

Dieter stared at the table. Keiko, he thought. Gone.

Georg was pouring hot water on to the coffee. He had more news. The British Prime Minister was due in Munich this afternoon. He'd decided to fly to Germany and pay a personal call on the Führer to sort out all the Sudeten nonsense. Goering had personally ordered a *Luftwaffe* fighter escort for the last half hour of the trip.

'It seems the man's never flown before. It's our job to make him realise what he's been missing.'

'Our job?'

'You and me, *compadre*.' Georg put a cup of coffee on the table in front of Dieter and gave his shoulder a squeeze. 'A 109 each. Just like the old days, eh?'

*

The British Airways pilot bringing Chamberlain to meet Hitler had already filed a flight plan. He'd be taking off from Croydon Airport at mid-morning and tracking south-east along the Franco-Belgian border before entering German airspace north of Metz. With the predicted tailwind, he should be on the ground in Munich by 13.30. Time for the welcoming party to position themselves was therefore short.

Georg drove Dieter to the airfield at Johannistahl. On Goering's orders, ground staff had already checked and fuelled two of the new Emils. A take-off at ten o'clock should put them on a *Luftwaffe* base just kilometres inside the western frontier by half-past eleven. After refuelling, they'd be airborne again in time to intercept and escort the incoming flight from London.

It was months since Georg had last sat in a fighter plane and watching him fold his long frame into the cockpit, Dieter felt a hot gust of kinship from their time together in Spain. He'd loved the simplicity of those days. He'd loved the scruffiness of the villages and the slow rhythms of life amongst the mountain people. These were the toughest of men and often the happiest, too. When the big Atlantic depressions rolled in from the west, and the winds and the cloud base made flying impossible, he and Georg would find a local *bodega* and settle in for the evening. He remembered the guttering candlelight, and the draught through the ill-fitting door, and the howl of the wind down the rough stone chimney, and the endless toasts to God and Franco. Those winter nights in front of a roaring fire had a simplicity and an almost animal warmth that he'd known even then was doomed to disappear.

And Keiko? Dieter shook his head. Even then, even before he'd met her, the woman he loved had probably been pledged to some greater cause. Her father? Her family? The Emperor? Japan itself? He'd no real idea but what hurt most of all was the knowledge that she must have seen this coming. One day the regime would find her out. And so it had proved.

'Major Merz?' It was the base controller. Merz and Messner were cleared for take-off. Wind 12 kph from the south-west. Barometric pressure 997 mb.

Dieter adjusted his altimeter and signalled to his engineer that he was ready. Georg had begun going through his start-up drills, head leaning forward in the cockpit, an attitude of intense concentration. With a cough and a splutter his engine caught, tiny puffs of black smoke quickly shredded by the wind. Then Dieter did the same, hitting the starter button and feeding in maximum boost until he could feel the airframe quivering around him.

An hour and a half later they performed a low pass in front of the control tower at the *Luftwaffe* base near the border, and then circled around to land. That morning, Goering had put his entire fighter force on combat-readiness, a tactic calculated to spice the coming negotiations over Czechoslovakia, and the lines of 109s were visible on the airfield below.

After Dieter and Georg had landed, the *Oberstleutnant* in charge brought them the news that the British Prime Minister's flight was on track and on time. The pilot anticipated crossing into German airspace in forty-seven minutes.

Perfect. Dieter and Georg drank coffee while ground crews refuelled the aircraft. A young woman from the local paper made an appearance to quiz Dieter on what it felt like to be on screen in every cinema in Germany. Last week's performances over the Zeppelinfeld had already found a place in newsreel reports and Dieter watched her pencil racing over her notepad as he detailed the sequence of loops and rolls he took from display to display.

'He makes everyone think it's easy,' Georg told her. 'He even fools my wife.'

Fools my wife? Dieter wanted to know more. They were walking out to the 109s. Georg was studying a curtain of grey on the western horizon. There'd been no mention of cloud in the earlier forecast.

'She wants you to be godfather to the little one,' Georg said.

'Godfather? *Me?* You're serious?'

'That's what I asked her.'

'And?'

'She's dead set on the idea. God knows why.' He came to a halt beside Dieter's aircraft and looked down at him. 'So what do you say, *compadre*? Shall I tell her yes?'

*

Dieter and Georg took off minutes later. They climbed at full power, heading for the distant overcast, quartering the sky for sight of the British aircraft. It was a Lockheed Electra, two engines, twin rudders at the back, and Dieter spotted it first, high and slightly to the right. It was a dumpy little thing, reliable, pedestrian, perfect, Dieter thought, for a British politician about to get his first taste of Adolf Hitler.

'Your two o'clock high,' Dieter told Georg.

Dieter led the way, still climbing. He let the Lockheed pass and then hauled the 109 around until the British aircraft was on the nose, still heading south-east. Over breakfast, they'd agreed Dieter port and Georg starboard, and as they closed on the Lockheed, Dieter called the split. Moments later, Dieter was nicely positioned fifty metres off the Electra's left wing. Through the side of his canopy he could see the surprise on faces at windows in the fuselage and he lifted his hand to acknowledge the pilot's greeting. At the briefing, he'd been told that this man spoke a little German.

'*Wilkommen in Deutschland*,' Dieter said.

'*Vielen Dank*,' came the reply.

'Your passengers are OK? We're not too close?'

'My passengers are fine.' The pilot seemed amused. 'They'll do what they're bloody well told.'

Dieter laughed, trying to imagine what awaited them once they'd landed.

According to Georg, Ribbentrop would be waiting for his visitors. There'd be a welcoming committee, a line of soldiers to inspect, maybe a red carpet, maybe even a band. A limousine would be ready to take the British Prime Minister to the railway station and thence south to Berchtesgarten. Another drive would follow, whisking Chamberlain up the zigzag road to the Berghof. There, in the late afternoon, he'd meet Hitler.

The three aircraft droned east, away from the thickening line of cloud. Below, to the left, Dieter tracked the shadows as they raced over field after field. Sooner than he expected, the dark mass of Munich began to fill his forward view.

Dieter checked on the Lockheed again. The British pilot was gradually losing height, riding a patch of turbulence.

The Führer, Dieter thought, waiting in his mountain lair. The voice in the tunnel. The madman who chews the carpet. Those soft, soft hands. And the eyes that give nothing away. There would follow hours, maybe days, of negotiation. Messages passed back to London. Pleas entered. Positions staked out. Compromises half-agreed. Concessions abruptly withdrawn. Then one last session, Hitler still on his feet, probably past midnight, everyone else exhausted, the Czechs abandoned, the world holding its breath while the men in the field-grey uniforms marched east.

Dieter took one last look at the Lockheed and then peeled off, dropping a wing and pushing the throttle lever to its limits.

Estocada, he thought.

30

LONDON, 15 SEPTEMBER 1938

Tam arrived back in London in the early afternoon. A car and a driver were on hand to meet the incoming flight and Ballentyne was waiting in the Mayfair safe house. Tam explained everything that had happened since his return to Berlin. The news that Tam had mounted a bid to resolve the Hitler issue on his own initiative drew a murmur of surprise from Ballentyne.

'You told them you tried to kill him? You admitted it?'

'I did.'

'Under duress?'

'Yes.'

'And yet they released you? In my book that makes you a very lucky man.'

'Meaning?'

Ballentyne wouldn't answer. When he offered a drink Tam shook his head.

'You think I've done some kind of deal?'

'It's a possibility. You have to admit it. Nothing in this world happens by accident. These people can be pretty persuasive. You wouldn't be the first to buy them off. Nor, I imagine, the last.'

Tam was staring at him. In the spirit of total candour he'd laid everything out, exactly as it happened, determined to settle his accounts and be on his way. Not for a moment had he appreciated that he himself might have become a security risk.

'So what happens next?' he asked. 'You want to lock me up? Pour water down my throat? Wait for me to drown?'

Ballentyne looked briefly pained. The operation to stiffen the German opposition, he admitted, had failed. Chamberlain, ignoring the advice of countless others, had elected to resolve the Sudeten problem in person. Ballentyne hoped some settlement might emerge from the days to come but suspected the worst. If you happened to be a Czech living anywhere near the border now might be the time to pack your bags and head east.

Tam nodded. He was angry. He wanted to know how long he'd be expected to stay in London. Would there be a full post-mortem? Days of incessant interviews? Checks and counter-checks? Would Bella be hauled back to attest on his behalf? Swear blind that he hadn't become a Nazi stooge?

'God, no. We've put you through far too much already. And for the record, we're truly grateful for what you've done.' Ballentyne checked his watch and got to his feet. 'Your father's not too bright, by the way. It might be wise to pay him a visit.'

*

Tam spent the night in a Bloomsbury hotel at Ballentyne's expense. Next morning he walked the mile and a half to his father's nursing home. The matron greeted him with the news that his father had taken a turn a couple of days ago and wasn't responding to treatment. He was refusing to eat and even getting liquids into him was proving difficult. She led him upstairs and paused outside his father's door.

'You've lost a good deal of weight yourself, Mr Moncrieff. Nothing serious, I hope.'

Nothing serious? Tam sat with his father for the rest of the morning, trying hard not to dwell on the last couple of days. The old man was skeletal, his face already a death mask. Twice the sunken, rheumy eyes flickered open but on neither occasion did he recognise the presence at his bedside. Finally, at lunchtime, Tam said his goodbyes to the staff and headed for the door to make his way to King's Cross Station. As a parting gift, the Matron pressed a packet of sandwiches into his hand.

'Something for the journey,' she said. 'We'll keep you informed.'

*

Over the next week or so, back at The Glebe House, Tam snatched what time he could to monitor the regular wireless bulletins on Chamberlain's progress in Germany. The first meeting with Hitler led to another round of negotiations, this time in Bad Godesburg. The radio reports were kind to the Prime Minister but Tam could sense that the ex-Lord Mayor of Birmingham was no match for a gangster of Hitler's pedigree. When the talks finally broke down and Chamberlain reported back to his Cabinet, it was evident that war could be imminent. Anti-aircraft shelters were readied in Central London. Plans were under way to evacuate children to the countryside. Then came the moment when the Italians intervened, offering to broker yet another meeting, and the country held its breath.

By now it was the end of the month and Chamberlain once again flew to Munich to confront Hitler. Two days later London erupted to welcome him home. He had, he said, headed off the near-certainty of war. In addition, he'd secured a written pledge from the German Chancellor guaranteeing peace in our time. And all this for the modest cost of three and a half million Czechs. On the first of October, with the blessing of Britain and France, Hitler's divisions marched into the Sudetenland.

Next day the London *Times* carried photos of *Wehrmacht* troops crossing the Czech border. Tam recognised the lie of the landscape, the softness of the Bohemian hills, the sullen peasant faces watching the Germans march by. A handful of MPs expressed their shame at the Czech sell-out but the rest of the country were only too pleased to believe Chamberlain's promise of a lasting peace. That night Tam sat up late with a bottle of malt whiskey. And wept.

*

The following week, early in the morning, Tam took a call from the nursing home. His father had died in the night. The matron offered her sympathies and enquired what arrangements Mr Moncrieff might have in mind. Later that morning, Tam phoned his sister and broke the news. Vanessa appeared to be unsurprised. Their father, after all, was seriously old. All things being considered, he'd had a thoroughly good innings. Alec was in South America just now and she thought it unlikely he'd make it back for the funeral.

Tam shipped his father's body north and paid a visit to the village rectory. A date was fixed for the funeral in the third week in October. Vanessa attended, together with a number of relatives and local friends who'd known Tam's father in his prime. As the mourners filed into the tiny granite chapel, awaiting the arrival of the hearse, Tam was surprised to spot

Ballentyne and Sanderson. The latter, sporting a deep tan, paused at the chapel door to shake Tam's hand and offer his condolences. Tam had arranged for a modest wake back at The Glebe House after the interment.

'Soup and sandwiches,' he said. 'And a little something to drink.'

Ballentyne and Sanderson exchanged glances. Tam could sense that Sanderson wanted to be on his way but Ballentyne seized on the invitation.

'Delighted,' he said.

The service was low-key, in keeping with what Tam suspected his father would have liked. A couple of hymns. A eulogy from Cally MacBraine and another from a local teacher who used to fly-fish with the old man in his retirement. Then came a final prayer and the slow procession through the dripping pines to the village graveyard.

By mid-afternoon, the wake was in full swing. Tam circulated with a bottle of Laphroaig, shepherding guests towards a display of photos he'd spent some care in putting together. Dad in his youth when he played competitive hockey, proudly receiving a trophy. Dad on his wedding day, his new bride standing beside him. Dad bent over the infant Vanessa, trying to tempt her with a buttercup. Heads nodded. Stories were shared. One woman, who'd regularly called on the old man before his departure to the nursing home in London, shed a tear.

By seven o'clock The Glebe House was near-empty again. Assuming he'd said the last of his goodbyes, Tam stepped into the dining room with the bottle of Laphroaig to find Ballentyne and Sanderson already seated at the table. Tam hesitated for a moment, taken by surprise. This was where the madness began, he thought, with Sanderson tucking into home-made scones. The memory of finding a stranger at this same table seemed to belong to another life.

'You did your father proud.' Ballentyne got to his feet and extended a hand. 'You must be relieved it's all over.'

Tam waved him back into his seat and murmured a thank you for helping out with the fees at the nursing home. Under the circumstances, the money had been more than welcome.

'Our pleasure. It was the least we could do.'

Ballentyne wanted to know how the business was bearing up, now that Tam was back at the helm.

'It's slow, I'm afraid. The Germans have stopped coming, as you might imagine, and no one else seems to have money to spend.'

'Difficult.'

'Indeed.'

Tam was looking at Sanderson. Something appeared to be troubling him. So far he hadn't said a word.

'I spent some time with your stepdaughter in Berlin.' Tam unscrewed the cap on the bottle. 'You must be very proud of her.'

Sanderson didn't respond. When the silence became uncomfortable, Ballentyne cleared his throat.

'A tot or two might be very welcome.' He nodded at the bottle. 'If you're offering.'

Tam fetched glasses from the kitchen and poured three generous malts. He had no idea what to expect next.

'There were two reasons we came up,' Ballentyne said carefully. 'One of them, of course, was your father.'

'And the other?'

'Bella, I'm afraid.'

'Afraid?' Tam felt the first prickle of apprehension. 'Something's happened to her?'

'Indeed.'

'Some kind of accident?'

'Probably not.'

'Then I don't understand.'

Ballentyne fell silent. He'd said enough. The rest had to come from Sanderson.

'The bloody girl's defected.' Sanderson at last looked Tam in the eye. 'She's bailed out. Joined the opposition.'

Tam stared at him. He didn't know what to say.

'You're serious? She's joined the Nazis?'

'Worse. The Russians.'

'The *Russians*?' Tam was trying to absorb the news. 'Why on earth would she do that?'

Sanderson shook his head. He couldn't say, couldn't begin to fathom it. You bring someone up. You lavish all that time and love and God knows what else on her, and then something like this happens.

'To be frank, it's a nightmare.' He reached for his glass. 'I still can't believe it.'

Ballentyne nodded. The news, he agreed, had come as a terrible surprise.

'We thought it best to have a quiet word in private,' he explained. 'Before the papers get hold of it. We understand you two were close.'

Tam nodded, said nothing. Bella had been on his mind ever since his return from Berlin and one of their conversations had been haunting him for weeks. They'd been in bed in her apartment. In a moment of seeming frankness Bella had told him about the importance of belief, of having something overwhelming in your life. Total commitment, she'd said. Total otherness. A kind of surrender. At the time he'd wondered exactly what she meant. Now, he knew.

'No one saw this coming?' he asked Sanderson. 'Even in your line of business?'

Sanderson wouldn't answer. Tam put the question again, this time to Ballentyne. He, after all, had known Bella well. Probably better than her stepfather.

'Alas, no,' Ballentyne said. 'Thinking back, there were all kinds of clues but what use is hindsight?'

'What kind of clues?'

'She had a boyfriend at Oxford. Nice lad. Committed Commie, of course, but that was nothing unusual. She was really keen on him. Really smitten. Her first love, really, and all the more powerful for that. She brought him up to Skye. We met the lad. He wanted to join the Marines for some reason. We never fathomed why.'

'So what happened to him?'

'He fought in Spain with the International Brigade and never came back.'

'Killed?'

'Either that or he ended up in Moscow. I don't think she ever got over it. Oliver. . .?'

'You're probably right,' Sanderson shook his head, still unable to grasp the scale of his stepdaughter's betrayal. 'Impossible. You think you know someone. You think you can trust them. They're kith and kin, for God's sake. And then something like this happens. Her mother affects not to be surprised. I must say that makes her a great deal wiser than me.'

Tam toyed with his glass for a moment. For some reason the revelation about Bella was beginning to raise his spirits. Someone with a cause, he told himself. Someone prepared to take a risk or two. Someone who had the guile and the guts to fool a great number of people who should have known a great deal better. In ways he couldn't explain, it was hard not to envy her.

Tam's eyes travelled from one face to the other. Then he raised his glass.

'Here's to my dad,' he said softly. 'And those lucky Russians.'

*

Snow arrived early that winter. A freezing Christmas came and went and the drifts in the mountains were still thigh-deep by the onset of spring. In early March the postman struggled up the lane to The Glebe House with a handful of mail. Amongst the bills and the booking cancellations was an envelope with a Russian stamp and an indecipherable postmark. Tam put a match to the kindling in the open fire and settled at the kitchen table. Bella, he thought.

The card was plain and black-edged, the kind he'd sent to friends and relatives after his father had died. Tam opened it. He recognised the handwriting from a note she'd once left at his Berlin hotel. There were no endearments, no hint of a memory worth sharing, nothing about the life she'd made for herself, just a curt, two-line message.

Hitler will take the rest of Czecho next week. Probably the 14th or the 15th. Never say we weren't warned. RIP.

We?

Tam stared at the card and then got to his feet. Bella was probably right. Reports on the wireless had been warning of a German move on Prague but nothing he'd heard had been this specific. Next week? The fourteenth or the fifteenth? He gazed down at the fire. The kindling, to his satisfaction, was well alight. He hesitated a moment on the icy flagstones and then ripped the card in half before consigning it to the flames. Half-close his eyes and he could see Renata's face. She was sitting at the table that first night when Tam had arrived in Karlovy Vary. Edvard was beside her. They were sharing a second bowl of his mother's onion soup. And they were laughing.

'RIP,' he murmured, watching the fragments blacken and curl in the heat.